"These stories have it all. Adventure, intrigue, romance. Loyal friendships and hidden treachery. The authors deftly weave plot elements that stretch across the known universe, while still remaining focused on the characters who drive the action. Ultimately this is a story about extraordinary people (both human and alien) who find in friendship, loyalty, and love the strength to face overwhelming challenges. You will want to buy two copies, one to keep and one to share with your friends."—Patricia Bray, author of Regency romances, whose work includes *An Unlikely Alliance* and *The Irish Earl.*

The Liaden Universe stories are very good space opera."—Sherwood Smith, author of *Journey to Otherwhere*

SHARON LEE
STEVE & MILLER

A Liaden Universe® Novel

Crystal
Soldier

Book One of the Great Migration Duology

Meisha Merlin Publishing, Inc.
Atlanta, GA

Crystal Soldier Copyright © 2005 by Sharon Lee and Steve Miller

Crystal Soldier

Published by Meisha Merlin Publishing, Inc.
PO Box 7
Decatur, GA 30031

Editing by Stephen Pagel
Copyediting and Proofreading by Trina Jackson
Interior layout by Lynn Swetz
Cover art by Danato Giancola
Cover design by Kevin Murphy

ISBN: Hard Cover   1-59222-083-5

http://www.MeishaMerlin.com
First MM Publishing edition: February 2005

Printed in the United States of America
0 9 8 7 6 5 4 3 2 1

SHARON LEE
STEVE & MILLER

A Liaden Universe® Novel

Crystal
Soldier

Book One of the Great Migration Duology

TABLE OF CONTENTS

Dedicated to

Butterflies-are-Free Peace Sincere

PART ONE

SOLDIER

ONE

On the ground, Star 475A
Mission time: 3.5 planet days and counting

JELA CROUCHED IN the dubious shade of a boulder at the top of the rise he'd been climbing for half a day. Taller rock columns on either side glared light down at him, but at least helped keep the persistent drying wind and flying grit from his lips and face.

At the forward side of the boulder, down a considerably steeper slope than the one he'd just climbed, should be the river valley he'd been aiming to intersect ever since he'd piloted his damaged vessel to the desolate surface four days before.

Overhead and behind him the sky was going from day-blue to dusk-purple while—on that forward side of the boulder—the local sun was still a few degrees above the horizon, bright over what once had been a ragged coastline.

In theory he should be watching his back; in theory at least one of his guns should be in his hand. Instead, he used both hands to adjust his cap and then to slip the sand-lenses off. He used them as a mirror, briefly, and confirmed that his face was not yet in danger of blistering from the sun's radiation or the wind's caress.

Sighing, he replaced the lenses, and craned his head a bit to study the mica-flecked sandstone he sheltered against, and the scarring of centuries of unnatural winds and weather. The purpling sky remained clear, as it had been all day, and all the previous days—no clouds, no birds, no contrails, no aircraft, no threats save the featureless brilliance of the star; no friends, no enemy spiraling in for the kill, no sounds but the whisper of the dry, pitiless, planetary breeze.

So certain was he that he was in no danger that the rescue transponder in his pocket was broadcasting on three frequencies...

He sighed again. Without an enemy—or a friend—it would take a long time to die in the arid breeze.

Friends. Well, there was hope of friends, or comrades at least, for he'd drawn off the attacking enemy with a reflexive head-on counterattack that should not have worked—unless the attacking ship was actually crewed rather than autonomous. He'd fired, the enemy had fired, his mother ship had fired...and amid the brawl and the brangle his light-duty vessel had been holed multiple times, not with beams, but with fast moving debris.

Both the enemy and the *Trident* had taken high speed runs to the transition points, leaving Jela to nurse his wounded craft into orbit and then spiral down to the surface and attempt a landing, dutifully watching for the enemy he was certain was well fled.

There was no enemy *here,* no enemy other than a planet and a system succumbing to the same malaise that had overtaken a hundred other systems and a hundred dozen planets in this sector alone. *Sheriekas!*

Sheriekas. They'd been human once, at least as human as he was—and, even if his genes had been selected and cultivated and arranged, he was arguably as human as anyone who didn't bear a Batch tattoo on both arms. But they'd willfully broken away, continuing with their destructive experiments and their...*constructs*...while they offered up a grand promise of a future they had no intention of sharing.

They'd named themselves after their own dead planet, which they'd destroyed early on in their quest for transformation—for superiority. In their way, they were brilliant: conquering disease after disease, adjusting body-types to planets, increasing life-spans...They'd been driven to achieve perfection, he supposed. He'd once known a dancer who had destroyed herself in the same quest, though she hadn't had the means to take entire star systems with her.

And the *sheriekas*—they achieved what his dancer had not. To hear them tell it, they were the evolved human, the perfected species. Along the way, they'd created other beings to accomplish their will and their whims. And then they'd turned their altered understanding back along the way they had come, looked on the imperfect species from which they had shaped themselves—and decided to give evolution a hand.

So they had returned from wherever it was they had gone, sowing world-eaters, robot armor, and destruction as they came...

It had been a big war—the First Phase, they called it, fought well before his time—and the after-effects had spread over generations. Those refusing the initial offer of *sheriekas* guidance had supposed they'd won the war rather than a battle. That assumption meant that

Jela was here, fighting a battle centuries later…and that there was no pretense from the enemy, now, of benevolent oversight.

Jela blinked against the glare, pulling his mind back from its ramble. There was a real danger, with your generalist, of feeding them so much info they got lost in their own thoughts and never came out again.

He couldn't afford that—not here. Not yet. He had time; he had duty. All he needed to do was get off this planet, back to a base and…

His timer shook silently against his wrist. Water.

He leaned into the warm boulder and dug into the left leg pouch, fingers counting over the sealed bulbs. Ten. That meant that there were still ten in the right leg pouch. He always drew first from the left, ever since the fight where he'd broken his right leg.

The leg ached in sympathy with the thought, as it sometimes did, and M. Jela Granthor's Guard, Generalist, finished his water, uncurled himself, stretched, and danced several fight moves to bring up his attention level. Feeling considerably refreshed—his was a resilient Strain—he moved around the boulder, heading down.

Behind him, his shadow was flung back across a day's walk or more as he strode across the ridge, but there was no one there to notice.

From orbit it had seemed clear that something…unusual…had been at work on the world and that a good deal of time and energy had been spent in this, the last of the river valleys likely to have retained life under the onslaught of meteor-storms and radiation bursts. After concluding that his vessel would not in fact leave the surface in its current state, there'd been little left to do but sit and hope—or explore the structures on either side of the river. Being a generalist—and an M—he'd naturally opted for exploration.

Moments after stepping around the boulder and moving on his way, he realized that, somehow, he was not exactly where he thought he should be. He was not overlooking the valley that led to the tip of the former river delta, but was instead on the rim of a side valley.

Curiosity drove him to check his position against the satellite sensors—and he sighed. Gone, or down to three and all but one on the wrong side of the planet at the moment. They hadn't had time to get the things into stationary orbits.

"Can't triangulate without a triangle…"

The breeze took his voice along with it and rewarded him a moment later with an echo.

He laughed mirthlessly. Well, at least *that* ranging system worked. It was, alas, a system he'd never learned to use, though he'd been told that on certain worlds, the experts could say a song across a snowy mountain range and tell, from the echoes, distance as well as the safety of an ice pack.

Ice pack! Now there was a dangerous thought! Truth was that this world used to have an ice pack, but what it had now for all its trouble were two meteor scarred polar regions and a star with so dangerously and preternaturally active a surface that it could be a candidate for a nova in a million years or so. His ship's geologist had speculated that at the height of planetary winter—five hundred or so local days hence, when the planet was nearly a third more distant from its star—there might be enough cold to accumulate a water snow to some significant depth—say as deep as his boots—on the northern plains and cap.

Checking the magnetic compass for north, he saw a nervously twittering display as the field fluctuated and he wondered if there'd be another round of ghostly electric coronas lighting the night sky.

As he walked across the rocky ridge, anger built. Within historical record—perhaps as recently as two thousand Common Years—this world had been a candidate for open air colonization. In the meantime? In the meantime the *sheriekas* conceived and mounted a bombardment of the inner system, setting robots to work in the outer debris clouds and targeting both the star and this world.

Kill. Destroy. Make life, human, animal, any—already improbable enough—impossible...

The *sheriekas* did this wherever they could, as if life itself was anathema. Overt signs of *sheriekas'* action were an indication that a planet or a system held something worthwhile...

And so here was Jela—perhaps the first human to set foot on the planet, perhaps the last—trying to understand what was *here* that so needed destroying, what *here* that the *sheriekas* hated enough to focus their considerable destructive energies on.

It wasn't useful to be angry at the enemy when the enemy wasn't to hand. He sighed, called to mind the breathing exercises and exercised, dutifully. Eventually, he was rewarded with calm, and his pace smoothed out of the inefficient angry stride to a proper soldier's ground-eating lope.

Suddenly he walked in near darkness, then out again, as the defile he'd entered widened. In time of snow or rain this would have been a dangerous place. It was as convenient a walkway as any, now that the plants were killed off or gone subsurface; now that the animals, if there had been any, were long extinct.

After some time he found himself more in the dark than otherwise, saw the start of a flickering glow in the sky to the north, and stopped his march to take stock. Underfoot was windblown silt—soft enough to sleep on.

He ran through his ration list mentally, pulled out a night-pack, selected his water, and camped on the spot. Overhead, the sky flickered green fire until well after he went to sleep.

The footing had become treacherous and Jela half-regretted his decision to travel with light-pack. The dangle-cord he carried was barely three times his height and it might have been easier to get through the more canyon-like terrain with the long rope. On the other hand, he was moving faster than he would have with the full pack and he'd have had no more rations anyway...

Now that he was below the ridges, rather than walking them, he found the grit and breeze not quite so bad, though the occasional eddy of wind might still scour his face with its burden. Too, not being constantly in the direct rays of the local star helped, though that might be a problem again as it approached midday. For the moment though, he was making time and was in pretty good shape.

Rations now. Rations were becoming an issue. It was true that his rations were designed to let him work longer on less, and it was equally true that *he'd* been designed—or at least gene-selected—to get by on less food than most people ate and to be more efficient in his use of water. Unfortunately, it was also true that he did require *some* food, *some* water, *some* sleep, and *some* shelter—or he, like most people in similarly deprived circumstances, would die.

Bad design, that dying bit, he thought—but no, that was what the *sheriekas* had thought to conquer—and perhaps had conquered. No one seemed to know that for sure. Meanwhile, he—Generalist Jela—had been designed with human care and he approved of much of the design. He could see and hear better than average, for instance. His reaction times were fast and refined and he was far stronger for his size than almost anyone.

It was this last bit of design work that had gotten his leg broken, despite it too being stronger than average. He just couldn't hold the weight of six large men on it at once. He'd gone over that fight in his mind many times, and with several fighting instructors. He'd done everything right—just sometimes, no matter what, you were going to lose.

He was rambling again. Deliberately, he brought his attention back to the job at hand. The next moment or two would bring him to the mouth of the canyon and into the valley proper; soon he should have sight of the structures he'd spotted on his recon runs.

The possibility that they were flood control devices had been suggested by the ship's geologists, as well as the idea that they were "cabinets" for some kind of energy generating stations that needed to be able to survive both flood and ice. Dams—for water conservation? Even the idea that they were the remains of housing had been suggested...

His stomach grumbled, protesting the lack of wake-up rations. He figured he'd be hungry for awhile. No reason to break that next pack open quite yet.

He slogged on, cap shading his eyes, watching for the first sign of the—

There! There was one!

It was silted in, of course, and beyond it another—but the form of it, the details of it, the stubs—

He ran—a hundred paces or so to the nearest—put his hand on it—

Laughed then, and shook his head.

And laughed some more, because he didn't want to cry...

TWO

On the ground, Star 475A
Mission time: 9 planet days and counting

THE TREES HAD been magnificent. Their crowns must have
reached above the canyon rim in spots and together they may have
shaded the valley below from the direct light of the local star. An
entire ecosystem had no doubt depended upon them. No wonder
the ship's geologists had thought them constructs from orbit…

What remained was still impressive. The base diameter of the
downed trunk he touched was easily six or seven times his own
height and he hesitated to guess how long a board might have been
sawn from its length.

The shadow caught his attention then, as light began filling the
area in earnest.

It was time to move downstream. If there was water left at all,
it would most likely be at the ancient headwaters—too far by days
for him to reach—or downstream. Downstream, he might make in
time for it to matter.

He walked, because he'd chosen to explore, and explore he would.
At night, he stopped when his augmented vision blurred, camping
where he stood. He went to short rations, cut them in half, and in
half again, stinting on water as much as he dared. So far, the rescue
transponder had guided no one to his position—friend or foe.

So, he walked. He strove to be alert, spending part of the time
analyzing his surroundings, part watching the sky, and part in an on-
going argument with himself—an argument he was losing.

"Not going to do it, I bet. They can't make me!"

"Will, can."

"Won't, can't."

The argument concerned the growing fashion among the newer
troops of putting their ID markers on their face. Fashion was something he didn't deal with all that much, and besides, he felt that a
commander should be making these kinds of decisions, not a troop.

And yet, he had to own it was convenient to be able to tell at a glance which unit, rank, and specialty defined a particular soldier.

"Shouldn't!"

He'd said this loudly—definitively—just before Tree Number Sixty-four. It was while using the base of that tree as shade—and checking the angle of its fall—that the position locator in his pocket chuckled briefly.

He grabbed the unit, watching the power-light—but there, that was silly. Unless things improved pretty soon, the unit's power would outlast him by quite some number of years. After all, it had been three days—four?—since he'd last had heard that sound...

Alive now, the sensor showed him to be somewhat closer to the pre-marked goal than he had expected. The map roughed in by the original orbital photos showed that he'd managed to miss an early valley entrance—likely by refusing to walk quite as boldly as he might have into the teeth of the gritty breeze—and had thus saved himself a half day or more of trudging down a much longer hillside.

The big question was becoming "saved" for what? There were no signs of life still alive, nor of water. The trees—

Maybe the trees *were* worth the walk, after all. There was a theory growing in his head—that he'd come in part looking for great works and that he'd found great works. In the days he'd been walking with the trees, he'd found evidence of purpose far beyond the probability of happy accident.

For one thing, in places—not random places but specific kinds of places—the trees had fallen across the ancient watercourse, high ground to high ground, just where there was no marching forward to the ocean on that bank. They seemed to have preferred the left bank—which was generally wider, when it existed at all—and they sometimes seemed to have rested from their march and made a small grove, while at other times they'd hurried, stringing a long line of solitary trees.

Too, they were getting smaller. It saddened him, but the later trees...sigh.

Sloppy thinking. He didn't have dated evidence. For all he factually knew, the first tree he had encountered was the youngest, not the eldest. And yet he persisted in believing that the trees had marched from the high ground down to the sea, and with purpose.

And what other purpose could they have but to live—and by continuing to live, fight the purpose of the *sheriekas*?

"As long as there is life in the Spiral Arm, especially intelligent, organized life, the *sheriekas* will not easily reach their goal!" The memory-voice rang in his ears, for the moment obscuring the sound of the wind.

That had been...who had it been, after all?

Song-woman.

Right.

Jela closed his eyes, saw the small troop of them standing on a hilltop like so many ancient savages, singing, singing, singing.

He'd been part of a survey team then, too, his very first, and he'd laughed at their belief that they were fighting some space-borne invader by standing there singing, singing in the light and long into the night.

In the morning there had been three fewer of the singers, and eventually word came down from the frontier that three *sheriekas* world-eaters had simply vanished from tracking—gone, poof!

The timer on his arm went off. He reached for a water bulb...and stopped before his hand got close to the pocket. Not yet. He'd been waiting a little bit longer of late, and longer still if he could. There wasn't a whole lot of water left and he'd stopped counting. That he was in the valley helped, since the cutting wind—though noisier—was much less in evidence here among the fallen trees at river height.

But he'd been thinking about something...

Trees.

That was it. Like the singers, the trees had helped hold off the *sheriekas*; he was sure of it. But why then had the *sheriekas* not taken the planet and the star system, the trees being dead? Why did they skulk about the edge of the system, rather than occupying the place? Why hadn't they blown up the star, as they had become so fond of doing the last decade or two?

The singer-woman and her ilk were needed every bit as was his ilk, if they could sing or pray or startle the enemy to a standstill. The trees, too, if they were on their own inimical to the scourge. The trees. Why, if the trees—without human help or human thought—had fought the *sheriekas* to a standstill, he should have them. He should take a piece for cloning, plant them throughout the Arm and—

He sat, suddenly, not noticing that he landed on rock. There was something here to be thought on. If worse came to worst, which it rapidly was, he would need to write this down, or record it, so that the troop could see this new ally in its proper light.

Before writing or recording anything, he reached to the left leg pouch and took hold of the water container. Beneath, in the next down, was one more. And then of course there was his right leg with its water...

He gently squeezed a drop or two onto his fingers first, carefully rubbing them together, then wiping his upper lip and clearing some of the grit away from his nose. Then he sipped.

As he sipped, he thought.

There had to be a connection between the trees, the pattern of their flight, and the attack from which the *sheriekas* had withdrawn. He almost had it, that idea of his. Almost.

Well. It would come.

One more sip for the moment. One more right now for the soldier.

He sighed so gently a lover sitting beside him might have missed it.

So he was a soldier. In various places, humans saw the fighting and withdrew, saw the fighting and played the warring parties against each other, fought as these trees had fought to draw every bit of water from the dying world, fought to hide and survive and perhaps outlast the madness of the battle.

In the end, the powers-that-were had permitted the experiments to resume. To fight augmented humans, one needed special humans. Not quite as adjusted and modified, perhaps, as the *sheriekas* or their manufactured allies, and perhaps lacking the power to sing away the death of worlds, but fighters who were more efficient, stronger, and often faster.

Did he survive this world and a dozen more he'd not live the life nor die the death of an ordinary citizen.

Retire? Quit?

"Not me!" His voice echoed weirdly against the grating of the wind. He sighed, louder this time, sealed the partial bulb and replaced it in its pocket. Then, he staggered—truly staggered—to his feet.

He centered himself, felt the energy rise—somewhat, somewhat—danced a step or two, did the stretch routine, settled.

Things to do. He had things to do. With or without his ID on his face, he was M. Jela Granthor's Guard, a generalist in the fight to save life-as-it-was. Who could ask more?

He laughed and the valley gave his laugh back to him.

Heartened, he followed the march of the trees.

He'd managed to wake, which he took for a good thing, and he managed to recall his name, which was something, too. Eventually he bullied his way through a two-day old partial ration pack, knowing there weren't many more left at all, at all, not at all, and glanced at his location sensor.

The map there seemed clearer and his location more certain. There were still just three satellites working instead of the ideal seven, but they were working hard—and all on this side of the planet at the moment, by happy accident, building exactly the kind of database a generalist would love to own.

The trees he'd been following for the last—however long it had been—now were downright skinny, as if they'd been striving for height at the expense of girth, but that was only six or eight times his own paltry height rather than a hundred times or two. Some of them were misshapen, short things, as if they'd tried to become bushes. He tried to use one as a bridge from the right bank back to the left, as he had done several times during his hike, and it broke beneath his boots, both frightening and surprising him since this was the first such bridge that had failed him.

He'd landed in the silted river channel, not too much worse for the fall, knowing he was at the delta he'd been aiming for since he first stepped out of his lander...

He climbed, slowly, onto the firmer soil of the bank, blinking his eyes against the scene.

Had he the water to spare he would have cried then. He'd come through the last bend of what had been a mighty river; before him, the channel led out into the dusty, gritty, speckled plain of what had been a vast and shallow salt sea. Here and there were great outcrops of boulders and cliffs and, when he turned around, he could see the distant hills.

There were a few more trees ahead of him, lying neatly in a row as if each had fallen forward exactly as far as it could; and a new one had sprouted right there and—

There was nothing else.

Wind.

Rock.

Grit.

Three thousand two hundred and seventy-five of the trees then, since he'd started counting—maybe one or two more or less as he'd walked some nights until he could see nothing.

"Finish the job, soldier."

He was the only one to hear the order, so it must be his to carry out.

Dutifully, he walked those few steps more, to see it to completion. To honor the campaign, well-planned and well-fought, which had nonetheless ended in defeat.

Afterwards, he knew, he'd need to find a shaded spot down in the dead channel. Above it, he'd build a cairn, set his transponders to full power and put them on top—and then he'd settle in with his last sip or two of water to wait. The hill wasn't all that bad to look at and he'd be comforted by the presence of fallen comrades. It was a better death than most he had seen.

Reverently, Jela stepped over the last tree—like so many others it had fallen across the river, across the channel. It was hardly thicker than his arm and had scarcely reached the other side of what had been a skinny riverlet, where its meager crown lay in a tangle over a rock large enough to cast a shadow.

His boot brushed the tree, snagged in a small branch, and he fell forward, barely catching himself, the shock of the landing leaving a bright flash of sun against pale rock dancing in his head. There was a green-tinged after-image inside his eyelids, a strange counterpoint to the speckled brown and dun of the ex-seashore.

He closed his eyes tightly, heard the sound of the wind, heard the rattling in the branches that still graced the dead trunk, felt the sun.

I could stay here, he thought, *just like this, sleep, perhaps not wake—*

He opened his eyes despite the thought, caught movement across the way, keeping time with the beat of the wind.

There at the root of the rock, just beyond the meager crown of the downed tree, was a spot of green. A leaf—and another.

Alive.

THREE

On the ground, Star 475A
Mission time: 14 planet days and counting

DUTY WAS A strange thing to think of in this moment, for he was giddy with a joy totally beyond reason—and he knew it. He felt as he had when he'd come back to the troop hall after serving seventeen days in detention for his single-handed fight against the squad from Recon. He came into the hall to absolute silence. No one spoke to him; no one said anything. He'd been so sure he'd be sent off—

And there on his bunk was his personal unit flag. Wrapped around the haft of it were green and blue ribbons of exactly the shade Recon preferred. When he had it in his hands and held it up and looked out at them, they cheered him.

And that's how he felt, looking across at the green life dancing in the wind—as if dozens stood about it, cheering.

And then, there was duty.

Though the tree was alive, and mostly green, some of the leaves were browning, and his first thought was to give it water.

Of course, he didn't have enough water to rescue it, really, just as he didn't have enough rations to rescue him. But he gave it water anyway—the last of the partial and a fourth of a new bulb, the same as he drank himself.

Duty made him wonder if the tree was poisonous.

It was a scrawny thing, barely half his height, with a fine fuzzy bark about it. Perhaps he could suck on a few of the leaves.

There was something else, among those leaves, and he knew not if he should consider it fruit or nut. He knew not if he should eat it, for surely anything that could live in this environment was—

Was what? *He* was living in this environment, after all. For a time.

The fist-sized pod was high on the tree, its weight bending the slim branch on which it grew; and he saw the thing now as yet another soldier carrying out its duty. All of the trees he'd walked beside had marched down to the river and then down to the sea, each with the goal of moving forward, each after the other bearing the duty of taking that seed-pod, high up in the last tree this world was likely to see, as far forward as possible.

Duty it was that made the little tree grow that pod...

And duty told him that this tree was far more important than he was. It and its kin had preserved a world for centuries, as the report he'd carefully written and repeated into voice record told those who would follow.

At this point, even with the tree withering in spots, it would—like the satellite sensor he carried—outlast him. Duty dictated that he should help keep it alive, it being life and he being sworn, in essence, to help things live.

He sat down, finally, for standing was taking its toll on him, and leaned against the rock where he could touch the tree, lightly. He was tired, for all that it was not yet noon, but he had shade—green shade—and could use a rest.

If only his pick-up would come. He'd grab the tree up in a heartbeat, and take it away, for there was nothing to keep it here, or him. He'd take it someplace where water was certain, some-place with good light and good food—and dancing girls. He was partial to dancers and to pilots—people who knew how to move, and when. They'd have a great time, him and the tree, and there'd be room for a dozen more trees—and why not?—dozens of dancers...

He fell asleep then—or passed out—and dreamed a dream of storms and floods and trees lying across swollen rivers and falling in the depths of snow and of landers coming down from the sky, unable to rise again—and behind it all both a sense of urgency and a sense of possibility. He dreamed of his dozen dancers, too, recalling names and lust.

He woke with the smell of food in his nostrils and a clear sense that he'd made a decision. He opened his eyes and saw the leaves rattling in the breeze.

He knew he'd die soon but, if he drank the last of his water and then—rather than going to shelter in a cave or a hole—arranged himself to die here, beside the tree, so he'd not be alone, it was likely that his fluids and remains would nourish the tree for some time and that would be the best use of what duty he had left to him.

And then maybe, just maybe, that seed pod would sprout; and the soldier born of it might have the chance to be found and taken away, to continue the fight.

Food. The smell of fruit. He eaten the last partial rations—when? A day ago? A year? And the smell of the pod so close left him hungry...

Guiltily, he got to his feet and moved a few steps away from the tree.

No, he couldn't. It would have been one thing if he'd found the pod beside the tree, with no chance of it growing, no rainy season to hope for at this latitude any longer, no winter. But now, at best, what could it do? Give him another hour? Or kill him outright?

He was hoping that his eyes deceived him, for the leaves around the pod looked browner now than when he'd first spotted the tree. He didn't want it to be failing so quickly. He didn't want to see it go before he did.

The tree moved slightly, and the leaves rattled a bit in the breeze. There was *snap*, sudden and pure.

Aghast, Jela watched the leaves flutter away as the pod tumbled to the silty soil.

The pod sat there for a dozen of his accelerated heartbeats. It seemed to shiver in the breeze, almost eagerly awaiting his touch, his mouth.

Jela pondered the sight, wondering how long such a pod might be fresh, considering how useless—and how senseless of duty—it would be to let it lie there unused and uneaten.

He moved carefully and bent to the pod, lifting it, cherishing it. Feeling the sections of rind eager and ready to peel away in his hand, he wondered if he had waited too long, and was even now hallucinating in the desert, about to eat a pebble found next to a dry dead stick.

He sniffed the pod and found an aroma promising vitamins and minerals and, somehow, cool juicy refreshment.

He saluted the tree and then, dragging from memory the various forms he'd learned, he bowed to it, long and low.

"I honor you for the gift freely given, my friend. If I leave this place, you will go with me, I swear, and I will deliver you into the hands of those who will see you as kin, as I see you."

Then his fingers massaged the pod, and it split into several moist kernels.

With the first taste, he knew he had done the right thing. With the second he recalled the joy of rushing water and spring snow— and the promise of dancers.

And then, considering the promise of dancers yet again, weighing the fragility of the inner kernels, Jela pushed aside the restraint which suggested he try to save one kernel out, just in case...and he devoured the entirety.

The in-between place—the plane of existence between sleep and consciousness—was a place Jela rarely visited. It generally took drugs or alcohol to get him there, and even achieving *there* he rarely stayed, as his optimized body sought either sleep or wakefulness, the latter more than the former.

His dreams, all too often, were also optimized: explicit problem solving, pattern recognition, recapitulations of and improvements on things he'd actually done or attempted to do.

So this was unusual, this feeling of being comfortably ensconced below wakefulness. Odd in the security of it, though he had a right to be tired, having laid out an arrow of rocks—actually a double row and more of his tracks and a row of the whitest stones— pointing to the tree and his fox-den nearby.

Perhaps it was completion he felt. He'd done the best he could, all considered, and if he were now to fall into the fullest sleep and never wake, it would not have been for lack of trying to do otherwise. Certainly, he was not one who might call to him ephemeral magics and gossamer wings to fly to the edge of space and command a comet to carry him, cocooned, to a place where others of the *sheriekas*-bred might find and thaw him...

That briefing came to him now, of how certain of the *others* created by the *sheriekas* as spies and weapons were able to move things so easily to their wills...That such were rare, and as erratically dispersed as the killer things, was to the good...

But there, the doze was both deeper and lighter now and he had truly not meant to sleep.

Not dream, he'd nearly said, all the while hearing the wind and its acts: the slight rustle of leaves near his head, the sound of gritty sand-bits rushing to fill an empty sea, perhaps an elegant thunderstorm distantly giving impetus to waves on a beach and wings that beat, perhaps the distant tremble of air as some flying thing cavorted...

Now *here* there was comfort, for there had been flying things once, of many sizes. If they'd fought amongst themselves at times, they'd done their work, too, moving seeds and pods about, taking away loose branches, warning of fires and off-season floods, sharing a measure of joy in the world until they were vanquished by some short-term calamity beyond the thought of trees.

What an interesting idea…

In his mind's eye, he soared with great wings above a world populated by trees and quiet creatures, above seas willing to carry rafts of the flood-swept for years, rafts where nests and young might travel in the shade of those still green, growing, and accomplishing. Very nearly he could feel the weight of such a pair, singing and calling, perched in his crown at sunrise, answering the call of others across the canyon and those passing on rafted currents along the sometimes untrustworthy coastal cliffs…

No! He knew he had never had a crown of green, nor had creatures perching in it! His mind took that thought, rejected it as it might a bad element in a dream, came back to the sounds, things that he might measure, rather than ones that might keep him comfortably immobile.

The sounds he was hearing were old sounds, echoed off of canyon walls last week or last month or last year or…or when?

If he'd been half asleep moments before, now he was one quarter asleep. His muscles still lounged, and his eyes, but his ears recalled a distant mammalian heritage and would have twisted like those of a fox if they could…for there was something there, something that hadn't been there in the days of his walk, or the nearer days of his hibernation—something he was hearing as if through a template.

He agreed with himself somewhere deep in the near-sleep: a template. A template not of sight, but of sound and vibration. An old template that shuffled a million years of experience and separated the sounds and shifted other templates to form a nearest match.

Flying thing.

Not a fox's template though. Not usually heard through ear, but through branches.

Flying thing.

He willed his eyes open, did Jela, who found his name then, and his duty, but his lids remained closed, so he listened harder, for this was a template recently used, despite its age, and he must connect it to the sound in the root and branches and—

Then there was thunder enough to open his eyes, and his ears were his, and to his wakeful mind the pattern came: sonic boom.

He shed sleep entirely then and glanced at the tree, which had been shading him as best it might.

"Flying things, my friend? And dragons?" He laughed, to hear his voice sounding remarkably like the dragons of the dream. "Dragons and now spaceships? What a fine delirium you bring!"

His eye caught the line of a single narrow contrail in the sky, floating with no obvious sign of an attached craft. It looked like they were heading away from him—to the place he'd touched down. Else they were headed in the other direction—directly for him.

Sighing, Jela the soldier reached for his sun shades, tapped the knife on his belt for comfort, and drew the gun to be sure the barrel was not full of sand, nor the charge useless.

"Field of fire," he remarked to the tree, "favors both of us. If it isn't someone we know and they can read the signs, they'll have an idea where I am, so I'll be just a little bit someplace else. If they're bright, they'll expect it, but hey, I've got the rescue beacons on.

"You…I'm going to camouflage as best I can."

His handiwork, when admired from a distance, appeared to be another random pile of debris, though his tracks around it were hard to disguise entirely. He'd used his vest to sweep the more obvious tracks into smudges and left the beacon on. He took one transceiver, leaving all the other powered items in the den, where they'd either not be noticed or, if detected, where they'd serve to convince anyone oncoming that he was sensibly in the shade.

He was not *exactly* sensibly in the shade, though he had some of it. That wouldn't be a problem for much longer today, in any case, since the sun would soon be on the horizon.

His choice was a gully where the meandering of the stream bed had made a short-lived branch. There, looking across at the tree, he laid out his pistol and his backup, and emptied his pockets of anything that might weigh him down if he needed to move fast.

He laughed mirthlessly, no doubt in his mind that he was running on adrenaline and hope, knowing too that his chance of moving with speed or stealth was pretty slim, this far into no rations.

It was then that he felt the ship, as if large welcome wings were overhead. There was a whine of the wind, and some slight hissing—remarkably like that of the CC-456s he'd known for decades.

It swept in low over the tiny campsite, its wings not all that large—indeed the ship itself was not all that large!—did a half-turn, displaying a single black digit on each of its stubby maneuvering wings, then another half turn—incidentally bringing the nose cannon to bear on the campsite. Then it hissed itself quietly into the empty ocean, and was still for very nearly eight full seconds, at which point Corporal Kinto jumped out of the open hatch, slipping on the shifting sand with an obscenity.

FOUR

On the ground, Star 475A
Mission time: 14.5 planet days and counting

"THAT'S AN ORDER, Jela. Prepare to embark." Chief Pilot Contado's voice was getting quieter, which was not a good sign.

"We're not done here." Jela's voice also got quieter. He was standing on top of his den, half-facing the tree, what was left of his kit packed into his pockets.

Contado stood beside the tree, towering over it, his permanent grimace accentuated by his squinted eyes in the shadows of the low sun. He was pointedly ignoring Jela's inclusion of the tree in the "we" of his intent.

Around Jela were the remains of the hasty moist meal they'd given him, along with discarded med-packs—they'd hit him with doses of vitamins, inhalants of stim, sublinguals of anti-virals—and three empty water bulbs.

Sated in many ways, refreshed naturally and artificially, shaded by his rescuers' craft, Jela felt stronger than he had in days—and as stubborn as the trees he'd followed to the ocean of sand.

"I *will* take the tree with me," he said, very quietly indeed.

"On board, dammit! Our launch window..." This was said loudly—meaning Jela had made a gain...

"That launch window is an arbitrary time chosen by the pilot. You're working with guesses. There's nothing yet on the sensors..."

"Troop, this is not a biologicals run. I'm not..."

"Chief, this tree saved my life. It and its kin fought off the *sheriekas* for...who knows how long...for dozens of centuries! There's no other reason I can think of that this system was left alone for so long, and why it's got so much attention now. We can't simply leave it unprotected."

From inside the ship—off-com but still clearly audible— came Kinto's voice: "He wants to protect it, give him another gun and put him in charge. I told you it wasn't worth coming back for him..."

There was a brangle of voices from within the ship and then:

"Just moments to sundown, Chief. I've set a countdown, and Kinto's doing the pre-flights in case we need to boost directly to rendezvous."

This new voice on the com was Junior Pilot Tetran and Jela bet himself that, in addition to the pre-flights, Kinto now owned either a bruise or a run of make-work when they got back to base—or both.

Chief Pilot Contado looked at the tree—and at Jela—and then at the ship and beyond, holding a hand above his eyes.

"Chief, as a bonus—I mean as recompense for being shot down while saving both the commander and the *Trident*, you can arrange it for me—" Jela murmured.

There was a gasp at that, that he should so blatantly claim such a thing, but he pushed on, defiant.

"And I promised, when I ate the fruit…I promised I'd save it if I could! All I need, sir, is…"

Contado cut him off with a slash of the hand and a disdainful grunt.

"Troop, if you insist on it, it's yours. You have until the ship lifts to take your souvenir. The quartermaster will charge carrying fees against your account—I'll not have that thing dignified as a specimen—and you'll report for trauma testing as soon as we arrive at an appropriate location."

"I'd prefer to lift in daylight!" came the junior pilot's voice, merciless.

Jela broke toward the tree, survival knife and blanket out, hoping he didn't kill the fool thing trying to save it!

"We lift with or without you, Jela," said the Chief Pilot, and the wind carried his voice elsewhere, unanswered.

Jela was not a gardener, nor a tree surgeon, and, if ever he'd felt a lack of training in his life, it was now, on his knees on an alien planet, battle-knife in hand, facing the tree that had intentionally saved his life. His utility blanket was laid out beside it and he fully intended to wrap the tree in that to carry it.

"Thank you," he said, bowing, and tried to recall a life's worth of half-heard lore of those who had tread the forests on other worlds.

And then, as there was absolutely nothing else to do, he began to dig a trench with the knife, cutting into the earth as he *had* been trained, recalling now the proper method of slicing through the outer roots quickly. The training—how best to avoid entangling the blade, how to get under the over-roots so that they might be preserved as camouflage or cover—came back, reinforced by the experience of digging for his life under fire.

He knew that he shouldn't take the tree entirely from the earth, that he needed to keep soil around some of the roots—but how should he know how much?

The dirt surprised him, being drier even than he'd been expecting. He trenched the first circle around the tree hurriedly, realized that the sandy soil wasn't likely to hold together anyway, and dug a new trench barely three hand-spans away from the spindly trunk.

As he dug he realized he was talking to the tree, soothing it, as if it could understand—as if it were a child or a pet.

What cheek I have, to tell the king of a planet to be calm while I dig it out of its safety!

Despite that, he continued to talk—perhaps for his own comfort, to assure himself that what he did was right and correct.

"We'll get you out of here soon," he murmured. "Won't be long and you'll see the dragon's eye view…"

The breeze began to pick up, as it always did at dusk, and the scents that played across his nose were those of sand and dirt and some sweetness he could not identify at first, until he realized it was the scent—the taste even—of the tree's gift he'd eaten…

Another turn around the tree, and Jela's blade was much deeper, but digging toward the center. The sounds from the ship were familiar enough, and they were the sounds of vents being closed, of the testing of mechanical components, of checking readiness for lift.

It was during the third turn around the tree that Jela could hear several of the hatches closing; and during that turn he realized that much of what he'd thought was a ball of dirt was in fact a bulbous part of the tree's tap root. It was easily twelve times the diameter of the portion above the ground, and as he dug away he could feel that it likely weighed more than the visible stalk above as well.

Finally he reached beneath, found several strong cord-like roots leading deep into the bowels of the planet. He hesitated, not knowing which life-lines were critical, nor even knowing how to test—and in that moment of hesitation he felt the tree shift as if some inner ballast had moved. Then, with a sharp snap, the tree lurched and the roots he'd been concerned about were severed, his blade a hand-width or more from the spot.

The full weight of tree and remaining roots descended into his hands, and he staggered, nearly pulled down into the pit he'd dug.

With back-straining effort he gathered the tree to him, feeling the unexpected mass of that head-sized bulb, shaped like some giant onion beneath his hands.

Now hearing the sounds of ship generators revving coming to him, he wrestled the tree out of the ungiving ground and, with a single motion, wrapped it in the blanket and stood, moving at a run toward the ship.

Corporal Kinto stood guard at the last open hatch, eyes studiously on the hatch's status display, hand on the emergency close button.

"He's in!" Kinto said to the air and then the Chief Pilot's voice came across the intercom. "We lift on a count of twenty-four."

Kinto glared around the branches at Jela then and smiled an ugly smile.

"Even a Hero shouldn't order a Chief Pilot about, Jela. I anticipate your trial!"

They lifted. The lander crew had allowed him to strap the tree into the jump seat beside him and then they ignored him. Ignored his careful dusting of the leaves, his positioning of the plant where it could reap whatever feeble grace the ship's lights might bring it; ignored his use of a camp cup to dampen the sandy roots...and they ignored his talking, for his words were all for the tree. To Corporal Kinto, he had nothing to say. Contado and Tetran being dutifully occupied at their stations, he—a passenger—should not distract them with chatter. So he whispered good tidings and calm words to the tree, which was departing not only its home world and its honorable dead, but the very soil that had nourished it.

The transfer to the *Trident* was awkward. He was left to negotiate himself and the tree through the transfer port. Emerging, arms full of trunk and branches, he'd been unable to properly acknowledge the captain. Then, as a pilot returning without his craft, there were the docking logs to sign, certifying his ship lost due to enemy action, which duty he performed clumsily, tree propped on a hip, log tipped at an unstable angle, while the quartermaster displayed an unlikely degree of interest in his secondary screens.

None of his wing met him, which he thought a bad sign, and he'd been directed not to his own billet but to the pilot's lounge, escorted by the assistant quartermaster.

"I should go to my quarters, change uniforms, clean myself..."

His escort cut him off sharply.

"Troop, you ought to know you're just about at the limit," she snapped. "Took the pilots a lot of jawing to convince the captain to come back this way long enough to pick up your signal. Besides, there's no guarantee you've got quarters to go back to..."

That last sounded bad—worse than being at the limit of what would be officially tolerated. He was old friends with the limit. No quarters, though—

With him up ahead in the corridor, there wasn't a good way to get a look at his escort's face, to see if she was having some fun with him. Just then they reached a junction in the passageway and had to make way for pilots wearing duty cards. Jela managed to hide his face in the branches, pleased that the youngsters—for they were both rookies—could not see his reaction to the gaudy tattoos they wore on their faces. It was while looking away that he saw two of the hatches in the passage dogged to yellow and another dogged to red.

"Took a hit?" he said over his shoulder as they continued. "I thought—"

"Your boat took most of it." Her voice was gentler now, as if she gave due respect to duty done, and done well. "But there was still some pretty energetic debris and a bad shot from one of ours, too."

Jela grimaced, partly from the news and partly from the exertion of carrying the tree. He'd have sworn it had been much lighter when he'd grabbed it out of the ground.

Forced to the side of the passage once more by through traffic, he leaned against the metal wall, resting for a moment, until a tap on the shoulder reminded him that he was on ship's business and not his own.

Moving forward, he vaguely wondered which—if any—of his belongings might have survived, then let that thought go. He was here; the tree was here; and that was more than he had a right to expect, after all.

They came at last to the pilots lounge. The hatch was uncharacteristically dogged—to green at least!—but, with ship's air at risk, it was only a common-sense precaution. He had time to note that his wing's insignia was pasted roughly to the door, then the assistant quartermaster reached past him to rap—which was her right, after all—to have a lesser open for her from within.

The hatch swung wide. An unexpected hand between his shoulders sent him through, half-stumbling, and he looked, quick eyes raking past the scraggly leaves of the tree, taking in the six empty helmets sitting with unsheathed blades beside them on a table, and five faces—familiar, strained, concerned—watching him.

His knees shook. He locked them, refusing to fall, but...

Six? Six gone?

Corporal Bicra it was who gently took the tree from him and Under Sergeant Vondahl who led the salute.

With Jela, they numbered six—the smallest number Command would recognize as a wing.

And as luck would have it, he was now eldest in troop and senior in rank.

He returned the salute uncertainly and sat heavily in the chair beside the tree.

"Report," he said, not at all wishing to hear the tale.

FIVE

Trident
Isolation Ward

THE MED TECH was adamant, all the while admitting Jela's basic understanding of the theory of contagion.

Yes, many diseases could be spread—*could have been spread already*—by the mere passage of an infected person, such as Jela, bearing an infectious object, such as the tree, through the ship.

That Jela had been escorted by the assistant quartermaster and welcomed into the temporary wing wardroom was unfortunate. That no one had yet died of some hideous, unknown disease since his return to the ship was not proof positive that no one *would*.

More to the point, several standard protocols had been abused and the med tech was voluble in their listing.

First and foremost, Jela should not have been permitted to land on the planet without a thorough reevaluation of the biological information from the old surveys.

Secondly, neither Jela nor the tree should have been permitted back into the pick-up ship without disinfection.

Thirdly and most annoying to the tech, as Jela read it, neither he nor the tree should be aboard *now* without having been disinfected.

The tech knew the rules and had the ear of *someone* on staff—and that someone had been appropriately notified, dignified, and horrified.

And so it was that the second day of Jela's reign as Acting Wingleader was spent in an isolation tunnel. The double-walled see-through chamber was inflated inside an ordinary infirmary room. The tree, within a double-walled flex-glass cubicle, was isolated all the more within that chamber while various tests were done on the dirt it called its own. At least they'd seen the wisdom of leaving the tree were Jela could watch it. If it turned blue or purple or became infested with bugs in its chamber, he'd be right there to see it.

He hadn't pointed out to the med tech that no one knew exactly how long it might take a scruffy-looking tree of unknown genus to exhibit signs of parasitism, decay or the like, but he had managed to get the tech to agree to a watering system for the plant so it wouldn't give a "false positive" that might have the fleet isolating the whole ship...

Luckily, the tech admitted the biotic sanctity of electronic communications, so Jela's small command was at least able to speak with him when required and otherwise keep his comm-screen active with the news and goings-on of the group.

Things might have been busier had Corporal Bicra also not been in isolation elsewhere, this news brought and left by a smirking Kinto. The corporal had touched the tree, carried her Wingleader's burden—as both proper and prudent!—after all. Bicra being the most organized of the remaining squad, some important details were sure to be missed.

Jela was inclined to consider Kinto a factor in the isolation as well, since he was known to be a friend of the med tech. What use any of the fooraw could be to Kinto was a mystery worth exploring at a later date; for the moment Under Sergeant Vondahl was too busy overseeing the maintenance and repair of the wing's ships to spend time on a vital-records search.

The med tech seemed a busybody of the highest order. Jela's three sensor packs reported ably to the room's central console, but the tech remained in the room nonetheless. More, he constantly checked Jela's rate of water intake and—

"Will you give me ten heartbeats to myself, Tech? You've already got cameras, body sensors, air-intake gauges, and two measurements of my weight. Do you think I'll grow wings and leave you behind if you don't check my color every tenth-shift?"

Most of Jela's attention was on his porta-comp, where he was following with interest the check on Sergeant Risto's ship. Risto was one of the three who'd died when the primary passage had been laid open to space while they were scrambling.

"Not likely," admitted the tech. "I don't think there's anything in the literature about a more or less standard human being able to fly—or even grow wings. The *sheriekas* are said to..."

Jela looked up when the phrase wasn't even finished.

"Are said to *what?*"

The tech looked down, rising blood staining sturdy cheeks a deeper brown. "I can't say. You haven't been confirmed as Wingleader and the information may be restricted to..."

Jela looked on with interest as the tech mumbled into silence and turned to busy himself with adjusting various dials that didn't need adjusting.

Understanding blossomed.

"I see," Jela said. "Until I'm scanned, rescanned, sampled and shown to be free of disease and healthy of mind—hah!—I might be an agent of *them,* magically cloned on the spot and released to destroy the defenders from within." He took a breath, decided that he was still irritated and that, furthermore, the tech had it coming and continued.

"Will it ease your mind to know that I was one of the generalists brought in to study the problem of how to spot *sheriekas* and *sheriekas*-made in their human disguises? That would be, *before* they sprout wings and—"

"Stop, Troop!"

This was a new voice—an entirely new voice, from a woman he'd never seen before.

Her uniform—

Jela slowly moved the keypad back, stood, and saluted.

"Commander, I have stopped."

She snorted delicately.

"I hear, Troop. I hear."

She pointed at the med tech.

"You may leave, Tech. Your monitors will warn you if there's a problem."

A quick salute from the tech, who nearly tripped in his hurry to leave the scene.

As the door sealed, the commander sighed, none too gently.

"*Wingleader.*" She said the word as if she tasted it, as if she *tested* it.

"*Wingleader.* Indeed, it would look good on your record, were that record reviewed but not much inspected—I may allow it to stay. May."

She moved closer to the wall of his enclosure, studying him with as much interest—and perhaps even concern—as the med-tech had showed disinterest and disdain.

In his turn, Jela studied her: a woman so near his own height he barely needed to look up to meet her eyes, strongly built, and in top shape. Not a Series soldier, but a natural human, her brown hair threaded with grey.

She continued as if there had been no pause for mutual evaluation.

"Wingleader...Yet, I'm not sure if that would be best for you, howsoever it might serve the troop."

She peered through the inflatable, studying his reaction.

"No comment, Troop Jela?"

"Wingleader has never been in my thoughts, Commander. It is an unexpectable accident..."

She laughed.

"Yes, I suppose it is. I *have* seen your record. You always seem to rise despite your best efforts!"

Jela stiffened...

"Stop, Troop. Relax. Understand that you *are* monitored here. You *are* on camera. You *are* being tested for contagion of *many* sorts. There's no need to bait the tech. He's too ordinary to be worth your trouble."

Jela stood, uncertain, aware that information was being passed rapidly, aware that levels of command were being bypassed.

"Sit," the commander said finally. "Please, sit and do what you can for the moment. As time permits, we will talk."

Jela watched as her eyes found the cameras, the sensors, the very monitors on his leg. He sat, more slowly than he'd risen.

"We will talk where we might both be more comfortable. In a few days, when you will be quite recovered from your trek, Wingleader."

She saluted as if that last word was both a command and a decision, and then she was gone.

The Commander made no more appearances in Jela's isolation unit— a unit he'd begun to think of as a cell after the third day schedule commenced in the vessel outside his walls and, by the start of the sixth ship-day, knew to be the truth, if not the intent.

He'd been in enough detaining cells in his time to see the similarities: he was on his jailer's schedule, he exercised when they told him to, he ate what they brought him, and he slept during a portion of the time after they turned the lights out on him.

He did have his porta-comp, which meant some communication, after all; and he had received a few visitors, though he'd had more visitors in some lock-ups than he had here. Then, too, most often his jail cells hadn't had the luxury of his very own green plant.

It turned out that the "alien plant" was under every bit as much scrutiny as he was—in fact it appeared that many of the sensors he wore or was watched by were duplicated for the tree.

Perhaps the most frustrating thing was that though he could see the tree—and was under orders to observe it and report any anomalies—he could not to touch it, or talk to it, or comfort it in what must be new and terrifying circumstances.

Shortly after the commander's visit, he gained an amusing rotation of warders to replace the solitary med-tech and his curious warnings—or perhaps threats.

What was amusing about the new set of keepers was that they each seemed guided by a printed sheet. They neither saluted nor acknowledged him other than directing him for exercise or tests. They also wore medical gowns without emblem, name, rank, or number.

What they did not wear were masks—thus baring the all-too-silly tattoos that were becoming the rage—and making each as identifiable in the long run as if they'd shouted out name, rank, birth crèche, and gene units...

For in fact, every one of the new keepers were of the accelerated, the vat-born, the selected, the so-called "X Strain"—able to work harder and longer on less food than even the efficient M's. Too, they had for the most part had similar training, similar instructors, similar lives. They spoke amongst themselves a truncated and canted artificial dialect and appeared to lump any soldier but those of the latest vat runs into a social class of lesser outsiders.

Despite the disdain and the tendency to seek only the company of their own kind, what had so far eluded the designers of soldiers was the sought-after interchangeability that would have made them— the Y Strains and the X—in the image of some committee-envisioned super-fighter: Physically perfect, identical, and above all amenable to command. It was the downfall of the M Series, so he had heard it said—they were too independent, too individual, much too prone to use their own judgment, and much too often, Jela might have added—right.

So, he found himself in the care of the proud yet still-flawed X Strains and he'd been annoyed in the night to wake as some one of the guardians attempted to enter the room without disturbing him. They were all of the blood, dammit! Would he have assumed them so lax...well, yes. He might have.

"You of Versten's Flight have no regard for the sleep of your brethren, eh?" He called out in the assumed dark of the infirmary's night. His reward was a not unexpected flash of light as the woman with a red lance crossing a blue blade tattooed on her right cheek reacted, alas, predictably.

"Wingleader," she gasped.

He'd *startled* her—and if he'd been of a mind he might just as easily have killed her—been through the transparent enclosure and had his hands around her throat before she'd known he was awake.

"Wingleader," she said again, recovering her voice, if not her dignity. "The monitors must be checked manually from time to time, and the calibrations..."

"The calibrations may be made just as conveniently from a remote station," he said, allowing his voice to display an edge. "It would be well if these things were done during ship's day, for who knows what one who has been abandoned on a near lifeless world might do in the midst of being startled awake?"

"Wingleader, I..."

"Enough. Calibrate. I will sleep again tonight, and some of tomorrow day as well..." which was unlikely, so he owned to himself, but minor, as he was no longer entirely on ship schedule.

This was an oddity he considered too minor to concern med techs of any ilk, though interesting to himself. It seemed he was keeping two clocks now. One was the ordinary ship-clock any space traveler became accustomed to. The other...the other was the daily cycle of the planet he'd been stranded on, though he'd kept planet-time for so few days he might still be expected to be in transition-timing.

The X Strain tech finished a half-hearted tour of the sensors, used her light to peer inside his cubicle and satisfy herself that he was not green and leafy, and that the tree was. She left then, without a word to him, leaving him wakeful.

And that, too, might have been her purpose.

Jela crossed his arms over his head, his thoughts on the planet of the trees, its sea, and other things he could not possibly remember from the place. No doubt he'd been very close to total exhaustion and on the verge of dementia when he'd been picked up. Perhaps the techs were right to be concerned after all.

Because he was a pilot, and an M, with all that Series' dislike of
being idle, he began to calculate. He checked his new sense of
time against the trip back to the mother-ship, knowing that the
breeze would about right *now* have been shifting to come at his
face if he stood on the hill over the empty sea.

That established, he calculated the entirety of his journey to
his best recall—brief time outbound, to taking on the enemy
vessel, to near automatic charting of course to the nearby planet,
to the landing...likely he spiked this or that spy-sensor as he
recalled the grueling and pitiless flight through that eventually
life-saving atmosphere—and then the walk. He recalled the
walk...vividly, recalled the valleys, treasured the long trip the
trees had undertaken from the side of a mountain to the ocean
so far away...

And that thought he put quickly away, tagging it mentally as a
mention-to-none, a category that by now seemed to include half
of his thoughts in any case.

Jela consulted the other clock in his head, saw that it would soon
be time for his breakfast and rose to do stretching exercises. When
the techs entered, en masse as they did at the beginning of each of
his days, he'd be good for a full schedule of work, sleepless half-
night or not.

The combat warning came before breakfast, and the transition
warning overlaid it almost instantly. Neither his bunk nor his chair
were attached to the deck within his isolation unit—nor was the tree
secured. His orders were clear—he was to observe the tree until
released to general duties.

Jela yanked his bunk against the wall of the wider room, ignoring the ripples in the flex-glass, and pushed the tree, still within
its own cocoon and attached to its various umbilicals, into the
corner thus made. Flinging himself against the bunk he hugged
the tree's base through the flexible walls, internal clock counting
the beats until—

"Go, dammit! Go!"

His voice rippled the flex-glass walls, and that was all the effect
it had. The ship shuddered with the familiar shrug of launching
fighters...but no stand down from the transition warning followed.
He did the calcs out of habit, assuming a nearby threat in the line of
travel—why else launch now?

There was another kind of shudder in the ship now—this one less familiar. Perhaps a jettisoning of mines…or an unusual application of control jets?

Maneuvering *was* starting. The direction of *up* shifted slightly; and then again; and, as if it hadn't already sounded, the transition buzzer went off again.

He ought to be with his wing! His duty—

He took a breath, and another, and did what he could to relax. Around him, the ship went absolutely still as it slipped into transition. He wondered, then and with an effort, how long breakfast would be delayed, and how many pilots they'd left behind so that breakfast was an issue.

Breakfast failed to arrive and it was nearing time for lunch. Jela remained close to the tree, concerned that any moment might bring them into normal space with unwanted, deadly motion. He was *still* sitting beside the tree when the commander arrived, four hurried helpers in tow.

"Take your samples, quickly," she ordered. She half-bowed, half-saluted Jela, who rose as quickly as he could.

"Wingleader, the medical department has been advised that they are no longer concerned with the possibility that you have become infected by contact with your tree. As they assure me you show no signs of physical abnormalities, other than those any M grade soldier might show at this point in his career, we shall shortly have an opportunity to discuss the matter I spoke of earlier. Please, Wingleader, prepare your computer for removal as well."

Jela went to the desk and snapped the unit together, watching with some relief as the technicians inserted a hosed connection to the outer lock of his chamber. In a few moments, the structure sagged around him and the outer flex-glass rippled as the technicians peeled apart the seal. A moment later, the inner seal sighed open and two technicians strode in, heading toward the tree. Only one was face-marked.

"The tree? I may take that with me?" he asked the nearest tech— the unmarked one—but was rewarded only with a half-formed shrug. He risked annoying the officer, whose attention was focused on a medical reader connected to the room's telemetry.

"Commander? The tree—I will take the tree with me as well, I assume?"

She didn't look up from her study of the reader, her answer heavy with irony. "Yes—the tree, the computer, your boots—whatever will make you comfortable, Wingleader!"

He nearly laughed, then wondered if he'd really put up that much of a fuss when they'd told him to leave his boots outside the isolation area. Yet as a soldier and a pilot he deserved certain politeness, and he was as aware as they that his treatment had misused his station.

The commander was quick.

"You, Corporal. You will carry this computer and walk with us to the Officer's Mess. You, Wingleader, may help the other tech as you will, or carry the tree if you prefer, and we shall together retire to the mess so that you may be fed."

In the end Jela carried the tree, while one of the techs carried his boots and his computer. They made a strange procession through a ship unnaturally quiet, and it had taken a moment or two of confusion to see everything placed when they arrived at the mess. At last, the techs were sent on their way and the Commander preceded him through the lunch line—open early, apparently for their convenience.

"So, Wingleader Jela, we have arrived at a place I'd hoped not to arrive at."

He looked up from his meal, startled, and she smiled a mirthless smile.

"No, it is not that I dislike the food onboard ship, as rumor might imply! Rather it is that our hand is forced—*my* hand is forced—and all of this ripples things set in motion long before either of us took our first breath."

Jela thought for a moment, waited until he was sure an answer was required.

"This is always the case with soldiers," he said carefully. "From the colors of our flags and uniforms to the names of our units to the choice of worlds we must defend, none of it is beyond the influence of what went before us. It is a matter of soldier's lore that we often die for the mistakes made generations before."

She was eating as if she, too, had been denied breakfast, but Jela saw that his remark had sparked something, for she put her fruit down and took a sip of her water, while raising a hand to emphasize...

"Which is the problem I deal with," she said, moving her hand almost as if she wanted to break into hand-talk. Jela followed her fingers for a moment, but she resisted or else failed to find the appropriate signs.

"You will not quote me to any on board this ship, Wingleader, but we have only a few days to prepare you. First, I must ask if you have made any plans for your retirement?"

He nearly choked, hastily swallowed bread in mid-chew.

"Commander, no, I have not," he admitted, stealing a hurried sip of juice. "I've always thought I would die on duty, else on penalty of some infraction..."

"Indeed? Then you have paid no attention to the information from the bursar's office about time due and funds due, of the rewards of taking up a farm?"

He looked at her straight on and then allowed his eyes to roll.

"Commander, there's not much retirement allotted for an M. True, true, some of us have retired—I've heard of three, I think, but it's not something I admire. I just spent several days too many watching a star set on a desert world—a sight I'm assured is restful and worth seeking!—and found it far from restful. I fret when I'm not busy. You've seen my record! When I'm idle, I am as much an enemy of the corps as any..."

"No, Wingleader, I will not permit that statement. The truth is that you are what you say. You know you are an M; you would rather march in circles for days in payment for having had your fun than sit staring at a wall doing absolutely nothing, and often you are better informed than your commanders, for you sleep very little and begrudge it besides."

She paused, sipped her water, went on.

"Still, there is in your record the information that you've taken your leaves on quite a few worlds, you've managed to survive in situations that killed your crèche mates, and you're a very quick study. More, when you have been in command situations, you've done well until faced with dealing with the—let us call it *the weight*—of decisions made above your head."

Jela permitted himself a hand signal of acknowledgment, to go along with a sigh.

"I have very much been a soldier, Commander. Alas, some 'above my head' have been raised to different rules and understandings about soldiers, duty, and necessity."

"A soldier's truth, plainly put." This time her hand did signal agreement; it was as he had supposed—whatever other training or duties she'd had, the commander was a pilot.

She paused, pushed her plate away from her as if it were a distraction, and leaned toward him, speaking quietly.

"Wingleader, I have for you some choices. There *are* times in a soldier's life when choice is available; there *are* times when it is preferable. So listen-up, here are some choices. Alas—you have no time but the time we sit at this table to make up your mind. I will not say that I do not *care* which choice you make, but I expect you will know."

Jela listened, swore he could hear the sound of a leaf, rattling in the breeze. Indeed, there was a breeze now—the ventilators were running at some speed, having come up unnoticed during their conversation.

"First, you may remain Wingleader of your small squadron. It is likely to be reassigned, given that the duties of this vessel are soon to change, but it is a respectable position, in which you would do well, to the benefit of the troop."

His hand-signaled acknowledgment—*information received in clear form.*

"Next, rather than remain as Wingleader, you may accept assignment to another squadron as a pilot. This choice I suggest in case you expect the duties of Wingleader might wear on you over time. You would be placed in the available pilot pool and we would have no way to know what or where you might be assigned, but you would have no responsibilities but those of a pilot, which are known to you and, I think, not overwhelming."

"Finally, you may take a long-term temporary assignment delivering a very nearly surplus vessel to a long term storage area, with appropriate adjustment of rank. You would oversee the delivery crew and be responsible for seeing the vessel properly shut down in case it must be redeployed. You would also assist in assessing local unit response readiness, from a pilot's viewpoint, in areas you travel through, to and from. In order to facilitate this, you would undergo a short, specialized, dangerous, and highly confidential training. It will not be an easy assignment."

She stopped. Looked expectant. Waited.

Jela hand-signaled, *check me—I repeat the information.*

Then he did that thing, nearly word for word, out loud.

"Yes," she agreed, "that's accurate."

He waggled his fingers—pilot hand-talk for feigned indecision—rolled his eyes, and began to laugh. He waggled his fingers harder and laughed harder, 'til tears came to his eyes...

"*That* funny?"

"Yes. Oh yes..." Finally he wiped his eyes on a napkin.

"Commander, I have one question. May I take the tree with me?"

"With which choice?"

"If you make me Captain Jela and have me deliver a ship, may I take the tree with me?"

It was her turn to do the pilot's waggle of fingers.

"If the tree is on board this ship when you leave, it will be spaced, I assure you. A captain is permitted a mascot after all."

"May I know your name, Commander?"

"If you pass the training, Wingleader."

SIX

Training Base
Mission Time: 34.5 days and counting

JELA CAME AWAKE in the night, the scent of sea-salt competing
with that of wind-driven fresh water, as if an electrical storm fresh
from the sea had burst upon the mountains behind, just before dawn.

A sense of energetic jubilation emanated from the youngers; a sense
of restrained relief from the elders upstream who knew that the combination of the early rain, rising sun, and the continued run of fresh
water from the hills would make this a wonderful day for growing.

Behind that relief, an under-note of melancholy drifted down
from the true elders, for in *their* youth, this would have been a
likely morning for the flyers to come and tend those whose detached branches or tangled seed-pods might cause difficulty later
in the season. The seed-carriers, the branch-tenders—they had been
with the trees since the dawn of awareness—had since vanished
from an awareness that yet grieved their loss.

Awake, Jela stood beside the tree knowing that, yes, it was just
about time for "sunrise" on a planet light years away from their
current billeting and knowing that in some fey fashion, the tree had
managed to dream *too loud*, so he had become encompassed as well.

The chronometer on the wall was adamant. No matter what
time the tree—or Jela, for that matter—thought it was, the duty
schedule indicated that breakfast, exercise, and class work were still
more than half his sleep-shift away. Alas, the schedule was obviously not designed for the convenience of an M Series soldier, but
to fit some administrator's concept of a busy day, or perhaps to
answer necessities a mere M had no need to be aware of.

Schedule or no schedule, he was awake and likely to remain so.
Sighing, Jela stretched and worked with a small weight set, all the
while trying to diminish the sadness he felt for the winged-things
he'd never seen, but whose touch was familiar and missed.

Despite the exercise, the sadness hung on, threatening to en-
compass the universe. He knew better than to wallow, and hoped

the tree did. But the tree might well still be in some in-between state of its own, and he felt no desire to disturb it.

Drawing a stim-drink from the small refrigerator, he broke the seal and stood sipping.

He'd spent the early evening reviewing troop strength charts; the attack patterns in the last wave of the First Phase; the siting of existing garrisons, their commanders, and their loyalties; the trading patterns and names of the major companies and players...

Now, he sat at the computer and began once again to go over the diagrams and intelligence...

First, though they controlled a good bit of the galaxy, Command was split on how to proceed, with a group allied largely with the inmost faction attempting to withdraw all forces from the Arm, in order to consolidate a line at the base.

This dangerously flawed plan had clearly been constructed by someone who had no sense of dimension—and no understanding of the nature of the enemy. For every time the *sheriekas* had been beaten back, they'd surged forward again, each time coming closer to claiming the right to control man's destiny.

And now? Now, the more observant of the High Commanders felt the war was almost lost, that the *sheriekas* were bare years away from being able to go wherever they wished, whenever they wished, to command, enslave, destroy...

Destroy.

It appeared that the enemy had less and less desire to control mankind and more desire to just be rid of it entirely. More, they seemed willing, or even eager, to destroy everything in existence in favor of some future where the very quarks trembled at their name.

The intelligence on this was spotty, though an M's intuition knew it for truth.

His drink done, Jela closed the intelligence data and opened what had lately become his most-accessed files. He was in a fair way to becoming obsessed with the problem they'd set him—two so-called math instructors his intuition told him he was unlikely, after all these days of duty, to see again.

He flicked through his data, frowning. Missing space craft were one thing; missing planets another. Both events were of course disturbing, though ordinary enough in a universe where black holes and novas and other such events were known, in a universe where the math—and hence the weapons—existed that could destroy a world with chain-reacted nuclei or the casual accidental flare of a burping solar-storm.

But lately, some other events were unfolding, as if *space* were unfolding, or as if the space where humanity lived among the stars was from time to time...dissolving.

The word *unfolding* had come from the younger and quieter of the two instructors; a sharp disagreement had followed its utterance.

It quickly became apparent to Jela that the disagreement was something more—and more serious—than simple professional sniping. The elder and more voluble instructor believed that the younger's *unfolding* was too simple a model; that if certain late developments were *mere unfolding*, the universe would simply get bigger—well, no, not bigger, not precisely, but that it would acquire another dimension, a dimension of so little moment that it would take five to ten times the known life of the universe for it to materially affect the spin of something as inconsequential as an electron.

No, the operative word, according to the voluble one, as he scribbled on the situation board—"Here! *This* is the math we have to work from!"—was *decrystallization*.

The instructor admitted that he had not the final proofs, that the math they were working from was the partial and not yet finished work of a mathematician who had unfortunately come to the notice of those who found his theories and equations anathema. The quiet instructor spoke of the mathematician as one honorably dead in battle and had turned to inscribe a series of equations that looked remarkably like piloting forms onto the situation board.

"The problem we face," he murmured, "is that someone—and we must assume that *someone* equals *the enemy*—is experimenting with dismantling the universe."

It was said so calmly that it was only in retrospect that Jela felt a flicker of dread.

The elder instructor tossed his pen from hand to hand pensively.

"Yes," he said finally, "that's a reasonable shorthand for the event, no matter what the full math may describe. It's rather as if you were able to set up a force field around a courier ship, attach it to a sector of the universe, and transition...forever."

"Good," said the younger, finishing up his notations and standing back. "That description allows us to use math that should be very familiar to our student." He gave Jela an uncomfortably earnest stare before waving toward the situation board. "Let's suppose, for example, that you wanted to visit the garrison at Vinylhaven..."

Unsurprisingly, the math was quite accurate for the mass of the proposed courier ship; the instructor then solved it for a location deep in the heart of the galaxy, on a heading that Jela recognized.

"Now, what we'll do for this mmm...trip..." the instructor murmured, as if talking to himself more than his increasingly puzzled student, "is restate the mass of the ship, drop it out of the locus defined by our standard five dimensions and into one defined by nine."

He did this, Jela checking the new equation on his pad...

"Now, the thing is..." the instructor said, suddenly turning away from the board, "no one really wants to go to Vinylhaven..."

Jela had been thinking the same thing himself, Vinylhaven being somewhat too close for comfort to the remains of the ember of a brown giant...

"...because," the instructor continued in his deceptively quiet voice, "it's not there."

Jela flat out stared. "*Not there?*" he demanded, wondering now if all of this had been some sort of elaborate hoax to test the gullibility of intransigent M's. "I've *been* there."

"Not lately," the elder instructor said simply. "I have been—or, say, I have attempted to go—within the last two Common Years. It is, as my colleague says, not there. Not the garrison world, not the brown giant. While we can use the coordinates that formerly brought us to Vinylhaven, in fact we can only come to the approximate vicinity, for pretty much everything out that way is gone. The nearest known destination we can raise is the yellow star three light years away, which is still there, though it has gone nova."

"Our guess," the younger instructor said seriously, "is that a sphere—and this *is* a guess; it may well be a more complex shape—approximating three-fourths of a cubic light year was—taken away. I say the space was folded; my associate says the space—actually a small portion of the universe—was decrystallized. Down to the photons and below, there is *nothing*. We can measure the event—are measuring it—by finding the wave front of light."

He paused for a moment's serious study of the situation board and the equations elucidated there, then looked back to Jela.

"Given the fact that Vinylhaven is gone," he murmured, "let's calculate the transport-can big enough to hold the missing volume and mass..."

The lesson was not lost on Jela. They did the math, several times.

"Your answer as to the power source?" the elder instructor asked Jela.

He sighed and pushed back from his pad, though his fingers still wandered lightly over the keys, looking for a solution that made sense, granting the data...

"Lossless total conversion?" he offered.

"Consider the multiple spin-states, and the mass of the photons..." The younger, that was.

Jela sighed again. "Are you sure there's not a black hole? I mean..."

"Absolutely no sign of one," the elder answered, "and insufficient to have cleared the zone. Lossless total conversion fails, as far as we're able to compute, if the mass actually moves somewhere else. We're talking energy levels above those in a super-sized galactic core black hole. With no trace."

"The nova you mentioned?"

"Likely not coincidence," the elder conceded, "but not nearly enough power to cause this. Perhaps there was leakage and we simply don't know what to look for."

"Not natural," Jela persisted. "You're *sure?* Not some rare, once-in-a-billion-year event?"

The two instructors looked at each other and a message passed between them as surely as if they'd used finger-talk.

The younger reached into a pocket and withdrew a datastrip.

"Vinylhaven is the seventh such event that we're sure of. We have been apprized of three more since. All in the Arm. This datastrip contains a summation of the ten events and what we can deduce about the physics, the geology, and the cosmology."

He laid the strip across Jela's palm. "Tomorrow, we'll want to see if you've found a pattern."

The elder instructor placed a second strip in Jela's hand.

"Background on the commanders and garrisons, native populations. The people..."

Dread nibbled at the edge of Jela's consciousness again, dread and sadness.

"Do you expect *me* to solve this?" he asked.

They looked away, almost as one. The elder looked back with a sigh.

"No. Not solve it. But we want your help. We're looking for special circumstances. For insight. For hope. And you must know, Captain M, that your mission, when you leave here, will be in part to keep the troops in place and fighting, whether there is hope or none. It's about all we can do right now."

However, the next day did not bring the mathematical pair back, nor the next several days beyond that. Rather, Jela was immersed in an intense round of training on surviving small-arms shoot-outs, of choosing the right weapon, of avoiding detection; as refreshers on ships, on engines and power plants, on intra-system navigation, and more history of the First Phase.

So, he kept to the project in his so-called "off-time," eating over study flimsies, exercising with computer screens and keyboards within reach, captured by the problem and hungry to see where the data led him.

He tried to understand the locations of the disappearances, drawing simple maps of the missing sections, and more maps, over time. He'd tried analysis by local population or lack of it, since only four of the now-missing locations had any population to speak of. He analyzed by political leanings of nearby garrison commanders, by system discovery or occupation date, by the colors of the stars, even by the alphabetical orders of the names of the stars or systems or planets.

The databases he had been given were large and flexible; but he strained them, joined them together and drilled through them. He pondered and set the computer to pondering...

In the meantime: exercise, classes, exercise, reading, exercise, classes, exercise, research, sleep.

Sleep proved its own mystery for there was no doubt that he'd found a pattern to his wakefulness that no longer matched a typical M's profile. As little as the average of the M Strain slept, he slept less. And there were the dreams, usually not so loud as to wake him, and behind them the conviction that he could almost smell the water, hear the surf on the beach, recall the dragons hovering over the world-forest, and know their names.

This last was the most perplexing—for he must assume that the dreams and wistful memories were the tree's, channeled to him by a mechanism he accepted without understanding—and how would the tree know the names of beings who rode the air currents?

He permitted himself little time to explore these personal mysteries, however, with so glorious and complex a problem before him.

It was the middle of the sixth day following his assignment to the task of the disappearances when the elder of the two instructors reappeared, interrupting a landing sim. Jela was a little disturbed by this, for the sim was decidedly trying to create unfavorable conditions and he'd yet to crash or hard-land—

"Captain," the instructor said briskly. "We will be sharing a quick meal with my colleague; our schedules will no longer mesh with yours after today, and so we seek a summary from you. In no case, by the way, will you divulge your analysis of the situation to the common troops you will be visiting as part of your mission. Most will lack your training and appreciation of nuance. Please follow me."

Though courteously enough phrased, it was an order, so Jela locked the sim and followed the instructor out of the connected rooms of his dormitory and tutoring hall, through a series of corridors on dark-time schedule.

They passed several people, none of whom acknowledged them, and arrived in a small cafeteria as the younger instructor hurried in from yet another corridor, carrying what appeared to be travel cases.

"We're set," he said to the elder. "When the interview is over, we go."

Jela's interest was piqued: for many days it had been as if the only concern of this place was him and his training. To see outside necessity now so much in view...

"Please," the elder instructor said to Jela. "Sit and eat. We're outbound in short order."

The meal was decidedly more ambitious than he'd been expecting, given the apparent imminence of the instructors' departure, and Jela fell to it with more enjoyment than he usually found in dining hall food. The initial discussion was near commonplace— questions about which information he'd thought most useful, which databases might as well be left out if the information were to be shared elsewhere...

There was, amazingly, real coffee to finish the meal, which suggested his instructors to be even more out of the ordinary than he'd thought. High-rank officers, then, or independent specialists beyond the direct control of the military—

"And so," the younger said at last, "as you have had an extra bit of time in which to consider, would you care to share with us your analysis?"

Eyebrows up, Jela glanced about the room and the several tables occupied by quiet-speaking folk.

The elder instructor smiled. "Of the secrets here, this is—like every secret here—the most important."

The younger moved a hand for attention.

"What we have is a series of potentially cascading situations," he said seriously. "Some discuss this type of event in terms of catastrophe. Things beyond our control and possibly beyond our ken have been set in motion and will continue in motion. And we? We are in a precarious spot, as if we stand on a high ridge of sand capable of sliding either to the right or to the left.

"The motion—let's call it a wind—may set off a slide, or it may not. If the wind carries more sand, the slide might go to the right. If the wind carries moisture, the slide may be delayed—or it may be to the left. If the winds gain strength slowly, an equilibrium may be reached for some time. If the winds, they bluster—well then, we may have an avalanche—and still we are unsure if we will slide left or right."

"So our words, heard or unheard," the elder said after a moment, "do not move us from the ridge. They may or may not permit us to jump in the most advantageous direction at the correct time. And that we know the wind is blowing—it is of no moment. The wind cares not."

Jela, from an impulse which felt oddly tree-like, saluted the instructors.

"In that case, yes, I have found patterns. Many of them. They perhaps point somewhere useful; they raise questions I would pursue if my time were my own."

"Have some more coffee, my friend," suggested the elder, pouring as he spoke.

Jela sipped appreciatively and placed the cup carefully on the table.

"I would summarize this way: the basic patterns of the settled worlds were such that trade peaked at about the same time for all of them. This makes some sense, after all, when one compares the ebb and flow of galactic economics and populations, and when one looks at what these worlds offered for trade. None of them ever rose above mid-level—but they're all somewhat removed from the most profitable of the trade routes.

"The pattern of the unsettled worlds was that traffic to and from peaked at about the same time as the settled worlds in question." He paused to look at the instructors, seeing only serious attention in their faces.

"These are misleading patterns," he continued. "There's a far more interesting underlying connection; and one far, far older.

"As near as I could tell, the star systems in question were all very nearly the same age. I mean this with an accuracy I can't properly express. Though listed in some catalogs as having a range in birth of several millions of years, it appears that they may have been more closely linked than that. My guess would be that they were exactly the same age."

The instructors sat as if entranced while Jela paused, picked up his cup, stared into it, trying to put thoughts, feelings, intuitive leaps into something approaching linear.

At last, he sipped his coffee, sighed. Sipped again, and looked at them hard, one after the other.

"The trade patterns were merely an accident of trade and technology; I doubt that they were anything more than a symptom."

He sipped again, still feeling for the proper way to tell it...

"Isotopic timonium," he said, at last. "Each of the systems had been sources of an isotopic timonium. The stars were known to retain a fair amount, the planets orbiting them contained some, the gas clouds beyond had it...I'm tempted to say a *unique* isotopic timonium—I can't, not having all the information to hand.

"The pattern I see most fully is that the matter in all of those systems was formed from the same cataclysmic event. They shared birth, perhaps in the intergalactic collision that helped form the Arm. Again, I can't—didn't have time—to do the retrograde orbital analysis, the spectrum comparisons, the motion component cross-sections, the..."

He stopped himself. After all, the instructors didn't care what he hadn't done, but what he had.

"Unique isotopic timonium?" the younger instructor murmured. "This despite the distances from each other?"

"It's the pattern behind many of the other patterns," Jela assured him, being confident on that point at least. "I've lately seen literature which indicates that timonium was long considered to be an impossible element, semi-stable despite its atomic number, radiating in an unnatural spectrum...all this early conjecture was news to me, since my education was practical rather than creative."

He shrugged.

"I can't guess all of it. But, given a unique proto block or proto cloud formed in part into a galaxy that collided with the one we now inhabit—we speak in billions of years now!—and this timonium, which has all decayed at the same time, so close as if it came from the same furnace."

He sipped the last bit of coffee in his cup, saw the glance between the instructors from beneath hooded eyes.

"The *sheriekas*," he murmured, almost as quietly as the younger instructor. "They use timonium as if it were the commonest of metals. If anyone can find it at a distance, they can. If anyone knows how to make it act, or how to act on it at a distance, they can."

A chime then, and the instructors looked to chronographs and hastily rose.

"Destroy your working files," said the elder tutor, "and whatever hard copies you may have made. Eventually, of course, others may see the same thing, assuming they can access the information."

The younger instructor sighed audibly.

"You have—given the information we brought together over our careers—duplicated our thinking. This information has been shared only at the highest levels. Your commanders understand and act upon it; all others ignore it and deny it."

The elder instructor picked up a travel bag and looked pointedly at Jela.

"Do not doubt yourself," he said sternly. "The particular crystal that we protect, that we live within, is in danger. You, Captain, are one of a few who know the depth of the danger, and one of the fewer still who might do something about it."

Then, with a most unexpected flutter of pilot hand-talk, signaling, *most urgent, most urgent, most urgent,* he continued. "My studies show that there are universes entirely inimical to life. And there are universes not inimical which yet have none…"

From without came the sudden snarl of an air-breathing engine. The speaker lost his train of thought in the noise and looked to his fellow.

A second chime sounded, and amid a checking of pockets and carryabouts, the instructors saluted Jela as if he were an admiral, and hurried off.

"Carry on, soldier," the quiet instructor said over his shoulder—and that was the last he heard or saw of them.

He carried on. He saluted the empty space, poured the last of the coffee into his cup, and sat with it cradled between his palms until it grew cold. Shaking himself, he rose, leaving a hint of a drop in the bottom of the hard-used cup, and returned to his interrupted sim.

SEVEN

Awaiting Transport

JELA STOOD QUIETLY in the arid breeze, fascinated—or so it might have appeared to an observer—by the pair of contrails crossing the cloudless blue-green sky on exactly the same heading, one perhaps a hundred of Jela's calm breaths behind the other.

There was no way that a man without instruments could positively say which was higher, though Jela felt he knew. The leader, he thought, would land and be on its way to rotating its wheels for takeoff before the second touched down. After all, that's what had happened when he'd landed here, many days ago.

Yet the observer—and there was no small chance that there was such, likely watching from a camera or sensor stand for one last bit of measurement, one last bit of information about this particular candidate—the observer would have been wrong.

Far from being fascinated, M. Jela Granthor's Guard had pitched his mind as close to a dream state as he might while continuing to stand upright at the edge of the runway, and was himself observing: listening to the keening echo of ancient, dead-and-gone flying things and concentrating on templates that fell almost visually across his concentration. The tree sat companionably by his side, its topmost leaves moving in a pattern not entirely wind-driven.

Leaning against the tree's lightweight traveling pot was the small kit he'd been given on his arrival at the training grounds. Anything else he owned was elsewhere, perhaps not to be seen again. He hoped, as he stood watching the contrails approach, that he'd soon be allowed his name back. The trainers had, without fail, called him Captain M and, while his name was nothing more than a quartermaster's joke, he was fond of it.

It could well be that they had been told no better name for him. After all, the fact that he was an M was there for all to see—and that he'd been training for duties and activity somewhat...above...those assigned a corporal, was also as clear as the air here.

There.

With an almost audible snap, the top branch fluttered and the template not quite before his eyes became an odd cross, the image half a small spacecraft and half a dragon gliding serenely on stiff wings.

Jela's back-brain applauded the attempt to match this relatively new experience with an unutterably ancient one and to adjust that template on the fly, as it were.

The scary thing—and it was scary, on the face of it—was that the template continued to evolve, as if the tree were able to reach into Jela's own store of memories and capture details it could never have known of for itself.

As he watched, the dragon's wings began to bulge at wing-root—but that was surely because Jela knew the craft on the way was an air-breather for much of the trip and would have engines buried there. Too, the keening of mighty dragons was giving way to not one, but two sets of incoming jet sounds, yet the approaching craft was still some moments beyond the range where any human ears might actually hear them.

He shivered then, did Jela, and let his attention return to the exact here and now that he breathed in, letting the template fade from his thought. The first craft was on final approach over the distant river and the second was making its turn—and *now* the engine sounds hit him, waking a touch of nostalgia for the first time he'd flown an air-breather.

There, the landing gear glinting, and *there*, the slight flare-out as a moment of ground-effect lift floated the graceful plane a heartbeat above the cermacrete runway.

A beautifully light landing then, with hardly a sound from the gear and barely a sniff of dust, and the underwhine ratcheting down quickly…

The fuselage hatch opened and two people stood inside, one to a side, as the craft rolled to a stop directly in front of him. The plane obligingly folded its gear to bring Jela within reach of the short step-ramp, and the two inside jumped the final knee height to his side to help him up, each flashing a salute, despite the fact he had no insignia on his near-colorless 'skins.

One of the assistants took his kit, the other considered the tree for a moment, decided on the proper way to hoist…

And that quickly was Jela within the plane, and the tree beside him, the only occupants of a small if comfortable passenger cabin. The engines began revving, the plane started rising on its gear to take-off height, and the assistants helped Jela snap into his belts.

Two more salutes and the assistants stepped off the plane, leaving the tree, taking the kit, and closing the hatch against the sound and the breeze.

On the wall before him was the flashing "Lift in Progress" sign, but he'd already felt the plane's gear lock and the motion of the completed turn. He settled in, envisioning—for the tree—what had just occurred, and then relaxed as the craft hurtled down the runway and into the air. The small *thwap* of the gear-doors closing mirrored a jolt of acceleration and the nose rose.

Through the cabin's small view port, he caught a glance of the second craft, now landing. Like this one, it bore no markings.

"Well," he said conversationally to the tree, "guess I get a new wardrobe when we get where we're going!"

He closed his eyes as the comfortable push of the ship's lift continued, indicating a pilot in something of a hurry.

Being neither pilot nor co-pilot, the best thing he might do for the troop at the moment was sleep—which he did, willingly.

As usual he woke quickly, finding the plane about him barely an instant after deciding to wake. The afterimage of his working dream was a reprise of his last meeting with the language team. Of all the work—ranging from new and surprisingly interesting methods of killing, to explosives, to studies of maths far beyond those that he'd aspired to—it was the language work which had been a non-stop challenge. And the dream left him with the impression that he still needed work, that his skills were not quite adequate for the task to hand.

It was then that the craft banked and the door to the piloting chamber slid open. A voice, somewhat familiar, drifted back.

"Captain Jela, welcome. Please come forward and take the second seat."

Jela unstrapped, pleased. He hated to be bored.

The flight deck was exactly like the trainers they'd tested him on—no surprise. Nor was the pilot's face.

"Commander." He nodded as he strapped in. Her 'skins, like his, were without markings, he saw.

She nodded in return.

"Your board will be live in a few moments. We'll hit the boost shortly—but there—see your screen for details. Soon we'll rendez-vous with a ship carrying your crew and you'll begin simming on your new command.

"Your board is live, Captain," she said quite unnecessarily. "And, as you'll find in your info pack when we arrive, I am Commander Ro Gayda. Welcome to the real war."

PART TWO

SMUGGLER

EIGHT

On Board *Spiral Dance*
Faldaiza Port

THE CARGO HAD been waiting, for a wonder, and the loading expeditious, for another. She was scheduled to lift out in what passed for early tomorrow, hereabouts, which meant she had twenty-three hours, ship-time, in which to please her fancy.

The last few ports had been something short of civilized, by even her standards, so it happened she had a fancy.

She shut the board down as far as she ever did, having long ago learned not to turn off all the tell-tales and feeds, and never to put all systems in suspend, where she couldn't grab them out again in a hurry. With her outbound so soon, it really didn't make much sense to go through the extra half-shifts of shutdown and boot-up, anyway.

While *Dancer* settled in to doze, she idly watched the local port feed. Some familiar names scrolled by—a bar she knew pretty well, or at least had known pretty well, and a couple jumping-jacks.

She considered the 'jacks and shook her head. She was too old to think of paper sheets as anything but a last resort that'd leave her needing to do things right next port. The problem with running a solo ship—and having a reputation for liking it that way—was some folks figured you were *always* solo, or else somebody whose interests weren't much in the public way. Mostly, she guessed, she fit that.

Not that she'd always run solo. Back when she'd been Garen's co-pilot and they'd done most of their work on the Rim—there'd been some grand flings, back then. She sighed and shook her head again.

Wasn't any use thinking about Garen, or about past lusts, either. Nothing good ever came out of thinking about the past.

Now. Now what brain and body were united in wanting was a time to relax and sleep naked-to-naked, after a couple heavy duty squeezes, some teasing and some sharing…*Now* was when it was hard on a body to be solo.

Truth told, there'd been more choices, back when. She wasn't ever going to be a beauty, but she *was* a pilot, and she damn well came out for fun with plenty of money in a public pocket so she didn't have to hold out for somebody else wanting to pay.

Back when, she didn't have the history of having killed a couple idiots who'd tried to take her ship; she didn't have a record of being fined and confined for taking on—in a fair fight!—the entire executive section of a battle cruiser and leaving them on hospital leave. Nor did she, then, know that this one beat her co-pilot, and that one stole virgins, and that other one robbed the people he slept with, every one.

And there she was, thinking about the past again. Brain melt, that's what it was. Happened when you ran solo too long. Likely, the port cops would find her in her tower, gibbering and wailing, crying over people long dead and vapor, like tears could ever right things.

She glanced back at the port feed, still scrolling leisurely through the various entertainment options, reached out to tap a key and zoom in on one section.

Beautiful. Beautiful girls, beautiful boys, beautiful couples. And, the ad said, they delivered. She could have one or a pair brought right here to her, health certificates and all.

The prospect of having a cute local pro—even a pair of cute local pros—on hand to talk to in the middle of her night warmed her not at all.

She needed to get *out*, off-ship, away from metal walls and the sound of her own thoughts. Away from the past.

A tap on the keyboard banished the port feed. Another put the lighting back to night-rest. She stood and stretched to her full lean height, then headed for the hatch, snagging her kit-bag out of the empty co-pilot's chair.

First, food from something other than ship's store, maybe with a mild stimulant, to keep the edge on. After that—not ale, not today. Today, she'd have wine. Good wine—or the best on offer. And that food—nothing out of some grab-a-bite. No. She'd have plates, and linens, and pilots. Top of the line, all the way. She could afford it today, which wasn't always the case.

By the time she reached the edge of the field, she'd almost convinced herself that she'd have a great time.

Finding a room had been easy enough. The clerk at the Starlight Hotel was pleased to reduce her credit chit by a significant sum in return for a room complete with a wide bed, smooth sheets overlain with a quilted coverlet dyed in graduated shades of blue. A deep-piled blue carpet covered the floor; and the personal facilities boasted a single shower and a hand-finished porcelain tub wide enough to hold two, this not being a world which was exactly short on water.

She stowed her bag, had a quick shower, hesitated over maybe putting on something a little fancier than 'skins, decided that safety came first on Faldaiza, and headed out. The sweet smell of the hotel soaps and cleansers clung to her, distracting until she forgot them in her search for the rest of the list which had proved unexpectedly difficult to fulfill.

The first fancy eatery she approached advertised all kinds of exotic and expensive food-and-drinkables, but she caught the gleam of armor 'skins as she approached and decided against. The next place, the woman holding the door acted like maybe pilot 'skins smelled bad, and the third place was standing room only with a line out the door.

She was about to give up on food and move on to wine and companionship, when she happened on The Alcoves.

It didn't look so fancy as the others, but the menu scrolling over the door promised fresh custom-made meals at not-ruinous prices, and a list of wines she recognized as on the top level of good.

She squared her shoulders and walked in.

The master of the dining room wore a sleeveless formal tunic, the vibrant green tats of his Batch glowed against the pale skin of his forearms, short gloves and hosen, all shimmering with embedded smartstrands.

"Pilot," he said, with a gratifyingly respectful bow of the head. "What service may this humble person be pleased to provide?"

"A meal," she said, slipping a qwint out of her public pocket. "Company, if a pilot's asked."

He palmed the coin deftly and consulted his log.

"There is one guest who has requested the pleasure of sharing his meal with a fellow pilot, should one inquire. Happily, he has only recently achieved a table, so your meals may be coordinated."

She felt something in her chest she hadn't known was knotted up ease a little and realized how much she had wanted another face, another voice, another *self* across the table from her. Someone who spoke the language of piloting, who knew what it was like to pour your life into your ship…

She inclined a little from the waist.

"I would be pleased to accept an introduction to this pilot," she told the master formally, and waited while he made a note in his log with one hand and raised the other, the strands of the glove glowing briefly.

From the curtain at his back, another Batcher appeared, also in smart formals, the same glow-green tats on her arms, her face an exact replica of the man's.

"This pilot joins the pilot seated in the Alcove of Singing Waters," the master said, and the waiter bowed.

"If the pilot would consent to enter," she murmured, and stepped back, sweeping the curtain aside with a tattooed arm.

She stepped into a wide hallway floored in gold-threaded white tiles. A subtle sound behind told her that the curtain had fallen back into place, and she turned slightly as the attendant approached.

"If the pilot will follow this unworthy one," the Batcher murmured and passed on, silent in gilded sandals.

Her boots made slightly more noise as she followed the Batcher, passing alcoves at measured distances. Across the entrance of each hung a curtain, heavy with sound absorbing brocade.

She had counted eight such alcoves on her right hand. At the ninth, her guide paused and placed her gloved palm against the drawn curtain.

Some signal must have been traveled from the brocade to the strands in the gloves and thence to the attendant herself, for she drew back the curtain slightly and made a bow.

"This one requests the guest's forbearance," the Batcher said softly. "A pilot comes to share food with a pilot, if this is still desired."

In the hall and some steps behind, for decency's sake, she heard nothing from the room in response, but the answer must have been in the affirmative, for the attendant pulled the curtain wider and beckoned.

"Pilot, if you please. The pilot welcomes you."

She went forward, walking easy, keeping her—specifically empty— hands out where they could be seen. On the edge of the alcove, she paused, letting the light outline her, giving the other pilot—and herself too, truth told—a last chance to have a change of requirement.

The man seated in the lounger next to the wall of flowing water that apparently gave the alcove its name was dark in the hair and lean in the face. From the breadth of his shoulders, she judged he'd top her not-inconsiderable height, but when he stood up to do the polite, she found herself looking down into eyes as black as the empty space beyond the Rim. His 'skins were dark, and it was hard to definitively decide where the man ended and the dim room began.

"Pilot," he said, and his voice was a clear tenor. "In peace, be welcome."

There weren't many who would violate the terms of peaceful welcome, and if the small big man was one, well—she had long ago learned to err on the side of mistrust.

So. "Pilot," she answered. "I'm pleased to share a peaceful interlude."

Behind her, she heard the curtain fall. Anything that was said between them now would be absorbed and erased by the brocades. Unless there were paid listeners, of course…

"The room sweeps clean," the other pilot told her, reading the thought on her face, maybe—or maybe just naturally assuming she'd want to know and looking to save her the effort of scanning.

As it happened, her 'skins were on auto-scan and, lacking a warning tone, she decided to take his word for the conditions.

"That's good news," she said and came another step into the room. "I'm Cantra."

"Welcome," he said again, and gestured toward the loungers by the water. "I'm Jela. I sent for a bottle of wine, which should be here soon. In fact, I thought you must be it. No doubt the house will provide another glass, if you'd care to share a drink before the meal?" He raised a broad, brown hand, fingers spread.

"You understand, I have a forgiving schedule, and set myself the goal of a leisurely meal. If your time is limited…"

"I've got a few local hours to burn," she said. "Wine and a relax would be—something a lot like nothing I've had lately."

He grinned at that, showing white, even teeth, and again indicated the loungers. "Have a seat, then, and listen to the singing waters, for if I'm not mistaken—" A gong sounded, softly, from the brocaded ceiling.

"Enter!" Jela called, and the curtain parted for the female Batcher, bearing a tray holding a bottle of wine and two glasses.

Cantra sat down and let the lounger cradle her body. Jela sought the chair opposite and the attendant brought the wine to the table between them. She had the seal off efficiently and poured a mite of pale gold into each glass, handing the first to Jela, the second to Cantra.

Passing the glass beneath her nose brought her a rush of scent and a growing conviction that she was in the right place.

She sipped: sharp citrus flavors burst on her tongue, followed by a single note of sweetness.

"I'm pleased," Jela said to the attendant. "Pilot?"

"I'm—pleased," she replied, handing her glass back to the attendant with a smile. "And pleased to have more."

This was accomplished without undue fuss. Both pilots being accommodated, the attendant bowed.

"This humble person exists to serve," she said. "What may it please the pilots to order from our available foods?" She placed her gloved hands together and drew them slowly open. In the space between her palms, words formed—the house's menu.

Jela ordered leisurely, giving Cantra time to peruse the offerings and settle on the incredible luxury of a fresh green salad, non-vat fish steak, and fresh baked bread.

The attendant bowed, closed the menu and departed, silently slipping past the brocade curtain.

Cantra sipped her wine, relishing the flavors and the layers of taste. Across from her, the man—Pilot Jela—he sipped, too, cuddled deep in his lounger, forcefully projecting the impression of a man relaxed, indolent, and slow.

She having projected just such impressions herself from time to time in the interests of not frightening the grounders—maybe she was a little too aware of what he was doing. It might have been polite, not to notice. But it irritated her, to be treated like a know-nothing, and she brought her glass down to rest against her knee.

"You don't have to go to all that trouble for me," she said. "Pilot."

There was a short space of charged silence, as if he weren't used to being called on his doings, then a nod—neither irritable nor apologetic.

"Old habits," was what he said, and lifted his glass to sip with a respect that she registered as real. The relaxation he showed now was properly tempered and much more restful to the both of them, she was sure.

They sat quiet for a while then, each sipping, and letting the water whisper its song down the wall and disappear.

"Where are you in from, if it can be told, Pilot Cantra?"

"Chelbayne," she answered. Nothing to hide there, now that she was away, the cargo delivered and the fee paid. "Yourself?"

"Solcintra."

Kind of an Inner world, was Solcintra, or near enough that somebody from the Rim might think it not quite on the Arm, proper. A kind of has-been old settle in a quiet area where everyone traded with neighbors, that was all. Not a place she'd normally find herself. Still, you never knew.

"Anything special?" she asked, and saw him shrug against the lounger's deep back. She hadn't asked what kind of pilot he was; he might be anything from a cruise liner captain to a freight hauler to a relief man. 'Course, his presence on Faldaiza Port kind of argued against the cruise liner.

"There's a military unit garrisoned there," he was saying carefully over his glass. "A good few dozen ships attached to it. Most of them seemed to be in twilight."

Well, and that was news, after all. Soldiers were inevitable, in Cantra's experience. Garrisoned soldiers—they were something of an oddity. And even more so, squatting down on a not-especially-prosperous world, trailing a buncha dozen sleepy ships...

"And how did you find things at Chelbayne?" he asked, taking his turn, which was polite and his right under peaceful welcome.

"Spooked," she said frankly. "Pilots doubling up on port. Rumors thicker'n star fields. Reported sightings of anything you like, including world-eaters, manipulators, and ancient space probes showing up with 'return to sender' writ on the power panels."

"Huh," he said, sounding intrigued in the way somebody would be by somebody else's craziness. "Anything stand up to scrutiny?"

She shrugged in her turn, feeling the lounger move to accommodate the motion. "The probes I heard about from somebody normally straight. On port for repair, she was, and looking to sign a new co-pilot. Could be she was ground-crazy. My inclination is to discount all I heard, no matter who gave it out. But maybe somebody really is collecting old space probes. Why not?"

"Why not?" he echoed comfortably. "See any yourself on the way in?"

She snorted. "Not to recognize." She sipped the last of her glass and put it on the table. "You been on port awhile?"

"A while," he allowed, finishing his own glass and leaning out of the embrace of the lounger. "More wine?"

"Yes," she said. And then, thinking that might have sounded too short, "Please."

He poured, splitting what was left equally between the two glasses, handed hers over, then sat back with his.

"Anything I should know, port-wise?" Cantra asked. "Don't want to be here past scheduled lift, paying for a misstep."

He was quiet—thinking—honestly thinking, was her sense, and not mumming. She sipped her wine and waited.

"There seem to be some odd elements on the port," he said slowly. "I'm not clear myself what makes them odd, or if odd translates into dangerous. The locals..." He paused to sip his wine gently. "The locals may have caught some of that spooked feeling from Chelbayne. Usual rules apply."

The last was said without irony, and with enough emphasis to move him well out of the passenger liner column on the pilot rating chart, as far as she was concerned. That was with the usual rules being: Watch your back, watch the shadows, and always expect trouble.

"That's something," she acknowledged.

He nodded, seemed about to say something more, but the gong sounded again, and he called "Enter," instead.

The Batcher attendant slipped into the room and bowed.

"Would it please the pilots to receive their meals?"

The food and the discussion of the food having both come to satisfactory conclusions, Cantra called for a third bottle of wine. It came promptly, was poured, and the two of them again sat deep into the loungers.

Cantra sighed, inert and content. The dinner talk, light on info as it had been, had finished unknotting the tension in her chest. She was in no hurry to move on; even the itch to find someone to share the upscale lodgings with had gone down a couple notches on the gotta list.

"So," said Jela from the depths his chair, and sounding as lazy as she felt. "Where do you go from here, if it can be told?"

That ran a little close to the edge of what was covered by peaceful welcome. Still, she didn't need to be specific as to when.

"Lifting out for the Rim," she said which was bound to be true sometime.

"Heard there was some military action in the far-out recently," he said, slow, like he was measuring how much info to offer. "Maybe even a world-eater sighted."

She moved her shoulders, feeling the chair give and reshape. "Rim's always chancy," she said. "All sorts of weird drifts in from the Deeps. Won't be the first time I've been out that far."

"Ship shielding doesn't even give a world-eater indigestion," he pointed out, sounding sincere in his concern. "And ship beams are just an interesting appetizer."

"That's right," she said, puzzled, but willing to play. "But a ship can run; a ship can transition. World-eaters are stupid, slow and confined to normal space."

"You talk like you've had some experience there," Jela said, which was absolutely a request for more, and danced well outside the confidentials guaranteed under peaceful welcome.

She took her time having a sip of wine, weighing the story and what might be got from it that she took care not to say.

In the end, it was inertia and a full belly that made the decision. She wasn't ready to move on just yet, and there wasn't much, really, to be gained from the tale, setting aside piloting lore which this Jela, with his big shoulders and noncommittal eyes, surely had, either from experience of his own or from training. He was no fresh-jet, in her professional judgment. Still, if he wanted to hear it...

"Not a new tale," she said, bringing her glass down at last.

"New to me," he countered, which was true enough—or so she hoped.

"Well, then." She settled her head against the chair and paused, letting the whisper of the falling water fill the silence for a heartbeat, two...

"I was co-pilot, back when," she began. "The pilot had some business out on the Rim, so there we were. Problem came up and we lifted in a hurry, ducking out a few klicks into the Beyond." She paused to have a sip.

"That's some problem," Jela said after her glass came down again, and she nearly laughed.

You might allow it to be a problem when the cargo was wanted by the yard apes who were all too ready to confiscate it and all the info there might be in ship's log and the heads of pilot and co-pilot. You might allow it to be a problem that the client wasn't particularly forgiving of missing deliveries and Garen having to make the call, was it better to lose the cargo out in the Deeps and maybe have a chance to collect it later, risking the client's notable bad grace, or chance a board-and-search?

She'd opted to dodge and jettison, a decision for which Cantra didn't fault her, though they never did find it again, worse luck, and wound up working the debt off across a dozen runs, the client having been that peeved by the loss.

"It was a problem of some size," she told Jela. "Understanding that the pilot was out of the Rim, original—and didn't maybe respect Beyond like she ought. Anywise, we're out there, beyond the Rim, just meditating, and giving the problem time to brew down to a lesser size, when an anomaly shows up on the far-scans." She shrugged against the chair's embrace.

"A pilot's not a pilot unless they got a curiosity bump the size of a small moon, so she and me, we decide to go take a look."

"In the Beyond?" His startlement seemed genuine. "How did you navigate?"

"Caught the Rim beacons on mid-scan and did the math on the fly," she said, off-hand, like it was no trick at all. Nor was it, by then. By then, she and Garen had been out Deep considerable.

"So, we went on out to look," she resumed. "And we got a visual on something that looked to be a bad design decision on the part of the shipwright. Big, too. Not much velocity, spill spectrum showing timonium, timonium, and for a change timonium. Tracking brain plotted its course and saw it hitting the Rim at a certain point, in a certain number of Common Years.

"The pilot hailed it on general band and I hit it with every scan we had."

She sipped. He sat, silent, waiting for the rest of it.

"Well, it didn't answer the hail, o'course. And the scans bounced. I'm thinking it was the scans got its attention, but it might've been the hail, after all. It started to rotate and it started to get hot. Radiation scan screamed death-'n-doom. We figured we knew what we had by then, and the pilot was of a mind to turn it back into Beyond, where it couldn't do much harm."

"Turn it?" *That* got his attention.

"Right." She raised her hand, showing palm. "Say the pilot was a fool, which I'm not saying she didn't have her moments. Can't say for certain if that was one of them, though, because the truth is she did turn it, playing easy meat, while I sat my board sweating and feeding everything I dared into the shields, which were peeling like old hull paint."

"So I'd think."

"We kept its attention until we was sure it was on course for Out-and-Away. Shields were just about gone by then, and I was starting to fear for the navigation brain, not to say the biologics, when the pilot decided we'd done what we could, and nipped us into transition."

"Transition," he repeated. "Using what for reference points? If it can be told."

"Had the Rim beacons on long-scan, like I mentioned," she lied glibly. "Did the math on the fly."

"I—see." He had a go at his glass, and she did the same, to finish, and put the empty on the table.

She'd come too close to a slip, she thought, half-irritated and half-regretful. Time to be moving on, before she got any stupider.

"I want to thank you," she said formally, and his Deeps-black gaze flicked to her face. "For your companionship. The time was pleasant and informative. Now, I must take myself off."

She stood, leaving the embrace of the chair with a pang. Paused for one last listen of the singing water—and very nearly blinked as the other pilot came to his feet.

"As it happens, it's time for me to leave, too," he said blandly, and moved a hand toward the curtained exit. "Please, Pilot. After you."

Pilot Cantra was an interesting case, Jela thought, following that lady down the tiled hallway toward the foyer and the front door. The tale about turning the world-eater had rung true, though there had been, he had no doubt, a certain few tricky facts greased in the telling.

She wasn't being easy to file, either. He'd've said prosperous free trader, from the quality of the 'skins and the fact that she was eating at a subdued place on the high end of mid-range. On the other hand, there was that story and the easy-seeming familiarity with the Rim—and beyond. According to his considerable information, Rimmers had a flexible regard for such concepts as laws, ownership, and what might be called proscribed substances. Not that all Rimmers were necessarily pirates. Just that none of the contributors to the reports he'd been force-fed had ever met one who technically wasn't.

Given that she wasn't at all who he'd been expecting—he'd been expecting Pilot Muran, who was now some local days overdue for their rendezvous—he counted himself not unlucky in the encounter. She was a fine-looking woman—tall, lithesome, and he didn't doubt, tough. Her weapon was quiet, but there for those who knew how to look—and he appreciated both the precaution and her professionalism.

He'd entertained the notion that she might be somebody sent on by Muran, when he found himself unable—and dismissed it when the meal took its course and she failed to produce either code words or a message from the tardy pilot.

That she was only a pilot who had wanted company over her meal—that seemed certain, and he made a mental note to chew himself out proper for supposing that any pilot who would choose such a restaurant would come complete with co-pilot, client, or companion. Getting civilians into soldier trouble, that was bad.

Though there was no guarantee that there was or would be trouble, he thought, trying *that* notion on for not the first time. Muran being late—that could be explained by a couple things short of catastrophe.

Muran not sending a reason or a replacement—that couldn't. Jela sighed silently and owned to himself that he was worried.

Pilot Cantra had reached the curtain, swept it away with one long arm and stepped to a side, holding the doorway clear for him.

"Pilot," she said, and it could've been irony he heard in her voice, "after you."

He nodded and slipped past her, fingering coins out of his pocket as he approached the console.

Behind him, he heard the curtain go down. He deliberately didn't turn, but finished counting the price of the meal out into a pile, and a few more coins, into a second, smaller pile, over which he held his hand, fingers outspread.

"For the attendant," he said to the master's raised eyebrow. "The service was excellent and I am grateful."

The master's fee had come off the top when he had made his initial reservations. Jela had made a point of tipping the attendant on every visit.

Nodding, the master gathered up the meal-price, thumbed his drawer open and deposited the coins.

"This humble person is delighted to hear that the pilot is pleased," he said.

Jela felt a presence at his side and looked up, expecting to see the female attendant. What he did see, to his somewhat surprise, was Pilot Cantra, leaning forward to offer a credit chit. Yellow, he noted, being in the habit of noting such details. Whatever Pilot Cantra was, she was in funds today.

"The meal was fine, the company welcome," she said, her husky voice giving the formal words an interesting texture.

"This humble person delights in the pilot's pleasure," the master assured her expressionlessly, running the chit through the console's reader. There was a *ping* as the amount was deducted, and the chit was passed back. Green now, Jela noticed, but still at a more than respectable level for a pilot on Faldaiza Port.

Cantra received her chit and slid it away without giving it a glance. When her hand came out of her pocket, she leaned over and put a stack of coins next to Jela's stack.

"For the attendant," she said. "She served well."

"The pilot's generosity is gratifying," the master said and raised his hand. His Batch-sister slipped around the edge of the curtain and came forward until she was standing behind the console, facing Jela.

She was a compact woman, efficient-looking without being at all lithe. She bowed, precisely, and gathered the coins into her gloved hands.

"Pilots. It is the pleasure of this humble person to serve. Walk safely."

He felt Pilot Cantra stiffen beside him and hoped he had masked his own shock more fully.

Turning, he looked up into the other pilot's eyes. They were green, he saw, which he hadn't been sure of, in the dimness of the dining alcove, and calm, despite her start of shock.

"Shall we proceed, Pilot?" he asked, expecting her to push past him and stride out into the port on her own—which would clarify one thing or another.

But it appeared it was his hour for surprises.

"Why not?" Cantra said.

Outside, the shadows were lengthening into the leisurely local evening. Jela hung back a step, intending to let the other pilot make the first move.

"I don't *see* anything worth worrying about," she said easily, dawdling by his side—just two friends, finishing up a chat started inside over food and wine. "You?"

"Not immediately," he said with a smile for the joke she hadn't made. "Maybe we should move on, in case they're running late?"

"Good idea." She turned to the left and he went along, matching her long stride easily.

"Now I'll ask you," she said, without looking at him. "Was the Batcher having a little fun with us?"

It was an interesting question, all things considered, and Jela did consider it, alongside of a couple other facts and oddities, among them the lack of Pilot Muran—and the presence of Pilot Cantra, who might be an innocent civilian, or who might be something else.

"No reason to believe she was," he said slowly, not particularly liking the direction his thought was tending, but letting it have its head.

"Other question being," Cantra mused, and he approved the way she scanned the street as they walked along—eyes moving, checking high points, low points, possible places of concealment. "Who's likely to be wanting to talk with you in a serious way? I can think of some couple who might want to have a cozy chat with me, but nothing that can't wait."

There shouldn't, he thought, be anyone wanting to talk to him in any serious way, excepting the absent Muran.

They'd set up the rendezvous carefully, that being how they did things. And they'd arranged for a back up, just in case the primary went bad. He'd checked the back up, and needed to do so again—now, in fact. All things considered.

He glanced at the woman beside him and found her watching him, green eyes—amused?

Not easy to scan at all, was Pilot Cantra. And it came to him that he'd better make sure of her, if he could.

"I'm after a bit of noise and maybe something else to drink," he said. "You?"

Slim eyebrows arched over those pretty green eyes, and he thought she might turn him down. But—

"Sounds good," she said easily.

"I know a place just a couple steps over there." He cocked his head to the left, and she moved a slim, ringless hand in the pilot's sign for *lead on*.

NINE

On the ground
Faldaiza Port

PILOT JELA'S "PLACE," a bar-and-drinkery calling itself Pilot's Choice, was considerably more than a couple steps, situated as it was in the shadow of the port tower. Giving the pilot his due, it wasn't a pit, nor showing any 'jack spaces on offer. What it was, was full of pilots, loud voices, and something that might've been music—in fact, was music.

There was pair of bouncer-types checking ID at the door, which was a good thing by her way of thinking, 'cause it meant the local lowlifes weren't allowed in—just them with proper Port clearance or genuine pilot-class credentials.

Cantra showed her ship's key and was gratified to see the hand motion from the sharp-eyed man requesting just a bit more…and so she flashed the flat-pic with numbers and such on it. He didn't bother to run-scan on it, though the machine was live—just gave her a half-salute and waved her into the dense noise and rowdy dance-and-brew scent.

Apparently Jela was in the same pod as far as looking legit on visual, which was a shame, 'cause all she saw was him slipping his card into a semi-public pocket, the woman on that side singing out with a respectful, "Thank you, Pilot!"—and still not a polite way to find out exactly what he was a pilot of. But some information you just didn't ask if it didn't come voluntary.

They pushed on, just like they were together. The crowd motion stopped them for a moment, 'til she could point out to Jela the direction of the bar from her greater height, which information he acknowledged with equanimity.

Now they were further in, she could see a couple almost-nakeds on a raised platform on the opposite side of the room from the bar, dancing, they might've been. Looked interesting, whatever.

She let Jela break trail, which wasn't any problem at all for those shoulders, and directly joined him at the bar proper, one foot on the rail, waiting for the notice of the bartender.

"There's a man here I need to talk to," Jela said to her, his voice pitched to carry under the general hubbub. "It's probable he'll have news, maybe make some sense of our friend's concern, if you'd want to wait?"

She gave him a smile. "I'll wait," she murmured, for his ears only. "Why not?"

"Good. Back soon." He was gone, moving quick and light through the crowd and she watched him go, considering the wide shoulders and the slim hips with a sort of absent-minded admiration. Not her usual sort, Pilot Jela, but a well-made man, regardless.

"What'll it be, Pilot?" The bartender's prosaic question brought her back to the now and here.

"Ale," she said, knowing better than to ask for wine in a pilot's bar this far in to the shipyards.

"Coming up," the 'tender promised, and up it came in a timely manner. She smiled for the quick service and slid a couple carolis across the bar.

"Keep the change," she said. He gave her a grin and went away to tend to other customers.

Having ale didn't mean having to drink it. Cantra kept the glass to hand, which was respectful of the house and the 'tender, and turned her back against the bar, surveying the room for possibles.

Problem was, the room was a little too full, a little too loud. She wasn't jumpy, not that, but say that the Batcher's warning had sharpened her edge. In the general way of things, Batchers kept strictly to this-humble-person. There was good reason for that, Batchers on most worlds in the Arm being not only "biologic constructs" but property, bought and sold. What there wasn't any good reason for was a Batcher to give clear warning to a couple o'strange pilots, or even to say more than the standard humble gratitude.

Unless, she thought, and it wasn't a thought that made her feel any smoother, the Batcher's owner had ordered her to say what she had. And if that was so—

If that was so, there were 'way too many unknowns in the equation. Anyway, she thought, what's it matter, warned trouble or unexpected? The usual rules applied.

She had to admit that, after the quiet time at The Alcoves she was inclined to be a bit more aware of things; and if even so small a break from routine had energized her, *that* was a sign she needed to get a real break soon. Like maybe right now. She'd come off the ship looking for action, and it looked like action might be all about, if she put her mind to it, and took a lead from the dancers...

The couple on the platform was slow-dancing now, hip to hip and thigh to thigh. As she watched, they separated and went to opposite edges, calling for volunteers from the crowd to come up and join them.

This proposition was greeted with such enthusiasm that at first it seemed the bar's entire pilot population would be up on the platform. The dancers, though, they were pros, and managed to keep their company down to two each—one to an arm. A couple of the chosen had drunk a bit too much ale, and the dancers had their work scheduled, keeping their dainty bare toes out from under boots.

Watching them, she felt some heat building in her belly and recalled herself to the proposed task list.

It'd be a shame to let the lodgings stand empty, she thought, and tried to bring herself into a concentration on the available options.

Jela hadn't reappeared. It might, after all, be best if he didn't reappear, shoulders or no. He'd been a not-entirely-comfortable, if welcome, meal-mate, but she wanted something a little less—controlled—for the bed-sport side of the evening. That little redhead, for instance. Cute, quick, and not drunk yet, dancing all by himself in a vacant square of floor.

She watched him, feeling her blood warm agreeably, and just about cussed when the music ended.

The redhead stopped dancing and looked around like maybe he didn't know what to do now.

Cantra pushed away from the bar and went over to introduce herself.

"He was here, sure," Ragil said. Most of his attention was on the stim-stick he was rolling. Command frowned on soldiers using non-regulation stimulants. Not that Ragil had cared much for that particular reg when he was regular troop. Now that he was on the underside, he claimed the stim habit gave him "verisimilitude" in his role as bar owner. For all Jela knew, he was right.

"So he was here," he said now, working on holding his temper. "Where is he now?"

Ragil finished the stick and brought it to his lips, drawing on it to start the thing burning. He looked up, broad face worried.

"How do I know? I gave him your last, that you'd be at the prime spot an extra day, same time, same code." He drew on the stick, sighed out smoke. "You're asking because he didn't connect?"

"Why else?" Jela sighed. "Somebody else did connect, though. Scan the floor?"

"Sure." He left the stick hanging out of the side of his mouth, tapped a code into the top of his desk. "Center screen," he said.

Jela sat carefully back in his chair—no upscale lounger here— and watched the slow pan of the barroom. The stage was empty; the dancers where down on the floor, circulating—col- lecting tips, no doubt—and offers of companionship after hours. The room was crowded and he sharpened his focus, in case he missed her in the crowd.

"Busy," he commented.

"Damn place is always busy," Ragil returned. "And it's not 'cause the drinks are cheap. Owe you one, by the way. Your idea of getting a couple dancers in here paid off."

"Getting anything useful?" Jela asked absently, eyes on the screen.

"Who knows what's useful?" Ragil countered. "Rumor, hear- say, and speculation, most of it. What they do with it at the next level—how do I know? Heard one pilot the other day give as his opinion that there's no enemy now, nor hasn't been for longer than you or me's been fighting. Command, see, needed a reason to in- crease the production of soldiers, so they sorta invented an enemy."

"I've heard that one," Jela said. "What they never explain is why Command wants soldiers, if there's no enemy."

"Take over the Arm?" Ragil asked.

"And hold it how?" He was beginning to think that Pilot Cantra had left the bar without—

"There!" he said. "Grab and grow the tall woman there next to the redhead."

Ragil obligingly did this and Pilot Cantra's strong-boned face filled the center screen.

"Know her?" Jela asked.

The other took a deep drag on his stick while he considered the image. "No," he said finally. "Don't think I want to, either. What's your interest?"

"She came to the primary, asked for a meal-mate, if there was a pilot available."

Ragil whistled, soft and tuneless. "So—what? She's Muran's replacement?"

"Didn't say so," Jela said, slowly. "Didn't act anything but like a pilot half-crazy from running solo and looking to have a voice that wasn't her own to listen to. Didn't make any play to stay close; I invited her along. In case." He paused, thinking, among other things, of the Batch-grown's warning, which had shocked Pilot Cantra— but for what reason? "She's a hard one to peg, and I won't say she's not fully capable."

"So she might be a beacon?"

"Might," he said, still not liking the idea—not that it made any difference what he liked, or ever had. "Might not."

Ragil pitched the end of his stim-stick into the recycler, leaned forward and tapped a command into his console. The grow-frame vanished as the camera went real-time, keeping its eye on Pilot Cantra and her friend.

"What're you going to do?" he asked.

Jela sighed. "Don't know."

The red-haired pilot's name was Danby and he wasn't disagreeable to letting her buy him an ale. She got the 'tender's attention and settled that, then they leaned on the bar, arm against arm, and did the preliminaries.

His ship was nice and legit—belonged to the Parcil Trade Clan, from which there was nothing more legit—and him fairly new-come to first chair. They were on-port for three local days, of which this was the evening of the second day. Trouble was, they ran watch-shifts on-board, instead of shutting down and letting all crew loose at once, and he was due to take his turn at watching inside the next couple hours.

"There's a 'jack down the road, here," he said with a bit of hope in his voice, tipping his head toward the door.

Cantra considered it—he was that cute, funny, too, in a by-the-law sorta way—then shook her head.

"Got lodgings rented up-port," she said, apologetic, since there was no use hurting his feelings. "Just in from a long run. Figured on a long, slow night to make it seem worthwhile."

He looked wise and nodded. "Sometimes quick won't do it," he agreed, not noticeably cast down by her refusal. "Too bad we didn't meet up earlier."

Across the room, the dancers came back on stage, and the music started up again, almost overwhelmed by the hollering and whistles from the pilots on the floor. Danby put his hand on her arm and she looked over to him, slow and careful, wondering if she'd misjudged—

"Let's dance," he said.

She blinked, and—hesitated, not having been much in the way of dancing lately.

"It'll work out some of the kinks, anyway," he urged.

She remembered, back when she'd been younger than Danby looked to be, dancing whole leaves away. Back when, dancing had in fact worked out some of the kinks. She tried to remember when she'd stopped—and why—then figured it didn't matter.

"Sure," she said, with a smile for his wanting to help. "It's been a long time, though—fair warning."

Floor space being at premium, closer in toward the platform, they hung back along the edge of the crowd and claimed themselves a rectangle of floor by the simple process of facing off and starting in.

Dancing came back pretty easy, once her muscles got over the shock. Danby jigged and high-stepped and she copied him, letting her body get reacquainted with the notion.

"Doin' pretty good for somebody who doesn't remember how!" he yelled in her ear—yelling being the only way he could make himself heard in the general exuberance. "Try this!"

Hands on hips, he executed an intricate and rapid triple crossover, legs scissoring and boots hardly seeming to touch the floor. He finished with a jump and a spin, and threw her a grin that was pure dare-you.

She grinned back and put her hands on her hips, swaying with the music for a few bars, letting the movement pattern seep through the pilot brain and down into the shoulders, arms, hips—

Her legs moved, boots beating out the count, then she was up and spinning, the room circling 'round her—the high-stepping dancers; pilots, stamping; pilots jigging in place; pilots leaning against the bar; the 'tender pouring a glass; two not-pilots in armor 'skins walking in from the street—

She saw what looked like some resistance from the doorman who'd ushered her through, but that was guessing, since she kept moving, had to, with the momentum and—

She touched floor, twisting back toward the door before her feet were properly set. Her height gave her an advantage—she could see the door, just, over the heads of the combined pilots. The armored pair was inside, now, hesitating—no. Scanning the room.

Bounty hunters, she thought, or charity agents. Amounted to the same thing: Trouble.

She reached out and grabbed Danby's arm, hard. He blinked at her, pretty blue eyes going wary and sharp. Likely he was a bit pinched, though he kept it to himself if he was.

"Trouble in the door," she growled into his ear, and felt him tense under her hand.

"What kind of trouble?" he asked, and she let him go, moving her shoulders in frustration.

"Can't tell," she muttered. "Might be bounty. Might be—" She stopped then because the two had decided to make it easy on themselves.

The first pulled her gun, aimed at the ceiling and pulled the trigger. It was an explosive charge and made a bit of noise. Enough to put all the rest of the noise in the room into remission. On the platform, the two dancers sank to their knees, arms around each other, faces hidden against shoulders.

Into the sudden silence, the second woman shouted, "We're looking for two people. We know who they are, and we know they're here. Everybody just stay peaceful while we do a walk-through and collect them, then you can go back to having fun."

Bounty hunters, then. Cantra stifled a sigh. It didn't advance commerce or do anything else useful, but she hated bounty hunters. Always had.

There was muttering, but nobody went for a weapon—wasn't any sense to it, being what the second 'hunter had said was true. Unimpeded, they'd sort through the crowd, round up their prey and be gone. All very efficient and no trouble for anybody, except the ones they'd been paid to collect.

The first 'hunter started on the bar side of the room, the second on the dance platform side. The dancers visibly cringed when she walked past, but she never gave them a glance.

The first had finished with the bar sitters and was wading into the crowd of sullen pilots, her eyes moving rapidly, her face intent—a woman who had a pattern in mind and whose only thought was a match. She worked her way along, dismissing everybody she passed—then her eyes lit on Danby and got wider.

Cantra tensed, remembering her weapon, riding quiet and accessible, and reminding herself forcibly there was no profit to be had from putting herself between a 'hunter and her bounty. She didn't know Danby, she didn't owe him. But—

The 'hunter lunged, Cantra felt her fingers twitch toward her gun and killed the move—just as the 'hunter's hand came around her wrist, snapping the bracelet tight.

Too late, she jerked back, swinging with her free fist—*stupid*, she snarled at herself—impeded by the press of people. The 'hunter grabbed the fist as it skinned past her cheek, snapped a bracelet on it, too, twisted the two lead wires into a single, and clipped the tail end into her belt. Then she reached out and pulled Cantra's gun from its quiet pocket.

Cantra snarled, caught movement out of the corner of her eye, which was Danby coming in, and made herself go limp.

"What the hell's this?" he yelled at the 'hunter. "She's as legit as I am!"

Not quite, though it did warm her to hear him say it. She moved her head; caught his eyes on hers.

"Easy, Pilot. Don't want to be late to your watch."

"Listen to her," the 'hunter advised. "No difference to me if I get somebody on aid-and-abet, too."

He stepped back, bright lad, and threw Cantra a look. She made her face into something representing calm and nodded to him.

The crowd around had started to come back, and that could get dangerous on its own, if she wasn't careful. Wouldn't do to have him call in a friend or two and start a riot on her account.

"It was fun—the dancing," she said, letting him see that she was calm about it, and then the 'hunter jerked on the wire and she was moving, trying to keep her arms from being dislocated.

The second 'hunter came up, empty-handed. They exchanged a glance and wordlessly turned toward the door, Cantra in tow like a wreck bound for salvage.

"Next time you pull a gun in here somebody'll shoot you!" promised the woman who'd scanned Jela in. The man was off to the side, a small callphone to his ear, talking earnestly.

Outside, the 'hunters kept walking—and by necessity, Cantra, too—down the street proper, then into a smaller one—a service alley, maybe. Something was definitely out of true, Cantra thought. Leaving aside the question of whether or not she deserved to be arrested, any bounty hunter worth her license would not be dawdling in alleyways when she had a prize on the leash and payment due.

On the other hand, an alleyway was going to suit her purposes admirably. The fact that they hadn't searched her was interesting, but not particularly useful, with her hands bound like they were.

What was both interesting and useful was the fact that they'd used smartwire to bind and seal her. Made sense for them, o'course. Besides being industry standard, smartwire was—call it impossible—to break, which was close enough to true, given the usual conditions under which bounty arrests were made. The other thing about smartwire was that it was—call it virtually impossible—to escape. It only rated a "virtually" because a frequency existed which interfered with its process, briefly, allowing the alert captive to slip free. The window of freedom was small, smartwire being able to repair and reroute itself, but it was there.

"Where's the other one?" The first 'hunter asked the second, who shrugged, plainly aggravated.

"Not there."

"Must've been there. He didn't leave."

"That's why we sent Kaig to take care of the back room, wasn't it?"

Cantra almost sighed. Three of them, assuming Kaig survived his adventure to the back room, which she didn't consider likely, if the "other one" was Pilot Jela, as it must be. Still, it wasn't any use waiting to find out.

She brought her hands up, resting the bracelets against her breast, fingers folded together. She jerked her chin, hitting the hidden toggle, felt a ripple in the fabric of her 'skins…

The bracelets fell away. Cantra dodged back, slapping the seal on her thigh.

The first 'hunter yelled, bringing her noisy gun around. Cantra shot her in the eye, landing hard on her shoulder on the alley floor, rolling for the scant cover of a trash bin, as the second 'hunter fired, fired, fired—and stopped.

Cantra peered out from beneath the bin, hideaway at ready—two more darts left, which ought to be enough if—

"Pilot Cantra?" The voice was familiar and not unexpected.

"Pilot Jela?" she replied.

"Yes," he said, rueful, she thought. "The field is ours, Pilot."

As it happened, she'd been wrong about Hunter Kaig's chances of survival. He was alive, twisted up in his own wire and sound asleep on the floor.

"I'll send him on up to the next level," the man named Ragil said, rolling a dope stick one-handed while he talked to Pilot Jela. "Won't be much help in present conditions, though." He brought the stick up, drawing on it hard to get it started, and glanced over to Cantra, where she had taken up a lean against the wall, the better to watch the room.

"Want one?" he asked.

"I'm fine," she said, forcefully agreeable.

"Owe you," he insisted. "My people are supposed to keep the riff-raff out."

"No favor in a stim-stick for somebody running on adrenal high," she answered, still agreeable. "I'm fine."

She got the right answer this time. Ragil gave her a look and turned back to Jela, who was working with the computer, idents from the three 'hunters on the table next to him.

They were a study, Ragil and Jela, and Cantra took her time about studying them. Ragil's hair was brown, which matched his eyes. And while he was another one built like a war-runner, his shoulders weren't quite as broad as Jela's and he was about a head taller. Not natural brothers, she'd decided. Not Batchers neither. Not, she thought, kin at all, though there was something —undefinable and undeniable— that put one of them in forcible mind of the other.

Part of the similarity, she considered, was bearing—both were proud, tall-standing men.

Another part was age—or lack of specific age, other than the ever-slippery "adult"—but that could just mean they'd done a lot of ship-time. Truth was, she didn't look her own years, quite, having started in on ships at a tender age.

The rest—might be they'd been shipmates once—they seemed to have that kind of understanding between them. Neither one calling senior, both comfortable in their talents.

Shipmates, she decided, watching Ragil drag on his stick, eyes narrowed as he read Jela's screen through the drifting smoke.

"That doesn't look good," he said. Jela grunted, and sat back.

"What's not looking good, if you don't mind sharing?" she asked from her lean, and the pilot spun his chair around to face her. He might've been worried, or he might not, for all the info she could read off his face.

"It happens that our friends weren't necessarily registered," he said and she shrugged, which got her a bite from the bruised shoulder.

"Freelancers, is all," she said.

"Not on Faldaiza." That was Ragil. "Freelancers gotta register for a non-resident license and get listed in the public files, along with the text of their writs."

She considered that, then used her chin to point at the cards on the table. "What're they?"

Jela grinned. "My money says forged."

She frowned. "Forged 'hunter tickets—for what? I'm not wanting to pry into your private affairs, Pilot, but I don't have any shame in telling you there ain't no bounty out on me—"*for at least two Common Years now*, she added silently—"so even if they'd been registered, it'd be an illegality to come in and arrest a righteous citizen of the Spiral Arm during a certified pursuit of happiness. Which is what they done." She took a breath, looked from Jela's face to Ragil's, seeing identical expressions of placid waiting.

"So when I'm saying freelancers," she said, just in case the brains behind those noncommittal eyes hadn't processed the thought. "I'm saying *freelancers*. I understand Faldaiza's feelings regarding the slave trade, but that don't mean those taken here need to be sold here."

"Well," said Ragil, and took a heavy drag on his stick. Jela tipped his head.

"That would fit," he allowed, "except they knew who they were looking for—you."

"And you." She sighed. "So—what?"

"So—the piece of news you don't have," Ragil said, "is there's another pilot in the mix. He was set to meet Jela this evening, except he never showed. Me, I saw him—talked to him—no further out than local yesterday."

Cantra looked at him, then back to Jela.

"He fell or got taken," she said, watching his face, "and before he filed his last lift, he said something that made you sound interesting to whoever was listening."

His mouth tightened, not a smile, she thought. "Who then came looking for me at the restaurant, since that was the arranged meet, but you'd already claimed the open invitation."

"Putting me up high on the interesting list, too. And the Batcher warned us to walk careful 'cause she'd seen the come-lately and thought he smelled bad." She sighed. "Well, at least that hangs together as a tale. Got any idea who?"

"No."

"Not helpful."

"I agree."

She shifted against the wall. "What's the odds the Batcher knew the come-lately?"

"That's an idea," Ragil said to Jela, who looked up at him.

"Right. I'll swing by on my way back."

"Back from where?" Cantra asked, thinking that she was glad of the dance with Danby, because it looked like that was going to have to do it. Whoever was trying to get Pilot Jela's attention had her linked to him, which meant her place was on her ship—just as soon as she could get there.

"From your ship, I'd imagine," Jela said, seriously. "I got you into this—whatever it is. Least I can do is give you backup to a defensible point."

"Think I can't take care of myself?" She snapped at him, and he held his big hands up in front of his face, fingers spread.

"I think you can take care of yourself just fine, Pilot Cantra," he said, and it was respect she heard in his voice. "But I'll ask you to do the math. First time, they sent one—we think. This time they sent three. Next time they send six, or nine. Do I scan?"

"If they send," she countered. "Might be three was all they had. Might be they lost interest and found something else to do what's fun."

"And might not," he answered, which he hadn't needed to do, her brain already having said the same.

She sighed and shoved away from the wall, feeling her recovered gun in its quiet pocket and the needler with its depleted charge hidden back behind seal.

"All right then," she said, not in any way pleased by the ruination of her plans. "I got my kit to get, if you're wanting a tour of the town. But before that, I'll come along with you to The Alcoves and see what the news is there."

"Why not?" he said, and levered out of his chair. He had the cheek to smile at her, too.

TEN

On the Ground
Faldaiza Port

THE ALCOVES WAS closed, the door opaque, the menu over it dark.

"They never close," Jela said, and Cantra felt a shiver start at the back of her neck.

"Maybe repairs?" she asked, but not like she believed it herself, nor did the other pilot bother to answer.

What he did do was step up to the door, put his big blunt fingers against it and push. Nothing happened. Cantra could see the strain in his shoulders as he exerted more force. She looked up the street and down—empty. So far, so lucky.

The door gave a small groan and began moving back on its track. Jela continued to exert pressure until he had opened a small gap. The foyer was dark, which fact slowed Jela not at all: He squeezed through the gap and became one with the darkness beyond.

Cantra sighed, tried to think *generator failure*, but her heart wasn't in it.

She followed Jela, and sometime between passing over the threshold and coming to rest inside the dark foyer, her gun slid out of its quiet pocket and into her hand. The dark was too thick for her to decipher much more than a blacker blot on the blackness to her left, which might have been Pilot Jela, breathing so quiet she couldn't hear it, which irritated her for some reason. Frowning, she touched another seal pocket and slipped one of the several lightsticks out, snapping it inside her fist. Feeble bluish light leaked between her fingers, enough for her to see the empty console and Jela approaching on sneak-feet, his far arm held down against his side.

At the edge of the console he paused, looked—and moved on, his near hand rising to wave her along behind.

She followed, not liking it, but not inclined to let him go on alone. He'd put himself out for her, coming into the alley and taking care of the second 'hunter, for which act of lunatic generosity she owed him…even though she'd had the situation under control.

She paused, looked around the edge of the console—and wished she hadn't. The master of the dining room was crumpled into an improbably small ball on the floor, his formal tunic dyed with blood, a wide ragged gash in his throat.

Swallowing, she moved on, past the wadded up curtain, which had been ripped down from its hanging over the doorway, and caught up with Jela just inside the hall.

The third room down was nasty—eight identical corpses displaying the remains of various unsavory forms of persuasion. Two wore formals, while the rest, by their clothes, had been kitchen workers. It was well-lit, unfortunately, and Cantra slipped the lightstick into her public pocket.

Jela swore, quietly and neatly. Cantra held her peace, not thinking immediately of anything she could usefully add to the motion.

"All Batchers," she said after he'd prowled a bit and had a chance to work off some of his bad mood. "No guests."

"There are other rooms," he answered, and she sighed, jerking her head at the curtain.

"So we'll check 'em out," she said and after a heartbeat or two he brought his chin down, which she took for "will do." She swept the curtain back.

Most of the other rooms were found to be empty and intact, saving the one that held what had once been a woman of some substance. A neat hole had been made in the center of her forehead; the skin 'round the hole was just a little burnt, which you'll get with your pin-lasers.

This time, Jela didn't say anything, just went down to a knee and started going through pockets, quick and efficient. Seeing that he had the way of it and didn't need her help, Cantra set herself to guard the hallway, the curtain hooked back just a bit, so he'd be able to hear if she shouted.

The hallway was dim and quiet—not much different than it had been earlier in the day. If you didn't know that one of the rooms held eight Batcher bodies, and the one behind her was occupied by—

There was a noise—a very small and stealthy noise—from the left, where the hall ended at a flat white wall, barely two dozen paces from Cantra's position. She frowned, staring at the area and finding nothing to see, save the hall and the wall.

She'd almost convinced herself that the noise had come from behind, inside the room where Jela was relieving the woman's body of care, when the sound came again, slightly louder this time, and from the same area.

Carefully, she moved forward, slipping the still-glowing lightstick out of her pocket, holding it high in the hand not occupied by her weapon.

The section of hall she went through was certifiably vacant. The wall at the end was white and blank. She went over to the left, where end wall met side wall, lifted the lightstick high and began to scrutinize the situation.

She hadn't got far along in the scrutiny when the noise made itself heard again—well over to the right and sounding a shade impatient. Cantra moved down-wall, light still high and illuminating nothing but wall, flat, white, seamless, and—

Not entirely seamless.

It took a professional's eye to see it, but there it was—a thin line along the blank face of the wall, shimmering a little in the lightstick's blue glow.

The noise came again, just beyond the tip of her nose, a scratching sound—fingernails against plazboard, maybe. Mice.

She marked the position of the line, slipped the 'stick away, unsealed another hidden pocket and pulled out a ring of utility zippers. Frowning, she fingered through the various options. The ring was a portable, o'course, armed with the most common polarizers. If this particular hidey hole were sealed with anything out of the way, she'd need the full kit from her ship. Still, it was worth a—

"Pilot Cantra?" His voice was barely louder than his breath, warm against her ear. "What do you have?"

"Stashroom," she said, keeping her eyes on the line, fingers considering the merits of this zipper, the next, a third…

"Think I've got a way in," she said, weighing the third zipper in her hand. "Somebody inside, is what I think." Her fingers decided in favor; and she nodded to herself.

"Cover me." She slipped her gun into its pocket and activated her chosen tool, reaching up to run the needle-nose down along the line in the wall. The zipper's path was marked by a gentle peel, as if the skin of the wall were rolling back from an incision.

Cantra knelt on the tile floor, brought the tool down until its nose caught on the second line, followed that one along parallel to the floor, snagged on the third and went up again, the skin of the wall rolling up in earnest now, almost as high as her waist. Big enough for someone to come out of, if they were so minded. Big enough, absolutely, to shoot through. Big enough—

A body leapt through the opening, curling as it hit the floor and going immediately into a somersault, showing a flash of green among a blur of pale arms, pale hair, pale tunic.

Jela extended an improbably long arm, caught the Batcher by the back of the tunic and hauled her—for it happened to be "her", Cantra saw—up, feet not quite making contact with the floor, which didn't stop her from squirming and twisting.

Cantra slid her weapon free and pointed it. The Batcher stopped struggling and hung limp as a drowned kitten in Jela's grasp.

"Pilots," she gasped. "This humble person is grateful for your aid."

"Right," Cantra said, and looked to Jela, giving him leave to ask what he would with the quirk of an eyebrow.

He was silent for a moment, then spoke to the Batcher. "You gave us warning earlier in the evening, eh?"

"Yes, Pilot," the Batcher said submissively, which could as easily be truth or a lie told in order to placate him.

"Tell me," Jela said, inexorably calm. "What you said, to warn us."

The Batcher hesitated, then raised her face, though she stopped short of actually meeting Jela's eyes.

"Walk safely," she whispered.

"Why?" Cantra asked, which might not've been the question Jela wanted the answer to next, but which had damnall bugged her since it happened.

The Batcher licked her lips. "There were those who had taken the other pilot," she whispered, "as he was about to enter our establishment. I saw this. They were many, he was one. I thought to warn pilots that there was danger in the streets. The master—" Her voice caught. She took a hard breath and hung her head again. "The master did not forbid this. The master said hoodlums in the streets are bad for business."

There was a short silence, then Jela said. "I'm going to put you on your feet. I expect you to stand and answer the questions this pilot and I ask you. Try to run away and I'll shoot you in the leg. Am I understood?"

"Pilot, you are."

"Good." He set her down. She stayed put, head hanging, gloved hands limp at her sides.

"Tell us what happened here," Jela said.

She swallowed. "They came here during the slow hour. Uno, at the desk—he had time to hit the emergency bell. Many of us ran, but in the kitchen, they were prepping for the busy hours upcoming and were caught. Also, the master—the master had been in the wine cellar and did not hear the bell. When we came to this floor, they had already killed Uno and captured the kitchen staff. The master told me to run for aid, and I did try—but they were at all exits, even those not generally known. I came back and they were—they had killed the master and left her. I—I hid myself in the wall, but I could not open the secret door from the inside. And then you came."

"I see," Jela said in a tone that conveyed that he might not actually believe everything he'd just been told. "Do you know—"

Back toward the front of the building, there was a sound—a large, unfriendly, sound.

"You know a way out?" Cantra snapped, not being in any way wishful of meeting the people who had killed a pilot, eight Batchers and their owner—*For what gain?* she asked herself, then put away that wondering for another and less fraught moment.

"Pilot," the Batcher said, "I do, if they are not deployed as before."

"Go, then," Cantra snapped, over a second noise, louder and less friendly than the first. "We'll follow."

The Batcher looked at Jela.

"You can move now," he told her. "Lead us out of here."

The Starlight Hotel sat on its corner, dark walls showing glitters and swirls of silver and pale blue deep inside, like looking out an observation port and seeing the starfield spread from one end of night to the other. Cantra was standing in the dim, recessed doorway of a closed dream shop. She'd been there for some time, just one shadow among many, watching the entrance to her lodgings. Jela and the Batcher were watching the back door, the Batcher having refused to be parted from the pair of them after they'd shaken the dust of The Alcoves off their boots.

It was beginning to look like prudence was its own reward. Whoever had her linked with Pilot Jela only had a face, not a name. And certainly not the location of the lodgings, rented only hours ago with such high hopes. She gave herself a couple of heartbeats for wistful consideration of those hopes, then shrugged it all away. Staying alive was more important, as Garen used to say, than staying sane. Not that Garen had been anything like sane, as far as Cantra had been able to observe. There was something about the Rim that was unproductive of sanity. It was the weird seeping in from the Deeps that did it—that'd been Garen's theory. Cantra's was simpler: Rimmers made Rimmers crazy.

The past, again. Like she didn't have enough present to occupy her.

Shaking her head, she slid out of the doorway and ambled down the walk, one eye on the Starlight. People continued to enter and exit, and there were no signs at all of anybody waiting at stealth.

Directly across from the front entrance, she paused, then quick-walked across the street when the traffic thinned, and jogged up the wide steps. The door slid open and she stepped jauntily into the lobby, heading for the lift bank just beyond the desk.

Abruptly, she swung to the side and approached the desk, fingering a flan out of her public pocket.

"Change this for me?" she asked, slipping the coin across the counter.

"Surely," the clerk said, and counted out a certain number of qwint and carolis. "Will there be anything else?"

The guard on the lift bank was looking at her. She watched him out of the corner of her eye as she swept the coins into her palm, and saw his lips move slightly, as if he was talking into an implanted talkie.

"That's all, I thank you," she said to the desk clerk. She dropped the coins into her public pocket, turned and walked back toward the front door, not running, not hurrying, though she could feel the guard's eyes boring into her back.

Out the door, walking calm, down the front stairs, with a little jog in the step, finally slipping into the crowd moving along the public way. At the corner of the building, she left the crowd and dodged into the shadows, heading for the back entrance.

Very shortly thereafter, she was behind the generator shed, in concealment that was a bit thin for three.

"Got it?" Jela asked, though he must've seen she didn't.

"Abort," she said. "Watcher on the lift bank. He saw me and reported in. Nothing in the kit that can't be replaced." *For a price.* "Now what?"

A small silence, then.

"My lodgings," Jela said. "Then a strategic retreat."

"If they're on me, they're on you," she argued. "Time to cut your losses."

"There's something at my lodgings that can't be lost," he answered, and there was a note in his calm voice that she didn't find herself able to argue with. "Cover me?"

"I can do that." Had to do it, he having performed that same service for her. She looked over to the Batcher woman, silent and attentive by the edge of the shed.

"Time to go home," Cantra told her. "This is more trouble'n you want."

"This humble person will remain in the company of the pilots," the Batcher said—a repeat of her earlier communication on the subject.

"This humble person," Cantra said, sharp, "belongs to whoever's come into being master—which ain't neither of us."

The Batcher crossed her arms over her breast. "This humble person will remain in the company of the pilots," she said, making three on the evening.

"It's her life," Jela said, rising up onto his feet.

Technically not true. On the other hand, as long as neither of them damaged, killed, or moved her, the law had nothing to say to them.

"Makes no matter to me," Cantra said. "We better go, though, before unwelcome company finds us here."

"Right," said Jela and faded into the dark. "Follow me."

Jela's lodgings were back toward the shipyards, in a plain boxy building formed out of cermacrete. The surface showed cracks and a few craters, which gave witness to its age. Inside, Cantra thought, it was probably more of the same—clean and spare. The showers would work; the beds would be sleepable; service and questions would be minimal. Transient housing, that was all. She'd stayed in places just like it herself, more than once. She owned some surprise to find Jela quartered here, though. She had him pegged a couple notches higher up the food chain.

In addition to the front door, the back door and two side doors, there were a good many giving windows, all rigged out with safety nets. Three bridges connected the hostel at varying levels to a larger building next door, which on closer inspection proved to be Flight Central, where those pilots who found themselves to be respectable went to register the news of their being on-port, and whether they was wishful of taking berth, or had a berth on offer. There'd be eatables and a local info office, scribes, brokers, moneychangers, shipwright, and honest folk of all stripe. She'd been in two or three like establishments, over the course of her career.

Could be it made sense for Pilot Jela to bide close to work and news of work. She hadn't asked him where he was next-bound— and there was still that vexed question of what sort of pilot he might be—having somehow received the impression that the answer would've been an uninformative shrug of those wide shoulders.

Which line of thought did produce an interesting question: Where was Pilot Jela *going*, once he had recovered his unlosable? She had the *Dancer*; the Batcher had her master's home which she'd see sooner or later. But Jela? If he didn't have a berth, it was going to be hard going for him on Faldaiza Port.

Which concern was none of hers. She was well out of it just as soon as the good pilot picked up his kit and was away. Which event she hoped would come about quickly.

"So," she said to Jela, who had been quietly and intently regarding the building from his place next to her at the mouth of a convenient alley, the Batcher hovering behind them both. "How do you want to play it?"

"I'd like you and our friend to wait here," he said slowly, like he was just now working out his moves. "I'll go by the Central's bar and see if any of my acquaintance can bear me company. Company or solo, I'll go in by one of the bridges, and by-pass any left to guard the lift bank, the desk or the call-clerk. Bridge access is limited to those who have a key."

"They'll have set guards on the bridges, too," she pointed out.

"Likely, but not proven. I'm counting on the guard at the bridge being less able than those at the more likely places."

"Could get messy."

He grinned, not without humor. "It could, couldn't it?"

She gave him his grin back, and jerked her head at the building. "Coming out the same way?"

"Depends on how many they are and how they're deployed. Might have to go out a window, though I'd prefer not to. There are a couple of interior routes that would serve me better, and I'll aim for one of them. What I want you to do is give me cover when you see me. If you don't see me in an hour, then it's probable you won't and you're free to strike for your ship."

That was cool and professional. She tipped an eyebrow at him. "You got an idea who's responsible for all this, I think."

This time the grin was thinner. "I have too many ideas of who might be responsible. What I don't have is a reasonable way to filter them, and I'd rather not be used for target practice in the meantime."

He sounded seriously put-out by recent events, for which she blamed him not at all, being just a little annoyed herself.

"We got a problem of scope," she said, nonetheless. "Whoever's after having a chat with us thought enough of themselves to kill eight Batchers and a freewoman back at The Alcoves, not to say your piloting brother. The reason they're after me is because of you, not the other way around. If one of your ideas is more likely than another, I'd appreciate hearing it."

He sighed and pushed away from the wall. "If anything comes to me, I'll let you know," he said. "An hour. If I'm not out, jet."

He faded out of the alley. Cantra put a cautious eye around the edge of the concealing wall and saw him already well up the walk, one of a group of law-abiders moving purposefully toward Flight Central.

She thought about swearing, and then didn't bother. Her curiosity bump was unrelieved, but she'd live. Once this business here was settled and she was back on *Dancer*, the game, whatever it was, ceased to be important. Faldaiza wasn't a regular stop, though it wasn't unknown, either. Whatever ruckus she was currently enjoying the fruits of would die out completely between tomorrow's lift and the next time she hit port.

She hoped.

Behind her, she was aware of the Batcher's quiet breathing.

"You," she said, not gently.

"Pilot?" The Batcher stepped forward to take Jela's place next to her.

"You got a name?"

"Yes, Pilot. This humble person is called Dulsey."

"You heard what Pilot Jela said, Dulsey? He's figuring it to get dangerous hereabouts within the hour. Now's your best moment to scoot along home and make a bow to the new master."

"This worthless one heard what Pilot Jela said, and what you yourself said," Dulsey answered in her inflectionless voice, "and understands that danger may soon walk among us. The new master will not easily forgive one who had been favored by the previous master and then allowed her to be slain."

"Huh." Cantra considered that, one eye on the street. Jela was going up the stairs to Central, his shoulders silhouetted against the building's glow.

"If you get yourself killed," she said to Dulsey. "It's nobody's fault but your own."

"This humble person is aware of that, Pilot."

He began to worry about the time they stepped off the bridge into the third floor hall of the Guard Shack, so called because it had been a garrison back in the First Phase, before the *sheriekas* had retired to regroup.

He'd crossed the bridge in company with three pilots known to him from the Central's bar. Two were port security, on rotation, the third a gambler who spent most of her time dicing with new arrivals at a discreet back table. She was on easy terms with the cops, as she wasn't technically operating on-port, and found Jela a challenge, since he would neither dice with her nor bed her.

"There was a lady asking for you at the bar today," she said as they approached the bridge. "Shall I be jealous?"

Jela grinned. "More than enough of me to go around."

She'd laughed, and the two cops, too. They all mounted the steps and started across to the Guard Shack, the lighted deck throwing weird shadows ahead of them.

"What did she look like," Jela wondered, "this lady?"

"Do you not know?" asked the gambler playfully. "Surely, she would not have come without invitation. It was a sorrowful woman, indeed, who heard that you had not been seen so far this day."

"There are so many, it's hard to keep track," Jela apologized, to the loud appreciation of the cops. "Let me see…" He feigned considering thoughtfulness, then snapped his fingers. "It was the bald lady with the long-eye and the demi-claws, I'll warrant." He sighed wistfully. "It's too bad I missed her. She'll punish me proper, the next time we meet."

"I am certain that she will," the gambler said cordially. "And the moreso when she finds you've been seeing another on the side, and she a mere port tough, with a gun on her hip and no more finesse than to bellow your name in a public place, as if she were calling a hound to heel."

Jela eyed her. "She did that? Not one of mine, then. My ladies are always polite."

"Even when they're punishing him," one cop told the other, to the loud delight of both.

"Did she leave a name?" Jela asked the gambler under the cover of the cops' laughter.

"She did not," the gambler answered, looking as serious as he'd ever seen her. "She did, however, state that she was the envoy of one Pilot Muran." She looked up into his face, her being a tiny thing. "This is bad news, I see. Should I have given it earlier?"

He shrugged and manufactured a rueful grin. "It wouldn't have changed anything."

"Ah," she said wisely, and then said nothing more.

By that time, they'd reached the end of the bridge. One port cop stepped forward and used his key; he and his partner ducked beneath the gate as it started up. Jela and the gambler passed through next; he had to bend his head to clear the spiked ends. She walked beside him, head high.

He was sure of his weapon and of his companions. The one who had been sent to watch for him was about to have some trouble.

Except—there wasn't a guard. No one overt or covert watched the end of the bridge or the hallway stretching away into the inhabited regions of the Guard Shack. His 'skins likewise failed to warn of any mechanical snoopers.

"You were expecting someone?" the gambler asked, with the fine perception that assured her success in her chosen field.

"I thought there might be someone here," he said slowly, and added, "…related to the lady who missed me at the bar."

"That would have been unfortunate," the gambler said seriously. One of the cops looked over her shoulder at them and paused, putting a hand out to stop her partner. "But perhaps not as unfortunate as it could be. Where else might they seek you?"

"His room," said the first cop and looked to the gambler. "How ugly was that particular customer?"

She considered, head tipped to one side. "She was indelicate," she said at last, "in the extreme."

The cop slapped her partner on the arm. "I'm going down and collect that money the pilot owes me," she said. "He says he's got it in his room and I believe him."

Her partner pursed his lips. "I don't like you going with him alone," he said. "What if it's a set-up? I'll come along and keep an eye on you."

"Think you're my mother?" the first cop asked.

"Think I'm your partner," the second answered, which seemed to clinch the argument, for the first cop shrugged and looked over to the gambler, who smiled brightly.

"As this may be the only opportunity I have to behold the good pilot's bed, I will of course accompany you," she said gaily and skipped forward. Jela was trailing behind, feeling the hairs on the back of his neck stirring.

"I met some of the lady's relatives earlier today and seen their work more recently still," he said, as the four of them continued down the hall toward his quarters. "They're nasty, they're sloppy, and they seem to be numerous."

"In which case," the gambler said. "We hold the advantages of pure heart, neatness and quality."

"Our duty," said the second cop, who might have been talking to his partner or to himself. "Our duty is to enforce the peace."

They followed the curve of the hall and Jela stretched his legs, taking the lead as they came closer to his rooms. He wasn't really surprised to find the gambler keeping pace with him.

"This could get bad," he said to her, softly. "Or it could be nothing."

"Let us then hope for nothing," she murmured in return, "and carry loaded weapons."

There was no one watching the door. His 'skins noted an anomaly as he approached the door, key out. He paused, but no warning solidified. Sighing, he slipped his key out and went forward, the first cop at his side. The gambler continued down the hall and took up a position near the lifts. The second cop moved back the way they had come, slipping into the convenient shadow of a drinks dispenser.

Jela used his key, pushed the door open and went with it, moving fast and low, gun out and aimed—

At the tree in its pot next to the open window, precisely where he had left it that morning.

"Everything fine?" the cop asked from behind him and he straightened up slowly, letting the rest of the room seep into his awareness. It looked all right—his kit rolled and ready where he had left it, the book he'd been reading last night on the table under the lamp, the bed as tight and as shipshape as he had made it that very—

"Someone's been in," he told the cop, frowning at the rumple on the corner of the aggressively smooth coverlet.

"They take anything?" she asked.

"Appears not." If they'd been after info, he had it on him. He didn't touch the sealed leg pocket where his log book rode and frowned again at the rumpled cover. His 'skins were still insisting on that anomaly. He moved across the room, stood to one side and yanked the privacy curtain back.

The 'fresher was empty. He sighed, crossed the room, picked up the book, slid it into the kit, slung the kit over his shoulder and went to the tree.

"I'm leaving," he said. "I'm feeling exposed." He hefted the tree—bowl and all. The tree had found its new life good; it was full of leaves; and the girth of its trunk had increased. These things filled Jela with a sort of wondering joy, except when he had to carry it.

"Not conspicuous or anything," the cop commented. "Back slide?"

"I'm thinking that's best."

"We'll escort," the cop said. "Let me alert—"

From the hall came the sound of a bell and then the gambler's light, clear hail—followed by a single shot. Jela stumbled, fighting a lifetime of training that would have him dropping the tree and running forward. His duty—

His duty.

"Go!" snarled the cop. "I'll cover you!"

Kit over his shoulder, arms circling the pot, trunk pressed against his cheek, leaves rustling in his ear, Jela moved.

Out the door he ran, spared a glance down the hall toward the lifts and saw the gambler still in her watching place. She gave him a jaunty salute. Something huddled on the floor beyond her—

The lift bell rang.

"Go!" shouted the cop coming into the hall behind him, weapon at ready.

Jela went.

At the mouth of the alley, Cantra straightened out of her lean, eyes suddenly sharp on the pattern of people moving along the walkway between the Guard Shack and Flight Central.

"Here it comes," she said to Dulsey. She turned her head and met a pair of determined gray eyes. "Last chance to shrug out of this and make your peace with the new master."

"This humble person," the Batcher said, like Cantra should've known she would, "will remain in the company of the pilots."

"Have it your own way." Cantra sighed and asked the next question anyway, though she was pretty sure she knew what the answer was going to be. "You got a weapon?"

"The master found this one to be worthy," Dulsey said.

Cantra looked at her. "That mean yes?"

"Yes, pilot," came the stolid reply. "I have a weapon."

"Good. Keep it handy and you might live through this after all."

'Course, then she'd still have to face the new master, which Cantra understood dying to be preferable to and which Dulsey should've thought of before she went and hid in the stashroom instead of getting her brain toasted alongside the old master, like a faithful Batcher ought to have.

Across the street, more people were moving against pattern, taking up this and that spot of cover; some others stopped in the shadow of the Guard Shack, small knots of friends pausing to talk.

Cantra counted maybe fifteen and chewed her lip. "Cover" was what the man had said he'd wanted—if and only when she saw him. Fifteen on the job, though—he might not've expected so many. She considered the numbers excessive herself—and that was only the front door. Who knew how many they had watching the back and the sides?

She slid her gun out of its pocket and checked the charge. Good to go, not that she'd expected elsewise. Always paid to check, though.

From across the street, 'round toward the back of the Guard Shack, there came a flash of red light, followed by a low and drawn-out *bo-oo-oo-o-m*. The clusters and knots of chatting friends turned and ran toward the sound and the intermittent red flickering. The concealed watchers stayed concealed, but the attention of most seemed to be on the commotion.

"Let's go," Cantra said to the Batcher and strolled out of the alley and down the street. When they were across from Flight Central, she paused, waiting 'til traffic allowed; then ambled across the street.

Once across, she turned up toward the Guard Shack, then left the walk and angled between the two buildings, her pace increasing. Overhead, the three bridges glowed with a golden light, illuminating the empty passway.

As they neared the back of the building, sounds other than respectable street noise could be heard. Some sounded remarkably like shots, others like people yelling. Cantra stretched her legs until she was running lightly toward the commotion, gun in hand.

Just before she reached the corner of the Guard Shack, another low explosion disturbed the peace, a simultaneous flare dying the walls and the passway red. More yelling made up for a sudden pause in the shooting.

Cantra dodged close in to the wall, crouched and kept on. At the corner, she paused and, keeping low, carefully eased out to have a look.

The back lot was full of smoky red light. Far down toward the other side of the building, the illumination was eye-burning bright: a solid bar of flame from the edge of the building to the utility shed, from the surface of the walk to the windows three levels up. Nearer to hand, trash bins and runabouts loomed, their shapes wavering in the smoke.

And in the mid-distance, moving at speed, came a short, wide-shouldered figure, massive arms wrapped around a bowl clutched 'gainst his middle and over it all, something long and vegetative.

Cantra swore briefly and brought her gun up, acquiring the range *behind* the running figure about midway to the wall of flame. Anything longer was shooting at shadows and pursuit was sure to materialize just the instant the fastflame burned low enough to jump. Already, she could see figures through the flames, though they still reached high enough to discourage gymnastics.

The bulky runner came briskly on, despite the handicap of his burden. Whether he was running faster than the flames were dying, though—

"Here!" she shouted and he heard her. She knew he had because, incredibly, he picked up speed, skidding 'round the corner so fast the plant he carried snapped like a whip and lost a couple leaves.

"All this for a *vegetable?*" she yelled at him.

"We'll talk about it later!" he yelled back. "Go!"

He took his own advice, leaves blowing in his wake. Cantra waved Dulsey after.

"Cover him," she snapped and the Batcher flung herself down the gold-lit passway.

At the corner, Cantra dropped to one knee and turned her attention to the back trail.

The flames had thinned, though they were still more than she'd care to jump through, lacking a compelling reason. Could be that the pursuit considered Pilot Jela just that, for as she watched, three of them came through the flames, arms folded over their faces, and hit the ground running.

Cantra dropped them—one, two, three—as soon as they came into range, and by that time, four more were through. The flames weren't looking so threatening any more.

She repeated the first exercise with similar results, glanced over her shoulder and saw that the passway behind her was clear. Duty done. Debt paid.

A peek 'round the corner showed that the fire had grown low enough to jump over. Time for her to start moving on her own behalf.

She got her feet under her—and ran.

ELEVEN

On the Ground
Faldaiza Port

WHEN SHE WAS certain her back-track was clean, she set her course for the port proper, *Dancer*, a clean-up and a well-earned nap. She thought of the big tub in her abandoned hotel room and sighed. It would've been nice to sit and soak, maybe another bottle of wine to hand and some interesting company to share it all with.

As it was, she'd had interesting company right enough and too much of the wrong kind of excitement.

"Might as well been working," she muttered to herself, checking her back-track again. Far as she could scan it, far as her 'skins could scan it, too, she was alone in the world at present—which suited. Port was quiet anyhow, it being about five local hours ahead of busy-time for the daily paper-pushers and cits. Not being stared at by the cits—"Look, kids, there's one of those space pilots!"—suited, too.

She wished now that she'd had a chance to get out of Pilot Jela the name of whoever he'd annoyed. Anybody who could field the number of players she'd seen tonight likely had the means to operate elsewhere than Faldaiza. She could do without meeting them or theirs again on her next set-down—or ever.

Once again, she checked her back. Still clean. Heartened, she continued on her way, keeping to shadows when she could, but not being fanatical about it. There wasn't any sense calling attention to herself by being too stealthy. Extra caution would pass, pilots being who and what they were. Even extra-jumpy caution would pass, there being some pilots who just naturally did better on-ship than on-ground.

Not that she particularly argued with that better-on-ship stuff. Once you got the hang of the sound and vibrations, there wasn't anyplace you could be on a ship and not have a good idea of what was going on.

Not like here, as a quick sample, where part of the listening was wasted on identifying high squeaky sounds she'd never heard before—could be birds, could be equipment—to identifying the deep, low, shaking rumbles—might be light ground tremors, might be a storm coming in, might be equipment...hell, might be some clubband practicing with their enviroboards! If she jacked the 'skins a bit, she might get some directionals and figure the noises out, but then she'd be standin' stock-still to listen, which would gain her attention she didn't want or need.

Could be she was just gettin' that tired, which ought to warn her not to run quite so close to the edge, a lesson she thought she'd learned a dozen or two times over.

She'd come into the shipyards some distance from her exit point, on the day-side, now closed up tight for the local night. She was on approach to *Dancer's* location, passing a strip of low cermacrete buildings—cargo brokerage office, repair-and-parts shop, automated currency exchange, and a grab-a-bite—looking a degree scruffier than most.

Cantra sighed. Inside a local hour, all going well, she'd be back on her ship. Safe, as the saying went.

She strolled on past the grab-a-bite. Away near the center of the yard, she could just make out the lines of her ship. Despite herself, she smiled and stretched her legs a little more, feeling the cermacrete under her boots.

Her 'skins gave a yell, audible to her ears only, but she was already turning, hideaway sliding into her palm—and found herself facing a too-familiar stocky woman with determined gray eyes, wearing a pair of mechanic's coveralls neither new nor clean, with conveniently long sleeves, clipped tight at the wrists, and "J.D. Wigams" stenciled on the breast. A work hood had been shoved up and back, hanging careless-seeming over one shoulder.

"If the pilot would follow this—" There was a marked break-off and a sharp intake of breath. "If the pilot would follow," she repeated, firmer this time.

Cantra sighed, hideaway still enclosed in her fist. "No sense to it. I'm for my ship and a lift out. You're on your own, except if you're wanting a last piece of advice, which is—don't startle people who've got cause to carry protection."

"I am grateful for the advice," Dulsey said stolidly. "As I understand the transaction, advice balances advice. So—my advice to you: Take care not to walk into a trap, believing harm has lagged behind you."

Cantra stared at her. "You reading me good numbers, Dulsey? If not, I'll make sure you never have to face the new master."

"The pilot is generous. I have seen evidence. That same evidence is available to you. Follow me." She turned and walked back toward the row of sullen shops, not looking back.

Cantra sucked air deep into her lungs and exhaled, hard.

Then she followed Dulsey.

Down along the shops, and back a small alleyway, no more than seventy or eighty paces from where she'd been stopped, there was a small shop—"Wigams Synchro Repair and Service." She'd been all but dragged inside by Dulsey, past the sign showing the place wouldn't be open for business for another couple hours.

There wasn't any sign of forced entry, and Dulsey had carefully turned the mechanical lock behind them before heading for the stairs beside the work bay. Cantra sighed gently. It looked like she wasn't the only one around with proper tools and improper training.

She hadn't been particularly surprised to find it was Pilot Jela and his vegetative friend that Dulsey had led her to and had not been particularly surprised to find him sitting comfortably in a deep leather chair behind a shiny real wood desk with a wonderful view of the window on the top level office of Synchro Repair. The window in turn had a wonderful view overlooking the port.

Jela hadn't bothered with a greeting, just pointed at the spy-glass sitting on the sythnwood work table beside the big desk.

Cantra eased onto a stool and picked up the 'glass, finding it already set to study a circle 'round *Dancer's* position. Not hard to find a ship, after all: a quick search on her name against the roster of ships down during the last day local would net the info fastest.

She sat for a heartbeat, just staring down into the black surface, then put her hands on the wake-ups.

The surface cleared and she was looking at the yard, *Dancer* so close on her right hand she could read the name and the numbers on the pitted side. The view panned back, showing a range of ships, energy overlays on two of them.

"Get on the portmaster's bad side, holding weapons live on the yard," she commented.

Jela didn't answer, except to say, "To the right about thirty degrees, if you might?"

Which she obediently did and the view changed, displaying a piece of construction equipment lazily moving behind a distant fence in its storage yard, like it was looking for a place to park.

"Up the magnification a notch."

She shrugged...

Right. She had him figured now for some kind of security pro, so he'd notice what she might miss. And she would have, too. Not construction equipment after all, the armored crawler was a dark wolf among the yard's more regulation equipment, staying a prudent distance back from the fence. The energy overlay on that flickered as it moved, as if it were shielded.

"Check the ships again."

She drew a ragged breath, did so, and the screen showed those ships and the energy overlays still on high, then faded to black as she thumbed the power.

Eyes closed, she sighed, then spun the stool and glared at Jela.

"So?" she asked.

He shrugged his big shoulders, showing her empty palms.

"Didn't seem neighborly to let you walk into that," he said, projecting a certain style of soothing calm that she found particularly annoying.

She took another deep breath.

"One," she said. "Like I said before—you don't need to go to all that trouble for me. Two, I'd appreciate an explanation of what the pair of you think you're doing snooping my ship."

"Looking for a lift out," he said.

Cantra snorted. "I don't take passengers."

"Understood," he said, still projecting calm, which was going to get his nose broke for him sometime real soon. "Nobody expects you to take passengers. Hate 'em myself. But nobody here's a passenger. I'm willing to sit second. If you don't mind my saying it, Pilot, you were looking to be on the wild side of edgy when we met for dinner. Could be a run with some downtime built into it is just what you—and your ship—need."

"I'm the judge of what me and my ship need," Cantra snarled. "And what neither needs is to be taking up a man whose friends are shyer than his enemies and a Batcher on the run from her owner."

"This humble person," Dulsey said, "is fully capable in cargo handling, communications and outside repair. Also, this person has received some small training in the preparation of foods, which the pilot may find of use during the upcoming journey."

Cantra looked at her.

"Repair, comm, and cargo?"

"Yes, Pilot."

"What was you doing working in a restaurant?"

Dulsey looked aside. "The manufacture of our Pod was commissioned by Enclosed Habitats, which specialized in constructing and maintaining research stations. When the cost of maintaining the stations exceeded the contracted sums, the company failed. All assets were sold at auction, including the worker pods. The master purchased those of our Pod who remained for The Alcoves."

"How many of your Pod're left now?" Cantra asked, although she didn't really have to.

"One." Dulsey whispered.

Right.

"That's too bad," Cantra said. "Doesn't change that you're a runaway Batcher—or will be, pretty soon—which puts you on a course to there being none of your Pod left by—call it mid-day tomorrow, local."

"There is benefit to the pilot in accepting the assistance of Pilot Jela and this—and myself." There was a note of panic in the Batcher's voice, despite the bravura of "myself;" and the gray eyes were wide.

Cantra cocked an eyebrow. "I'd argue opposite, myself, but there don't seem to be a need just now." She glanced over to Jela.

"I need a roster, a comp, and a talkie."

He pointed beyond her, at a stand next to the work table. "Lift the top of that. It's all right there."

The name of the ship was *Pretty Parcil*. Cantra spent a few moments jinking with the feeds, not wanting to be interrupted in her conversation, nor particularly needing the garage day-shift to take delivery of trouble that wasn't theirs. Jela watched her, silent in his borrowed chair. He was still projecting calm, but he'd either eased up some or she was getting used to it.

Satisfied at last with her arrangements, she opened a line to the piloting station on *Pretty Parcil.*

There was a click and a voice, sounding sterner and older than he had earlier in the day.

"*Parcil.* Pilot on deck."

"Is that Pilot Danby?"

A pause about wide enough to hold a blink, followed by a specifically non-committal ack on the ID, then, "Pilot. What happened?" No more than that. Likely he wasn't alone in the tower. That was all right.

"Turned out to be a mistake," she told him. "I'm at liberty and mean to stay that way."

"Mistake?" He was a bright boy, and not too young to understand that there were mistakes—and mistakes.

"I give you my word of honor," *for what it's worth*, she added, silently, "that there's no bounty out on me."

She heard his sigh—or might be she imagined it. "Good. What can I do for you, Pilot?"

"I'm wondering if you can confirm for me," she said. "I've got two ships on scan showing live weapons. Don't want to think my scanner's gone bad, but..."

"I'll check," Danby said, and over the line there came the sound of various accesses being made, then a bit of silence...

"Nothing wrong with your scanner," he said eventually. "You protest to the portmaster?"

"Not yet," she said, and Jela leaned forward on his stool, black eyes showing interest.

"I'm wondering," she said to Danby, "if a protest from a Parcil Family ship might get a little extra snap into the belay order. I'm small trade, myself. Just me and my co-pilot, like I told you..."

"Got it," he said. "I can file that protest, Pilot. Stay on line?"

"Will do."

She heard him open a second line, and request the portmaster's own ear for "First Pilot, Parcil Trade Clan Ship *Pretty Parcil.*" There was silence then, which she'd expected—and much sooner than she'd hoped, his voice again.

"Portmaster, we've just completed a security scan and have identified two vessels on-yard with weapons live." A pause, then a calm recitation of the coords of both ships and, "Yes ma'am, I am filing formal protest of these violations. I request that you issue a cease-and-desist to those vessels immediately, to be enforced as necessary."

Another short silence and a respectful, "Thank you, ma'am. We will monitor. *Parcil* out."

Cantra smiled. Jela came of the chair and moved to the work table, doubtless to have a look-see via the spy-glass.

"Protest filed, Pilot." Danby was back with her. "The portmaster promises a shut-down inside the local hour."

"Much obliged," she said, and meant it. "I'll get back to my prelims then and hope I won't have to ask you to verify my long-scans."

"We've been watching long," he said. "Pilot's Undernet has reports of pirate activity in-sector. Faldaiza shows clear to out orbit. So far."

"Obliged again," she said. "If I catch anything suspicious on the long, I'll pass it on."

"I'll be here," he said. "Thanks for the heads-up, Pilot. Good lift, fair journey."

"Fair journey, Pilot," she answered, just like she was as legit as he was, and closed the line before folding the desktop down.

Jela had a hip hitched on the edge of the work table, black eyes intent on the image in the spy-glass.

"One's off-line," he said without looking up. "The portmaster doesn't like the Clans upset."

"Makes sense to keep the money happy," Cantra returned, considering him. "What about that armor?"

"Nothing lit," he said, head still bent. "Might not be anything to do with us at all."

"On the other hand, it might be," she finished what he didn't say and sighed. "Man, *whose* ugly side did you get on?"

"Second one's down," he said and looked up, his face about as expressive as she'd expected.

"Am I getting an answer to that, Pilot? Seems to me I'm owed."

He frowned. "By my calculations, we're even."

"Not if you leave me open to more of the same, elsewhere." She felt her temper building and took a deliberately deep breath, trying to notch it back. Her temper wasn't her best feature, being enough to sometimes scare her. She didn't figure it would scare the man across from her, though it might lose her bargaining points.

"The reason I'm in it at all is because we had dinner together. Honest mistake—on both our parts. I had no right to the particulars of your business up to the point my hands are 'wired together and I'm being hauled out of a public place on a bogus bounty. At that point, you owed me info—and I ain't been paid yet."

He looked thoughtful. "You won't like the answer."

She blinked. "So I won't like the answer," she said. "Plenty of answers out there I don't like."

He sighed, lightly. "All right, then. The answer is, I don't know who's involved, if they're local or more—connected."

"You're right," Cantra said, after a moment. "I don't like it. Do better, why not?"

He spread his hands. "Wish I could."

Her temper flared. "Dammit, we got a double-digit body count out of this night's work, including Dulsey's Batch, and you *don't know* who thinks you done 'em wrong?"

"That's right," he said, imperturbable.

"It is possible that those who ultimately seek the pilot are off-world," Dulsey said surprisingly, from her seat on a closed toolbox. "The ones who came to The Alcoves were local odd jobbers."

Cantra spun on a heel to look at her, sitting with her hands gripping her knees and her pale face seeming to glow in the dimness.

"How you figure off-world?"

Dulsey moved her head a little from side to side. "Odd jobs are done for pay. Had the pilots paid for protection against harm, then the local chapter would have split—half to fulfill the contract to…discommode…the pilots; half to ensure that the pilots were not in any way impeded."

"They don't act on their own is what you're saying?"

"Pilot, that is correct."

Cantra looked over at Jela.

"Light any dials for you?"

"Sorry."

She sighed, then shrugged, giving it up as a hopeless case. "I'll watch my back. Business as usual." She nodded to Jela. "Be seeing you, Pilot. Safe lift."

She was halfway to the door before she heard him say, "About that armor, Pilot Cantra…"

Red at the edge of her vision. She stopped, keeping her back toward the two of them, closed her eyes, forced herself to breathe in the pattern she'd been taught.

"Pilot?" Jela again. She ignored him, breathing—just that—until the urge to mayhem had receded to a safer, pink, distance.

She turned and met his space-black gaze straight on.

"It's been what I count as a long day, Pilot Jela, and my good nature's starting to wear a bit thin. If you got info bearing on the safety of my ship and her pilot, share it out short and sweet."

"The info's nothing special," he said, and she could hear a certain care in his voice, though he'd given over the stringent projecting of calm. "Just a reminder that ground-based armor can bring weapons on-line faster than space-based."

"By which you're meaning to tell me that armor there—" she nodded at the spy-glass sitting quiet and dark on the workbench "—doesn't have to reveal its feelings until I'm rising without challenge."

"That's right."

"I thank you for the reminder," she said, feeling the quiver starting in the roots of her bones, which meant the last of the adrenaline had run its course. Too long a day, by all the counts that mattered. She eyed the pilot before her, with his tell-nothing face, his big shoulders and solid build.

"Military?" she asked, wondering how she hadn't quite managed to get him pinned down on that either.

"Not quite," he gave back, which was answer enough in its way.

"What do you want?"

"What I said—transport out, for me, the tree, and Dulsey. I'm good for co-pilot and, yes, I do know the avoids for that class of armor."

"Might be manned."

He hitched a shoulder—qualified denial. "Not much room in those for personnel. Not to say there couldn't be a couple of smalls running crew. In which case the assault's randomized, making avoids more difficult, and less accurate, which assists avoidance."

"That a fact?" This asked against a rising shake. She tried to make the follow-on sound stronger. "That stuff can be evaded?"

"Experience shows it can."

Cantra closed her eyes. The shaking was more pronounced, now. She was headed for a crash and no mistake. Granted, she had more than enough Tempo in stores to keep her up and fully able for some number of ship's days. Having flown that course more than once, she knew that all the drug did was put the time of the crash out, interest compounded hourly.

And, truth told, she didn't have room for downtime on this leg—not now and not later. She had cargo; she had a deadline. And there was no way she could justify taking anyone lawful aboard her ship, nor trust anyone not.

She flicked a look at Dulsey, sitting frozen on her toolbox, and another at Jela, standing calm and quiet, letting her think it through. What his answer might be if the product of her thought didn't match his had-to's, she couldn't guess. And, after all, it was *her* ship.

She jerked her head toward the door.

"Right. Experience. Let's go."

There wasn't any way to tell how the ships and the armor gained their info, so there wasn't any use going roundabout to the ramp of Pilot Cantra's ship. Thus the pilot ruled. As it happened, Jela didn't disagree with her reasons or her decision. He was beginning to develop some serious respect for Pilot Cantra, even though the day was beginning to visibly wear on her.

They marched in order—pilot first, himself and the tree next, Dulsey in her stolen coveralls and not-stolen gun covering the rear. It was interesting to note that they encountered no armed lurkers or outliers. Not so much as a panhandler impeded their progress. Jela walked on, senses hyper-alert, and revised his opinion regarding the likely involvement of the armor. It wasn't especially good strategy to depend on the equipment to the exclusion of soldiers on the ground. On the other hand, he hadn't seen much good strategy in this op—present company excluded.

The air had cooled rapidly with the setting of the local star. However, so brisk was their march that it was unnecessary for his 'skins to raise the temp. Above his head, the tree's leaves were still, despite the breeze of their passage, allowing him to use his ears to listen for possible enemy movement.

They came to the ramp of the pilot's ship in good order. She mounted first, which was her right as captain, her long, light stride waking not a whisper from the metal deck. He followed, the tree cradled in his arms; and Dulsey came at his back, metal ringing under her deliberate steps.

The hatch began to slide back as Pilot Cantra reached the top of the ramp. She never paused, crossing the landing in two of her strides and ducking through the gap into the lock beyond.

By the time Jela—bearing the extra inconvenience of the tree—reached the landing, the hatch was wide open, the lock beyond spilling pale blue light onto the decking. The plate over the door read *"Spiral Dance.* No home port."

He paused, waiting for Dulsey.

She reached his side, throwing him a wide glance out of gray eyes. "Pilot?"

Arms occupied with the tub holding the tree, he used his chin to point.

"The minute you cross into that ship, a bounty goes on you," he said.

"Yes, Pilot. This—I am aware of that," she answered and it might have been impatience he heard. He hoped so.

"You didn't discuss with Pilot Cantra where you might like to be set down," he continued. "There aren't many worlds where those Batch-marks will go unnoticed."

"I am also aware of that, Pilot. I thank you for your concern, but my immediate need is to depart Faldaiza. Deeper plans—deeper plans await event."

Two "I's" and a "my" in the same couple sentences, and nary a hesitation before any of them. She might, he thought, make it—provided she could find some way to neutralize the Batch tats. There might even be a way to do it, short of amputating the arms and regrowing. He'd never heard of any undetectable method besides the amputations—acid baths only removed the first two or three layers of skin and left behind telltale burns; attempts to camouflage the tats with others, done by needle, were doomed to failure.

"We should not," Dulsey said, "keep Pilot Cantra waiting."

"We should not," he agreed, and jerked his chin again at the open hatch. "After you."

She hit the pilot's chair, hands already on the board, opening long eyes and short, slapping up wide ears. Pilot voices began to murmur—groundside chatter, as it sounded. Nobody sounding frantic; no tightness in the banter. Good.

Her hands were starting to shake and a high whine had started in her ears, damn it all to the Deeps. She thought about the stick of Tempo in the utility drawer. Left it there.

A racket from behind announced the imminent arrival of her crew, speaking of arrant stupidity. She pushed on a corner of the board—a hatch slid silently open, revealing a minute control panel. She snapped three toggles from left to right, pressed the small orange stud. The hatch slid shut, merging invisibly with the metal surface.

Cantra spun her chair around to face the incoming.

Dulsey came first, slipping her weapon away into a pocket of the coverall. Pilot Jela came next, massive arms wrapped around a biggish pot, apparently not at all bothered by the leaves tickling his ear or the twigs sticking into his head. He took in the piloting room with one comprehensive black glance, walked over to the point where the board met the wall on the far side of the co-pilot's station, bent and set the pot gently on the decking. He slapped open a leg pouch, pulled out a roll of cargo twine and pitched it to Dulsey, who caught it one-handed and stood holding it, head cocked to one side.

"Secure that," Jela said. The words fell like an order on Cantra's ringing ears.

Apparently it sounded that way to Dulsey, too. She dropped her eyes, mouth tightening. "Pilot," she murmured and walked over to do what she'd been told.

Jela put himself into the co-pilot's chair without any further discussion, his big hands deft on the controls. Seat adjusted to his satisfaction, he pointed his eyes at the board, giving it the same all-encompassing look he'd given the pilot's tower.

"We have a scheduled lift?" he asked. "Pilot?"

"We do," she answered, spinning back to face her screens. "We'll be departing some earlier."

He was opening co-pilot's eyes, his attention on the readouts; touched a switch; and brought the chatter up a mite.

"If we refile, we give warning of our intention to anyone interested," he said, just offering the info.

"That's so," she agreed, "which is why we're not refiling." She eyed the readouts—nothing glowing that shouldn't be; and the armor just where and how they'd last seen it. The chatter was staying peaceful, and long eyes brought her nothing but the serene turn of stars. She reached to her own instruments and started the wake-up sequence.

"What we're going to do, as soon as Dulsey has that damn vegetable secured and gets herself strapped down, is grab us out and lift."

"Tree," Jela said, so quiet she could barely hear him over the chatter and the ringing. He sent her a glance, lean face absolutely expressionless. "If we wait a bit, we might lull whoever could be watching into thinking we'll keep to the filed lift."

If we wait a bit, Cantra thought, feeling the shake in her muscles, *the pilot won't be fit to fly.*

She fixed him with a glare. "You sign up as co-pilot on my ship?"

Black eyes blinked. Once. "Pilot, I did."

"That's what I thought, too. We go now. Pilot's choice."

Another blink—and a return to the studious consideration of his area.

"Pilot," he said, and there might or might not've been an edge to his voice—not that she gave a demi-qwint either way.

"Dulsey," she snapped. "Can you take acceleration?"

"Yes, Pilot," came the cool response. "More than you can."

Now *there* was an assumption. Cantra grinned, feeling it more teeth than humor. Navigation brain was awake. She set it to scanning for safe out-routes and shot a fast look down-board. Dulsey was finishing up with the cord and the vegetable. Tree. Whatever.

"Get yourself strapped into the fold-out. You got ten from my mark." She took a breath. "Mark."

Suggested routes were coming in from navigation. She belatedly added the co-pilot to the report list, copied the first batch manually and did a quick scroll. Beside her, Jela was heard to make a sound amounting to *tsk.* She shot him a look while her fingers initiated engine wake-up.

"Prime thinkum," was all he said, his big hands steady on the controls. "How do you want to run it, Pilot?"

She glanced at the nav screen, scrolled through the new offerings, moved a finger and highlighted a particular course. It hung there, gleaming yellow, awaiting the co-pilot's consideration.

"We could do that," he said, and the screen showed a second highlight, blue, two choices further down. "This one gives us more maneuvering room, in case anybody wants to throw flowers at us."

She frowned at the suggested route, found it not inelegant. A little sloppy if the armor kept to itself, but nothing to endanger. The portmaster was going to be irritated, but that was the portmaster's lookout.

"We'll take it," she said, and pressed the locking key. "If we wake up the armor, first board goes to you, since you got the experience and I don't, at which point I'll grab second." Her hands moved, setting it up, except for the final confirm, which was one key within easy reach. "If nobody cares we're leaving, saving the portmaster, I'll stay with her. Scans?"

"Scans clean," he replied.

"Dulsey, you in?"

"Yes, Pilot."

"Ten," said Cantra and gave *Dancer* the office.

She flew like a bomber pilot, did Cantra, and with as much regard for her passengers. The acceleration didn't bother him, of course, and it seemed to not bother her at about the same level, which was—almost as interesting as a nav brain that based its simulations on lifts pre-filed and stored in the central port system. He did spare a quick glance at Dulsey, strapped down in the jump seat. She looked to be asleep.

They were up for full seconds before Tower started howling. Neither the order nor the language in which it was couched interested Pilot Cantra, by his reading of the side of her face.

More seconds. Tower continued to issue orders and other voices came on-line quickly—pilots on the yard, they were, some siding with Tower, others urging *Spiral Dance* to more speed, still others laying wagers on the various angles of the thing—elapsed time to orbit, probable fines, the likelihood of collecting them, number of years before *Spiral Dance* dared raise Faldaiza again...

He rode his scans, seeing nothing hot behind them on the fast-dwindling port, and was beginning to consider that the armor had never been in it at all, that local talent wasn't going to trouble themselves to pursue off-world, in fact, might be applauding their departure—when three bright spots blossomed on the screen. Not energy weapons—missiles!

"Trouble in the air!" Jela spat, and reached hands toward a board not yet his.

In short order, just ahead of them, a glare of light, and then the port-ward scans lighting up at the same instant as the ship's collision alarm went off. He took it in, didn't swear.

"Con coming your way." Cantra's voice was firm.

Another burst, and the pilot slapped the transfer button, swapping her board for his. His hands moved, feeding in avoids, hoping the pattern he had in his head was going to be good enough.

"Three," Pilot Cantra said meditatively. "And the man don't know who loves him."

Being engaged, he let the debate go, kicked the engine up another notch, and felt the ship surge while screens one, three, and five showed explosions.

Though they were still in atmosphere, he slapped up the meteor shields, then played the controls a moment to check reaction time...let the ship spin about the long axis, the modest airfoils working just fine at this velocity.

Tower came over the open comm, ordering the armor to cease and desist, which would do as much good as ordering any other robot unit to do the same.

"Ships coming on line behind us," Cantra said quietly. "Main screens going up as soon as we're clear."

Ships coming on line—that could be bad, or good, and in either case not on his worry plate until any of them actually fired. He slid the throttle up another notch, felt the instant response in his gut as the acceleration kicked in, and then quickly backed off power as the collision alarm went off again.

"Tiny!" was what Cantra said, and she was describing the munition struggling to change course, to catch them...

Jela slammed the control jets, bouncing the ship and occupants around ruthlessly as the missile seemed to skitter along some unseen barrier. One final burst of acceleration now and the projectile slid helplessly behind them.

Another cluster of bursts, below them now, and—

"Shields up! Got us a ship burst—"

He frowned at his screens, reached to the reset—

"One armor gone," Cantra said. "Tower can't decide whether to be happy or not. ID..." An audible in-drawn breath. "*Pretty Parcil.*"

"Not bad," Jela said. "For a civilian."

She didn't say anything, loudly. He notched the engine back, reached to access the next item in the navigation queue—

"Nothing close, now," he said. "I think we'll do."

Suddenly a blast of noise, internal, as Cantra brought the audio to the speakers.

Jela sighed. So much for a quiet departure. Ships calling for weapons, pilots demanding information, the local air defense group issuing contradictory orders…and all thankfully behind them.

Cantra nodded at him, with a quick hand sign that was *thanks*, in pilot hand-talk.

"I'll rig that up for auto-run," she said, and the lights flickered under his hands—swap back. He sighed to himself, fiddled with the comm, checked the screens and said nothing. Her ship, her rules, her call.

Pilot Cantra fed the silence, fingers moving with deliberate purpose, locking in the auto-run. At last, she sat back, unsnapped the shock straps, and leaned her head against the chair.

"Dulsey!" she called.

"Pilot?" Languid. Sounded like she'd been asleep, for true. Jela grinned. Nerves spun out of steel thread. She'd do, all right. Maybe.

"You ride a board, Dulsey?"

"No, Pilot. I regret. The Batch-grown are not allowed to hold professional license."

Cantra sighed. "Replay what I asked you, Dulsey. I don't care if you got a license, scan?"

Silence. Jela shot a glance over his shoulder. The Batcher woman was sitting on the edge of the jump-seat, straps pushed aside. She bit her lip.

"Pilot, I can ride a board," she said slowly. "But I am the very most novice."

"Just so happens you'll have Pilot Jela on first, and he's something better than that, as we've seen demonstrated. Do what he tells you and you'll be ace."

She turned her head and glared at Jela, who considered the lines etched in by her mouth and the discernible trembling of her arms and her fingers, and forbore to bait her.

"And you'll ring me, if something comes up except a clear route and easy flying, is that right, Pilot Jela?"

"I'll do just that, Pilot," he agreed, and touched the green button at the top of his board with a light forefinger. "That'll be this?"

"That's it." She reached to her instruments, assigned control back to him, and came to her feet, swaying slightly. "If you have to vary for any reason, it better be good, and you'll be checking with me. Right, Pilot?"

"Right," he agreed, amiable as he knew how.

"I'm going to my quarters," she said. "Chair's yours, Dulsey."

She took two deliberately steady steps toward the hatch, stopped, and turned to stare at the tree.

Jela watched her, not saying anything. She stood like a woman caught in a freeze-beam. He snapped his webbing back, noisier than it needed to be.

Her glance flicked to his face, green eyes wide. "What *is* that?"

He felt the hairs shiver on the back of his neck and produced a smile.

"A tree, Pilot," he said, easy as he dared. "Just a tree."

Had she been in strength, she'd've asked him more, he could see that. In her present state, though, it was sleep she needed, and she knew it. *Questions later*, he could see her decide, and she jerked her chin down, once, letting it go.

"Orders. You ring me," she said again. "If anything shows odd."

"Aye, Pilot," he returned, and the hatch snapped shut behind her.

TWELVE

On Board *Spiral Dance*
Departing Faldaiza

PILOT CANTRA'S AUTO-RUN leaving no room for vary, nor any way short of physical tampering to take the thing off-line and just fly the ship himself, Jela amused himself for a time by running Dulsey through a series of board drills, the while keeping an eye on the screens and the scans.

Dulsey completed every pattern he called for with competence, but without flair, her pale face displaying a tense seriousness that eventually brought to mind the fact that she had also suffered a long day.

He stretched in his chair, and waved a hand.

"You'll do," he said, striving for a tone of easy satisfaction. "Lean back and talk to me. Unless we get pirates on the screens, we've got nothing to do until transition."

She leaned back, tension ebbing, leaving her serious and puzzled. "What shall I talk about, Pilot?"

A Batch-grown question if ever he'd heard one. So perfectly Batch-grown, in fact, that he suspected Dulsey of having fun with him—unless he looked stupid—which, he conceded, was probably the case.

"If it's going to be up to me to choose the topic," he said, still genial and easy. "Then I'll ask you to retrace your logic for me."

Her face tightened. "Which logic, Pilot?"

"The reasoning which brought you to assert to Pilot Cantra that the gentlefolk responsible for making the latter part of our evening so entertaining were working for off-world interests."

Dulsey frowned. "I believe my reasoning is linear, Pilot."

Outright irritation. Jela raised a hand and waggled peaceable fingers.

"Grant that I'm having trouble with it," he said. "I can go along with you, to a point—the abduction of my original contact, the people following us to the bar, the guards on our rooms. But what I can't figure is—why did they make the mess we found at The

Alcoves? Local forces wouldn't have a reason, or the initiative, to vary from orders—"

"Ah." For a split-second, it seemed that Dulsey would actually laugh. She managed to restrain herself, however, and spun her chair so she faced him.

"It is sometimes true that unrelated events run in parallel," she said. "It is also sometimes true that the parallel-running events may share some components which make it tempting to theorize a connection which does not, in reality, exist. Such is the case with the events of the evening, and the pilot's puzzlement may be laid to rest by understanding that what appears, from his perspective as a shared component, to be one mega-event is in fact two unrelated occurrences."

He considered her. "The business at The Alcoves had nothing to do with us, is what I'm hearing you say."

"The pilot hears correctly," Dulsey said. "The fact is that the— the master had long been an...aficionado...of data. The pilot will have noted that the several alcoves in which he dined were data-mined. That the harvesting devices did not operate during the pilot's tenancies was a source of amusement for the master, who pronounced the pilot a very able fellow."

He blinked. "I'm flattered."

"The pilot displays appropriate respect for the master," Dulsey said, and he could've sworn it was irony he heard in her bland voice. "Unfortunately, there were others who were not so respectful, among them her heir, who, though it is not the place of this humble person to say so, is not an able fellow. The master's devices thereby harvested data which he would rather they had not, and she had begun the process to have him disbarred from inheriting. As his debts are high and his prospects otherwise limited, he took steps to insure that the master's property passed to him intact."

"With the exception of your Pod," Jela commented. "I'd've thought you were valuable."

Dulsey shrugged. "The master had allowed us much and we knew him for what he was. Though we could not have initiated legal proceedings, nor even made a complaint to a constable, yet he would not have us. He knew the master armed some of us. He knew we had built the harvesting devices and—other—apparatus, that we assembled the records and were often required to listen to them. We were a danger to him, and best accounted for."

Jela took a moment to consider the screens and the scans. Sighed. "In that case, Dulsey, he can't afford to let you be unaccounted for." There was a short silence. "Pilot, I believe you are correct. However, I also believe that there exists significant opportunity to escape him."

"Not likely. All he has to do is let it out that the one missing from among the dead had a gun. Obviously, she's the culprit—a Batcher gone bad. He could even get off with offering a mid-figure bounty with a story like that."

Dulsey closed her eyes, opened them, and stood up out of her chair.

"Would the pilot care for a hot snack?" she asked distantly. He studied her face—closed—and her posture—tense; met her eyes and smiled.

"Sure, Dulsey. A hot snack would be fine."

He spun his chair back to face the board and pointed his eyes at the instruments, pilot-mind primed to shout out at the first sign of a problem. That left a good bit of mind on its own, unfortunately, and he was tired, too. He took a breath, centering himself, and put the part of him that wasn't watching into a doze.

"Pilot?"

He started, grabbed a look at the instruments, then spun his chair to face Dulsey, standing with a mug and a bowl in her hands.

She stepped closer, offering both; and he took them, slotting the mug into the chair-arm holder and snapping the bowl into the board-edge restraints. The bowl gave off a pleasantly spicy steam.

"Thank you," he said, meaning it. "Feed yourself, too, right?"

"I've eaten," she said, sounding irritated. "There is something that you must know."

He raised his eyebrows. "Go."

"We are locked in," she said, even more irritated, to his ear. "The piloting room, and the hall beyond that door—" she pointed at the interior hatch—"we are allowed. The second hatch, further down the hall, is locked, and another door, across from the galley, is also locked."

"That bothers you, does it?"

Dulsey frowned. "Does it not bother you?"

He pulled the mug up and had a sip. Tea, hot and sweet, just what a tired pilot needed. He had another sip, somewhat deeper, before looking back to her.

"Not particularly," he said. "Pilot Cantra didn't exactly ask for our help, though she did realize she needed it. It only makes sense for her to lock us out of the places she doesn't think we need to get into." Another sip of tea—damn, that was good.

"Besides," he said to Dulsey's angry eyes, "I'd rather be locked in the pilot's tower than out."

"There is that," she said after a moment, and went to the vacant chair. "I will watch, Pilot, while you eat."

THIRTEEN

Outbound, Faldaiza Nearspace
Approaching Transition

SOMEWHERE, FAR AWAY, a two-tone chime was going off. Cantra rolled onto her stomach and pulled the blanket over her head. Not that it would do a bit of good. Ilan would be by too soon to enforce the wake-up call. She'd heard that in other dorms it was possible to bribe the top girl for a couple hours' sleep-in. Not Ilan, though. Oh, she'd take the bribe, all right—she wasn't a fool, was she? And then she'd write it up and hand it in to the Super and there'd be a short, intensely miserable time, during which you learned to wonder what sleep was, to have made you want more of it. And when you were well and truly beyond thought, feeling or—

Damn chime should've finished its cycle by now. Might be an emergency drill. She struggled with the thought, trying to call the various drill-tones to mind. Which process tipped her over the edge from mostly asleep to mostly awake, whereupon she recognized the chime as her own alarm clock, which she'd just managed to set before crashing into her bunk, 'skins, boots, and all.

There are strangers on my ship.

Recent memory got her eyes open and her legs over the side of the bunk, blanket sliding to the deck.

She sat there a moment, taking stock. Her head ached, her thoughts were fuzzy, her throat and eyes were dry, and her stomach felt queasy. On the other hand, the down-deep shaking was gone, and her ears heard clear, meaning that the alarm was irritating. All in all, a four hundred percent improvement over her state of—she squinted across the room at the clock—three ship-hours ago.

She was in shape to fly, if she had to—and she did. After a bit of clean-up.

Sliding to her feet, she crossed the room and slapped the alarm into silence, stripped off 'skins and boots, dropped them into the decom drawer, and stepped into the sanitation closet.

She emerged dry cleaned and somewhat less queasy, opened her locker, and pulled on ship clothes—a close-fitting sweater and pants—and a pair of ship slippers. The polished metal interior of the locker showed fleeting reflections of a tall, thin woman, her beige hair cut off blunt at the jaw line, her eyes misty green under thin winged brows. The rest of the face was sharp—cheekbones, nose, and chin—skin the uniform golden-tan prized in the higher class courtesans. The reflection moved with spare economy, one motion flowing effortlessly into the next—a dancer's grace. Or a pilot's.

Cantra slammed the door, picked up the fallen blanket, and began to put her bunk in order, thoughts on the piloting room and the strangers aboard her ship.

No sense now second-guessing the line of logic that had led her to such folly in the first place. Done was done. She had a situation which called for some care and some planning, neither one of which she had been in shape to handle—and arguably still wasn't.

She owned that Jela had called the problem on Faldaiza Yard accurately, and that he hadn't stinted on his answer to it. He was also the devil's own pilot—as good as the best she'd ever seen. What he was doing without a ship was a mystery—a worrisome mystery, if he took it into his head that *Dancer* suited him.

Well, she thought—tucking the blanket tight and reaching up for the webbing—if he took that notion, he'd have to kill her to fulfill it. More than a few had filed that course and failed at lift. Jela being a better pilot than she was—he might manage the thing. In which case, her worries were over. Best she could do was stay awake, stay on guard, and hope she got lucky if matters fell out that way.

Assuming that they didn't…She sighed. The cargo was expected by a certain someone, on a certain date and time, there on Taliofi. The course was set in—she glanced at the clock—transition coming up soon—and even with the early lift the schedule wasn't generous. So, Pilot Jela and Batcher Dulsey were with her 'til then. After she'd collected her money, and delivered the goods—that was when she'd lose them. If it came to lifting without cargo—she could do that. Take on something at Kizimi, maybe. Or Horetide—that was an idea, in and of itself. She hadn't seen Qualee in a ship's age.

She finished with the webbing and stepped back from the bunk. Ditch Dulsey and Jela at Taliofi and lift for Horetide. As a plan, it was simple, straightforward and not too likely to go wrong. It might get dicey if it came known she'd aided and abetted a runaway Batcher—but it *was* Taliofi they was bound for, a port that 'hunters wishful of living long tended to avoid.

In the meantime—another glance at the clock. Right. Time for her to relieve her crew, who were probably more than ready for their own naps. First, though...

She opened the locker once more, ignoring the flickering reflections, and pushed on a corner of the right-hand wall. The concealed door slid away and she considered the pattern of light-and-dark, flicked two toggles, closed the hidden door and the public one and left the cabin at a brisk walk.

She made a short detour through the galley for a high-cal bar, found the tea caddy warm, poured some of the contents into a mug, and sipped. Strong and on the edge of too sweet. Perfect. She filled the mug and carried it and the high-cal with her into the piloting chamber.

The door snapped open, revealing a scene of ship's tranquility, both pilots sitting their boards, attentive to the duty at hand.

Mostly.

Dulsey, alerted by the sound of the door, spun her chair around, her face neutral to the point of accusation.

Pilot Jela, now, he merely lifted his eyes to the forward screen, tracking her reflection as she came across the room.

"Pilot," he said, nice and polite.

"Pilot," she answered, in the same pitch and key. She included Dulsey in her nod. "I appreciate the two of you keeping us on course while I had some down time." She hefted her mug with a slight smile. "I also appreciate the tea."

"You are welcome, Pilot," Dulsey said softly. "If you like, I can make you some soup."

"Not right now, thanks," Cantra answered. "Right now, it's time for the shift to change. I'm rested enough to fly her and the two of you have got to be on course for exhaustion yourselves." She took another step forward, and now Jela spun his chair, too, looking up at her out of black, ungiving eyes.

"We're coming up on transition," he said, calm and easy on the surface, but showing tense beneath it. Cantra felt a flicker of sympathy for him, inclined her head and squared her shoulders.

"So we are. The board is mine, Pilot. Get some rest, the two of you."

"Where shall we rest, Pilot?" Dulsey snapped. "We are forbidden the ship, save this room and the galley."

Cantra tipped her head. "Don't like to be locked out of things, Dulsey?" She shrugged, flicked a glance to Jela and saw her own image in his eyes. "I've reconfigured," she told him, trusting Dulsey would follow his lead, and trusting that he wouldn't chose to make trouble now, if trouble was on his flight plan.

"The quarters across from the galley are unlocked now. I suggest the two of you get some rest." She stared deliberately into Dulsey's eyes and was mildly amused when the Batcher's glare did not falter.

"I *strongly* suggest that the two of you get some rest," she said softly.

There might have been a hesitation. If so, it was too brief for her to scan. Jela came to his feet and nodded, respectful.

"The shift changes, Pilot," he said formally.

"Thank you," she replied. "I'll see you on the far side of sleep."

A measuring black glance swept her face before Jela turned and moved toward the door with his light, almost mincing steps. The panel slid aside as he approached—stayed open as he turned.

"Dulsey?" he said, and it was clear from the tone that he could and would carry her, if she wanted it that way.

For a heartbeat it seemed as though Dulsey would stay stubbornly in her chair. She glared at Cantra, who gave her a smile and sipped her tea. Goaded, she transferred the glare to Jela—

And levered herself out of the chair, walking heavily. At the door, she paused, like she'd just remembered something, turned and bowed deeply.

"Pilot. Good shift."

Almost, she returned the bow. Almost. In the event, she simply nodded, and watched the two of them out the door.

When they were gone, she opened the secret hatch on the board and flicked a toggle, locking herself in.

The door opened to his palm, revealing quarters not much smaller than standard transport quarters. There were two hammocks—one high, one low—and compact sanitary facilities, including a dry cleaner. Floor space was at a premium, and he took up most of it.

Dulsey sidled in between him and the door. It shut as soon as she cleared the beam, emitting a peevish-sounding sigh, and the status light went from green to red.

They were locked in.

Jela kept the curse behind his teeth. Of course she'd lock them in, he thought. The same reasons that had seen them confined to the tower and the galley applied.

Dulsey sighed, sharply, but surprisingly enough didn't say anything; just turned and considered the cramped quarters, her face Batcher-bland.

"You have any preference for high or low?" he asked when it seemed like she wasn't disposed to speak or move on her own.

"If the pilot permits," she answered distantly. "I will take low."

"Makes no difference to me," he said, remembering to keep his voice easy. "I've slept worse."

"So have I," she said, and slipped past him, rolling into the hammock like a spacer, and yanking the webbing tight.

He considered the top bunk—two pair of handholds were molded into the ship's wall by way of a route; he used them, rolling into his hammock like a spacer, too, and pulled the webbing snug. He looked around, finding it no more roomy at the top than the bottom, and located the sensor within an easy sweep of his hand.

"Want me to dim the lights, Dulsey?"

Silence. Then the sound of a hard-drawn breath.

"If the pilot would be so good."

The pilot would. He waved his hand; lighting obligingly fell to night levels. He closed his eyes and deliberately relaxed, which should have triggered his sleep process. Granthor knew he was tired enough to sleep.

Despite that, he lay awake listening at first to the small sounds that Dulsey made and, after her breath had evened out into sleep, his own thoughts as he moved, not into sleep mode, but into problem-solving.

While he hadn't minded limited access while he was in the pilot's chair, he found he minded it more than a little now. Easy enough for Pilot Cantra to lock them both into this tiny cabin until she raised her next port and handed them over to whatever passed for law locally. Easy enough, if he was of a mind to be morbid, for the pilot to evacuate the air from this same cabin and save herself any planetside inconvenience at all.

He wished he had a better reading on Pilot Cantra, truth be told. That she traded Gray—or even Dark—was near enough to certain. No honest civilian pilot had reason to fly like she did—and that was before taking into account her choice and number of weapons, her specially-rigged 'skins, and her highly interesting ship.

Balancing all that was the fact that she had held to peaceful welcome and paid her share when it came down to cover and be covered. In point of fact, she had been entirely well-behaved and civilized right up to the time hostilities were specifically brought against her. At which point, she had acted efficiently and well.

Until she'd hit the end of her energy allotment, and he'd thought he was going to see a tall, grim woman fall face flat to the deck. By his estimation, considering the muscle tremors, staggered breathing, and elevated adrenal levels, she *should have* gone down. The fact that she hadn't was—interesting. As was the fact that a relatively short nap had returned her to functioning—if not optimum—levels.

That she didn't trust strangers—a lapsed military and a runaway Batcher—on her ship only showed her good sense. That she would allow them to stay long on her ship—was unlikely.

Full circle. He wasn't problem-solving. He was worrying—he was that tired. As if he needed proof.

Fine. This called for measures.

He breathed, filling his lungs fully and then fully exhaling. Before his mind's eye rose an image of a task screen, cluttered with tasks, and showing generous sections of red and yellow. With each inhale he focused his attention on one section of the screen. With each exhale, he wiped that portion of the screen away, leaving only blackness.

Half the screen cleared, he abruptly remembered something else. The tree. He'd gotten used to having the tree by his side while he slept, to protecting it, and imagining it protecting him.

In fact, he hadn't slept without the tree in the same room with him—since when? Since he'd returned to the *Trident*. Not even when they'd put him in isolation.

Concern began to grow. He remembered...

The tree was still anchored in the piloting chamber, along with someone who—

Moist greenness filled his senses, soothing him, lulling him into—

Jela slept.

FOURTEEN

Spiral Dance
Transition

THE HIGH-CAL BAR was gone. Cantra checked her numbers for transition, found nothing to adjust and sat back in her chair, sipping what was left of the tea.

She considered opening the intercom into the guest quarters, and decided not. Jela and Dulsey'd already had plenty of time alone to talk and go over plans, if plans they had. If they were smart—and she allowed both of them to be smart—they'd catch the naps she'd recommended, maybe after taking a little mutual comfort.

Her stomach clenched at the thought of mutual comfort and an unwelcome memory of Pilot Jela's wide shoulders and slim hips flickered, which she was having none of.

"*Three* armor," she reminded herself loudly, and had another sip of tea, putting her attention wholly on the screens and the scans.

It seemed that they'd gotten away clean, leaving aside the questions of who, how and why they were being pursued. If the pursuers were outworld, like Dulsey thought, then there was the possibility of a welcoming party at Taliofi. She didn't much like the idea of that, but she liked less the idea of missing the delivery deadline. An agreeable amount of hard coin came with meeting that deadline, and a deal of grief she neither wanted nor would likely survive came with a late delivery.

So, they went to Taliofi, exercising due caution. The vulnerable moment would be at the end of transition, when it would take the screens full seconds to come back online, and weapons only as fast as the pilot understood the situation.

It wasn't possible to translate with the shields up, but it *was* possible, though risky, to go in with weapons live—and emerge with those same weapons still live and eager to answer the pilot's touch.

Prudence, as Garen would say, plots the course. Not that Garen had ever in her life acted with what anybody sane'd call "prudence." Of course, Garen hadn't necessarily been sane.

Cantra finished her tea, slotted the empty cup and leaned to the board, accessing the weapons comp and inserting the appropriate commands. The timer at the bottom of her forward screen revealed that they would reach the translation point in a quarter clock, which gave her time to stretch, fetch more tea, and—

A green flutter tickled the corner of her eye. She turned and looked down-board at Pilot Jela's veg—tree, its leaves moving in a pattern approximating the Dance of a Dozen Scarves, inspired no doubt by the flow of air from the duct under which it sat.

Sighing, she came out of the chair, closed her eyes and did her stretches, the while seeing shadows of leaves dancing on the inside of her eyelids. Talk about prudence. Last thing she needed was for that pot to leave its moorings, if the translation happened to be a rough one, which, going in with the weapons live, it was likely to be.

Stretches done, she moved down-board and stood before the plant in question.

It wasn't much to look at, now that she had the leisure. It was considerably shorter than she was, and its main trunk wasn't any thicker than a dueling stick. Straight like a dueling stick, too, until near the top, where four slender twigs branched off on their own. The branches held a goodly number of green leaves, and, nestled among them, what looked to be three fruits, encased in a green rind. The whole thing smelled—pleasing, moist and minty.

None of which changed the fact that it was a stupid thing to have in a piloting room.

She shook herself and bent to the restraints, finding in short order that Dulsey had done a job which couldn't be improved upon, short of rigging up a restraining field or spacing the thing. Not that she had time to do either.

Good enough would have to do, she thought, straightening and giving the tree one more hard look before she went back to her chair, glaring at the screens as she unslotted the cup.

Clear all around, for a wonder. She carried the cup with her to the galley, filled it from the carafe, snapped the lid down, and gave the little room a fast once over, looking for things left loose.

More credit to Dulsey—everything was where it belonged, the latches engaged on all cabinets and doors. She touched the carafe, making certain it was secured, and left the galley. In the hall, she flicked a glance to the door of the guest room. Red and yellow lights glowed steady, signaling that not one, but two, locks were engaged, Pilot Jela having impressed her as a man handy with a toolkit and inventive besides.

'Course, the room hadn't been locked that couldn't be escaped, but Jela had also impressed her as cool-headed, not to say sensible. There wasn't any use to him in irritating her right at present. Much more productive to just take a nap and bide his time, being sure that they'd outrun whoever wasn't after him. No, the vulnerable moment with Jela would be when *Dancer* was on Taliofi Port. She'd have to be slick in her ditching, which she was confident she could be. What wasn't known, of course, was if she could be slick enough.

Well, that was a worry for later. She turned and went back to the piloting chamber, slipping into her seat and making the straps secure just as the timer in the forward screen went to zero.

The weapons came up; the shields went down; the screens went gray; the timer reset itself and began counting down from twelve.

...eleven...ten...

Spiral Dance shivered.

...nine...

...calmed...

...eight...seven...

...twisted like a Sendali contortionist. The straps tightened across Cantra's torso; at the far side of the board Jela's little tree snapped a bow, its leaves in disarray.

...six...five...

...calm again, but Cantra wasn't believing it...

...four...three...

Dancer twisted again, with feeling. The pot containing Jela's tree thumped hard against the bulkhead, despite the restraints. Cantra gasped as the straps pressed her into the chair...

...two...one...

Normal space.

Her hands moved, one for the weapons board, one for the scans and shields, ready, ready—

The screens showed stars, all around; the scans showed clear, likewise. The image unfolding in the navigation screen showed her course overlaying the pattern of stars, with an estimated time of arrival at Taliofi in just under twelve ship-hours. Ahead of schedule, thanks to the early lift. Still, she didn't feel like taking the scenic route. The quicker she got down—even at Taliofi—the better she'd feel.

She sighed, notched the weapons back to stand-by and scanned again, just being sure.

If there were any ships with hostile intent inside the considerable range of her eyes and ears, they were both cloaked and cool— which made them watchers, dangerous in their own ways, but not needful of her immediate attention.

A blue light lit on the edge of the navigation screen. She touched it, and info flowed down the screen, the short form of it all being that one and one-quarter ship hour's could be shaved off real-space transit to Taliofi, if she was willing to fly like a Rimmer.

She grinned, fingers already feeding in the amended course.

The hammock swung hard and Jela woke, felt the ship steady, and took a breath, expanding his chest so the webbing wouldn't grab too tight on the next bounce.

"All right down there, Dulsey?" he asked.

"The pilot is kind to inquire," her voice came, breathlessly. "This humble person is well."

"Good. Stay put, hear me? I don't think we're done dancing ye—"

The ship bounced again, gratifyingly on cue. The straps snapped taut, and the hammock swung out and back, smacking Jela's hip against the metal wall hard enough to sting through padding and 'skins. He scarcely noticed it, himself, but his cabin-mate didn't have his advantages.

"Dulsey?"

"What transpires?" An edge was added to the breathlessness; Jela figured she'd taken a pretty good bump herself.

"My guess is we're translating with weapons on-line," he said. "With a ship this size, that's bound to introduce a bobble or two."

"Bob—" she began, and stopped as the ship settled around them once more. "We are out."

He considered it, listening with his whole body in a hammock that hung calm from its gimbals.

"I think you're right," he said at last.

"The door is still locked."

He was sorry to hear that, but the info didn't surprise him.

"I figure the pilot has other things on her mind," he told Dulsey, keeping his voice easy despite his own dislike of the situation. "Even given that we lifted out early and should be ahead of whatever delivery schedule she might have, she doesn't know who might be coming after. If I was in the pilot's chair, I'd want to minimize my exposure. It might be Pilot Cantra's going to do some flying—" That was what they had said in his training wing, when a pilot needed to produce the impossible. "I'd expect us to be in here until the ship's on port."

Grim silence for a count of five.

"What shall we do?" Dulsey asked finally.

Jela sighed, quietly, trying not to remember how very much he disliked doing nothing; and did not wish for a computer, a database, or a stack of reports to read.

"Sleep?" he suggested.

She didn't answer and the grimness lingered for a bit. Then he heard her breathing smooth out and knew she'd taken his advice.

Now, if only *he* could take his advice, he thought crankily and moved his head against the hammock's pad.

Well. Enough of sleep and dreaming memories. What was needed was analysis and a plan. It was not to Pilot Cantra's benefit to keep him with her, so she would think and she was quite possibly correct to think it.

However, Pilot Cantra's benefit was secondary to his own. His departure from Faldaiza had been strategic retreat—remaining would not only have been foolhardy but would have endangered himself and his mission, those two elements being inseparable, and Pilot Cantra and her ship had been available. The question now became: what was best for him to do in order to recover the ground he had lost?

It was a knotty question, he thought with some satisfaction, as he began to assign decision priorities.

He hoped he had an answer by the time Pilot Cantra unlocked the door.

FIFTEEN

Spiral Dance
Taliofi

TALIOFI WASN'T EXACTLY the garden spot of the Spiral Arm, nor was it quite so law-bound as, say, Faldaiza. It was by no means the worst world on which to put down a ship carrying irregulars, and the lack of an interested local constabulary generally made it a likely port for a pilot in Cantra's line of trade. The fact that it wasn't one of her favorite ports had less to do with the various briberies involved, which could go as high as ten percent of receipts, and most to do with it being home to Rint dea'Sord.

In a business where the faint of heart failed and the ruthless prevailed, Rint dea'Sord was known as a man not to cross. He paid well for his commissions, if not always at full price; and he paid well for errors, too, with interest. A bitter enemy was dea'Sord, so the word went, and a man with a galaxy-wide reach. No one cheated Rint dea'Sord, but the same could not be said for himself.

Garen had refused to deal with the man at all, which might have said something positive about her sanity after all. Cantra's dealings with him had been exactly two. Both times, she'd come away with enough of her fee in hand that she thought three times whenever a deal involving a Taliofi delivery came up—once for the money and twice for Ser dea'Sord.

This instance, she'd thought four times, the money was *that* good. And in the end, it was the money that had convinced her, despite the client's known tendencies. If she actually received even a third of the promised fee, it would represent a tidy profit. Profits being what motivated the pilot and fueled the craft, she'd taken the job.

And now here she was, thinking a fifth time, which was a plain waste of time and thought-channels. She was down, a fact that couldn't fail to escape the notice of those with a tender regard for her cargo. Lifting now got her nothing but ruined. Best to collect her pay, off-load, and commence about ditching her so-called crew.

She might should've had qualms about leaving them in such a . port, but she judged Jela able to take care of himself and, while Taliofi wasn't a nexus, it wasn't back-system, either. A pilot with Jela's skills should have no trouble hiring himself onto a ship heading for his favorite coordinates.

The other matter was a little less certain, but Dulsey's chances of long-term survival were in the negative numbers no matter how you rolled it. Cantra found as she locked the board down that she did feel something bad about that, which was another side of senseless. Dulsey'd made her choices and Taliofi was as good a place for a runaway Batcher as any—and considerably better than some.

Lock-down finished, she released the webbing and stood. She was well ahead of her appointed time. Might be best to switch her priorities and get her crew up and gone before Rint dea'Sord took note of them. With that detail taken care of, she could lift directly after she'd off-loaded, which did appeal. She'd go on to Horetide and pick up work there.

Half-a-dozen steps brought her to the little tree. There was a dent in the pot from where it had smacked into the wall and it had lost three leaves to the decking. Loss of leaf wasn't likely to do it harm, she thought and bent a little closer. The branches and the thin trunk appeared intact—and the fruits still hung in their places. So far, so good.

Time to skin-up and see if her passengers had fared as well.

Cocooned in his web of calculation, Jela felt the ship come to ground. He let the current probability analysis run itself to an outcome he liked even less than the previous one, and opened his eyes.

"We're down, Dulsey," he said, neither loud nor soft. The walls rumbled a little when his voice struck it.

"Thank you, Pilot; I am awake," came the composed answer. "Do you think Pilot Cantra will let us out now?"

"I think that's the most likely scenario," he said, and released the webbing, taking a moment to be sure that it was untangled and ran smooth on its rollers, in case the next tenant of the bunk needed to strap down in a hurry.

Satisfied, he eased onto his side, face pointed toward the door, and told himself that it took time to lock the board and file pilot's intent with the port and—

There was a sound—small in his super-sharp hearing—and the door opened, framing a long, lean figure. Her face was amiable, which he knew by now meant nothing with Pilot Cantra; and her head was cocked to one side, tawny hair brushing the shoulder of her 'skins.

"I'm glad to see the two of you looking well-rested," she said, her voice smooth and unhurried, the Rimmer accent just a tickle against the ear-bone. "Time to get up and do some errands."

"Where are we?" Dulsey asked, surprisingly sharp.

One of Cantra's winged eyebrows lifted, but she gave answer calm enough. "Taliofi. That inform you, Dulsey?"

There was a pause, long enough for Jela to read it as "no," but Dulsey surprised him.

"Yes, Pilot. What errands are required?"

"As it happens, I've got a list." She raised her head and fixed Jela in her foggy green gaze. "Ace, Pilot?"

"Ace," he agreed, and produced an agreeable smile, there being no reason not to.

"Good." She jerked her head to her left, toward the hatch. "Let's go."

She'd considered leaving the tree where it was, in the interests of misdirection, but had decided against. Jela'd gone to considerable risk and trouble to bring this particular plant out of Faldaiza, and she had no intention to rob him. So, she'd untied the thing and got it—pot, dirt and fruits—onto a cargo sled, by which time she had developed a whole new respect for Pilot Jela's physical attributes, and dragged it down to the hatch.

Jela eyed it as he entered the area, and she drew a subtle breath, ready with her story about the pot being broken and dangerous in high acceleration. But he'd only shrugged, did Jela, and bent to pick the thing up, cradling it like kin.

"Pot took a beating, I see," was what he said. "I'll tend to it, Pilot."

"'preciate it," she'd answered, matching his tone. If he'd planned on making a move for *Dancer*, now was the time; and he couldn't well make that move with his arms full of tree. She didn't doubt that he'd already understood the situation with regard to his lack of continued welcome, and she was unaccountably relieved that no fancy-work was going to be needed on his behalf. She turned.

"Dulsey," she began, but the Batcher held up a hand, cutting her off.

"Pilot, there are those whom I would seek out on this port. If I do not return in time for lift, please understand it is not from disrespect for yourself or your ship, but because I have made other arrangements."

So Dulsey had contacts on Taliofi, did she? That was a piece of luck. Cantra inclined her head gravely.

"I understand," she said, and the Batcher bowed.

Cantra turned and opened the hatch. The day beyond showed gray and cold and raining.

"Right," she said, and sighed as she waved them out and down the ramp. "Welcome to Taliofi."

Thing was, she *did* have a list, a habit going back to Garen's insistence that "ship shape" meant something more than neat-and-clean. She stood at the top of the ramp and watched Dulsey lead the way down, saw Jela striding steadily away, looking from this angle like someone who might be able to make a night warm after all, carrying his potted tree like it weighed nothing at all.

Cantra sighed a bit against that thought and the feeling that she was watching the best pilot she'd seen in some years sashay right away from her, and she forcibly turned her attention to the list.

First was to do an in-person prepay for lift-off—in case news of her last lift-out had got this far already—and then do a little shopping, to top off the needfuls, no more'n that, not at Taliofi. After that, she'd scout up someplace quiet and have herself a meal, with herself for company. All this eating with crew had her half-imagining she was too old to work solo.

Once the eating was done, she'd find a private place, check her 'skins and her weapons, and go pay her respects to Ser dea'Sord.

It was a wonderful thing to be a generalist, Jela thought, as he and the tree made their way across Taliofi Yard. For instance, a generalist, with his horde of beguiling and unrelated facts and his valuable skill at putting those facts together in intriguing and uncannily correct ways, would recall that…interesting numbers…of diverted *sheriekas*-made devices seemed to have passed—oh-so-anonymously—through Taliofi, their previous ports, if any, and their places of origin muddied beyond recovery. A generalist would recall that Taliofi

crouched at coordinates easily raised from the Rim—and Beyond—
and that trade undoubtedly went both in and out.

And a generalist would conclude, against his will, for the woman
had covered him and had held away from trying to kill him or do
him any harm other than cutting him loose to pursue his own business on a port that might in charity be considered Dark—a generalist would conclude, in the non-linear way typical of the breed, that
he knew what was in Pilot Cantra's hold, which it was a soldier's
duty to confiscate, along with detaining the pilot and her buyer.

The weight of the tree was beginning to drag at his arms, and
the cold rain was an irritation on his face and unprotected hands. He
scouted ahead for a place to get out of the weather, spied what
looked to be a cab stand a few dozen strides to his left and made
for it, passing a goodly number of civilians about their daily business, none of whom spared one glance for a man carrying a tree. It
was that kind of port.

He shouldered his way into the cab stand, kicked the door shut,
used an elbow to punch the privacy button, and put the tree down
on the bench. Straightening, he stretched his arms and let them fall
to his sides with a sigh.

Dulsey had set out on her own course the instant her boots hit
the Yard's 'crete. He hoped her contacts here were solid. At least
the likelihood of bounty hunters was slim, which had to count in her
favor. He hoped.

On a personal note, though, he had a problem. While it might
be a soldier's duty to confiscate and arrest, to attempt to carry out
that duty without back-up was a fool's game.

The most effective thing he could do was collect evidence and
send it on to Ragil to pass upstream.

Not being exactly military, he also theoretically had the option
of ignoring the whole thing and getting on with the business of
finding a lift out for a man and a tree.

He considered it, because he had to, weighing the benefits—and
then gave it up. His whole life had been spent fighting *sheriekas* and
their works…

From the tree, a faint rustle of leaves, though the air was still
inside the cab stand, and Jela grinned.

"That's right. Both of us have spent our lives on that project,"
he murmured, and stretched one more time before taking the pot

up again and bringing the heel of his boot smartly against the door's kick-plate.

Outside, the rain had increased. Jela sighed and turned back the way he had come.

"Pilot, you honor my humble establishment."

Rint dea'Sord swept a showy bow, sleeves fluttering, right leg thrust out, shiny boot pointed straight forward, left leg behind and slightly bent, boot pointing at right angles. His hair fell in artful gilt ringlets below his slim shoulders. The shirt was silver starsilk, slashed sleeves showing blood-red. The breeches, tucked into high boots, looked to be tanned viezy hide and probably was, though the probability that Ser dea'Sord had followed tradition to the point of personally killing the donor reptile with the ritually mandated stone knife was vanishingly low. Very tender of his own skin, Rint dea'Sord was, though he didn't care if yours took a scar.

He straightened out of his bow with boneless grace, the right leg coming back just a fraction too slow, an error that would have gained him a turn in the phantom lover, had he been trained in her dorm which, naturally enough, he hadn't, being self-taught. For that level of education, he did well enough, Cantra allowed and answered his bow with a Rimmer's terse nod.

"The cargo's ready to off-load, pending receipt of payment," she said.

Rint dea'Sord smiled, which he did prettily enough, but he really should, Cantra thought critically, either learn to use his eyes or camouflage them with a sweep of the lashes or—

"All business, as always, Pilot!" He laughed gently and sat himself behind his desk, waving her to a chair with a languid hand. "Please, rest a moment and tell me your news. Will you take some refreshment?"

When Taliofi's star froze, that was when she'd take refreshment from the likes of Rint dea'Sord. Not that she'd be so rude as to tell the man so; she'd been trained better than that. She put her hand on the back of the chair she was supposed to sit in, and smiled, using her eyes.

"I just ate," she said, pulling the Rim accent up a little. "And my news ain't special or interesting. Took the cargo on at Faldaiza, lifted, transitioned, and came down on Taliofi Yard a while back.

Looking to collect payment due, off-load, and lift." She smiled
again, rueful. "A courier's life is boring, which is the way she wants it
and her clients, too."

He folded his hands carefully atop the black ceramic desk, and
considered her, his eyes blue and hard, belying his tone of courteous
and civil interest.

"Come, Pilot, you are too modest! When a courier performs
an unscheduled lift amid cannon-fire, surely that is news? As your
client, I can only applaud the skill which allowed you to win free
unscathed. It will of course be awkward for you to return to Faldaiza
for the foreseeable future, but that must be accounted to the side of
necessary action, must it not?"

"Right," she said, laconic, keeping her face smooth.

Rint dea'Sord smiled. "As your client, I must ask—please do
not think me discourteous!—if the contretemps surrounding your
departure from Faldaiza in any way touched upon the cargo you
have brought to me?"

"Separate issue," she assured him.

"You relieve me. Would that separate issue have had to do with
your passenger?"

Cantra showed him a face honestly puzzled. "Passenger?"

Rint dea'Sord clicked his tongue against his teeth, his face smooth
under the gold-toned makeup. "Come, come, Pilot! Passenger, of
course."

"I'm not recalling any passenger," she said. "Maybe your info
got scrambled."

Ser dea'Sord sighed, gently. "Pilot, surely you know that I have
eyes all over this port."

"Goes without saying—man of your position," Cantra answered
soothingly.

"Then you will know that I am reliably informed regarding
your passenger."

Since when did Rint dea'Sord concern himself with extra cargo,
crew or passengers, so long as his interests weren't put in jeopardy?
She wondered, stringently keeping the wonder from showing in her
face, eyes, voice or stance, and shrugged. Holding to honest puzzlement, she met the cold blue eyes, her own guileless and wide.

"Sir, I don't doubt you're reliably informed about everything
that transpires on this Yard, and would be about my passenger, if

I'd had one, which I didn't." She cocked her head to a side. "Got time for a let's pretend?"

The pretty gilt eyebrows arched high, but he answered courteous enough. "I am at your disposal, Pilot. What shall we pretend? That I am a two-headed galunus?"

"Nothing that hard," she said. "Let's just pretend that, instead of the two of us talking about your cargo and how I'm going to get paid real soon now so I can off-load and lift—let's pretend I had two clients on this port and I'm with the second. And let's pretend that this second client, having paid her shot and arranged the off-load, starts inquiries into your cargo, which it ain't any business of hers. And so she says to me, 'I'm a big noise on this Yard and I'm reliably informed that you're carrying cargo for Rint dea'Sord. Tell me about it.' Now," Cantra finished, watching him watch her out of those hard, cold eyes, "what's my proper response, given the cargo isn't got the young lady's name on it, but your own?"

There was a small silence during which Rint dea'Sord unfolded his hands and put them flat on the top of the desk.

"Let me see…" He murmured, and raised one finger in consideration. "Would it perhaps be, 'Cargo? I'm not recalling any cargo.'"

Cantra smiled. "You've played before."

"Indeed I have," he said, and didn't bother to smile back. "While I value your discretion—and your warning—I believe that the nature of this particular passenger warrants my attention as a—what was the phrase? Ah!—as a *big noise* on this Yard. Certainly, my attention must be aroused when a courier whom I am known to have employed is seen abetting the escape of a renegade Batcher."

Cantra visibly stifled a yawn. "Renegade Batcher," she said, on a note of reflection.

"It is possible of course," said Rint dea'Sord, "that you were deceived into believing her a natural human, such as yourself. A Batcher traveling alone, without the rest of her Pod, would seem to be as individual as you or I."

"Might've been traveling on behalf of her owner," Cantra said, by way of stalling him, while she tried to think it through. He was focusing on Dulsey, acting like she'd been the only one coming off *Spiral Dance*, saving Cantra. Had his bragged-on eyes somehow missed the substantial fact of Pilot Jela? Or had Jela decided to ingratiate himself with the Yard boss? Fast work if he had—and she didn't put it beyond him.

"Is that what she told you?" dea'Sord asked. "That she was traveling on behalf of her owner?"

Cantra sighed silently, bringing her full wits back to the conversation in progress.

"She can't have told me anything, since she doesn't exist," she said, letting aggravation be heard. "Ser dea'Sord, there's the matter of payment sitting between the two of us. Your cargo's secure in the hold of my ship. As soon as I have the promised coin, I can offload and we can both get back to the business of turning a profit."

This time Rint dea'Sord did smile and Cantra wished he hadn't.

"As it happens, Pilot, I am pursuing a profit even as we speak." He moved a hand to touch a portion of his desk top. A door opened in the wall behind him, and a burly man in half-armor 'skins stepped through, a limp form wound in cargo twine tucked under one arm. dea'Sord beckoned and the fellow walked up to Cantra, dropped his burden at her feet, and fell back to the desk, hand on his sidearm.

Cantra looked down. Dulsey was unconscious, which was maybe a good thing; her face was swollen and beginning to show bruises; her nose was broken, and there was blood—on her face, in her hair, on those bits of her coverall not hidden by cargo twine.

The cargo twine was a problem, being smartwire's dimmer cousin. Cargo twine could crush ribs and snap vertebrae. Not that anyone would care what damage a Batcher picked up for bounty took, so long as she was alive—stipulating that the contract called for it.

"Your passenger, I believe, Pilot?" Rint dea'Sord was having way too much fun, Cantra thought, suddenly seeing all too clearly where he was going with this.

"No, sir," she said, her eyes on Dulsey—still breathing, all the worse for her.

"Pilot—"

She raised her eyes and looked at him straight. "Much as I'd like to accommodate you, she wasn't no passenger."

The thin mouth tightened. "What was she then?"

"'prentice pilot. Sat her board neat as you'd like. 'Course, being an engineer…"

"An engineer." He laughed. "She was a restaurant worker before she turned rogue, murdered her owner, and terminated the others of her Pod."

Cantra glanced down at Dulsey. "Why'd she do that?"

"Who can know what motivates such creatures?" He gave a delicate shudder. "Perhaps she believed that, with the others gone, she might pass as a real human. *Why* scarcely matters. In a short while Efron here will be taking the Batcher across the port, where a bounty hunter will receive her and pay him our finder's fee."

"Right," she said, keeping her eyes on his face. "What's it got to do with me and my fee?"

"Pilot." He looked at her with sorrow, as if she were a favorite student who had unaccountably flubbed a simple question. "I think you are well-aware of the penalties attached to giving aid to an escaped Batcher. Whether she was an apprentice pilot or passenger really makes no difference."

Nor would it to those who were only concerned with collecting their bounties. And as for the penalties for aiding and abetting, she did know them: three years hard labor, and confiscation of all her goods—which would be *Dancer.* By the time her years at labor were done—assuming she survived them, which wasn't the way the smart money bet—she'd be broken and broke. She also knew that an aid-and-abet charge against a natural human, which in unlikely fact she happened to be, was subject to an appeal before an actual magistrate. The odds of her coming out a free woman on the other side of that appeal were laughable, and the accumulated penalties for her various crimes and sins against the law-abiding would add up to more and worse than the aid-and-abet.

Which simple arithmetic Rint dea'Sord had done, and then exposed himself and his operation to considerable risk by summoning a bounty hunter. Cantra supposed she ought to be flattered, that he thought her worth so much.

She smiled at him, wide and sincere.

"What do you want?" she asked, thinking the important thing was not to let Efron get twine around her. That likely meant a discussion of weapons right here and now—in fact, it would be best if it were here and now. She made a mental note to save a dart for Dulsey.

Rint dea'Sord was smiling again.

"Excellent, Pilot. *Do* allow me to admire your perspicacity. While it is true that I would enjoy owning your ship and your effects, I would enjoy having you in my employ even more."

Cantra frowned. "Ser dea'Sord, you don't need a Dark trader in your employ."

He laughed, gently, and fluttered his fingers at her. "Pilot, Pilot. No, you are correct—I *don't* need a Dark trader in my employ. I do, however, find myself in need of an *aelantaza.*"

Cantra felt her blood temperature drop. She jerked a shoulder up, feigning unconcern.

"So, contract for one."

"Alas, the matter is not so simple," he said. "The directors do not look upon my project with favor."

The projects the directors refused to write paper for weren't many, the directors being conveniently without loyalties and wedded to their own profit. If she hadn't already been chilled, the information that they had turned Rint dea'Sord down would've done it.

Well. How info did change a life. Cantra sighed to herself and eyed Efron. She counted four weapons, in addition to the showpiece on his belt. Two were placed awkwardly, but that wouldn't count as a benefit unless they had a much longer conversation that she was planning for.

Rint dea'Sord was another matter. He was the man at the control board, and he'd have to go first. If she were quick—

There was a loud noise on the far side of the wall behind the desk. Rint dea'Sord reached to his desk, frowning. Efron stood as he had—damn the man—and tested the slide of the gun, his eyes very much on her.

She smiled and showed him her empty, innocent hands. He relaxed, mouth quirking at the corner just a bit—then spun as the door went back on its slide, screaming wrongful death the while.

Cantra pulled her number one hideaway and pointed it at Rint dea'Sord's head just as Jela cleared the door.

Efron's gun was out and leveled, no boggles, fast and smooth.

Jela, however, was faster and smoother. A kick and Efron's gun went one way; a slap and Efron went the other, landing in a crumpled, unmoving heap. Jela kept walking, not even breathing hard, and knelt next to the unfortunate mess that was Dulsey.

"Cargo twine," Cantra told him, being not entirely sure of his state of mind, though he looked as calm as usual.

"I see it," he said, and set to work, not sparing a glance over his shoulder. Trusting her to cover him. Again.

Rint dea'Sord sat, hands flat on his desk, his eyes on Cantra's.

"Who is this?"

"My co-pilot," she told him, mind racing. Killing Rint dea'Sord was an extraordinarily good way to ruin herself in the trade. On the other hand, he held info—info he shouldn't have had—and where he'd gotten it, and who he might share it with, had to be a concern. And he would never forget that she'd drawn on him. So, the choice: ruined with a live enemy or a dead one on her back trail?

"A co-pilot and an apprentice," dea'Sord said. "That's quite a lot of crew for a woman who reportedly runs solo."

"I missed the notice that I needed to clear my ship's arrangements with you." Damn it all, there was no choice. Rint dea'Sord was going to have to die.

She saw him realize that she'd taken her decision, which was nothing more than idiot ineptitude on her part.

He lunged across the desk, and she fired, hitting him high, the force of the impact slapping him backward to the floor. Swearing at herself for clumsy shooting, she moved forward to finish the job—and found Jela there before her, hauling dea'Sord up by his silken collar and throwing him none-too-gently back into his chair.

Rint dea'Sord grunted, and shuddered, his hand pressed hard to the hole in his shoulder. He met Cantra's eyes with a glare.

"What do you want?" He gritted, the pretty Inside accent gone now.

Cantra sighed and lifted her gun.

Jela held up his hand. "Hold."

"We can't deal with him, Pilot," she said, keeping her patience with an effort. "Best to get it over with."

"I think we can deal," Jela said. "In fact, I think Ser dea'Sord will be happy to deal."

Until he has reinforcements on the way, Cantra thought, and kept the gun pointed in the right direction. dea'Sord flicked one fast glance at her, licked his lips and addressed himself to Jela.

"What's your deal, Pilot?"

"Just this. You pay the pilot here her fee. All of her fee. We'll take our comrade with us, go back to our ship and off-load your goods. We will then take ourselves out of your sphere of influence. Deal?"

Rint dea'Sord was no fool, though Cantra was beginning to have doubts regarding Jela. Her finger tightened, and he shifted, bringing a wide shoulder between her and her target.

"I can make that deal," dea'Sord said. "Just let me get the money—" Jela held up a hand.

"Tell me where the money is and I'll get it," he said, calm and reasonable. "The pilot will guard you."

Rint dea'Sord took a deep breath. "In the bottom drawer of the desk. It needs my fingerprint…"

"Fine," Jela said. "Open it."

Open it he did and there was no trick, which was, Cantra thought, a fair wonder of itself. She spared a glance at Dulsey, who wasn't looking as much the better for being free of the twine as she might have. Jela, damn him, had the wallet open and was doing a fast count.

"Eight hundred flan sound about right, Pilot?"

Fifteen hundred flan had been the agreed-upon sum, but Cantra had never expected to see that much.

"It'll do," she said, and he nodded, sealing the wallet and tossing it to her in one smooth motion. She caught it one-handed and slid it into a thigh pocket. "Now what, Pilot?"

"Now, we tie him up," Jela said, and produced the cargo twine.

He carried Dulsey and Pilot Cantra took rear guard, in which formation they reached the ship in good order and without incident. That they were under observation was a given, but without any word from command—and he'd made sure there would be no outgoing from command before he'd gone in—there was no reason for the spotters to pay them particular attention.

The hatch slid back a bare crack and Cantra waved him past, which was a nice blend of giving the wounded precedence and taking no foolish chances. He went sideways, easing his shoulders through and taking care not to jostle Dulsey.

"I'm in," he called as soon as he gained the narrow lock. Behind him the hatch reversed, Pilot Cantra slipping through the improbably thin opening, and stood watching 'til it sealed. Shoving her weapon into its pocket, she snaked past, managing not to bump him or to disturb his burden.

"Follow me," she snapped. "We'll get her in the first aid kit. Then you can cover me while I off-load."

He looked down at Dulsey's battered face and didn't say that she needed a good field doctor. A first aid kit was better than nothing and both were better than the 'hunters.

They crossed the piloting chamber, passing the yellow-lit board and the tree in its pot, the pilot making for the wall that should have been common with the tiny quarters where he and Dulsey had taken their "rest." A notion tickled at the back of his brain, and Jela looked ahead, down low, and—yes, a beam, very faint, where it could not fail to be tripped by approaching feet—or by a pilot, crawling.

Pilot Cantra's boots broke the beam, and a section of wall slid away, revealing a low box, its smooth surface so deeply black it seemed to absorb the surrounding light. Cantra bent, touched the top and up it went, the interior lit a pale and disquieting green.

"Put her down there," she said, stepping back to give him room.

He hesitated, knowing, in his generalist's tricksy mind—*knowing* what it was.

In his arms, Dulsey groaned, a feeble enough sound, and there was the chance that the cord had done damage beyond whatever she'd taken from the beating. And she wasn't a soldier, dammit, bred to be hard to break and lacking a significant number of the usual pain receptors.

"Pilot." There was a noticeable lack of patience edging Pilot Cantra's voice. "I want to off-load and have space between my ship and this port before Rint dea'Sord gets himself cut loose."

"Yes," he said, and forced himself forward. The area immediately surrounding the box was noticeably cooler than the ship's ambient temp. He knelt and put Dulsey down as gently as he could onto the slick, giving surface of the pallet, taking the time to straighten her arms and her legs.

"Hatch coming down," Cantra said quietly, and he pulled back, the cool black surface almost grazing his nose.

"All right." There was a sigh in Pilot Cantra's voice. "Let's get rid of the damned cargo."

SIXTEEN

Spiral Dance
In Transit

THIS TIME, AT least, there wasn't any cannon fire to speed them along, though what might be waiting at the next port in terms of surprises was enough to put a pilot off her good temper. Not that there weren't other things.

Cantra released the shock webbing and spun her chair around.

"Pilot Jela," she said, mindfully keeping her voice in the stern-but-gentle range.

He looked over, then faced her fully, eyes as readable as ever—which was to say, not at all—lean face pleasant and attentive, mouth soft in a half-smile, arms leaning on the rests, hands nice and relaxed—a portrait of pure innocence.

"Pilot?" he answered. Respectful, too. Everything a pilot could want in a co-pilot, saving a bad habit or twelve.

Cantra sighed.

"I'm interested to note, Pilot, that your damn vegetable was lashed in place in my tower when we brought Dulsey in to the first aid kit. As I distinctly remember you taking it and its pot with you when you left ship at Taliofi and, as I distinctly don't remember giving you a ship's key, I'd be interested in hearing how that particular circumstance came to be."

He closed one eye, then the other, then used both to look at her straight on, face as pleasant as ever. Rint dea'Sord, Cantra thought grudgingly, could do worse than take lessons from Pilot Jela. Too bad he was more likely to commission them both killed—but she was getting ahead of herself.

"I'm waiting, Pilot."

"Yes, ma'am," he said, easily and paused before continuing at a clear tangent. "You've got a good brace of guns on this ship."

"I'm glad they meet your approval." Stern-but-gentle, with a slight icing of irony. "You want to answer my question?"

"I am," he said, projecting goodwill. She held up a hand and he tipped his head, questioning.

"Point of information," she said, stern taking the upper note. "I don't like being soothed. It annoys me."

He sighed, the fingers of his right hand twitching assent. "My apologies, Pilot. It's a habit—and a bad one. I'll take steps to remember."

"I'd appreciate it," she said. "Now—the question."

"Yes, ma'am," he said again. "Your recollection is correct in both particulars—I did take the tree with me when we debarked earlier in the day and you did not give me a ship's key." The right hand came up, showing palm beyond half-curled fingers. "I didn't steal a key or gimmick the comp. But, like I was saying—those guns you've got. Military, aren't they?"

She considered him, much good it did her. "Surplus."

"Right." The hand dropped back to arm rest. "Military surplus. Not that old, some military craft still carry those self-same guns. I trained on them, myself."

Cantra sighed, letting him hear an edge of irritation. "This has a point, doesn't it, Pilot?"

"It does." He sat up straight in his chair, eyes sharp, mouth stern. "The point is that you're not fully aware of the capabilities of your gun brace. Pilot. Where I come from, that's lapse of duty. Where you come from, I'd imagine it'd be something closer to suicide."

Well, that was plain—and not entirely undeserved. "They didn't exactly come with instructions," she told him, mildly.

"Small mercies," he retorted. "As I said, I trained on guns like yours and believe me I know what they can and can't do." He leaned back in his chair, deliberate, and kept his eyes on hers. "So, I sweet-talked them into letting me in."

Cantra closed her eyes. "I'm understanding you to say that you came into this ship through the gun bays."

"That's right."

She wanted to doubt it, but there was the fact of the tree waiting for them, and *Dancer* reporting no entries between the time she'd sealed the hatch behind them in the early planetary day and the time she opened it again some hours later to admit Jela, Dulsey, and herself.

"That involve any breakage?" she asked. "Or, say—modifications?"

"Pilot," he said reproachfully. "I'm better than that." A short pause. "I wasn't entirely sure that we wouldn't be needing the guns again on the way out."

A pragmatist, was Pilot Jela. That being so—

She opened her eyes, saw him sitting calm and easy again in his chair. "I'll ask you, as co-pilot, to give me training on the guns to the full extent of your knowledge," she said.

There was a small pause, then a formal nod of the head. "As soon as we raise a likely location, I'm at your service, Pilot."

Not if I shake you first, she thought at him. Granted, she owed the man—again—but she didn't have any intention of making Pilot Jela a permanent fixture on *Dancer.* Still, so there wasn't no sense to putting him on notice. So—

"That'll do, then," she said, turning to face her screens—and stopping at the sight of his big hand raised, palm out.

"I've got some questions myself, Pilot."

"Oh, do you?" She sighed, sharply. "Lay 'em out and let's see which ones I care to answer, then."

"I think it'd be best if you answered them all."

That struck a spark from her temper. She gave her attention to the screens—showing clear, and the countdown to transition in triple digits.

"I think," she said tightly, "that you've got a very limited right to ask questions, *Pilot* Jela. You gimmicked your way onto this ship at Faldaiza, and engineered an unauthorized entry at Taliofi. Not to mention cutting a deal with a man who needed to die and ruining my rep into the bargain."

"If I hadn't ruined your rep," he said, voice deliberately placid, but not, at least, projecting calm good feelings. "You'd have been dead, and Dulsey, too."

"Dulsey, maybe," she said. "He wanted me alive so's I could do him a favor."

"And you were happy to be of service," he said, irony a little heavy. "At least, that's not how I read it, listening in."

She spun her chair back to face him.

"You were listening in on Rint dea'Sord?" She'd tried to crack dea'Sord's comms—twice, in fact, nor was she unskilled at such things, having received certain training. "How?"

He smiled at her, damn him. "Military secret." He touched the breast of his 'skins. "I have a datastrip which I request permission to transmit, via secure channel."

"No," she snapped.

He sighed. "Pilot, the information on this 'strip will guarantee that Ser dea'Sord will be too busy for...some number of years...keeping one jump ahead of the peacekeepers and bounty hunters to care about your rep or your life."

"That's some datastrip," she said, and held out her hand. "Mind if I scan it?"

"Yes," he said, which wasn't anything more than she'd expected he'd say, nor anything less than she'd've said herself, had their positions been reversed. Still, the notion of giving Rint dea'Sord enough trouble to keep him occupied and out of the business for years did have its appeal.

"You're asking a lot on trust," she told Jela "and I'm a little short where you're concerned."

His face hardened. "Am I supposed to trust a woman who carries a can full of military grade ship-brains into such a port as Taliofi, and has a *sheriekas* healing unit in her ship?"

She held up a fist, raised the thumb. "You should've checked the manifest before you signed on, if you're as tender-hearted as all that." Index finger. "You got moral objections to the first aid kit, you're free to open the hatch and save Dulsey's soul for her."

"It's her well-being I'm concerned with." There was more than a little snap there. She supposed he was entitled, there being the likelihood of a personal interest.

"Where did you get that healing unit?" he demanded.

She moved her shoulders and arranged her face into amused lines. "It came with," she said, and spread her arms to include the entirety of *Dancer* .

He stared at her. She smiled at him.

"Whoever acquired that thing was trading 'way over their heads," he said, still snappish.

She raised her eyebrows, giving him polite attention, in case he wasn't done.

He shut his mouth and looked stubborn.

"Leaving aside ship's services," she said after she'd taken a leisurely scan of her screens and stats and he still hadn't said anything else. "Is there a description of the cargo just off-loaded on that 'strip you think you want to transmit?"

"There is." Right grumpy, that sounded.

"And that's going to keep my rep clear with the 'hunters and other interested parties exactly how?"

Silence. A glance aside showed him sitting not so relaxed as previously, his eyes closed. As if he'd felt the weight of her regard, he sat up straight and opened his eyes, meeting hers straight on.

"It happens I'm in need of a pilot who knows the back ways in and out, and maybe something about the Beyond."

"I'll be sure to put you down at a port where you might have some luck locating a pilot of that kind," she said politely, and spun back full to face her board.

"I'd rather hire you," Jela said, quiet-like. "The people who receive my transmittal, they'll keep any…irregularities…to themselves, if it's known you're aiding me."

She let that settle while she made a couple of unnecessary adjustments to her long-scans.

"I thought you weren't exactly military," she said, first.

"I'm not," he answered, and while she didn't have any reason to believe him, she did anyway.

"What you're doing here is coercion," she said, second.

Jela didn't answer that one—and then he did.

"Maybe it is," he said, slow, like he was working it out as he went. "What I know is I've been fighting my whole life and the war's going against us. There's a chance—not much of a chance, but I specialize in those kinds of missions—that I can accomplish something that will turn the war back on the *sheriekas*. Or least make the odds not—quite—so overwhelming. If you agree to help me, then you have that chance, too."

"So what?" she asked, harsher than she should have.

"If we don't stand together," Jela said, still in that feeling-his-way voice, "then we'll fall separately. We need to face the enemy now—soldier, smuggler, and shopkeeper."

The war had been a fact of her entire life. The concept of winning it—or losing it—was alien enough to make her head ache. The notion that she might have a hand in either outcome was—laughable.

When the cards were all dealt out, though, Pilot Jela held the winning hand, in the form of his datastrip. If he could buy her free of Rint dea'Sord and gain her a promise of blind eyes from those who might otherwise be interested in curtailing her liberty—she'd be a fool not to go along with him.

At least for a while.

She sent him a studious glance, then gave him a formal nod. "All right," she said. "Transmit your data."

It appeared that Pilot Cantra had levels between her levels, Jela thought as he addressed his board and began setting up a series of misdirections. He didn't expect such precautions to thwart a determined attack, but then he didn't expect a determined attack, merely a snoop, the same as any pilot who didn't entirely trust her second might do.

He'd already established that *Spiral Dance's* brain was as familiar to him as her guns—one of the earlier of the Emca units, considerably smarter and more flexible than the Remle refits just off-loaded at Taliofi.

Fingers deft and quick, he set the transmission protocol: validate, send, validate, wipe original on close of transmission, no copy to ship's log.

A glance at the screens—clear all around, scans showing the appropriate levels of busy energies, nothing exotic or overly active, transition still some ship-hours ahead of them—and a look out of the side of his eye at the pilot sitting her board serene, long, elegant fingers dancing on the numbers pad, like as not discussing possible exit points with the navigation brain.

If it had been his to call, he'd have opted to wait and send closer to transition, to minimize the risk of a trace. The choice not being his and the likelihood of a trace being, in his estimation, low. The pilot possibly with her attention on something other than on him, he checked his protocols a second time and hit "send."

The query went out; the answer came back; the data flowed away. Query again, answer—and the thing was done, beam closed. Jela tapped a key, accessing the datastrip, which showed empty, just as it ought. Good.

He pulled it out of the slot and crumbled it in his fist. The flexible metal resisted at first, then folded, tiny slivers tickling his palm.

The sense of being watched pulled his eyes up—and he met Pilot Cantra's interested green gaze. He waited, with the clear sense that he'd just given information out.

But—"Scrap drawer's on your left," was all she said, calm and agreeable; and she turned her attention back to her calcs.

"Thank you," he muttered and thumbed the drawer open, depositing the strip and making sure his palms were free of shred before closing it again and putting his eyes and most of his attention on his own board.

Screens and scans still clear, timer ticking down to translation. Transition to *where* was apparently not a subject on which the pilot craved his input. He considered introducing it himself, then decided to bide his time, pending consideration of recent discoveries and events.

If Ragil's people up-line moved fast on Rint dea'Sord's operation, they might even recover most of *Spiral Dance's* recent off-loaded and lamentable cargo. He'd handed the man and the cargo to others better equipped to deal with them—nothing more he could or should do there. He therefore put both out of his mind.

Pilot Cantra, however…

He hadn't listened long, being more interested in downloading various fascinating data regarding dea'Sord's business arrangements, but he'd listened plenty long enough to hear the by-play around the need for an *aelantaza*.

It was apparently Rint dea'Sord's belief that Pilot Cantra, whose ship called her "yos'Phelium," was one of those rare and elite scholar-assassins.

Jela admitted to himself that the proposition explained a good many puzzling things about Pilot Cantra. Unfortunately, it also raised a number of other, equally good and valid questions.

Such as, if she were indeed *aelantaza*, was she presently on contract?

Or, if she were indeed *aelantaza* and *not* on contract, who was looking for her and how much of an impediment were they likely to be to his mission?

Or, if she was not *aelantaza*, as seemed most likely, why had Rint dea'Sord, a man with access to a broad range of information that he shouldn't have had, thought that she was—and what did *that* mean in terms of impediments or dangers to Jela's own mission?

And there was, after all, the matter of the name. Cantra yos'Phelium. Certainly, a name. Certainly, every bit as good a name as M. Jela Granthor's Guard. *Exactly* as good a name, as it happened. "yos" was the Inworld's prefix denoting a courier or delivery person, and "Phelium" bore an interesting likeness to the Rim-cant word for "pilot."

Cantra Courier Pilot, Jela thought. Not precisely the name he'd have expected to find on an *aelantaza*—contracted or free. On the other hand, what did he know? *Aelantaza* were known for their subtlety, which didn't happen to be a trait he'd've assigned to Pilot Cantra. But, if the Dark Trader persona was a cover for something else—

Not that he was over-thinking it or anything.

He sighed to himself and sent a glance to the tree—receiving an impression of watchful well-being. That would be the tree's reaction to the *sheriekas* device in which Dulsey presently slumbered—and he owned that the fact of the thing tied into this ship disturbed him, too. All very well and good for Pilot Cantra to say it had "come with," thereby loosing another whole range of questions to tangle around the *aelantaza*/not *aelantaza* question, and—

Stop, he told himself.

Deliberately, he invoked one of the templated exercises. This one restored mental acuity and sharpened problem-solving. There was a moment of tightness inside his skull, and a brief feeling of warmth.

He'd need to construct a logic-box, assign everything he knew about Pilot Cantra and—

"Pilot." Her voice was low and agreeable, the Rim accent edgy against his ear. More of an accent than she had previously displayed, he thought, and put that aside for the logic box as he turned his head to meet her eyes.

"Pilot?" he answered, respectful.

"I'd welcome your thoughts regarding a destination," she said.

Just what he'd been wanting, Jela thought, and then wondered if she was playing for info—which found him back on the edge of the *aelantaza* question, tottering on his mental boot heels. He sighed, letting her hear it, and gave a half-shrug.

"I thought you might have a port in mind," he said. "It'd be best not to disrupt your usual routes and habits. At least, not until I've seen a chart."

"Usual routes and habits," she repeated, a corner of her mouth going up in a half-smile. "Pilot, I don't think you're a fool. I think

you know we lifted out of Taliofi empty of anything valuable—
excepting yourself and Dulsey, neither of which I gather are up
for trade...and even if you were, I ain't in the business of warm
goods. One can's carrying generic Light-goods for the entertainment of any port cops we happen to fall across. That means we
can go wherever your fancy takes us, with the notable exception
of any of my usual stop-overs. It might be that the two of us're
cozy kin now, but I see no reason to introduce you and your troubles
to my usuals."

Reasonable, Jela thought, and prudent. Especially prudent if
Pilot Cantra expected to dump him and retreat to safety, which had
to be in her mind, despite her apparent surrender. He was beginning
to form the opinion that the pilot's order of priority was her ship
and herself, all else expendable. It was a survivor's order of priority,
and he couldn't fault her for holding it, though duty required him to
subvert it. Not the greatest thing duty had required of him, over a
lifetime of more or less obeying orders.

Yet, he couldn't help thinking that it would have been better for
all—the mission, the pilot, the soldier if it mattered, and the Batcher—
if Pilot Muran had made his rendezvous.

In point of fact, it would've been better for all if the *sheriekas*
had blown themselves up with their home world—while he was
wishing after alternate histories.

He looked to Pilot Cantra, sitting unaccountably patient, and
showed her his empty palms.

"We have a shared problem in need of solving, first," he said,
which was true, and bought him time to consider how best to follow up a rumor and a whisper, lacking the info Muran had been
bringing to him.

The pilot's pretty eyebrows lifted. "Do we now. And that
would be?"

"Dulsey," he said, and the eyebrows came together in a frown.

"I'm thinking Dulsey's your problem, Pilot—or no problem.
She's likely to go along with whatever you say."

"I don't see it that way," he said. "She couldn't leave me fast
enough at Taliofi. You remember she said that she had business and
might not make it back in time for lift? She was so intent on that
business she missed the fact that her further services as crew were
being declined."

There was a short pause while the pilot looked over her board, and twiddled a scan knob that didn't need it.

"You're right," she said finally, her eyes staying with the scans. "Dulsey was plotting her own course soon's she heard we was down at Taliofi. Rint dea'Sord intercepted her before she made her contact, I'm guessing." She moved her shoulders.

"Not like him to plan so shallow," she said slowly. "That favor he wanted—he wanted it from *me*. Thinking on it, damn if it don't look like the whole deal was rigged. Easy enough for a man with his connections to learn where my last-but-one was taking me. Dulsey—that must've been a vary, cheaper than whatever else he had planned on. Gave him a reserve." She got quiet then, the picture of a pilot attending her board.

Jela took a breath, and by the time he'd exhaled had decided on his plan of attack.

"He thought you were *aelantaza*," he said. "Any truth to that?"

That got him a look, green eyes a trifle too wide.

"No," she said, and spun her chair to face him square. "I don't think I heard what Dulsey has to do with your choice of a next port o'call. She's a deader wherever she goes, unless she can lose the tats, which you know and I know she can't."

"She can regrow, if she gets to the right people."

"She can, but they're looking for that dodge now. One arm younger than the rest of you—that's rehab, all legit. Two arms— you're a Batcher gone rogue, and better off dead."

That was, Jela thought, probably true.

"What else, then?" he asked her. "Not all runaway Batchers get caught."

"Well." She wrinkled her nose. "If they're willing to limit themselves to the RingStars, or the Rim, or the Grey Worlds, all they need is to hang paper, work up some convincing files, and maybe a dummy control disk. Expensive. No guarantees."

"But it can be done," Jela said, watching her face.

The green eyes narrowed. "Anything can be done," she said, the Rim accent hard, "if you got money enough to buy it."

"Do you—" he began and stopped as a chime sounded from the rear of the chamber.

Pilot Cantra jerked her head toward the alcove where the first aid kit sat.

166 Sharon Lee and Steve Miller

"Hatch'll be coming up soon. You might want to be standing by, in case there's a problem. I'll take the scans."

She spun back to her board.

Jela got up and walked, not without trepidation, back to the first aid kit.

The hatch was up, the greenish light giving Dulsey's pale hair and pale face an unsettling and alien cast. Her eyes were closed and he could see her breathing, deep and slow, like she was asleep.

She lay like he had put her, flat on her back, arms at her sides, legs straight, the bloodstained coverall—

The blood was gone and much of the grime. The green-cast face was evenly toned, showing neither bruises nor swelling; the nose, last seen bent to the left, was straight. Her hair was clean.

Her eyes opened.

"Pilot Jela?"

"Right here," he said. "You're in what Pilot Cantra styles a first aid kit. You're looking better than you did when you went in. You'll have to tell me how you feel."

She frowned and closed her eyes. He waited, his own eyes slitted in protest of the unnatural light, until she moved her head against the pallet.

"I feel—remarkably well," she said slowly. She raised a hand and touched her face lightly, ran a finger down her nose. Took a deliberately deep breath. Another.

"I believe I am mended, Pilot. May I be permitted to stand up and test the theory more fully?"

He realized with a start that he'd been hanging over the device, blocking her exit. Hastily, he stepped back.

"Might as well try it."

She sat up slowly, from the intent expression on her face, paying attention to each muscle and bone. Carefully, she got her legs over the edge and her feet on the floor, put her palms flat against the pallet, pushed—and stood.

"Ace?" he asked.

She took a step forward. "Ace," she answered.

Behind her, the hatch began to descend, hissing lightly as it did. She turned to look at it.

"A remarkable device," she commented. "Am I correct in believing that it was constructed by the Enemy?"

"I think so," Jela said. "Pilot Cantra doesn't deny it."

"Remarkable," she said again. She turned to face him and held up her left hand, palm out.

"Pilot, you have, I believe, very fine eyesight. Do you see the scar across my palm?"

Her palm was broad and lined. There were no scars.

"No," he said. "Was it an old scar? They fade, over time."

"They do," Dulsey said. "But it was a recent scar, still noticeable. Will you look again? It was rather obvious—from the base of the thumb very nearly to the base of the little finger, somewhat jagged, and—"

"Dulsey," he interrupted. "There's no scar."

She took a long, hard breath. Her face, he saw, was tight, her eyes sparkling.

"Thank you, Pilot." Her voice was breathless. She raised her other hand, fumbled a moment with the wrist fastening, then peeled the sleeve of the coverall back, exposing pale flesh, smooth, hairless, unscarred.

"It's gone," Dulsey breathed. Fingers shaking, she unsealed the other wrist, pushed the sleeve high.

"And it." She looked up at him. "Pilot—"

"They're both gone," he said, keeping his tone matter-of-fact, despite the fact that his neck hairs wanted to stand up on their own. He raised a hand.

"Use your brain, Dulsey. You know those tats are cellular. Just because they've been erased on the dermis doesn't mean they're gone."

"True," she said, but her eyes were still sparkling.

"Dulsey—" he began...

"Transition coming up," Pilot Cantra called from the wider room. "Pilot Jela, you're wanted at your station. Dulsey, strap in."

They transitioned with the guns primed and the passage was just as bad as it could be.

As a reward, they reentered calm—empty space, not a ship, nor a star, nor a rock within a couple dozen light years in any direction.

"Well," said Cantra and looked over to her co-pilot, sitting his board as calm and unflapped as if he hadn't been bumped and jangled 'til his brain rang inside his skull.

"Lock her down, Pilot," she said when he turned his head. "We'll sit here a bit and we three can have that talk about where we're going, now that we're nowhere in particular."

"Right," he said, briefly, fingers moving across his board.

Cantra turned to look at Dulsey, who was already on her feet by the jump seat. The coverall's sleeves were rolled up, showing pale, unmarked forearms. Cantra didn't sigh and met the Batcher's sparkling eyes.

"Trouble with that first aid kit," she said, conversationally, "is it don't think like you an' me. There's no deep reader on this ship, Dulsey, and you dasn't believe that what you got there is more than a simple wipe. Keep your sense hard by."

"The pilot is prudent," Dulsey said. "Shall I make tea?"

"Tea'd be good," Cantra answered, and added the polite. "Thank you."

"You are welcome, Pilot. I will return." She went, her steps seeming somewhat lighter than usual.

Cantra spun back to her board, letting the sigh have its freedom, and began to lock down the main board.

"We got eyes," she said to Jela, "we got ears, we got teeth. We're giving out as little as possible, and while we aren't exactly in a high traffic zone, I want to be gone inside of six hours."

Finished with the board, she spun her chair, coming to her feet in one smooth motion. She moved a step, caught herself on the edge of her usual calisthenics, and instead twisted into a series of quick-stretches, easing tight back and leg muscles.

Behind her, she heard the co-pilot's chair move, and turned in time to see Pilot Jela finishing up a mundane arm-and-leg stretch. He rolled his broad shoulders and smiled.

"It's good to work the kinks out," he said, companionably.

"It is," she returned, and was saved saying anything else by the arrival of Dulsey, bearing mugs.

They'd each sipped some tea and all decided that standing was preferable to sitting. So, they stood in a loose triangle—Cantra at the apex, Jela to her left and ahead, Dulsey to his left.

"This is an official meeting of captain and crew," Cantra said, holding her mug cradled between her hands and considering the two of them in turn. "Input wanted on where and how we next set down, free discussion in force until the captain calls time. Final decision rests with the captain, no appeal. Dulsey."

"Pilot?"

"Some changes while you were getting patched up. Me and Pilot Jela have consolidated. He's got some places he feels a need to visit, except he wants to see you settled as best you might be, first." She glanced aside, meeting his bright black eyes. "I have that right, Pilot?"

"Aye, Captain," he answered easily. "Permission to speak?"

"Free discussion," she said, lifting one hand away from the mug and waggling her fingers. "Have at it."

"Right." He turned to face the Batcher. "Dulsey, Pilot Cantra here tells me that there's a way to establish you—"

"If the pilot pleases," Dulsey interrupted. "I will ask to be set down on Panet."

Jela frowned and sent Cantra a glance. "Pilot? I'm not familiar with this port."

"I am." *Unfortunately.* She fixed Dulsey with a hard look, and was agreeably surprised to see her give it back, no flinching, no meeching.

"What's to want on Panet, Dulsey?"

The Batcher lifted her chin. "People. Contacts who can aid me."

"Ah." Cantra sipped her tea, considering. "Any kin to the contacts you didn't make on Taliofi?"

Dulsey bit her lip. "On Taliofi, the—I had the incorrect word, perhaps. Or perhaps that cell no longer exists. On Panet, however, I am certain—"

Cantra held up her hand.

"Dulsey, you won't last half a local day on Panet, even with the tats smoothed over. Your best course is to tell us what your final goal is, if you know it. It might be we can help you. Pilot Jela don't want all his trouble going to waste by seeing you taken up by bounty hunters six steps from ship's ramp, and I don't want to have to answer personal questions about did I know you was Batch-grown and what kind of hard labor I'd prefer."

Dulsey bit her lip, every muscle screaming tension, indecision. She raised her mug and drank, buying thinking time. Cantra sipped her own tea, waiting.

"I——" Breathless, that, and the muscles were still tight, but her face was firm, and her eyes were steady. Dulsey had made her decision, whatever it was. *And now*, Cantra thought, *we'll see how good a liar she is.*

"It is," the Batcher began again, "perhaps true that the pilot will know of the port I seek. I...had not considered that it might be possible to simply *go* rather than——" A hard breath, chin rising. "It is my intention to go to the Uncle."

The truth, curse her for an innocent. Cantra closed her eyes.

"Uncle?" Jela's voice was plainly puzzled. "Which uncle, Dulsey?"

"*The* Uncle," she answered him. "The one who has made a tribe—a world—populated by Batchers. Where we are valued for ourselves, as persons of worth and skill; where——"

"There ain't," Cantra said, loudly, "any Uncle."

"The pilot," Dulsey countered reproachfully, "knows better."

Cantra opened her eyes and fixed her in the best glare she had on call.

"I do, do I? You want to explain that, Dulsey?"

"Certainly. The pilot survived a line edit, I believe?"

Cantra fetched up a sigh. "You was awake enough to hear Rint dea'Sord theorize, was you? He was out, Dulsey. Do I look *aelantaza* to you?"

Dulsey bowed. "The pilot is surely aware that the *aelantaza* do not share a single physical type. It is much more important that the pheromones which induce trust and affection in those who are not *aelantaza* are developed to a high degree."

"That a fact?"

"Pilot, it is. It is also a fact that an *aelantaza* could not survive a line edit without outside intervention. Much the same sort of intervention——" She raised her unmarked arms—"necessary to wipe the Batch numbers not only from my skin, but from my muscles, bones, and cells." She lowered her arms and addressed Jela.

"There is an Uncle, and Pilot Cantra knows where to find him. If you would see me safe, see me to him."

"Pilot Cantra?" Jela said quietly.

Pain, in her head, in her joints, in the marrow of her bones. Garen's voice, grief-soaked, weaving through the red mists of shutdown, "Hang on, baby, hang on, I'll get you help, don't die, damn you baby..."

"Pilot Cantra?" Louder this time. The man who held her ship ransom to his have-tos. And wouldn't the Uncle just be pleased as could be to welcome a genuine soldier, not-exactly-military or—

"Pilot." Back to quiet. Not good.

She sighed and gave him a wry look.

"There was an Uncle, years back. He was old then and near to failing. Told us so, in fact. He's died by now for certain, but the story won't do the same. If I was a Batcher, I'd sure as stars want to believe there was a benevolent Uncle leading a community of free and equal Batch-grown. But it just ain't so—anymore, if it ever truly was."

"The pilot surely does not believe that the Uncle would have died without arranging a succession." Dulsey again.

Cantra sipped tea, deliberately saying nothing.

"Do you know where the Uncle's base is?" Jela asked, still on the wrong side of quiet.

She lifted a shoulder. "I know where it *was*. Understand me, Pilot, this was back a double-hand of Common Years. Uncle's dead, and if he did arrange for a transfer of authority, the way Dulsey's liking it, anybody with a brain would have moved base six times since."

"I'd do it that way myself," he agreed, and his voice was edging back toward easy. "But, as you say, the info's still out there, and it's not impossible that somebody might strike straight for the base instead of risking an intermediate stop where they might be noticed. Even if this Uncle or his second has shifted core ops, they'll have to have left something—or someone—at the old base, to send people on—or to be sure that they don't go any further."

That made sense. Unfortunately, it was looking like a trip to the Deeps in her very near future. Pilot Jela was going to be no end expensive, unless she could persuade whoever might be at the Uncle's old place of business that he was an unacceptable risk, while keeping her own good name intact. That was possible, though not certain. Still…

"Where is it?" Jela asked.

Cantra sighed. "Where would you put it, Pilot?"

His eyelashes didn't even flicker.

"In the Beyond."

"Ace," she said, and drank off the rest of her tea.

"I'd like a look at the chart," he said then, and she laughed.

"You're welcome to look at any chart you want, Pilot. You find the Uncle's hidey hole, you let me know."

"I hoped you'd be kind enough to point it out to me," he said, in a tone that said he wasn't finding her particularly amusing.

"I'd do that," she said, pitching her voice serious and comradely, "but it's not fixed. Or, say, it *is* fixed, though built on random factors."

"The rock field," Dulsey breathed, and Cantra regarded her once more.

"There's a lot of detail in that story, Dulsey."

"It is not one story, Pilot, but legion."

"Is that so? Stories change as they migrate—you know that, don't you? They get bigger, broader, shinier, happier. Might be, if—and in my mind it's a big 'if'—the Uncle I met did manage to pass his project on to another administrator, and if—another big one—they managed to be clever and stay off the scans of all who wish rogue Batchers ill, it might still be that the community of free and equal Batch-grown ain't as equal or as free as the stories say."

Dulsey bowed. "This humble person thanks the pilot for her concern for one who is beneath notice," she said, irony edging the colorless voice. "Indeed, this humble person has been a slave and a chattel and resides now under a sentence of death."

Meaning that the Uncle's outfit would have to be plenty bad before it came even with what she'd been bred to and lived her whole life as, Cantra thought, and lifted a shoulder.

"I take your point," she said, and looked at Jela.

"My business is nearer the Rim than Inside," he said, which she might've known he would. "First, we'll take Dulsey out to the old base and see if the Uncle's left a forwarding address."

"All the same to me," Cantra said, doing the math quick-and-dirty and not liking the sum. They couldn't run empty all the way to the Far Edge. She had padding, but a Rim-run would eat Rint dea'Sord's eight hundred flan and the ship's fund, too, like a whore snacking through a packet of dreamies. There was cargo—legit or, all right, Pale Gray—that could be profitably hauled to the Rim. It would mean buying at markets where she wasn't known—and where her info was thinner than she liked. But it was that or run empty and she'd rather not find herself broke at the end of Pilot Jela.

"Need goods," she said, giving both of them the eye—Dulsey first; then a stern lingering glare for Jela. "Eight hundred flan is all very nice, but the ship needs to sustain itself."

He inclined his head. "I agree that the ship should continue to trade and to behave, as much as is possible, as it always does." One eyebrow quirked. "I said that earlier, if you'll recall, Pilot."

"I recall. And you'll recall that I'm not taking you to my usuals. That means some bit of extra care, though I'm intending to carry legits rather than high risks. There's profit to be made on the Rim, in small pieces. Coming out of the Rim, that's something else."

"First, we go in," Jela said.

"That looks to be the case," she agreed. "If there's nothing else to discuss, then the captain declares this meeting at an end. Pilot Jela, I'll be spending some time with the charts, if you'll attend me. I'll need what info you might have on some possible destinations."

"I'm at your service, Pilot," he said, and gave her a smile. It was an attractive smile, as she'd noticed before—which was too bad, really.

"If the pilots have no duties for me," Dulsey piped up. "I will prepare a meal."

The words were on the tip of Cantra's tongue—*Don't bother; ration sticks'll be fine.* Second thoughts dissolved them, though, and she inclined her head a fraction.

"A meal would be welcome," she said formally. "Thank you, Dulsey."

"You are welcome, Pilot Cantra," the Batcher said softly. "I am pleased to be of service."

SEVENTEEN

On port
Barbit

THREE-AND-A-HALF cans were full of the lightest cargo *Dancer* had carried since—well, ever, if Cantra's understanding of her pedigree was correct. Not that Garen had ever actually come out and said she'd killed a *sheriekas* agent and took their ship for her own. Garen hadn't said much as a general thing and, when she did, more'n half of it didn't make sense. The bits that did make sense, though, had outlined a history that would have broken stronger minds than hers by the time she came to work as a courier for the Institute.

Come with me, now, baby. You gotta get clear, get clear, hear me? Pliny's gone and struck a teacher. Now, I said! You think I'm gonna let you die twice?

Cantra shook her head. The memories were getting worrisome, popping up on their own like maybe there was some urgent lesson embedded in the past that she was too stupid to learn. She had a serious case of the soft-brains, that was what, though she'd never heard it cited among the faults of her line. On the other hand, there'd been Pliny.

She'd have given a handful of flan to know how Rint dea'Sord had uncovered his info—and another handful to learn how Dulsey had gained her own and independent judgment of the situation.

All Garen's care. All those years. And the directors must have been sure she'd died in the edlin, along with the rest of her line. If they'd thought for an instant there were any survivors—

She took a hard breath and forcefully banished that run of thinking. *Life ain't dangerous enough, you got to think up bogies to scare yourself with?*

Deliberately, she focused on the here-and-trade, doing a mental inventory of the filled cans. Jela'd shown himself to be good about not grabbing extra room for "his" part, though she certainly didn't begrudge him his space—especially when he had such a knack for the felicitous buy. They'd hit five worlds so far, slowly trading their way from In-Rim to the Far Edge, specifically not attracting attention, according to Jela, and they'd come in to more than one port with exactly what was in high demand.

Two of those lucky buys had been hers, if she wanted to be truthful—and if she wanted to continue the theme, she was finding the trade—the honest trade—interesting. She was even getting used to wearing the leathers of a respectable trader on-port, rather than pilot's 'skins.

Almost, she thought, *I could go legit.*

Don't want to get too high-profile, baby, Garen whispered from the past. *Don't want to cast a shadow on the directors' scans...*

Right.

So, the trade, for now. Despite they had a good mix, there was still an empty quarter-can with her name on it. She could take a random odd lot, but there was still some time to play with and she wanted to do better than random, if she could.

Trouble was, nothing on offer in the main hall had called out for her to buy.

Shrugging her shoulders to throw off some of the tension of unwanted memories, she moved out of the main hall, heading toward what was the most boring part of any trade hall—the day-broker room. Odd how that was, 'cause on almost any vid feed of market action the image most shown was this: a couple rows of tiny booths, tenants wearing terminal-specs or half-masks, with four or five keyboards and three microphones in front of them. Day-brokers. Made an honest gambler look sane and saintly and a dishonest gambler look smart.

Day-brokers bought and sold at speed all day long, breaking lots, building lots, mixing cargo in and out. They were willing to sell down to handfuls, or discounted stuff that needed delivery two shifts before a ship could possibly get there.

Some of them were desperate; most made a living. A few were unspeakably rich—or would be, if they survived long enough to enjoy their earnings. Day-traders didn't often quit, though—it appeared that those who took to the trade at all found it addictive. What the attraction was, Cantra had never been able to figure.

They stuffed themselves into booths barely wider than their seats, with risers overhead or behind proclaiming names or specialties or preferences; some even had small bowls of trust-me smoke, or give away candy, or free-look vids for the senses, just stop and say hello...

Hard to know what might be found, hard to figure which booth to call the start. Some of the brokers were pay-box pretty, some just plain sloppy. Some looked like what they were: rich and bored and bored by getting richer—

And then there were the ones who paid attention to passersby, so the room was near as noisy as a livestock market.

"Pilot, what can we..."

"If you have three cans empty I can..."

"Only sixteen cubes and you ought to triple your money..."

"Go ahead, pass by! Pass up cash, pass by..."

"Sector fifteen or sixteen, I'll pay you, quick trans-ship..."

"Guaranteed to..."

She slowed, ran the sounds back through her head and turned. The skinny, bearded, bejeweled man smiled and repeated the magic words, "Guarantee, Trader? We can..."

She hand-signed him off, watching the hope fade on his face even as his hands jumped between keyboards, and he muttered into a mike tangled in his beard—

"That's a sell to you and theft it is. Forty percent..."

Cantra drifted back a couple paces, glanced up for an ID— which was an overhead banner with a blue light flashing first around a circle, then through, then back around.

Interesting design.

"I can pay you before lift," the broker was saying to a couple of traders who had come up and paused, maybe also lured by the promise of a "guarantee."

"Credits," the broker crooned, "gems, fuel rights..."

He wore a head-ring with a short visor, and she guessed he was reading info from that even as he appeared fully interested in the traders before him.

Interesting design, that.

The elder of the two traders said something Cantra couldn't pick out of the general ruckus. The day-broker whipped out a card and handed it over extravagantly. Ah, a fumble there—too many cards. The younger trader had his hand out, though, and neatly caught the extra as it fluttered away. He returned it; the other card disappeared into big hands. A nod, smiles all around, and the traders moved on, the broker carefully tucking the extra card away...

The day-broker looked at her now, even as he mumbled into his mike, "Live, seventeen, drop orders five-five and five-six, pay the penalty and get it off my dock."

"Now, Trader," he said pleasantly. "A profit before you start interest you? I have goods that need moving. I'll pay you up-front to load, and you'll get a delivery bonus from the consignee as well. I have…" He paused, squinting slightly as he apparently read the info off his visor—

"Double can loads transhipping to most Inward sectors, I have three one-can loads needing to transit the Arm, I have fifteen half-can loads going regionally including some transships, I have three half-can loads going Inward, one going to the Mid-Rim. I have one-quarter can transsshipping to Borgen, I have…"

"Pay up-front can always sound good," she admitted, while trying to place the man, his accent, or his type. It wasn't that he looked familiar, but that he didn't look familiar at all.

"Indeed, it can. Are you a rep for another, or do your own trades?"

"Indy," she nodded, "with a partial can needs filling. You got a hardcopy list of what-and-where I can peer at so I…"

"The trades move so quickly—but, I hardly need tell you, do I?—there is no hardcopy list, but if you can merely give me an idea of your direction I'm sure we can…"

A flash of something odd went across the man's face, his voice stumbled, and she felt rather than saw Jela at her side.

"Pardon, Broker," he said, overloud even in this loud place, "I'm afraid the trader's attention is needed elsewhere immediately."

She turned, sudden, and felt the pressure of Jela's knee on her leg. While not offensive of itself, the sheer audacity of it surprised her, as did the near fawning line of nonsense that came out of his mouth.

"Trader, I swear, this isn't just jitters this time. There's a problem, and you're needed! Quickly, before—"

Her gut tightened, thinking it might be real and there was active danger to her ship—but there was Dulsey on-board and watching, and the talkie in her belt hadn't beeped. And Jela looked serious, damn him—which meant nothing at all.

"Broker," she called, holding out a hand, "your card? As soon as I—"

"*Now*, Trader!" Jela cried, and she caught the quick flutter of fingers at belt level, read *touch not jettison flee* just before he dared to take her arm...

"I return!" she called to the broker, over Jela's continued babble—"Trader, I'm sorry. Broker, my pardons. Trader..." and followed his insistent tug.

Jela's back was *not* what Cantra wanted to see right now, nor did she intend to watch him walk in those damned tight leathers he preferred for his dock-side rambles. Since she wasn't going to run to catch him, the best thing she could do was try to cut him off when they turned the corner—

But that quick he spun about, fingers fluttering low like he thought someone might have a microphone or a camera pointed in their direction.

Next right quick time. Left and left. Safe corner door.

She snapped a two-finger assent and he took off again like there was an emergency at the end of the walk.

They made the door right quick at the pace he set, and then out into the wide common hall that acted like a street in this section of port, and she did have to stretch her legs a bit to keep up. How he made it look easy to move quite so fast without drawing attention to himself was—

He signaled that he was slowing, and she caught up to walk at his side.

"I was about to finish settling the cargo for that last quarter-can," she said, letting it sound as irritated as she felt. "This better be a quick answer..."

"Is. That's a really bad place to be getting involved with."

"What, you think picking up an extra bit of cash is going to hurt us? You must have more credit than I know about."

Jela looked her full in the face as he strode on, and the look was so full of genuine concern that it shocked her.

"What I can tell you is, best analysis, that man's operation runs at a loss, and he's been running it for the better part of a long-term lease. It's a loss," he added quietly, "that would keep you in wine and boys for the rest of your life."

She thought about that through the next six steps, then brought her hand up, fingers forming *repeat?*

Jela sighed and slowed his pace again.

"About what I can say is he's on a really quiet watch list. Looks like he must be selling IDs, shipping info out to—somewhere. Part of the reason there's no hardcopy is that he'll send something wherever it is you say you're going. There's a pattern—ships he deals with have some problems. Some pilots or traders end up in legal hassles a port or two down link. Some have cargo problems. Some...just don't show up."

"Legal hassles?" She frowned. "What could he do—"

"Forges contracts. Fakes tape. Fakes DNA seals—or breaks them..."

Cantra played the day-broker's actions over in her head. He'd looked straight—nothing had smelled wrong to her, with her highly-developed nose for trouble. And those two traders who—

"Damn." She shot a glance at Jela. "Breaks DNA seals? How, do you know?"

He finger-waggled something that might have been *captain's knowl-edge*, and gave a short and barely audible laugh before waving his hands meaninglessly, and chanting lightly, "Lore of the troop, Pilot. Lore of the troop."

She harrumphed at that, then had to do a quick half-step to get back onto his pace.

"So, why're we in a hurry?"

"Can't tell if he sent a runner after us or not, yet."

"Runner? For what? And if he's so bad, why's he still in business?"

"Second son of the second spouse of the ruling house."

He almost sang it—she wondered if this was another one of his seemingly endless store of song-bits.

"For real?" she asked.

"Close enough for our purposes. I expect the locals think he's spying for them."

"If he is, he's good and I hope they pay him what he's worth. Look, I didn't sign nothing, but I saw him stash a card a trader handled..."

"Right. Doesn't take much if you're not careful. But, I think all we need to do is act like you solved the problem your idiot junior couldn't, and then got busy. So, let's get busy. Buy you a drink?"

Some days, she wondered what Jela's head was stuffed with. Other days, she was pretty certain it was ore.

"What about that quarter-can that needs filling?" she asked him. "Besides, the last time we ate together in public, we had a bit of trouble."

"Nope. We had a good meal, and nice wine. I still think about that."

She shot him a glance, but he was busily scanning the storefronts they were passing, so she didn't know how she should take that. Hard to figure him, anyway.

She glanced over at him again, and saw his face brighten like he'd spotted a treasure.

He looked at her, grinning. "Really—are you up for a big helping of brew and a quiet lift-off in the morning? If worse comes to worst, that pod ought to be able to suck in some air..."

That was a point she hadn't considered, and it was true. The next step out was a station where they could probably sell excess air, and they could run up the pressure in the can pretty good without hurting a thing.

"You think like a trader, for all you got soldier writ all over you."

He gave a short laugh.

"Call me a soldier if you like, but tell me if you want a brew before we walk by the place!"

"Sure," she said, thinking that a beer would taste good, and if there was trouble at the ship, Dulsey would call.

"Wait..." she said, blinking at the bar they were on approach for.

"It's here," said Jela, and there was an under note of something excited in his voice, "or buy a ride back to the ship, I think. This is the last place on port they'll send a runner, if they've got any sense at all."

If the day-broker sent a runner at all, which wasn't proven, or in Cantra's opinion, likely.

She stopped on the walk, looking carefully at the doubtful exterior of the place Jela proposed for a quiet brew and a wait-out. It was decorated in antique weapons in improbable colors, the names of famous battles scrawled in half-a-dozen different scripts and languages across what looked to be blast-glass windows.

One Day's Battle was written a little larger than the rest, in red lumenpaint...

"You want me to go into a soldier's bar? *One Day's Battle* sounds kinda rough for a friendly drink..."

He grinned. "Too rough for *you*, Pilot?" he asked, and then, before she could decide if she wanted to get peeved or laugh, he continued.

"It's the title of a drinking song long honored by several corps. I'm sure you can hold your own, Pilot—don't you think?"

Well, yeah, she did think, and she'd done it a few times in her wilder youth, but those days were some years back.

"Safest place on port, ship aside," Jela said, earnestly.

Damn, but the man *could* be insistent.

She looked down at him, which meant he was that close to her, which he usually kept his distance, and closed her eyes in something like exasperation and something like concentration.

It wasn't always easy being candid with herself, training or no training, but the boy was starting to get tempting.

Well, she'd not let him hear her sigh about it, but the truth was, she didn't want him quite that close. Oughtn't to have him as close as he was, acting like co-pilot and trade partner. She of all people ought to know about acting. Might be a little distance could be got inside, where there'd be noise and distractions for them both.

So she pointed toward the door with a flourish and laid down the rules.

"We split. Any round you buy, I buy the next. Don't buy a round if you think you can't walk back to the ship from the next."

His grin only got wider—which, Cantra thought resignedly, she might've known.

"Wohoa!" he cried, shoving an exuberant fist upward. "Yes— a challenge from my pilot! I'm for it!"

"Sure you are. You break trail."

He stepped forward with a will—and then stepped back as a pair of tall drunks wandered out, each leaning on the other, which complimentary form of locomotion was suddenly imperiled when the taller of the two tried to stand up straight and bow to Cantra.

"Pretty lady," he slurred with drunken dignity, "take me home!"

Cantra shot a glance to Jela, but he only laughed and led the way in.

Despite her initial misgivings, *One Day's Battle* was—on the surface— a fine looking establishment, with a good number of people at tables, not as much noise as might be supposed, and lots of space to relax in. That the overwhelming number of patrons were military was a little unsettling, but nobody seemed to mind the entrance of an obvious civilian.

The place was laid out in three levels. They came in on the top level, and at the far end was a long bar manned by two assistants and a boss. A quick glance showed one of the reasons for the noise level being quite so low—there were a dozen or so noise-cancel speakers set about between levels.

To get to the next level, they went down a ramp on the left, with a glass wall about thigh high on Cantra and a good bit higher on Jela; at the end of that ramp was a fan-shaped area with a bar at the wide end and more empty tables than full. Two additional ramps led still lower, where a crowd was gathered around a big octagonal table.

That big table seemed to be where the action was. From a quick glance between the players, Cantra thought it looked like some kind of gambling sim…

Jela, however, was headed for the other side of the room, where he claimed an empty table overlooking the lower levels—including a view of the octagonal table and its denizens.

Cantra followed him more slowly, noting that the seats were more luxurious than those in the bar upstairs and that the tables were topped with some rich-looking shiny substance. The slight sounds of her footsteps was silenced by springy, noise-absorbing carpet. The lighting, too, was more subdued on this level.

"Officers' section?" she guessed. "We up to that?"

"Officers' mess, of sorts," Jela agreed, "but off-duty, and thus not official. It'll be just a bit quieter, though, and easier for us to note someone who doesn't necessarily belong."

He handed her into a seat, which surprised—then she realized it was proper. Co-pilot sees to the pilot's comfort first, after all. Too, by slipping her into the seat he chose for her, Jela got the chair with the best view of the entrance ramp, which was a habit she'd noted in him before—and couldn't much fault. A lot of his habits were like that—couldn't be faulted if you were a pilot who sometimes walked the wrong side of a line.

Cantra leaned into the seat, realized it was a bit oversized for her. Jela's legs threatened to dangle, except that he sat forward, leaning his elbows on the table. Cantra could see him reflected in the dark surface; he was staring into it, perhaps looking at her reflection in turn.

Then the table top shimmered, and Jela's reflection disappeared within the image of a battle sim.

He looked up, grinning wryly.

"Sorry, looks like it's autostart. This'll be the battle of the day, is my guess."

Cantra glanced into the table, recognizing some of the icons, but not all. Frowning, she bent closer—and then looked up as a tall group of soldiers walked by, talking between themselves as they headed for the bar. Their voices were easily audible, despite all the sound-proofing, and she frowned even more. It wasn't what they were saying that bothered her as much as the fact that she couldn't pick words out of the sentence flow—and that the sentence flow itself was—off-rhythm for any of the many languages, dialects, and cants she spoke...

Losing your edge, she told herself and tapped the top of the table, drawing Jela's attention.

"Why is this here?" she asked.

"Ah. Anyone who wants to—and who has credit enough—can play against the sim. Most prefer, as you see, to use the large table downstairs, but some of us like our comfort, and some prefer only to watch.

"This particular sim is of a battle fought some time back, so there's always a chance that someone in the crowd may have studied—and come up with something better. Of course someone else who has studied may be sitting at another panel...and thus learning may take place—and wagers."

"Great." She sat back. "Not sure I'm up to trying to outfight history..."

"Sometimes," he said, his voice sounding oddly distant as some change on the screen caught his attention, "there are battles which ought be re-fought a time or two—mistakes unmade. And some mistakes not made."

He pointed at the screen, touched some table side control and turned it toward her.

"You see in action exactly such a case. In this battle, a new weapon was all the rage on the side of the blues; and in the actual battle brought the other side to a nearly untenable position very early on. But you see, someone down there—" he pointed to the deepest pit—"who happens to know one of the now-proven weaknesses of this weapon, has attempted an early turning of the lines here and—" he swept his hand to the other edge of the board—"over here."

He sighed. "This is an easily refutable attempt to win the battle by guile rather than by true force of arms. The sim, if no one else will jump in, will take quite awhile to react, since it is required to work from the actual situation and toward the original goal..."

He stared into the screen a moment longer.

"No, foolish Green," he muttered, "you've overcommitted..."

Suddenly, he laughed, and folded both arms atop the screen, partially obscuring the play.

"My apologies, Pilot. If this is what the corps is teaching, the Arm is in danger for truth!"

Another pair of uniformed soldiers passed their table just then— faces animated under the gaudy tats—and they, too, walked inside the odd rhythm of a conversation she couldn't quite grasp.

Cantra looked to Jela, nodding toward the group of them.

"They from around here?" she asked.

"I couldn't read the insignia..."

"Me neither. But I got good ears, and I couldn't pick up a word they was saying."

"I was distracted," he admitted ruefully. "But to answer the question you asked—they are not from 'around here' by the look of their tattoos. To answer the question you meant—yes. They feel that they are at home here, and so they speak the language the troop wishes them to speak, which is not one you will likely be familiar with."

She shifted in the too-big seat—big enough, she realized, for one of the tall soldiers to sit in comfortably—turned around, caught the bartender's eye, and waved.

"If they're gonna have tattoos on their faces," she said to Jela, "and their own language, too, it might be hard for an ordinary citizen to take to 'em much. If I may be so bold."

He glanced away for a moment, scanning the room, she thought, then looked back to her with a slight lift of one shoulder.

"See for yourself. There are groups of those wearing tattoos, and there are groups of those *not* wearing tattoos. There are some solitary examples of each. You, I expect, will be perceptive enough to follow on these observations and..."

"Right. What I see is that there's only one place where you can see both tats and no-tats together…"

She completed her scan of the room; looked back at him, indicating *condition is* with her free hand as she watched a rowdy bunch striding down the ramp to the big board.

"Condition is they ain't what you'd want to call together down there, they're competing…"

Condition is, he agreed in hand talk as a tall and extremely straight-backed man in what was almost a proper uniform came to their table.

"Comrades," he began, speaking to Jela, then looked hard at Cantra.

"Comrade *and lady,*" he corrected himself. "How may we serve you?"

Jela's face went to that place Cantra categorized as *one step from dangerous,* and he answered firmly.

"*Pilots* will do, comrade."

There was a pause, then a sketch of a salute.

"Pilots," he agreed amiably enough, "your drink or meal?"

Cantra flashed *your choice,* and without hesitation Jela told the server, "The local commander's favorite brew, with a platter of mixed cheeses and breads."

After a slight pause—but before the question was asked—he added, "That will be a pitcher."

It was a big pitcher and it was good beer, but for all of that Cantra wasn't best pleased with her co-pilot being willing to stake out quite so much time at *One Day's Battle* at her expense. Her figurative expense, anyway, because he hadn't had the sense to see that she'd want to be back to the ship as soon as could. How long, after all, did he think this possible-but-not-proven "runner" would look for her?

She'd figured that they'd have a couple glasses…but now they'd be looking to about four or five each if she kept to her promise, and by damn she wasn't gonna not keep to her promise.

The cheese was decent and so was the bread. The beer was more than acceptable, and, unfortunately, so was the company.

"Don't much care for military art?" Jela asked, correctly reading her reaction to the over-done specimen of same hanging behind the bar.

She moved a shoulder and had another taste of beer.

"Not much in favor of this school, anyway," she answered. "Could be there's another?"

He took a couple heartbeats to study the painting.

"Could be. If there is, though, they all learned to paint the same things in the same way." He reached to the platter and slid a piece of the spicy-hot cheese onto a slip of dark bread.

"What do you find objectionable? If it can be told."

"Well, leaving aside the subject, the colors are too loud; there're too few of them; the figures are out of scale and out of proportion…" She heard her voice taking on a certain note of passion and cooled it with a sip of beer, waving an apologetic hand at her companion.

"No," he said, "go on. I'm interested in such things. Call it a hobby."

"It depends," Cantra said slowly, "what the art was meant to do. Me saying some certain piece is too garish or too…primitive— that has to stand against the question of the intent of the artist. If I was an honest critic—which you'll see I ain't—I'd be talking in terms of did yon offender make its point."

Jela had paused with his glass half-way to his lips, his eyes fixed on her face. As she watched, he turned his head and gave the painting under discussion a long hard stare.

Cantra helped herself to some bread and cheese and wondered what was going through his head.

"I see what you're saying," he said at last, and finally had his sip—and another one, too. "I'd never thought of art in terms of intent." He smiled and his fingers flickered.

Owe you.

"My pleasure," she said aloud, her eyes drawn down again by the damn' sim.

She moved her gaze by an effort of will, only to find Jela absently watching a couple their server would undoubtedly address as *ladies* wend their artless way down the ramp to the game level.

Neither one was her style, so she found herself looking again at the battle sim and trying to work out the icons and the situation.

Damn, if it was her that was general, she'd've realized that turning the battle line wouldn't really work, on account of the fact that the defenders could use the planet as a shield, and likely they must have had *some* secret of their own because they were fighting like there wasn't any particular point—or that the planet wasn't any more important than any other, which didn't make all that much sense, since she gathered it was a home world...

There was a sound that she realized was Jela's half-laugh. She glanced up to see a half-smile, too.

"It does grab the attention," he said, indicating the scene before her. "If you like we can buy into the observer mode..."

It was her turn to laugh.

"It's like trying to ignore somebody messing up their piloting drills. It *hurts* to see it going so stupid."

"Oh, you think so, too? I'm assuming you think Blue is..."

"I think I could whip Green pretty good if any of the ships I see over here are what they look like."

His smile grew, and with a flip of a credit chip he bought them the full observer feed. By the time the second pitcher had been delivered, she'd added a bit more to the sim's takings and bought their table a commentary slot, so they could drop public and private notes to the combatants. Jela'd commented at the time that they might as well go to full combatant, but she'd thought not, and called for another round of bread and cheese.

"You're absolutely correct," Jela was saying in all seriousness. "Blue has willingly got themselves set up just about backward now. See, that's because you came to this fresh, and without benefit of assuming anything. Green did very nearly the same thing in the real war, you know, and—well," he said, looking at the screen. "Well, I think they're just about to be toast..."

Green was very loud in the pits and apparently sure of a victory by now, and the other side was quiet. Much of the joyful noise was in the language Cantra didn't know, so she felt sure which side was which.

"Eh," came a loud voice from the depths, speaking to the whole establishment at once. "And what shall we do now, witnesses?"

"I'd say Green should ask for terms," Jela suggested to Cantra, as he looked over the rail at the action well below, "and beg that their officers will be allowed to keep their weapons..."

As it happened, they agreed on the point, and, it being her turn at the keyboard, Cantra tapped that good advice into the system, which dutifully displayed it on the screens below.

The sounds of joy and laughter from the pit plunged into silence, and in reaction all other conversation in the bar died almost instantly. An order for a double-grapeshot rang incongruously from the upper bar.

"Madness!" howled the soldier in the game pit. "Who dares? Who *dares?*"

All stared up from the pit as eyes around the room settled on their spot.

"We can make the door," Cantra said, putting the keyboard aside, dread rising in her stomach. "You start..."

Jela grinned at her and stood, but rather than jumping for the door he leaned over the rail and spoke down into the pit.

"*I* dare."

There was a moment of what Cantra believed to be stunned silence, then a minor roar of laughter.

"*You* dare, little soldier? *You?* Do you know who you speak to?"

"Yes, I do," Jela said calmly. "I speak to one whose mouth runs faster than his mind."

Cantra picked up her beer and had a sip, allowing herself to go back over the brief good time they'd spent. If they survived what was surely coming next, they ought to try it again sometime.

Or maybe not.

"Come down here and tell me that!" howled the soldier in the pit.

Jela laughed.

"No, I needn't. You've heard the truth; it would be the same wherever it was spoken. Go back to your little lost game and..."

There was some motion going on, Cantra saw. At the bar, a couple of the servers were pulling breakables back behind the counter and some of the other soldiers were moving to get a glimpse of the one on the mezzanine who would be getting pulped soon.

Down in the pit, half-a-dozen soldiers were pushing their way out of the crowd to 'round the game table and head for the ramp.

Jela looked at Cantra and spoke low and quick.

"You'll likely see blood. If you see too much of it is mine, it will be time for you to leave."

"Not a chance," she said. "If you're gonna break up the bar, I want my share of the fun, too."

He grinned at her, more than half-feral; and there was a gleam of anticipation in the black eyes.

The soldier from the pit cleared the upper end of the ramp and strode over to their table, where he stood, breathing hard, his mates not far behind. His right cheek carried a colorful tattoo of a combat whip, throwing sparks—or maybe it was stars—and he looked to be at least twice Jela's mass.

"You, little soldier." His snarl suffered somewhat from his ragged breathing. "What do you do here? You have no right to be where real soldiers drink!"

Jela moved slowly from the rail toward his antagonist.

"Child," he said, softly, "I was drinking and fighting before you suckled your first electric tit. Return to your games or have at me, but please do either before you fall over from breathlessness!"

That looked to do it, thought Cantra dispassionately, if what Jela wanted was a fight. The first closing ought to be coming soon, if she was reading the big soldier right, and—

It might have been a sound that warned her—she didn't know herself.

Whatever, her hand was in the air, snatching the incoming by its handle and swinging it down onto the table with a *thump*. Jela's glass jumped and fell over, spilling beer onto what was left of the cheese and bread.

She turned in her chair; spotted the offender three tables back.

"Fair fight is fair," she yelled to the room in general, "but this—" she hefted the would-be missile—"*this* is a waste of beer!"

She held the pitcher up for all to see and there were chuckles. The boy who'd come to pulp Jela was standing uncertain, his hands opening and closing at his sides.

Cantra waved the pitcher in the direction of the man who'd attempted to blind-side Jela.

"Bartender," she sang out, "that soldier's pitcher is empty and he'll pay for a refill. He'll pay for a refill for us, too!"

There was a hush then, but came a voice from behind the bar. "Yes, Pilot. Immediately!"

There was some outright laughter then and the chief antagonist dismissed his would-be champion with a wave of a long, improbably delicate hand.

"I need no help against this old midget." And to Jela, "Fool. I will show you..."

The bartender appeared, carrying two full pitchers. He placed one in front of Cantra and passed on to leave the second with the sneak.

That done, he stepped back and stood tall, drawing all eyes to him.

"I will personally shoot anyone who pulls a weapon," he yelled, showing off what looked like a hand-cannon. "Fatally!"

Jela glanced at Cantra, grinned, and hand-signed *seven, six, five…*

And indeed, on the count, the large soldier came round the table in a rush, seeking, it seemed, to merely fall on—

Jela was gone, not with the expected small sidestep but with a leap. The soldier whirled and in doing so faced—no one, for Jela had kept moving, staying behind him. The soldier stopped.

Jela was behind him again, but close.

This time the big soldier expertly swept out a leg, bringing the kick to Jela's throat—which wasn't there. Then the big man was down, leg jerked out from under him by a twisting form in black leather, in and out.

The soldier was quicker than his size foretold—he rolled and came up spinning.

The recovery put Jela uncomfortably close to the rail, or so Cantra thought, and the big soldier, seeing this same advantage to himself, pressed in. Jela moved—fake, fake, fake, fake, strike the shoulder, *bam*!

The big soldier bounced off the rail to cheers and moans of the onlookers, coming on in a rush—nothing daunted—and abruptly stopped, stretching deliberately, showing off his size to the crowd. Cantra, at the table, yawned.

The soldier glared at her. "Do I bore you so much? Wait your turn."

"Tsk." Jela moved a hand, drawing his opponent's attention back to himself. "A word of wisdom to the hero-child: do not threaten my pilot."

The big soldier smiled. "You are correct. My first quarrel is with you." He opened his arms, as if offering an embrace. "Now I know your tricks, little one. Just close with me once and it will be over…"

Jela danced in slowly, his posture not one of attack, but of calm waiting.

From her ring-side seat, Cantra could see the size of the problem—the big man's arms were almost as long as Jela's legs. If Jela couldn't get a single quick strike in—

She grimaced with half the crowd as the large solider threw a punch toward Jela's face. There was the inevitable sound of breaking bone and a yowl of pain, and she was out of her chair and three steps toward the action before she realized there was no need.

Jela stood fast, legs braced wide, the big soldier's right fist in his slowly closing hand. There was no sign of blood on either of them and for a long moment, they were simply frozen in tableau. Jela calmly continued to close his fingers, the soldier's mouth open in amazement or agony. Then, all of a sudden, he moved, putting every muscle in that long body into a lunge— which Jela allowed, dropping the ruined hand and pivoting as the soldier went by him.

The big soldier cuddled his broken hand against his chest, breathing hard. His shoulders dropped; the left hand twitched—

Cantra moved—two steps, slipping the dart gun out of its hideaway inside her vest.

"Pull that and I'll shoot your kneecaps off!" she snapped.

The big soldier froze amidst a sudden absolute silence in the bar which was just as suddenly shattered by the bartender's shout.

"I cede my board to the pilot!"

"Drop it," Cantra told the big soldier. "Now."

Slowly, he opened his hand and a slim ceramic blade fell to the carpet. Jela swept forward and picked it up, then fell back into a crouch, knife ready.

"Good boy," Cantra said to the wounded soldier and looked over the crowd, picking out a familiar insignia on two jackets.

"You two—medics! Take care of him!"

They exchanged glances, their faces stunned under the tattoos.

"Are you two med techs or aren't you?" yelled the bartender. "I told you, the pilot has the board!"

One of the techs ducked her head. "Yes, Pilot," she mumbled and jerked her head at her mate, both of them moving toward the injured man—pausing on the far side of Jela.

The second medic threw Cantra a glance.

"If the pilot will be certain that the—that the soldier is satisfied?"

Right. Cantra considered the set of Jela's shoulders and the gleam in his eye, and decided she didn't blame them for being cautious.

"Jela." She gentled her voice into matter-of-fact. "Stand down. Fun's over."

He didn't turn his head. She saw his fingers caress the hilt of the captured knife meditatively.

Cantra sighed.

"Co-pilot, you're wanted at your board," she said sternly.

Some of the starch went out of the wide shoulders; the knife vanished into sleeve or belt; and Jela took one step aside and turned to face her fully.

"Yes, Pilot," he said respectfully with a half salute.

In the pit there was the sound of groaning—and cheering.

On the way out the door Cantra heard someone say, "Never argue with an M..."

She'd have to remember that.

They were in a cab and on the way back to *Dancer* when the talkie in Cantra's belt beeped.

She yanked it free and pressed the button.

"Dulsey? What's wrong?"

There was a short lag, then the Batcher's bland voice.

"I only wished to tell you, Pilot, that the delivery from Blue Light Day Broker was taken at my direction to the port holding office. It awaits your signature there."

Cantra blinked. So Jela's "runner" wasn't a play-story, after all, though what the second son could want with her was a puzzle indeed.

"Your orders, Pilot," Dulsey said, sounding unsure now, "were not to accept any package or visitor unless it came with you."

Standing orders, those and trust Dulsey to stand by them.

"You did fine, Dulsey," she said into the talkie. "Pilot Jela an' me'll be with you in a couple short ones."

"Yes, Pilot," the Batcher answered. "Out."

Cantra looked over to Jela, who was sitting calm and unperturbed next to her.

"Now what?" she said, snapping the talkie onto her belt.

"Leave it," Jela said. "Somebody whose duty it is to watch that day-trader will show a proper interest, if they haven't already."

"Why target me?" she asked, which was a bothersome question, but Jela just shrugged his wide shoulders.

"You talked to him; you looked hungry; you might take the bait," he said, like it wasn't anything to worry on. "Man can't get ahead unless he takes some risks."

Which she had to allow was true.

EIGHTEEN

On Port
Ardega

"WHAT ABOUT STOCK seed?" Jela asked from beside her.

Cantra eyed the rest of the list on the theory that she was the elder trader.

Ardega wasn't a world known to her. Its rep was good, if it happened you were trading Lights. The on-offers here at the agri fair, for instance, included a wide range of basic genetically stable growables, the price-per's well into the reasonable range.

"Price is right," she said. "Might want to take on a pallet of the stasis-sealed embryos, too."

"They're not claiming to be gen-stable," Jela protested, and she pointed her chin at the board.

"On offer from Aleberly Labs," she murmured. "I'm betting they're stable."

"I missed that," he admitted. "They're a possibility, then. The price—"

"It's a little high per, but if we take the whole pallet, we get a discount from the dockworkers guild on the transfer fee."

"That makes it reasonable," he agreed, eyes on the offer board. "Do we want any of this whole leaf tea?"

She frowned. Where was he—oh. Garnet leaf. Good price, too. She sighed with real regret.

"It degrades too fast. Be gone by the time we raised Phairlind."

"They stay here, then," Jela said, and turned his head to look at her. "If we take the seed and the embryos, we've still got half-a-can to fill."

"Little more." She gave the board one last read, finding nothing that caught her by the trade sense and demanded to be bought—and looked back to Jela.

"Let's reserve our decideds. Then we'll go 'round to the arts fair and see what they have on offer," she said.

"Art?" he repeated. "Is there an art market on the Rim?"

"There's a market for damn' near everything, anywhere there's people," she said, turning and threading her way through the cluster of other traders, all oblivious to anything but the boards and the info displayed there.

Jela stayed at her back, which she'd gotten used to. Her nerves no longer processed him as "too-close-about-to-be-dangerous," but as "extra-protection-safe" which proved that her nerves were just as idiotic as her brain which, despite her having reasoned it out several times, continued to produce words like "co-pilot," "partner," and other such traps to describe Jela and his relationship to her and her ship.

Well, she'd pay that tariff when it came due. In the meanwhile, it was...comforting...to feel his solid presence at her back and know there was another honed set of survival skills on the lookout for trouble.

"yos'Phelium," she said to the reservations clerk, and slid her trade coin across the counter to him.

"Yes, Trader." His voice was high, and he spoke the Common Tongue with a lisp, which could have been accent, or an accident of nature. "How may I be of assistance?"

She tapped her finger on the counter, the goods on offer scrolling across its surface. The scrolling stopped and a highlight appeared under her fingertip. She moved down the list until she came to the ID for the seed, tapped once to highlight the line, moved down to the embryos and tapped that line, too.

"Very good," the clerk trilled, his eyes in turn on his private screen. "Quantity?"

"A pallet of the embryo," she said and shot a glance over her shoulder at Jela. "Three of the seeds?" He inclined his head.

"One pallet stasis bound poultry embryo guaranteed by Aleberly Labs. Three pallets mixed crop seed, gen-stable SATA inspected and warrantied." He looked up. "Anything else?"

"That'll do," she said. "Hold delivery until I call. My partner and me're still on the boards."

He worked with his screen, lower lip caught between his teeth.

"Delivery hold, will call," he said finally. "The goods revert, fee forfeit, if delivery is not taken by local midnight."

"I understand," Cantra told him and he spun the screen around.

She thumb-printed the order; he pressed the trade coin against the sensor. A sheet of hard copy curled out of the top of the screen. He pulled it free and handed it and the coin to her.

"Your receipt," he said. "Please retain it, in the unlikely event that a dispute should arise regarding your reservation. Thank you for your patronage of the Ardega Agricultural Fair and please come again."

"Thanks," Cantra said, sealing the paper away into an inner pocket of her vest. She left the counter, Jela behind her, and headed for the door.

The arts fair occupied a massive cermacrete shell, booths and tables stretching out to the horizon, and sparse of buyers, compared to the agri fair. Though that could, Cantra thought, have been an illusion born of the much larger space.

She paused on the edge of the floor, and frowned at the directory.

"Not a lot of money on the Far Edge of the Rim, in a general way," she said, running her eye down the long list of luxuries and frivols. "There are some who can afford whatever there is to buy— at Out-Rim prices. I'm thinking we've got room in that can for something interesting in textile. Rugs. Wall hangings. Bolt cloth."

"One-ofs?" Jela asked, leaning over her shoulder and putting his finger on a listing for stone carvings.

She wrinkled her nose. "We got the room, but is there enough of a market? We'd have to hand sell, and I'm not seeing us setting up a booth on Port Borgen, say, for a Common Month."

"It could happen," he said, in the way he did sometimes that made her think she wasn't the only one who bye-n-bye forgot to remember that their partnership was a matter of his convenience.

"How much credit left?"

She fingered the trade coin out of its pocket and held it up; he glanced at the number and grunted softly.

"Reserve a quarter of that for me?" he murmured. "I want to cover the possibility of having to spend a month on Borgen."

In pursuit of his wandering info, whatever it was. For a man who said he knew what he was looking for, he was awfully fuzzy on its probable location, despite his continued—and unauthorized— use of *Dancer's* long-comm. He hadn't discovered the sentinel—or he had and had made the decision to pretend it wasn't there, in the cause of preserving ship-board peace.

As long as a copy of the outgoing was caught and shunted to the private screen in her quarters, she had no complaint. Or no complaint that she was willing to voice, given the circumspect nature of the intercepted communications.

Incoming messages—and there were those—did present a problem, Jela having worked a block that she was reluctant to disturb for reasons that were likely close to those that kept him from interfering with the sentinel.

"Quarter's yours," she told him now. "Meet you back here in two hours?"

"Will do," he said and with a nod was gone, moving out with that easy stride that covered ground quick and never seemed to tire him.

Cantra watched until he turned a corner, admiring the stride, which was just nothing short of dangerous—to ship and to pilot—and forcibly put her eyes back on the directory board.

Textile was on the Avenue of Weavers. She touched the listing and a map opened on the screen, a green line showing her the path straight down the main hall, across six intersections, and a right at the seventh. She touched the map over the avenue and the image enlarged, showing a long row of booths, with names and annotations.

She identified several bolt cloth dealers and also several rug merchants. Good. The sooner the last can was full with honest trade goods, the sooner they could lift out of here bound for Scohecan, which port had been Jela's call, and a sorry world it was, too. Still, it did own a port there and a market, though they weren't likely to either sell or buy there.

And after Scohecan, a gentle jump off the Farthest Edge and into the Out-and-Away for to pay a social call on the Uncle. If she came out on the other side of that visit with Pilot Jela still by her side, then she could concentrate her whole mind and heart on getting her ship and her liberty restored.

Right.

Sighing, she straightened her shoulders, had one more look at the map and took off toward the Avenue of Weavers, swinging out with a will, thoughts firmly on textile.

She committed half the remaining credit, less Jela's reserve, on a quarter-can of mixed compressed textile. The transaction was completed at the booth and a time for delivery was set. Still room for a few rolls of rugs, assuming Jela wasn't buying life-sized carvings for his portion.

Mind more than half on double-checking her capacities, she came to the first rug booth on her list. It, like the textile booth, was thin of company. A bored young person she took to be the 'prentice merchant lounged behind the counter, arms crossed over his chest, staring across the avenue with a slightly glassy look in his eye.

Cantra turned her head, following the direction of the young man's gaze, and found it was a young lady of voluptuous habit in the scarf booth across the way under study. The lady was draped in numerous of her diaphanous wares—very likely a dozen of them—in complimentary shades of blue, and clearly thought herself very romantical.

Someone, thought Cantra, had neglected her education badly, judging from the way the scarves were arranged. She hoped the young lady didn't take it into her head to attempt to perform anything she might fondly believe to be the Dance of a Dozen Scarves. She doubted the arts fair was ready. Though it looked like the 'prentice merchant was.

"Good day to you," she said, approaching the rug booth.

The boy started badly, and came out of his slouch with a gasp, bowing hurriedly.

"Trader," he murmured, the Common Tongue pleasantly burry in his mouth. She didn't immediately place the accent—and then did: the lad was from The Bubble. "How may I be of service?"

"I am interested in rugs, sir," she said, bringing the Rim accent up a notch. "Good rugs, not necessarily in the first line of art, but durable and pleasing to both the eye and the foot."

"I believe we may have precisely what you are searching for," the boy said, moving down the booth. "If the trader will attend me here, I will undertake to acquaint her with our mid-line rugs. It is on these rugs that we base our reputation as manufacturers of the first rank. Durable, attractive, stain and dirt resistant. Here—" He put his hand on a sample. "Feel the nap, Trader. Not so deep as to trap dirt, yet deep enough to comfort feet tired from a day on-port in boots."

Cantra felt the nap, as directed, and found the boy to be correct with regard to the rug's tactile virtues. Unfortunately, he was dead wrong regarding attractiveness, it being warning-light orange. She flipped an edge up and considered the backing. Machine-loomed, sturdy, nothing special to commend it; color to discommend it. She sighed and flipped the edge back down.

"I wonder," she said, "if there might be a less—robust color available."

"Trader, I am desolate. The color is the hallmark of this particular rug. Now, if the trader would be willing to aim a step higher, we have these to offer—"

He moved up-counter, displaying a slightly larger specimen woven from variegated rose thread. The 'prentice flipped the edge up before she could get her palm against the nap, displaying the back for her.

Machine-loomed again. Cantra reached out and flipped the corner down, sliding her hand against the nap.

Stiff and unpleasant, cut far too close. She sighed and moved back from the counter, letting her eyes rest meditatively on the boy's face.

"Young sir, it would appear that you have no rugs that you wish to sell me."

He had the grace to blush, round cheeks darkening.

"Trader, it was you who asked to see cheap rugs."

She moved a hand in negation. "You misheard me, sir. I asked to see durable, comfortable and useful rugs at a good price. I have no interest in art pieces, nor in rugs so flimsy they lose their knots at the first suggestion of a boot. However, I see that you cannot accommodate me. I will search elsewhere. Fair profit to you."

She strolled away, leaving the 'prentice staring, hot-faced, after her. Cantra sighed. It was an old game—guide the customer to the goods carrying the highest mark-up by being unable to produce anything suitable at the lower price levels. The boy hadn't played it particularly well and had likely earned a tongue-lashing from his master for ineptitude, more the pity. Light traders, being law-abiding by fiat, ought not to display such tricks, even given that the Light version of the game was hardly more than a parlor trick, with only money at the risk. The same game played at a Dark port could well involve lives and ships.

The next rug booth on the list sported customers—no surprise, if they'd all encountered the boy with the Bubble accent first. The senior merchant behind the counter gave her a quick flutter of fingers—hand-sign for *be there soon*—which Cantra acknowledged with a dip of the head. Mooching through the displays not involved in the merchant's presentation, she located two possibles, both machine-loomed, durable, and soft against the skin. One was deep blue, the other a blend of quiet greens, and by the time the senior merchant came down-counter, Cantra had decided on the green, should price and availability favor her.

"Trader, how may I help you?" The merchant had a good, solid Insider accent, and a pleasant cast to her face. Her body language conveyed that she considered this to be the most important transaction of her day and she met Cantra's eyes openly, her own a lucent brown.

"I am interested in good, serviceable rugs," Cantra said, with an easy smile. "They need not necessarily be in the first line of art, but they must be durable and pleasing to both the eye and the foot."

The other woman smiled back, and reached to stroke the nap of the blue rug.

"The trader has a good eye. These and these—" the palm moved to the green rug—"are our most durable offerings. As you see, they are soft, both—" a practiced move of the hand and the corner of the green came up—"machine made, of course. They have been treated with SATA standard stain and dirt guard—to clean the rug, merely shake it out. Also, as you will see, all of our rugs have anti-skid strips at each corner, for added comfort and safety."

"The rugs please," Cantra said, flipping up the corner of the blue and running her finger over the skid stopper. "As well-made as they are, I wonder if they might be above my touch."

The senior merchant smiled. "Surely not. For a half-pallet of either, I ask only six hundred carolis."

"Entirely above my means, alas." Cantra sighed, and smoothed the blue rug with her palm. "I had been hoping that we might meet at three hundred carolis."

"Three hundred?" The senior merchant's brown eyes gleamed. "The trader jests, of course. Why—"

And so it went, until each was certain that they had the advantage of the other, and Cantra eventually handed over her trade coin, from which the brown-eyed merchant deducted four hundred carolis. A time was set for the delivery of the half-pallet of green and they parted amicably.

As pleased with her purchases as if she were legit and ultimately about lawful business, Cantra ambled back toward the entrance-way.

She did the calcs in her head as she walked and took time to hope that Jela's carvings were compact and not needful of specialized packing. Some stone was fragile, despite it all, which she should've thought to say to him, and if he came in with a deal on a crate full of breakables—

He'd be a bigger fool than you know him to be, she snapped at herself. *The man's a pilot; he knows about acceleration.*

Acceleration, in fact, was only one of the fascinating things that Pilot Jela seemed to know. Nothing like the encyclopedic training she'd survived, in which the aim of the directors was to cram all known history, cultures, languages, and arts into the skull of the student.

No, Jela seemed to specialize in the odd bit of knowledge, the random snip of lore. He had a truly awe-inspiring library of songs available to him—many of them obscene on one world or another—which he sang softly while he worked at whatever small task he had set himself to.

She had so far, and by constant reminder to herself, managed to avoid discounting him as a mere pack-dragon, hoarding his pieces and oddments without understanding—or caring about—their wider connections. Jela had surprised her more than once during their short acquaintance and she was allergic to surprises.

At the intersection with the main avenue, she turned left, taking it easy, there being some while left 'til the meet-time. It was, therefore, with some startlement that she bespied a short, wide-shouldered figure in respectable trade leathers walking purposefully in her direction.

She paused by an avenue sign and waited for him to join her, which he did in good time.

It was on the edge of her tongue to ask him how the carvings deal had gone, but something in his face dissolved the words, and another set fell out in their place.

"What's wrong?"

"I heard something—unsettling, I'd guess you'd say. I'll need to check it when we get back to the ship." A ripple of those wide shoulders. "It's probably just rumor."

A distinctly upsetting rumor, if it had Jela forgetting that she wasn't supposed to know about his indiscretions with *Dancer's* long-comm. Or maybe, she thought, and the thought made her stomach

hurt, the news carried on the rumor was dire enough to have Jela
thinking again—and figuring that the time for let's pretend was past.

"Carvings?" she asked then, and he jerked his chin over his shoulder.

"I've got a reserve on a case lot of hand-carved telomite. Each
piece unique. Good, hearty rock—won't splinter or crack under
acceleration. I told them I had to clear it with my partner."

Partner. She shook the word away and smiled agreeably.

"Sure," she said, easy and calm. "I've got us a lot of compressed
textile and a half-pallet of personal rugs. All paid for and delivery set
up. Let's get yours settled and go on back to the ship. You can check
out your rumor while Dulsey and me balance the can."

He looked at her out of unreadable black eyes and gave her a
smile of his own. It was about as sincere as hers had been, and
nothing like the genuine article.

So, whatever the rumor was had Jela out of sorts, Cantra
thought, walking with him toward the Avenue of Sculptures. That
was interesting.

NINETEEN

Spiral Dance
Ardega

THE CAN WAS balanced, sealed and checked quick-time, which was a definite benefit of having an engineer on the job. Cantra sighed and leaned against the wall of the cargo corridor, giving Dulsey a nod.

"That was almost painless," she said. "'preciate the help."

"You are welcome, Pilot." Dulsey said primly, and made to move on.

Cantra held out a hand, palm up, and Dulsey stopped, gray eyes going wary.

"Pilot?"

"I'd like to know," Cantra said, keeping her voice easy and calm, "on what facts you base the theory that I'm an *aelantaza* who survived a line edit—if it can be told."

A moment of silence. "And if it cannot be told?" Dulsey asked, sounding breathless and defiant at once.

Cantra flipped her hand, palm now toward the deck. "Then there's an end to it."

Dulsey sighed. "I believe you," she said, "and that should be proof enough that you are *aelantaza*."

"Why not believe me?" Cantra asked. "I'm telling the truth."

Dulsey laughed.

"Yes, certainly!" The laugh faded into serious. "It's scarcely a secret any more. The pilot will be familiar with the fact that many corporations contract persons to discover the secrets and weaknesses of the competition."

Industrial espionage was among the most common jobs contracted for graduates of the Institute. Cantra inclined her head.

"I've heard of such things," she acknowledged.

"Then the pilot will not be surprised to learn that Enclosed Habitats contracted for an *aelantaza* to spy upon their competition. In the way of things, we came to know this *aelantaza*, for it was the habit of Master Keon to interview her in those sections under construction or repair, as they could reasonably be assumed to be lacking surveillance of any kind."

"He debriefed her in front of you and your Pod?" Cantra demanded. "What kind of security is that?"

Dulsey bowed. "This humble person has no existence in the common law, save as an object to be bought or sold. This humble person may not testify against one's masters, nor will she be heard should she speak against the masters. This humble person may be killed out of hand by her rightful owner for no reason whatsoever."

Cantra sighed. "I take the point," she said. "So you got to know the *aelantaza*."

"We did. And she came to know us: she knew our names and took note of the differences between us, so that she never greeted me as Ocho, nor mistook Uno for Seatay. From the rear, in repair 'skins, she knew us, each from the other. It was from her—from watching her observe and learn, from listening to her report to and…*manipulate* Master Keon, that I came to understand that I needed to think beyond protocol, to take chances, and to—to seize opportunity, if and when it should ever come to me."

"Sounds like a learning experience," Cantra said dryly. "What's it got to do with me?"

"Two things," Dulsey said briskly. "First, she looked a great deal like you—not as much as Ocho and I, but there was definitely what natural humans style a 'family resemblance' between you and she."

She paused. Cantra flicked the hand-sign for *go on* at her.

"Secondly, there came a time when another *aelantaza* arrived instead and Master Keon interviewed him as he had always interviewed the other. And so we learned that the first *aelantaza*—whose name was possibly Timoli, though that may have been an alias—that Timoli was of a line which had lately been found inferior and was thus edited from the *aelantaza* breeding tables. This was, the new *aelantaza* told Master Keon with great sincerity, in order to insure that flaws would not be passed on, and was to the customers' benefit, assuring them of the very best service."

Timoli. Cantra kept her face smooth. She hadn't known her well, there having been something on the order of thirty years between them, but Timoli had been a full sister. Damn right there was a "family resemblance."

She inclined her head.

"I thank you for the information," she said formally. "I have one more question—again, if it can be told. How did you deduce that I had knowledge of the Uncle?"

Dulsey took a deep breath.

"That, Pilot, was a leap into the Deep. I surmised that editing a line which must have included dozens of very able and canny adults would have a potent delivery mechanism, and that the mechanism could be disarmed by one with access to the appropriate technology. It seemed to me that the Uncle might find the plight of a lone *aelantaza* marked for destruction...compelling."

"So you guessed." Cantra grinned. "Not bad, Dulsey."

"I am pleased that the pilot approves of my methods."

"I wouldn't fly that far. Still, it's good thinking—and good bluffing. You'll need both where you're bound."

Dulsey tipped her head. "Is it so ill a place, Pilot?"

Cantra came away from her lean against the wall and took a heartbeat or two to consider.

"The Uncle wants to control all, and there's no one to control him," she said eventually. "That's bad business, as far as I'm concerned. I won't say he spends lives without cause, on account he has a cause. And spend lives for it, he surely does. I wouldn't want to be under the Uncle's care, speaking personally. On the other hand, I've never been trade goods. It could be you'll find him and there everything you want." She paused, weighing it—and decided she might as well say the rest, for what it was worth.

"The Uncle will want you to devote your whole self to his project—for the good of all Batcher-kind, it is, or so he says. You still won't have anything like a free life."

Dulsey bowed. "It has been the observation of this humble person that all lives are confined by birth, skill, and circumstance. It is the degree of confinement only which is at issue." She straightened and gave Cantra a direct look from serious gray eyes.

"If the pilot has no more need of me, I will refresh myself and then prepare a meal."

Cantra inclined her head. "It's your course," she said. "Fly at will."

Another look, this one on the speculative side.

"Thank you, Pilot," Dulsey said and headed back toward quarters. After a moment, Cantra followed her.

He considered erasing the message—and decided against. There was no particular reason for Cantra to take his word for what had happened. Not that there was any more reason for her to take the word of a unknown X Strain commander, no matter how straightforward the report.

The fact that he'd been making free with the ship's comm for some time now would come as no surprise to the pilot or she wasn't the capable, conniving woman he knew her to be. There might be some interest to pay, now that he was out in the open—or not. Either way, she needed the info—and as co-pilot it was his duty to see that the pilot had the info she needed.

So he left the message, carefully trimmed of all IDs saving the commander's name, on the pilot's forward screen and took himself off to quarters for a quick clean-up and a change into ship civvies.

The tiny shower wasn't conducive to dawdling and, in any case, he wanted to be done and clear before Dulsey came in wanting her own refresh. The ship civvies—a long-sleeved black sweater woven from *skileti*, which hugged him like a second dermis, and long black pants made from the same fabric—were warm, durable and easy, with nothing trailing to get caught in machinery or to obscure a section of the piloting board.

He slid his feet into slippers and turned, careful in the tiny space, just as the door chuckled and slid back, revealing his bunk mate.

"Hey, Dulsey," he said easily. "How's the balancing going?"

"Done," the Batcher said, inching into the room. "Pilot Cantra is able with her numbers. She scarce needed my help at all." The door closed and she leaned on it, hands behind her back.

"Pilot Jela," she said, unwontedly serious, even for Dulsey.

"Right here," he answered.

"I wonder, Pilot—do you *trust* Pilot Cantra?"

Now, that was a meaningless question, wasn't it? Except it seemed apparent from Dulsey's face that she considered it full to overflowing with meaning. Well, maybe he'd misunderstood.

"Trust her in what way?" he asked.

Dulsey blinked. "There is more than one way?"

"In my experience," he said. "The Enemy, for instance—you can trust them to obliterate life wherever they find it. Back when I was active, I could trust a certain one of my team-mates to get bored and unruly when we were at leave and take to breaking up the bar by way of relieving his feelings. On duty, I could trust that same team-mate to be solid at my back and not let so much as a flea through to me." He shrugged, considering her. "That wasn't what you were asking, I take it?"

"Not…in so many words, no." She took a deep breath and met his eyes. "I specifically wonder if you believe that Pilot Cantra tells the truth, that she will keep her word and stand your friend, no matter what should happen."

"Ah." He thought about that, then shrugged again. "I think Pilot Cantra has her priorities, in this order: ship, then pilot—and I trust her to act in ways which are consistent with those priorities. So, no—I don't believe she'll stand my friend or at my back, if doing either puts her priorities at risk. No reason she should. Keeping her word? As a general thing, I think she does. On specific topics—again, there're those priorities to add into the equation." He tipped his head.

"Afraid the pilot won't take you to this Uncle of yours, Dulsey?"

She chewed her lip.

"It had occurred to me that it was not to Pilot Cantra's benefit to assist me and that it was perhaps not entirely to her benefit to continue her partnership with you." She sighed. "Unfortunately, these thoughts only concern me when I am absent the pilot's company. In her presence, I find myself thinking it impossible that so likeable a lady would lie."

"I see where this is going." Jela grinned. "You're worried that the *aelantaza* glamour will erode my judgment. Eh? That in Pilot Cantra's presence I'll lose what prudence you might suppose I have, being a once-soldier, and put me and you in danger?"

"You must admit," Dulsey almost-snapped, "that the 'glamour,' as you have it, is a potent weapon in the pilot's defense."

"It would be, if it worked," Jela said soothingly, and showed her his palms, fingers spread wide. "The M Strain—that's me, I'm an M—we're resistant to a long list of the known manipulations, including sabotage by pheromone."

Dulsey's face lost a little of the tense seriousness. "You are immune, then."

Well, no, he wasn't precisely immune. Pilot Cantra *did* smell nice; he'd noticed that. He'd also noticed that she moved like a dancer, possessed a quick and insightful mind, and had a well-developed appreciation of irony. Noticing those things was inescapable, but it didn't follow that his guard was down because he'd noticed them.

He had a feeling, though, that explaining any of that to Dulsey would only put on her the course to worry again, which wasn't useful for any of them.

So—"Immune," he agreed. "Most people aren't, but I've never been confused with most people."

She smiled slightly. "I am much relieved, Pilot Jela."

"Glad to be of service," he told her. "If it helps you, I believe Pilot Cantra goes out of her way to be cantankerous and irritating. She keeps people at a distance that way, where they're less likely to fall under the influence of things she can't control."

Dulsey's eyes widened. "*Can't*...I had not considered that aspect of the matter, Pilot."

"It's worth spending some thought on," he said, and gave her another grin. "Is there anything else on your mind or should I clear out so you can get a shower?"

"I believe my concerns are answered, Pilot. I thank you." She slid along the door until she reached the corner, giving him room to navigate.

"Any time," he said, and slid sideways toward, and then out of, the door.

Cantra was in the tower when he arrived, her arms crossed along the back of the pilot's chair, attention on her forward screen. She'd cleaned up and changed into ship civvies, and he paused for a moment to admire the poised grace of her slim figure.

"Who's Commander Loriton and why should I believe his info?" Her husky voice conveyed something like bored curiosity; her body language suggested that bored had the upper hand on curious. You had to admit, Jela thought, the woman was a pro.

"Commander Loriton's the military officer in charge of the sector where Rint dea'Sord's operations were consolidated," he said easily, walking toward her. "Upon receipt of my report of Ser dea'Sord's activities, Commander Loriton sent a task force to Taliofi."

"And now the task force and Taliofi are gone," she finished, and looked over her shoulder at him. "It says here."

"It does," he agreed.

Cantra straightened out of her lean and turned to face him, her movements smooth and unhurried.

"I don't want to disrespect him, but maybe Commander Loriton's charts aren't up to date?"

"That would account for Taliofi going missing on him," Jela allowed, "but it doesn't quite explain the task force. It goes bad for commanders who mislay ships, see."

"This is what you heard on the port that had you double-checking your info?"

"I heard Taliofi was gone," he said, stopping a comfortable arm's distance from her. "Loriton's memo was in-queue when I opened the comm. My other source confirms."

"The planet was mined, so says this commander." Her voice was expressionless. "What he doesn't say is why and who."

"Who—*sheriekas*," he said. "Most likely *sheriekas*, though it could've been dea'Sord himself. The info I nipped out of his system suggested he had the tech and the ability. Why—to keep the task force from finding what there was to find."

"Taliofi's pretty far in for the Enemy to reach," she said, which was true.

"It's long been identified as one of the nexus points in the undertrade. A good bit of *sheriekas* wares come through Taliofi." He cocked an eyebrow. "Unless Rint dea'Sord didn't trade with the Enemy?"

"Rint dea'Sord traded with whoever and for whatever brought the most profit." Her voice was lazy, like they were talking about things commonplace. "Mining the planet—doesn't strike me as like him. He'd've just pulled back to one of his other worlds and set up ops there," she said lifting a shoulder, "which he might've done anyway, there being no way of telling which particular atoms in a floating cloud of debris happened to have been him."

"Loriton says they got surveillance on him quick," he pointed out. "It doesn't look like he moved on. It does look like the *sheriekas* thought an example was in order."

The winged brows drew together in a frown.

"Example?"

"*We can reach in and crush you whenever and wherever we like,*" Jela intoned, making his voice deep and loud enough to come off the decking like a bell. "*Your world could be next. Fear us.*"

Cantra's lips twitched. "Tactics, is it?"

"Some of that. More, I'd think—and this is me, I don't have access to Commander Loriton's analysis—to destroy whatever was there that we'd be interested in and that they couldn't hope to hide, once the task force was down and searching."

"Well." Cantra glanced over her shoulder at the forward screen. "I didn't dislike the notion of holding Ser dea'Sord too busy to pursue a disagreement. I don't know that I find as much favor with a world going missing for my convenience. Our argument was with one man's ops. Extensive they were, but I have my doubts that Granny Li or Baby Ti took part in or benefit from them."

"Rint dea'Sord was trading with the Enemy," Jela said carefully. "That put him against us—by that I mean those of us who aren't *sheriekas* or *sheriekas*-made—and upgraded his actions from merely illegal to acts of war. He knowingly put that world and its people in harm's way. He knew what the *sheriekas* are and what they're capable of doing. Those deaths aren't yours—or mine—they're his."

The green eyes met his and he caught a flicker of—something, gone too fast for him to read. Her face was smooth and uncommunicative—which he knew by now was the expression that covered her retreat into the depths of herself. He waited, there being nothing else he could usefully do.

"Do the *sheriekas* have a line on this ship, then?"

The question surprised him—and then it didn't, as he recalled her priorities. He gave it the serious consideration it deserved, taking into account the things that Loriton hadn't said, and which his secondary source had touched on.

"In my estimation, the *sheriekas* have seen your ship, but there's no reason for them to have paid special attention to it, or to have it marked for reprisal. It was just one ship among many that happened to pass through Taliofi Yard."

"Not quite," her voice had a slight edge to it. He looked at her carefully.

"If you have info, Pilot, now's the time to share it with your co-pilot."

She sighed, lightly, reached behind her and spun the chair around; dropped into it; and waved him to the co-pilot's station.

He sat, and spun to face her, arms on the rests, deliberately at ease. Almost, he began to project a line of goodwill, but caught himself, and raised an eyebrow instead, waiting.

A corner of her mouth lifted—maybe in appreciation. There wasn't any harm thinking so, at least.

"I ever tell you how I happen to be master of this ship?" Cantra asked. She must have known she hadn't but, if she was in a mood to trade camp tales, he had no objection to that.

So—"No, Pilot, you never have. I'd be willing to hear the story, though. If it can be told."

"It can be told," she answered, her voice taking on a certain, not-displeasing, rhythm.

"For some number of years, I sat co-pilot to Garen yos'Phelium, out of Clan Torvin. Garen being the very last of Clan Torvin—and for all I ever found, the first, too—when she died, the ship passed to me. No secrets there, and as straightforward and by-the-legal as you could ask for.

"Where the story gets murky and interesting, though, is a few years further back again. And the question you'll be wanting to ask yourself is this: Where did *Garen* get this ship? A pilot as fine as you are will have noticed there ain't nothing shabby or second-rate about this vessel. It has some interesting features, not the least of which is that first aid kit back there in the wall."

She sent him a sharp green glance. He lifted a hand, fingers framing, *go on.*

"Right. Now, it's well to remember that Garen didn't say much, and of those things she did say, you'd do well to discount half. Problem was knowing which half, if you take me."

"I knew somebody like that once," Jela said, to show that he was following her. "The war had taken him, shaken him up and pitched him out. He didn't have any context for the experience, couldn't put together what had happened inside his head. Worse luck, he was the only witness to an event of some interest to the military. Intelligence tried to get the info out of him by talking him through it." He raised both hands, showing empty palms. "They used drugs finally and then had the generalists sort out the data-dump. Same problem—how to decide which was hard info and which was an attempt to rationalize what had happened."

"That would've been Garen," Cantra said, and sighed lightly. "What I pieced together—over years, now—from what she said and what she didn't, was that this ship came to her through captain's challenge and that the captain defeated had been actively working for the Enemy, from which he had gotten the ship and all its glittery toys."

Jela inclined his head, not really surprised.

"And what Garen had used to say to me, as often as she said anything, was that the things built by the Enemy, they never forgot who made them, and they called out—and were heard."

He considered that, taking his time.

"There are ways to clean out *sheriekas* homers," he said finally.

Cantra lifted a hand, let it drop. "She cleaned house. Every time we got new snoop-tech, we cleaned house. That would be one of the reasons we have those guns you dote on, instead of the pretties that came with. The first aid kit—that we took our chances with, it being useful beyond the maybe of being heard. But now I'm wondering if there had been *sheriekas* listening at Taliofi—and if they might not have heard *Dancer* singing to them, and known her for one of their own."

He felt the words filling his mouth—the easy, comforting, not-quite-true words that soldiers said to civilians who were asking about things they had no capacity to understand. There was no doubting Cantra's understanding—and she wasn't one to value comfortable lies over hard truths. Tough didn't begin to describe Cantra yos'Phelium, heir to Garen, out of Clan Torvin, whoever and wherever they might be.

Sighing to himself, he swallowed the easy words, his fingers sketching the sign for *thinking...*

Across from him, she leaned back in her chair, relaxing bonelessly, apparently satisfied to await the outcome of his thinking, if thought took him fifty years.

It wasn't quite that long before he shifted straighter in his chair; the movement drew her eyes; and she gave him a comradely nod.

He returned it and sighed, letting her hear it this time.

"The ship itself isn't *sheriekas*-made, though from what you tell me, they had the refitting of it. You're right to think that they would have seeded it with homers and tracers and all manner of listeners. Some would have been visible to our scans—more, as time went on. My 'skins did a scan when I first boarded—that's a military grade scan, and it might be that I have some things on-board that haven't made it out to the Dark Market yet—and the ship scanned clean. Whether we *are* clean..." He snapped his fingers.

"If we could read, discover, subvert or destroy everything the *sheriekas* can, have, or will produce, then we wouldn't be losing this war."

Silence for a beat of five, during which he was very conscious of the weight of a cool green gaze against his cheek. She leaned forward in the chair, hands cupping her knees.

"So you think it's possible, but not likely, that *Dancer* was heard at Taliofi," she said. "And undecided on the issue of whether there's anything in fact to hear."

He inclined his head. "That's a fair summation, yes."

"And we're bound for the Uncle," she murmured, then gave him one of her wide, sudden grins, which was enough to make a soldier's heart beat faster, even knowing that it was more likely than not bogus.

"Does it occur to you, Pilot Jela, that life is about to get interesting?"

TWENTY

On Port
Scohecan

THE GARRISON WAS a scarred survivor of the last war, its cermacrete gates patched and re-patched, the guard shack nothing more than a cermacrete-roofed nook wedged between the front wall and the forward shield generating station.

The generator itself was of slightly more recent vintage—a venerable OS-633, which was, in Jela's opinion, the most stable of the old-style units—meticulously maintained.

By contrast, the security scans were only a generation or two behind current tech. Though they were maintained with the same attention as had been lavished upon the generator, it was obvious that the template library was outdated.

The M Series guards at least were aware of the deficiencies of their equipment. One approached him as he stepped off the scanning dock, holding a civilian issue security wand in one hand.

"Arms out at your sides, legs wide," she said. He complied; she used the wand with quick efficiency; and he was shortly cleared.

"Specialized equipment?" he asked as the second guard dealt with his docs and credentials.

The first guard gave him a look of bland innocence. "Adjunct equipment, sir."

And very likely added into inventory and standard search procedures without recourse to such details as the commandant's approval. Though, if the commandant was also an M...

"Papers in order," the second guard said, holding them out.

Jela received the packet gravely and slipped it into an easily accessible pocket. The first guard spoke briefly into the comm, then turned with a nod.

"Escort's on the way. The commandant has been informed of your request."

"Understood," Jela said, and followed the first guard out into the yard to await the promised escort. Overhead, filtered through

Level One shielding, the sky was a slightly smoky green that re-minded him improbably of Cantra yos'Phelium's eyes. The star was approaching its zenith, and frost glittered in the shrinking pockets of shadow.

Jela sighed; his breath formed a tiny cloud of vapor, then dissipated.

"Pretty planet," he commented to the guard.

She lifted a shoulder. "It's pretty today. Come back during the rains and tell me what you think then."

"I think I'd like it better than no rain at all," he said.

"There's that." She jerked her head toward a two-man scooter heading toward them at a brisk clip. "Here's the escort. Make sure your pockets are sealed. Sir."

The escort was an X, his face bearing three modest diagonal stripes—green-yellow-green—and he appeared to treasure speed above all other things. Jela had scarcely gotten astride the scooter before they were off, blowers howling, dust and frost whipping off the paving in a glittering whirl.

The noise from the blowers made talking at anything less than battle-voice an exercise in futility, and even if conversation had been possible, Jela wouldn't have wanted to break the lad's concentration. It was clear he thought he was very good—and, measured by the ruler of speed and missed collisions, he was. What he was not, was a pilot, though his reactions were top-notch, for Common Troop. It also seemed to Jela that a couple of the near-grazes with walls and other traffic were done not so much in the interest of haste, but to maybe see if a rise could be gotten out of the old M.

Jela sat on the back of the scooter, hands cupped over his knees, swaying bonelessly with the scooter's rhythm and considered whether or no the corporal—the X was a corporal—was entitled to his game. It was a complex question, and he gave it serious thought as they hurtled noisily across the yard, zigged and zagged down a short series of ramps, and roared, with no diminishment of speed into the drop shaft.

There was a boggle at the edge of the shaft. The scooter wobbled and tried to skid—which was the excessive speed, of course. Jela shifted his weight; the scooter steadied. The escort ratcheted the thrust down, killed the lifters—and they were in, stable, upright and falling gently within a pall of blessed silence.

"Appreciate the assist," the X said over his shoulder. "Sir."

That was properly done, thought Jela, and decided that the kid had a right to his fun, as long as no harm came from it, and that the near-disaster with the scooter may have instructed him more than a lecture from an emissary, whose mind ought to be on the upcoming interview with the commandant, anyway.

Silently, he sighed. In his experience—which was now approaching considerable—the upcoming interview could play out along one of two broad avenues, with several minor variations of each possible, to keep things interesting.

Out here in what Pilot Cantra styled the "Mid-Rim," it was possible that the commandant would be willing to hear him—willing to hear his message, and might also know something that would be of use to his mission. The physical shape of the garrison, with its multiply-patched walls, crumbling cermacrete barracks and outmoded security system—it was clear what was going on, and unless the commandant was a fool—which had, he reminded himself, with a certain garrison commander further In foremost in his mind, been known to happen—unless the commandant was a fool, he had to know what this lack of proper care from Command foretold. Had to...

The scooter's fans came on, momentarily deafening, then they were out of the shaft and moving at a tolerably responsible speed down a wide access corridor. They gained the center hall, and hovered over a vacant scooter stand. The corporal scaled back the fans—and Jela was off and on his feet. The kid did all right with the resulting buck and snarl from the equipment and gentled it into the stand before killing the lift entirely, stepping off and giving Jela a terse nod.

"This way, sir."

Across the center hall and down an admin tunnel they went, the corporal moving at a lope, Jela at his heels. At the end of the tunnel was a door; before it stood a guard—another X, with the same green-yellow-green tattoo favored by his escort. She took the corporal's duty card, ran it through the reader, waited for the blue light, and waved them past. The door parted down the center as they approached and they entered the commandant's office at a spanking pace.

Two steps into the room, Jela halted, allowing his escort to go ahead an additional four steps, halt and salute the man behind the desk.

"Corporal Thilrok reporting, sir," he stated crisply. "I have brought the emissary."

The commandant waved an answering salute. "I see that you have, Corporal, thank you. Please leave us."

"Sir." The corporal executed a nice sharp turn and marched out, eyes front. The door sealed silently behind him.

Jela stepped up to the square of rug Corporal Thilrok had recently vacated and delivered up his own salute.

"M. Jela Granthor's Guard, Pilot Captain," he said, maybe not quite as crisp as the kid.

The officer behind the desk smiled slightly. He was a slender man, with sandy hair going thin, and lines showing around eyes and mouth—not a Series soldier.

Jela wondered briefly if the post were a punishment, then lost the thought as the commandant returned his salute and pointed at a chair which had apparently been carved from native wood back in misty memory and had applied all the time since to becoming quaintly decrepit.

"Sit, Captain, and tell me why you're here."

Gingerly, Jela sat, poised to come upright if the chair showed any immediate signs of collapse.

The commandant smiled more widely.

"The locals call that stonewood," he said. "It'll hold you, Captain—and two more just like you, sitting on your knees."

"No need for a crowd," Jela murmured, settling back. Not so much as a creak from the chair. He let himself relax and put his hands on the arms, agreeably surprised by the smooth warmth of the wood under his fingers.

He looked up and met the commandant's eyes—blue they were, and tired, and wary.

"I'm sent," he said slowly, "to give a quiet warning. The consolidated commanders advise that it may be wise for this garrison to have local forces and supply lines in place and at ready, and for the commanding officer to be prepared to act independently."

There was a small silence. The commandant put his elbows on his desk and laced his hands together, resting his chin on the backs.

"The consolidated commanders," he said eventually, with the inflection of a query. "Not High Command."

The man was quick.

"Not High Command, sir," Jela said. "No."

"I see." Another silence, while the commandant looked at him and through him, then a sigh. "You will perhaps not be surprised, Captain Jela, to learn that this garrison has for some time been on short supply. We have not been receiving necessary upgrades—you will have noticed, I'm certain, the security arrangements at the entry point. Requisitioned supplies and replacement equipment simply do not show up. We're already drawing on local resources, Captain. More than I like."

"Understood, sir, and I wish I was here to tell you that your supply lines have been re-opened, and there's a refurb unit on its way to bring everything up to spec." He paused, considering the man before him—the lined face, the tired eyes.

One sandy eyebrow arched, eloquently ironic.

"We don't often get our wishes, do we?" he murmured. "Especially not the pleasant ones. What else are you here to tell me, Captain?"

Good man, thought Jela, approving both the irony and the sentiment.

"The High Command will soon be issuing a fall-back order."

The commandant frowned. "Fall back? To what point?"

"Daelmere, sir."

Three heartbeats. Four. The commandant straightened, unlaced his fingers, and placed his hands flat atop the desk.

"Captain, Daelmere is two levels in, part of the Central Cloud."

"Yes, sir," Jela agreed. "It is."

Another pause—five heartbeats this time, then, in a tone of disbelief, "They can't be abandoning the Arm."

"Yes, sir. High Command's intention is to pull back, cede the Rim and the Arm, and establish a new boundary further In."

Silence.

Jela cleared his throat. "The consolidated commanders," he said, gently, "believe that the proper answer to the increased enemy attacks is to commit the larger portion of our troops to the Arm and the Rim, to stop the *sheriekas* here." *If they can be stopped*, he added silently, and maybe the commandant did, too.

"A temporary headquarters and a new command chain has been established," he added, though that was in the auxiliary information he carried. And if he was not mistaken, this commandant, with his tired face and wary eyes was going to ask—

"This could, of course, be a loyalty test," the commandant said, irony informing his tone. "Which I have doubtless already failed. In which case, I might as well make certain that my dossier is as damning as possible. I suppose you have something to back your claims up, Captain? A name, perhaps, of one or more of these consolidated commanders?"

"Yes, sir. I'm to say, if you ask, that Commander Ro Gayda vouches for me, and that she sends you these proofs." He touched the hidden seal on his 'skins, and withdrew a datastrip. Leaning forward, he placed it on the desk.

"On that strip, you'll find further information and proofs."

The commandant looked at the 'strip, made no move to pick it up.

"They take an enormous risk, do they not?"

Jela moved his shoulders against the chair. "They've taken precautions, sir."

"They send a single soldier, and a datastrip. What if I merely imprison you and ship you to Headquarters in chains?"

Jela grinned. "They send a single M Series soldier under orders to act with discretion and to answer no questions, unless they're put to him by his immediate superior." He nodded at the datastrip, sitting unclaimed on the corner of the desk. "The information might be transmitted. The encoding might also destroy the packet when it hits Command comm protocols."

"I see." The commandant put out a hand, picked up the 'strip. "Perhaps the consolidated commanders are not risking as much as they seem." He sighed, and slipped the strip away into his 'skins.

"Thank you, Captain. Is there anything this garrison can provide to you?"

Now was the time. Jela kept himself relaxed in the stonewood chair and tipped his head to one side, the picture of an M who had private thoughts about what duty required of him next.

"I wonder, sir...There's rumor of an engine left over from the First Phase maybe stashed out here in the Rim somewhere."

The officer's sandy brows lifted.

"Rumor has all sorts of odd and old tech stashed out in the Rim somewhere, Captain," he said dryly. "Most of it, happily, is built from vapor."

"Yes sir," Jela said respectfully. "This particular engine is reported to generate a field that will repel a world-eater."

The commandant smiled. "Well, that would be useful, wouldn't it?" He turned empty palms upward. "I doubt the engine exists, now, Captain. If it ever had an existence beyond wishful thinking, it was likely sold for salvage or scrap hundreds of years ago."

So much for that, Jela thought. Still, it had been worth asking the question.

"Is there anything else, Captain?" The question this time was pointed, and Jela took the hint.

"No, sir." He left the stonewood chair with real regret, and saluted. "With the commandant's permission?"

The officer moved a wiry hand—not a return of Jela's salute, but a flicker of hand-talk: *Information offered.*

"Yes, sir," he said, suddenly feeling a bit wary himself.

"That chair, Captain—remarkable substance, stonewood. When properly finished, it has the rather useful ability to detect a falsehood spoken by the person sitting in it." A second flicker—not hand-talk, but humorous deprecation. "I am aware that M Series soldiers possess extraordinary control of their biologic processes. I merely note that by the chair's report, you have been as truthful as a soldier on a difficult and dangerous mission can be." He smiled, very slightly. "The chair has been in my family for quite a number of years, and I am something of an expert in interpreting its signals."

Jela considered that, then raised his hand, fingers acknowledging: *Information received.*

"Good." The commandant rose and saluted, then leaned forward to push a button on his desk. "Escort will be provided to the gates. Good fortune, Captain."

The textile did something better than she'd expected; the embryos something less. All of which meant that Cantra left the halls with trade coins in her pocket, which she would shortly convert at the currency desk—taking half in cash, and half as a deposit to ship's fund.

She sighed as she made her way through the free trade zone, dawdling a mite down long lanes of tables rented out to day-traders, locals, and others who for one reason or another weren't able— or willing—to do business in the halls.

To hear Jela tell it, their next port o'call would be the Uncle's doubt-it-not former place of business. That being a given, and what came after by no means assured, she was wasting time shopping the free zone for trade goods.

Still, she did shop, in order to give the brain something to do other than dwell on memories that were getting more agitated, the deeper they went into the Rim.

No use thinking about the past, baby, Garen whispered from years agone.

Well, she'd been right about that, not surprisingly. The past was a sorrowful place, littered with mistakes and the dead. Best to ignore it entirely and keep the mind focused on the present and that small bit of the future that could be manipulated.

She came to a table covered with a black cloth, holding a spill of sadiline. The pale jewels blinked and flickered in the yellow daylight, and Cantra paused to admire the pretty little display.

She'd had a sadiline necklace once. All the students in her dorm had one—it had been the talisman of their class, so the instructors had told them.

"Natural gemstones, locally mined," a voice said softly. "Very fine quality."

She looked up into a pair of pale blue eyes, set deep in a face seamed, wrinkled and brown. A red scarf was tied 'round the trader's head, covering one ear, knotted at the back, the tails left to flow over her right breast. The uncovered ear bore a single earring—a large sadiline drop, blazing in the sun.

"The gem is said to improve memory," the trader went on in her soft, sibilant voice, "and to impart fortunate dreams."

Cantra glanced down, extended a finger and lightly stirred the scattered gems. "Maybe you'd sell more," she said, "if you said it dulled memory, and gave dreamless sleep."

"But that would be untrue." The trader said, gently reproachful. "And the gem would take its revenge."

Revenge. Cantra gave the gems another stir, lifted a shoulder and looked back to the woman behind the table.

"Not in the market today," she said.

The trader bowed her head. "Fair profit, Trader."

You saved my life, Garen, what can I do for you? There must be something...

Her own voice, young—how long since she'd been that young?—echoed out of her back-brain. She remembered the argument. She'd been raised to pay her debts. Raised to believe that all debts *could* be paid, more often than not in cash. Not an understanding Garen shared, exactly, though she'd been a stickler about paying her own.

You just be the best co-pilot you can be, baby. That's all. And if somebody should bribe the luck and take ol' Garen down—you do them the same, then. That'll make us square. 'til then, ain't no sense frettin'. I got everything I need or want.

Which might've been true, or might not've—Cantra had never quite figured that. And then what should Garen do but kill her own self and no way for Cantra to clear the debt.

Damn if she wasn't doing it again.

She took a deep breath and forcefully thrust both memory and regret out of her waking mind, putting her attention on the table she'd almost passed by.

The hand-lettered sign propped along the back edge read, "Oracle Odd Lots" and scattered on the scarred surface were several ceramic objects in various shapes—ship, ground car, and a unfeatured square that looked like a standard logic tile, all about the size of her palm.

Cantra paused and picked up the ship, smiling at the smooth feel of the thing against her skin.

"Learning devices," the woman behind the table said, her accent as hard as the sadiline merchant's had been soft. "If the trader will make of her mind a blank screen while she holds the item in her hand, she may have a demonstration."

Learning devices? Well, why not? Intrigued, Cantra curled her fingers around the little ship and with the ease born of long practice smoothed the surface thoughts away from a portion of her mind. The rest of her—what the instructors had called The Eternal Watcher—did just that, alert for any suspicious move from the vendor.

In the space between her ears, she heard a whispering, saw a shimmer of something, which solidified into the familiar pattern of a basic piloting equation, the last line missing. Cantra concentrated, trying to project the final sentence into the equation, saw another shimmer—as if she were looking at a screen—and the line appeared, as solid as the rest.

In her hand, the toy ship purred, imparting a feeling of warm pleasure.

Well.

Not without a pang, she placed the toy back on the table.

"That's something unusual," she said, looking at the woman's smooth face and bland eyes.

"They are specialty items," the other trader allowed. "We sell them in lots, from three to three dozen."

They were oddities, and it came to her that they *were* bound for Uncle, and that it might play well, her arriving with a gift.

"What's the price for three?" she asked.

The trader named a sum—much too high. Cantra answered with another—much too low. And so it went until the thing was done and the three toys—one of each shape on offer—were packed snug together in a gel-box.

Cantra took her leave of trader with a nod and continued on her way, a little brisker now, with less attention to the wares on offer.

Time was moving on, and Jela due to meet her at the administration hall pretty soon, now.

TWENTY-ONE

Spiral Dance
Twilight Interval

WHEN THE DOOR was unlocked, the quarters were surprisingly convenable. When the door was dogged open, the quarters were quite comfortable.

He relaxed there now, Dulsey bunked below him, both quietly occupying themselves while the ship moved—quietly and without turmoil—through what Cantra had styled "the long twilight."

He'd been working with his log book, bringing it up to date. It was...comforting to write out his notes and observations by hand, though some entries were necessarily in a code he held in common only with his commander. He had his doubts that the book would ever make it back into the hands of his commander, but it might. It might. And in the meantime, it was work and a balm to an M's active nature.

Below him, Dulsey was reading her share of the flimsies the captain had allowed crew to print out to pass the time.

Cantra was also reading in her quarters. If he craned his head one way, he could see her open door, and, beyond, a long leg stretched out on the bunk. If he craned his head the other way, he could see the tree in the pilots' tower, dreaming its own dreams.

Those dreams sometimes woke him from his own sleep cycle, as if a distant sun had come over the mountain just *now*. It had worried him for a while—the how and the why of it. Lately, he'd taken a more philosophic attitude. Ship time, tree time, what mattered it? Time passed—that was the fact no one escaped.

Dulsey seemed not to notice that his day wasn't quite in synch with the ship's. Cantra surely did notice, as she noticed everything that bore on her ship's state. She didn't remark it, though, which Jela knew she wouldn't do, unless and until he affected the ship's necessities.

Log brought up to date, Jela stowed the book and the pen, and reached for his own share of flimsies, which he'd anchored under his knee.

He didn't immediately begin to read though. Instead, he leaned his head back and listened to the sounds. The comforting, usual sounds of a well-maintained and ship-shape ship, her crew at ease and easy within the group.

Oddly enough, the easiness of their odd and randomly formed crew reinforced one of the tenets apparently espoused by the *sheriekas*—that "old humans" were herd creatures.

As a crew, Jela thought lazily, they were hardly a rousing illustration of the "old humans," when between them none had or could have met anyone approximating mother or father.

Still, he and Pilot Cantra *might* be said to have a mother and father; even if no one could ever have come forward to claim them. Met or unmet, there were progenitors of sorts.

Dulsey, though, was a full custom build, her and the rest of her Batch pulled from human genetic parts for a specific job, for profit.

That thought turned in his mind a moment, and he wondered briefly what motivated the *sheriekas*, for surely the universe that he knew and moved through was motivated by profit. Pilot Cantra's considerable skills were surely the result of desire for profit, as were Dulsey's. His own existence had been ruled by others, largely those who also obeyed others...and those others looking for little more than a quiet place to spin their webs and turn their profits.

Now, though, it might be that the profit motivation would finally fail the herd of men. When men like Rint dea'Sord traded with the Enemy, with thoughts of their own profit uppermost. When those Inside interests who ordered the High Command declared that their profit—their *lives*—were of more importance than the profits and lives of those who lived elsewhere...

The instinct for profit, thought Jela—personal profit. That instinct was maybe not a long-term survival trait.

The herd instinct, on the other hand, apparently permitted Pilot Cantra, who had not too long past locked him and Dulsey in and out at whim—to lounge, reading, while they did the same, in pursuit of goals that might transcend simple profit. Though it was never, Jela told himself, well to assume that Cantra's motives were either simple or apparent. And to remember that, if ever a woman held to her own profit above all else, it was Pilot Cantra—which led back to the question of what profit Cantra saw for herself in their present operation. Was it after all the herd instinct propounded by some ancient *sheriekas* philosopher, rising above the instinct for personal profit?

Well. Best not share that question with Dulsey, suddenly bereft of the life-long company of her Pod, nor with Cantra, who would surely laugh. The tree, now, might enjoy the puzzle, but it was presently in its more restful state, perhaps awaiting a dawn light years distant, so he forbore from passing it on.

TWENTY-TWO

Spiral Dance
The Little Empty

IT WAS QUIET in the piloting tower, both pilots at their stations, and the tree, Jela thought, at its. There was a tickle in the back of his mind, as if some intelligence beside his own was surveying the sparse starfield. If the sight awoke consternation in that other auditor, he didn't know it—though he wouldn't have been surprised. He'd been on the Rim more than once, and still the lack of ... *clutter* ... awed, amazed and intimidated him.

Pilot Cantra, now. If she felt awe or amazement, she kept both far away from her face. It wasn't to be expected, Jela thought wryly, that the pilot would be intimidated by anything.

From the jump-seat came the sound of small and shaky in-breath. Dulsey, at least, was impressed.

"Are we in the Deeps, then, Pilot?" she asked softly.

Cantra lifted a shoulder, her attention more than two-thirds on her board, which might at least indicate due caution.

"Say, the Shallows," she murmured. "When we come out of the next transition, then you'll have the Deeps." She finished fiddling with her board and released the shock straps.

"Rimmers, they call this the Little Empty," she said. "We'll take ourselves a pause here. Pilots'll do a complete systems check. Dulsey, if you're willing, a good meal to go into the next phase on would be welcome."

Truth told, it was that next transition that was giving Jela a bit of worry. The pilot might be enjoying her joke, pretending they weren't sitting in the Deeps, but he only had two beacons on con and some small star clusters on the screens, bright and hard against the velvet...

"I am more than willing to provide a meal, Pilot," Dulsey was saying. "Now?"

"Give us time to do the checks," Cantra answered, coming up out of her chair in a stretch. "Call it two ship-hours. Ace?"

"Ace," Dulsey said.

"Good. I'm also going to need eyeballs on the clamps and a diagnostic on the can system. You take that on, while Jela an' me get busy here."

"Yes, Pilot." Dulsey unstrapped and slid to her feet with a will, moving out of the tower with the determined stride of a woman with work to accomplish.

Cantra sighed and shook her head and gave Jela a look out of amused green eyes.

"Hope the Uncle's ready for this," she said.

"Dulsey's a hard worker," Jela answered. "If the Uncle's surviving 'way out here, he has to have a corps of hard, smart workers with him. She'll fit right in."

"Uncle's a bit further out, yet," Cantra said, leaning over her board and initiating a system-wide check. "Found this area too crowded, is what I heard." She straightened and gave him another look, this one straight and stern.

"Get your check running, Pilot. After, I'll thank you to recall that you were going to be showing me what those guns you dote on can do."

"Understand," Jela said, his big hands resting lightly on the edge of the co-pilot's board, "that you'll have to unlock the system all the way. I'll need complete access. I'll also thank you for sharing your codes so I won't have to use the system override."

She'd expected him to need gut-level access, but it was still hard to get her fingers moving in the sequence that would open the guns to him and send the codes to his work screen.

"Thank you." That was said soft, like maybe he had an idea how much of a struggle habit had put up against need-to-know.

"We'll begin," he said, of a sudden not soft at all, "with a complete system check, an inspection of records..."

She frowned, reached to the board—and pulled her hand back. *Need to know,* she reminded herself. *You need to know your guns, and this is the man to teach you.*

Which didn't mean he had the right to snoop her info.

"Right, Commodore," she said with asperity. "I'm guessing you'll need serial numbers, purchase dates, shell counts, and..."

He sighed, and she figured he was going to come all high-brass now.

Instead, though, he nodded.

"We'll want all of that, if you can give it to me. Then we can look and see what needs to be done to optimize things, and what rounds we might need to load up on."

Cantra sighed. If he'd yelled, she'd've yelled back. But him being reasonable...

She sighed again.

"This ain't a cruise ship, Pilot; it's a Dark trader. You think I keep copies of my receipts all nice and tidy for the port cops to look over at their leisure?"

There was a brief bit of tight silence—then he sighed, and shook his head, and said, quiet, "I take your point. Let's have some target practice, then."

She kept waiting for it, but he never did turn the brass on. He did insist that the best target practice they could get was from using a couple sets of what he called "underpowered rounds" as targets.

"I'm curious, Pilot," he said while she was in the midst of rough calculating in her head to back up the ship's computer, "how long you've had these Jaythrees and Jayfours on hand?"

The "Jaythrees and Jayfours" in question were currently loaded in Gun One, which he was using for his own, while she was firing general purpose tracking rounds with only a minimum of on-board guidance from Gun Two. It looked like he was practicing, too, because it was obvious he was calculating like mad and doing something special and antsy with the settings...

"You're making it hard for me to concentrate...," she muttered. He fidgeted briefly, and she sighed, giving up for the moment. "Which I guess is about right for combat conditions..."

He nodded, then fired the rounds; Cantra watched for his finger mark to indicate that she should start tracking, her mind maybe a quarter on his question.

"Garen bought 'em when she bought the guns," she said finally; "I never used them 'cause they was listed as close-in combat support in the docs, and I never had need." She moved her shoulders, and glanced at the side of his face.

"I'm a smuggler," she said, her voice sharper than she'd entirely intended, "not a pirate. The guns're defense."

The finger move came; she started the ranging, saw in her head that the shells were in a highly elliptical—no, make that a parabolic—orbit so tight it might even graze the distant star, would likely, in fact, fall right into it…

From the co-pilot's section, she heard a small sound, almost as if Jela was humming, which was nothing new, though why he was inspired to hum or sing now…but she could hear him busy on the keyboard, tapping queries or commands in a real hurry.

There! The computer and her calcs had reached an accord! She fired, let the computer take the next shot, fired the next on manual, let the computer have the next, and sat back to watch the tracks on the computer screen.

Even with Jela's rounds being "under-powered," it would take quite awhile for the interception, if she'd been accurate enough to—

Jela wasn't humming so much as growling. She turned her head to look at him.

"Can you tell me," he asked in a low, gravelly voice, "can you tell me *exactly* who sold you those shells and the manuals?" His face was so absolutely neutral that she felt dread rising through her, despite her training. Jela mad—really mad and out for balance—wasn't a sight she particularly wanted to see, she realized. Not that it would be smart to let him know he'd managed to unnerve her.

"Hah!" She shrugged carelessly and waved her hands in a casual *not my job.*

"Will the ship's log give us any idea?"

Her hands moved themselves; indication—*perhaps.* And expanded—*Maybe, low probability.*

"Garen was pretty careful about some stuff she didn't want me to know about…"

He looked away from her, fingers moving on the query pad, and spoke as if from a distance.

"At first opportunity—and you will remind me if I fail in this, please, Pilot! At first opportunity we will replace your documentation for these guns. We will also inspect—two sets of eyeballs so we're sure—the munitions themselves."

He paused, sending her a look out of hard black eyes.

"Try to remember where these shells came from, Pilot. Any clue would be good."

The man was serious, and—not mad, no. Something else, stronger and sterner than mere anger.

"Pilot, there's cause?" she managed, bringing the Rim accent up. "They out of spec?"

He rubbed his face with those broad hands, like he was trying to wipe away sweat, or a sight he wished he hadn't seen.

After a sigh he looked at her straight on again, not quite so hard.

"Jaythrees are rounds one might use to deny a landing ground to an enemy. A landing ground one wishes not to occupy for oneself. In addition to a fairly lethal explosive charge, they release a fine mist of plutonium powder. Jayfours..." He rubbed his face again.

"Jayfours are binary cleansers. The gas they release is... inimical...to most air breathing creatures and plants. In the presence of oxygen it will deteriorate to mere poison in about twelve days, and to an irritant in another twelve."

"Depending on the winds, one could cleanse half a continent."

Cantra blinked, swallowed and had cause to be briefly grateful for her early schooling.

"The docs?" she said, matching him quiet for quiet.

"Apparently someone wished to make you and your Garen into household names. Or else your seller, too, was tricked." She looked to the screen, where her shots, and the computer's, raced after the deadly payloads, and then back to him

"You aimed them for the star then..."

His hands fluttered into hand-talk.

Best course, she read.

And again—*best course.*

TWENTY-THREE

Spiral Dance
Jumping Off the Rim

TARGET PRACTICE WAS over, and so was the meal, eaten companionably together. The pilots were strapped in at their stations, while the third member of the crew sat in the jump-seat.

"All right, Dulsey," Cantra said, her eyes on her board, "I'll need those eighteen numbers now."

Dulsey stiffened, relaxed, shrugged diffidently.

"Pilot, I do not have eighteen. The numbers I was given come in three sets of twelve."

Jela, damn his hide, laughed. Cantra sighed.

"Let's have 'em, then," she said resignedly, and waited while Dulsey activated the jump-seat's tablet and tapped her info rapidly in.

They came up on the pilot's work screen—and the co-pilot's too—three neat rows of twelve, and anything more like plain and fancy gibberish Cantra hoped never to see.

"I'd guess," Jela said quietly, "that you'll be able to construct something reasonably familiar to you from those numbers. Maybe even something—" he wiggled his fingers in the pilot-talk for *comfortable.*

Comfortable. Right. Fuming, Cantra fed the numbers to the nav brain, not that she expected it to be able to do much with them—and she wasn't disappointed, damnitall.

"Easy for you to say," she snapped at Jela. "But out here, numbers ain't quite so casual as they are in the heart. Down there you got lots of reinforcement, including some places you just can't go, 'cause it'd take too much power, and lots of experience and references to let you know what's possible and what's not. Out here, almost any number'll get you *some*where. Twelve to five says most of where you can go is even safe. Sort of."

While she was talking, her fingers were busy shuffling and re-shuffling Dulsey's pack of thirty-six.

"Well, if we pile 'em up backwards and split 'em in two, we get one coord that'll take us into somewhere just a bit inside the wavefront of a gas pulse pumping out an X-ray beacon. So I guess we'll discard that one. If we stack 'em straight and divide in two, we get more gibberish. But..."

On a guess, she re-shuffled the digits the old way, the one that'd been real popular with the Dark traders along back years ago and—yes.

"If we do it this way," she said aloud, being careful not explain exactly *which* way, "we get two sets of honest coords, and one looks a lot like something I think I recognize." She spun her chair to face Dulsey.

"So, did you get any more of that key? Any way I can confirm? I might expect an engineer to know we was missing something here."

Dulsey sat up straighter—a good trick, considering how upright she kept herself as a matter of course.

"Pilot, understand that the information was not all given to th— to me. One of my Pod had the first set of numbers, which I be-came party to. The second set was mine to keep. The third...I broke a seal to get. It was assumed by our source that if we came, we would come all together."

"Hah!" Jela said. Cantra threw him a glance and a nod.

"Maybe," he said to Dulsey, "there were other numbers scat-tered among the rest of your Pod?"

But Dulsey shook her head.

"No, those were all we were given." She looked carefully at Jela, and continued almost inaudibly. "The others would not have been able to conceal the numbers and so were not given them."

Cantra grinned. "But you, not having all the numbers yourself, thought you ought to, and was ready to go with or without?"

Dulsey closed her eyes briefly, sighed, and faced her. "I cannot apologize for surviving," she said, and despite the brave words, her voice carried shame. "Nothing I did risked my Podmates, and there was nothing else I could have—"

"Stop!" Jela held up a hand. Cantra looked at him with interest, Dulsey with concern.

"Dulsey," he said, "I believe you. I believe you did the right thing. We've all become soldiers in this life—you as much as me or Pilot Cantra, here. You acted to preserve resources, which you have done; and you behaved with honor. You have nothing to be ashamed of. Your right to be alive is not in question. What Pilot Cantra must judge—as pilot and captain of this ship—is the safety of the routes you've given her. This is for the good of the ship, and the good of the crew."

Not bad, thought Cantra, admiringly. In the jump-seat, Dulsey shook her head again.

"I understand," she managed, voice shaking a little. "Truly, Pilot Jela, if I had more information, I would gladly—but these are the numbers. I have nothing else."

Cantra sighed. "Were you going to steal a ship, then? These numbers would've got you killed straight off, if you didn't know—"

"No, Pilot." Dulsey faced her again, chin lifting. "We were a group, before the bankruptcy, and in the group were pilots who had experience..."

Cantra lifted a hand, palm up.

"Dulsey, I'd be lying if I said I wouldn't steal a ship, given necessity. I'm thinking Pilot Jela's of the same opinion, is that right, Pilot?"

"That's right," Jela said comfortably.

"I wonder, though—how wide-spread was this attitude in your group? Were you going to depend on stealth, or on surprise?"

Dulsey's face hardened.

"They were depending on accident, coincidence, and rumor. With the application of reasonable energy some time ago, we could have all been gone."

Cantra barely avoided smiling. The girl wasn't a fool. Indeed, *indeed*, she hoped the Uncle was ready.

"I understand," she said, pitching her voice easy and calm. "In which case, I'll put the ship's back-up brain on the problem of a proof for those two sets of coords. In the meantime, since we're all strapped in and well-fed, let's get ourselves out to the Rim."

She was going to transition now? Jela looked to his board, in case he'd missed—but no.

"I've only got two beacons, Pilot," he said, keeping his voice gentle.

She was concentrating on her board, feeding that coord set to the "back-up brain," he supposed—whatever that might mean— and he didn't expect any answer, which would have been more informative than the one he got.

"Have faith, Pilot Jela," she murmured. "Have faith." And as if on-cue in some story-play, the nav-brain twittered, and a third set of coordinates marched across the center screen—Rathil Beacon, that was. They still needed one more, to balance the equation, and insure a safe and uneventful transition.

"Rathil's up," Cantra breathed beside him, and, louder—"Dulsey, strap in."

There was a tickle at the back of his mind, tasting something like a query—but he was too busy grabbing the coords off the screen, doing the math in his head and coming out with nothing good.

"Pilot," he insisted, keeping it gentle, "we're still down a beacon."

She shot him a look out of bright green eyes.

"When you don't got four, you fly on three," she said. "Hang on to your board, Pilot. This might be rough."

Her hands danced across her board with that light, sure grace he admired so much, and before he could draw a breath or begin to think an answer for the tree—

They hit transition.

And they hit it hard.

Radial velocity, he was thinking.

The math was a soothing balm against the frenetic vibrations the ship and crew were experiencing. A flash image inside his head showed that the tree knew what an earthquake was, and what it might do.

But no, radial velocity was not the whole answer. Part of it was the gravitational effect—a tidal effect almost—with the galaxy edge-on and the ship prying itself into *otherspace* against millions of stars and only the halo of diminishing dark energy a balance at this distance.

Cantra sat the board calmly, hands poised a moment, then stabbing a button, poised again, flipping a toggle—

They were out.

Cantra lounged at ease at the board, well aware that both Dulsey and Jela were much surprised.

Jela, for his part, recovered quickly, with a hand signal more to himself than her, Cantra thought—a long, slow *smooooothhh*—his only public comment.

Dulsey, cleared her throat.

"The pilot enjoys an excellent rapport with the ship," she said seriously; "and the ship enjoys excellent numbers!"

Cantra laughed.

"The ship goes where we send it, right? Just I do know some places to take off a bit and some places to add a bit to the equations. Them equations was done for the average ship on an average course somewhere down in the midst of that mess—" She pointed to the representation of the galaxy on the side monitor—"and if you look close, we're about as far as you can get from as much as you want to count of it and still say we're in the thing."

The Rim accent had come up hard all by itself, along with the side-drawl that helped make Rim cant both distinctive and muddy to some of the light-lappers who thrived down to the center of things. *Well, it comes with the territory*, she thought, and didn't fight it.

For effect she centered the galactic image…and sure enough, as the image shifted the blue dot representing their position moved way off to the left side of things before disappearing. She'd known that was going to happen, since the arm they were in was the longest of the three arms, and the most twisted. Some folks with a lot of time on their hands figured that *this* arm was what was left of an intergalactic collision somewhere on the far side of time. The truth was that once things got into the billions of years she, for the most part, lost interest because—as they said out here—her fingernails grew faster than that.

"If you would be so kind to keep the scale but center on our position, Pilot?"

Cantra looked up at Jela's voice, caught the notion that he'd apparently made the request first in finger-talk, and she'd missed it.

Smart of him, actually. No good could come out of directly interfering with a pilot staring down into that much of a think.

"Same scale?" she asked.

"Indeed."

And so now it was that there was all this near empty on the left-side of the screen. The arm they rode twisted back into the density of stars like a snake, coiling for a second strike.

Against that she upped the magnification a dozen clicks, and now there were a few smaller clusters yet showing out in the Deeps, and a couple places where stars had escaped from the embrace of others by a nova or supernova which had dashed into the darkness trailing gas, and the arm loomed big and important, like it ought to for folks and suns who spent their lives in it…

She upped the magnification again, and now—now they could see why it was called the Rim—that it was an actual rim of gravity and colliding grains of dust and gas. And since this arm was half-again as long as the others, this was the arm that spun itself against the intergalactic medium uncleared by the previous passage of the other arms, and here was the interplay of magnetic fields with the bow wave of light pressure, wild gas, and...

"The Uncle..." Dulsey's voice wavered a bit and ended on a gulp.

For all that, Cantra allowed as how she was doing better than most folks she'd seen when faced with the fact of the Rim, for who expected it to ripple with a glow of purple so deep you'd swear it wasn't there, and who expected—having learned about years and parsecs and light years and such—to find that there were things so much beyond them that mere billions was a kidstuff toy.

"The Uncle," Dulsey tried again, "lives—out there?"

"Almost there," Cantra said cheerfully, and shot a glance to Jela, who gave her his blandest face to look at.

"Now, we'll see how good those numbers are, Pilot," she said. "Ready for adventure?"

He smiled for that one and nodded. "Ready."

Transition was quiet this time, drop-out smooth and easy.

"Pilot," Cantra called, "shut down the running lights, the auto-hail, and active radar..."

His fingers flickered—*rock*—and she answered, though he hadn't seen her look his way.

"I know, but we'll take the first ten ticks as free and clear 'cause if they ain't, we should be able to slide in there anyway..."

"Pilot," he acknowledged, began to deactivate the systems, adding the dock-ranging equipment, and—

"...and anything else you think we ought to do to be quiet..." she said, over a sudden, head-rattling series of thumps, which would be the rocks, of course.

"Good thing sound doesn't transmit," he muttered, and Cantra laughed.

"It'll pass," she said—and that quick it was done, leaving behind nothing but smooth silence and the sounds of normal ship systems.

"Video!" Cantra called, but he was ahead of her, clicking on the infrared scanners just ahead of the video feed, hand poised above the meteor-repellor shielding switch.

The scanners began registering objects far away enough to be minor concerns; nothing close. Despite this, or perhaps because of it, Cantra spun the ship quickly on its axis, pressing Jela's aching left leg into the webbing.

He grimaced slightly; he hadn't noticed that complaint come on line, but there it was: transition was starting to affect his aches as much as dirt-side weather could.

A flitting image came to him—a tree, it must have been, as viewed from another, leaning into a prevailing wind.

That would be about right, he thought, *got my roots set and have to weather things as they come at me.*

That thought was swept away with the blink of light on the board—

Anomaly!

The infra-red scanners were showing multiple changing heat-sources...

"More rocks," he commented.

"I got 'em too," came Cantra's laconic reply, "and if we didn't I'd say we was in trouble. If my memory's at all good, rocks is about all there is out here, 'cepting the Uncle and his kindred."

There was time now for Jela to consider where they were. Cantra had the ship's brain doing a long-range comparison and analysis of the rock-field, looking for objects that she'd seen once before. Not that she was personally trying to identify this or that bit of stone or metal, but she had the ship trying to match images the former captain had been wise enough to capture and store in deep archives.

The process was time-consuming, and would have brought Jela to the edge of distraction had he not had both a practical and an academic interest in what the edge of forever looked like from the outside.

Where they had come from was not precisely visible now, with threads of dust and gas in the galactic disk obscuring where things had been multi-thousands of years ago and the more immediate pebbles, rocks, and gassed out-chunks of protocomets acting as a dulling screen to both vision and scanners attempting to use line-of-sight.

But around them, other than the thin scatter of what was—on galactic scale—negligible sandy left-overs, there was nothing. At this distance from the core there were no individual stars to act as beacons, and all the other galaxies were too distant to be seen as anything more than point sources, if they could be seen at all. The galaxy they orbited faded to a distant nebulous smudge...

Jela imagined all too vividly what it would be like to be suited up or in a canopied singleship here now, and felt the involuntary, perhaps instinctual shiver. There was no darkness like the dark of emptiness.

Cantra was muttering again, which Jela knew ought to have worried him, but it mirrored what he would have done had he been sitting in the pilot's spot with old information and a mission in peril for it.

He'd taken con for a short while as she grabbed a quick break and some tea, returning as renewed to his eyes as if she'd had a three day shore leave.

Now she was back at work, digging among files and archives that only she could access. That she added a running commentary was her choice, and if it helped the pilot think, why then, he'd seen pilots with worse habits.

He glanced at her—not for the first time since transition—wishing that he'd had her match in any of his units. She had an economy of movement and a wit as well, and for all her complaining there wasn't a bit of it that was an actual whine.

Too, he admitted, there was an underlying energy in her that was quite pleasing. Perhaps it was the training and background she so vociferously denied, perhaps it was the pheromones...

He wiped that thought away, or tried to, for there was no doubt that the night they'd met she'd been on the prowl for more than dinner company. Certainly if things had moved in that direction—and without the interruptions that had come their way—they might have had a good tumble. For his part, as someone willing to appreciate irony, metaphor, strength, energy, and honor...he knew he could have found some energy to share.

That this would not have been against orders he knew, for certainly, the troop understood that duty required nurture and recreation. And certainly, one could feel a certain amount of affinity for a pilot of excellent caliber who was also good when it came to hand-to-hand and had a clear eye and quick understanding with regard to who were enemies.

Hadn't she stood at his back? Guarded the tree? Was she not now engaged in a rather fine—not to mention out of the way—balancing of accounts in delivering Dulsey to a safe zone? Indeed, Cantra could be counted as comrade in truth...

From somewhere, a distant, whispery scratching sound, barely on the edge of perception. Jela started, blinking the momentary abstraction away, and sent a quick glance to the tree...

An image built inside his head, of a distant dragon in the sky, drifting away as the breeze brought haze...

"Dust," said Cantra lazily, and the image faded. "Carbon dust, with a bit of extra hydrogen. And that's a good sign, Pilot. You be ready to sing out when you got something to look at. Kind of amazing that a veil like this can hide the Uncle's little quarry for so long."

In the jump-seat, Dulsey stirred, eyes bright.

Cantra laughed, and even her laugh was loaded with accent, as if the weight of piloting had worn through a veneer.

"S'alright girl. Your numbers worked. Likely, though, if you'd have come in piloting yourself you'd have had to beg to be picked up, which is how the Uncle prefers things, I gather. Us now, we're going to be ringing that door chime on our own. Keep watching."

And as if Cantra had a cloud-piercing telescope to show her the way, the scans began to register, and video began to show distant objects vaguely outlined against the nebulous presence of the galaxy.

"Straps tight, now," she said, "each and all of us."

He'd thought once before that Cantra flew like a bomber pilot, and now, as the aches built up in his knee and his admiration grew, he was sure of it. He made a mental note to check on the training given to *aelantaza*.

The thing was that—within this strange space—her reactions were absolutely sure, and absolutely perfect. She threw the craft through crevices in the dust, around rocks and coils of rocks, sliding this way and that...for in this realm beyond the galaxy, action and reaction held sway, with but a nod and a twitch required to overcome the microgravity of the dust clouds or the trajectory of free-moving rock.

On the screen was the destination, a rather forbidding tumbling conglomeration of dust-stuck rock not even big enough to become a globe under its own gravity. The course to the target was irregular, with projected and suggested approaches appearing on-screen, being selected or deselected, or assigned back-up...

Jela watched and sat second, hands and eyes mostly in synch with the real action, though from time to time Cantra's choices were idiosyncratic at best. In some ways he was reminded of training games and mock-cockpits, where one could play a ship with abandon...

Here though, abandon was not what she was displaying. Here, Cantra was showing honed skill. If she flew it like it was a game, then it was her game, and not his. But then it was her ship, and she the one who had actually been to this unlikely bit of *here* before.

"Pilot," she said suddenly, "what we're going to do is to fly formation with this thing for a bit. There'll be another one around for us to look for, not a lot like it..."

And with that, she rolled the ship slightly and slung it around, slowly matching pace with the object—asteroid, dead comet, dustball...

Once they had achieved "formation," Jela saw it was too bright and speckled to be a mere dustball. In fact, it showed signs—

"See there," Cantra said carefully, her eyes on her screens, "we got a dozen flat surfaces or so here. One of them ought to be mostly red in visible spectrum, assuming we can shine enough of a light on it. It's been worked a bit, and it'll be obvious if we got the right rock. That's gonna be your job, and I'll tell you when to go to light. Same time, you're going to bring them guns up full, just in case."

"Pilot," he replied, and found the controls for the tracking light. They felt odd to his hands, and he doubted that he had touched anything like them since his long-ago days as a pilot trainee.

What kind of rock could have been "worked a bit" out here? Something else to add to his...

The spectralyzer flashed, and the infra-red too. There *was* an anomaly.

"Light it up!" Cantra snapped, but he'd already hit the switch, gotten the range—

They were following the rock formation, its weird slow tumble immensely weirder under the ship's spotlight. The rock looked like it had been sliced and grooved, as if whole slabs had been taken away. There was a flash of color—greenish—then gray, more gray, and—

"Red!" he said, exultantly.

"Right," Cantra agreed, lazily. "We got the right rock. Now all we gotta do is sit back and listen real hard. I'm punching the bands up now. Get me a directional on it if you can. "

There was a signal...so faint as to barely budge the meter. A chirping sound, in identical sets of three, filled the bridge.

The ship's computer struggled with the signal for some moments before Jela sang out.

"Got it!" He copied it to the pilot's screen, and heard her laugh, soft.

"Right," she said. "I'll just mosey us along in that direction for a bit. When you get a change in those bird-noises there, Pilot, just put the docking lights, and docking shields, and docking radar on." She sent a quick glance over her shoulder.

"Dulsey, this is your last chance to change your mind."

"I wish to be with the Uncle," the Batcher said firmly.

Cantra sighed, soft, but plain to Jela's ears, and her fingers formed the sign for *pilot's choice*. He signaled agreement in return.

"To hear is to obey, then," Cantra said to Dulsey. She cocked at eye at him and grinned.

"We're sitting on Uncle's back porch. We'll just knock on the door and see if anyone's to home. Whenever you're ready, Pilot."

TWENTY-FOUR

Rockhaven

"SHUT IT DOWN," Cantra said quietly.

Acknowledgment from the Uncle's pile of rocks had finally been received after an annoyingly long—perhaps calculatedly long—wait. Now they sat almost against the rock wall, tied to the haven by two light ship tethers and their own extendable gang tube to one of four observable access ports.

Jela paused with his hands on the board and considered her profile.

"Pilot? No need for all of us to go down. I can stay, if you want it, and keep the home fire burning."

She turned her head, giving him a steady, serious look, with nothing wild or irritable about it.

"Shut it down, Pilot."

There wasn't any arguing with that glance of calm reason, and Jela turned his attention to an orderly shutdown of his board, the while pondering the fact that it was impossible to argue with Cantra when she was unreasonable, and impossible to argue with her when she wasn't. Convenient. He'd also come to notice that she wasn't unreasonable nearly as often as she let it seem that she was.

The system lights went down one by one and in good time the ship was off-line, saving life-support.

Out of the corner of his eye, he saw her nod, once, then put her finger on the release and let the webbing snap noisily back.

"Up, up!" she said, spinning her chair around to grin first at him, then at Dulsey. "Best not to dally and make our escort irritable."

He mistrusted the grin, just like he mistrusted the total lock down of the board—in all his experience of her Cantra had never locked the board down tight. That she chose to do so here, at a docking she plainly distrusted was—notable. Coupled with the mandate that all three of them step off for a stroll through an asteroid habitat controlled by questionable forces, it became out-and-out worrisome.

On the other hand, there *wasn't* any arguing with her—she was ship's captain, and the only one among them who had previous experience of the Uncle.

Carefully, then, he unstrapped and stood, finding Dulsey already on her feet, face shadowed.

"Second thoughts, Dulsey?" Cantra asked.

Dulsey's chin came up and she met Cantra's eyes.

"Not at all, Pilot."

The grin this time was more amusement and less artifice, by Jela's reading—which didn't make it any more comforting.

"I'm glad to hear you say that. The Uncle I knew, he placed a certain value on boldness. For what it's worth."

Dulsey bowed slightly. "I am grateful to the pilot for her advice."

Cantra sighed, then abruptly waved a long hand toward the door and presumably the hall beyond.

"The two of you get on down to the hatch. I'll catch you in six."

Jela felt the hairs at the back of his neck try to stand up all at once. If this was a vary *now*—but he couldn't for the life of him see how, with the ship shut down into deep asleep, so he grinned, nice and easy, for the shadow across Dulsey's face, and nodded at the door.

"After you."

"Yes, Pilot," she said, subdued, turned—and turned back.

"Pilot Cantra."

The winged brows lifted over misty green eyes.

"What's on your mind, Dulsey?"

A hesitation, and then another bow, this one very deep, and augmented with the stylized gesture of the right hand which roughly meant *I owe you* according to particular civilian signing systems.

"The pilot has acquitted herself with honor," Dulsey murmured in the general direction of the decking. "I am grateful and I ask that she remember my name, should there come a time when my service might benefit her."

Jela held himself still, already hearing Cantra's pretty, sarcastic laughter in his mind's ear—

"Stand tall, Dulsey." Her voice was firm, and if it held any grain of sarcasm, it was too fine for Jela's ear to detect.

The Batcher straightened slowly, and brought her eyes again to the pilot's face. Jela, watching that same face, found it...austere, the green eyes bleak.

"*A person is worth as much as the value of their debts,*" she quoted softly. "You've heard that said, Dulsey?"

"Yes, Pilot. I have heard it said."

"Then you want to take some time to sort over who I am and what I'm about in the general way of things. Most would hold that an honorable freewoman shouldn't ought to devalue herself by standing in debt to the likes of me."

Dulsey smiled.

"A honorable freewoman must be the judge of her own worth, Pilot. Is this not so?"

Cantra's mouth twisted, unwilling, to Jela's eye, toward a smile.

"You'll do, Dulsey. Now the two of you get outta here. I'll meet you at the hatch in six. Ace?"

"Ace, Pilot," Dulsey said serenely, and turned to the door. "Pilot Jela?"

"Just a sec," he said, catching a ghost-view of dry sand behind his eyes.

He returned to his station, pulled open the hatch and removed a sealed water bottle from the pilot's emergency provision cache. Cracking the seal, he walked toward the tree, heard a murmuring inside his head, saw a flicker of visuals he couldn't quite sort...

"I know it's not much," he said, softly, dampening the dirt over the roots. "We're not intending to be long. You keep a good watch and let me know if anything odd happens while we're away."

Bottle empty, he straightened, reaching up to touch a couple of the higher leaves. Taller than he was, now. Not that that was such a trick.

There was a sudden quick rattle, along with image of a pair of dragons nipping at a tree limb to grab...

"Fair's fair, I guess," he said, catching the fruit pod as it snapped itself from the branch and fell.

"I hate to bother you, Pilot," Cantra's voice carried a payload of sarcasm now. "But the sooner we're gone, the sooner we're back and the less time your friend there needs to pine for your return."

Another image formed in back of his eyes, very precisely: A small dragon sitting on the grass at his feet, exercising its voice loudly—and even more loudly as a sudden fall of leaves came down over its head.

Jela laughed.

Behind him, he heard Cantra sigh. Loudly.

"Now what? It's telling you jokes?"

Still grinning, he turned, resealing the bottle absently.

"Pilot, the tree is learning irony from you."

Bland-faced, she considered him, then spun on one heel to address the tree in its pot, and executed as high-flying a bow as he'd ever seen, complete with a showy swoop of the left arm.

"It is my pleasure to be of service," she said, then straightened in a snap. "*Both* of you mobile units—outta here. Now!"

"Pilot Jela?" That was Dulsey, sounding nervous, and right she probably was.

"I'm behind you," he said, though he'd have given his accumulated leave, assuming he had any, to see how Pilot Cantra was going to gimmick the board. The tree's gift he happily consumed before they reached the lock.

The dock was just like she remembered—rock, rock and more rock—the floor unevenly illuminated by the white glow from several cloudy columns of candesa, the ceiling lost in darkness, from which the light, so-called, woke an occasional spark—like a star glimpsed through drifting debris.

At the base of the ramp stood a figure in light-colored 'skins, blond hair cut close to his head. The utility belt around his substantial waist supported a holstered needle gun.

Behind her, she almost heard Jela's watchfulness click up a notch, like maybe a man didn't have the right to wear a gun on his own dock. Feet still on the gang tube's ramp—technically still on her own ship and not yet on the Uncle's terms—she raised her hands to shoulder level, fingers spread. The status lights on the cuff of her 'skins thereby brought into view glowed green-green-green. So far, so good.

The guard sniffed, but didn't ask her to turn out her pockets, which was just as well.

"Names?" he snapped.

"Cantra yos'Phelium," she answered, giving him mild on the theory that it would probably annoy him. "Pilot-owner of *Spiral Dance*, just like I told Admin."

"You didn't tell Admin who else."

"That's right," she agreed, taking no visible offense. "Reason being they're here under my protection. We have business with the Uncle. I'd appreciate a pass-through."

The guard sneered. He had a good face for it, Cantra thought, critically.

"What makes you think he's here?"

"Only place I knew to look," she allowed. "Fact is, I didn't expect to find anybody here, excepting maybe a guard or two. So, if the Uncle ain't here, I'd appreciate a message sent, telling him Cantra yos'Phelium has something that belongs to him and where does he want it delivered?"

"What do you have?" The boy was going to go far with that kind of attitude.

Cantra sighed.

"You the Uncle nowadays?"

His face tightened. "No."

"Then it ain't your business," she said, all sweet and reasonable. "Send the message or pass us through—that's your piece of the action. Not so hard, is it?"

Another glare, which Cantra bore with slightly pained patience, then a sharp jerk of his head.

"This way." He turned and strode off across the dock without waiting to see if, or how, they followed, which just about shouted out the information that there were other watchers—armed watchers, make no doubt—in the shifty shadows.

Behind her, she felt Jela go up another notch on the wary meter, nor did she blame him. Glancing over her shoulder, she wasn't particularly surprised to find Dulsey directly behind her, with Jela's reassuring bulk bringing up the rear.

Protect the civilian, she thought, and deliberately didn't think what that made her, taking point like a damn' fool.

Their guide was apparently leading them toward a blank stone wall. Just before his nose hit rock, the wall split, the halves sliding apart. He strode briskly through, Cantra a couple steps behind.

She passed over the threshold, felt a shift in the air currents, and looked back. The doors were reversing themselves too quickly, sliding smoothly to shut just behind Dulsey—

Jela, at the rear, brought an arm up and pushed.

The right door panel faltered in its smooth slide toward the center. Jela moved forward, not hurrying, and under no apparent strain. When he was through, he dropped his arm and the door proceeded down its track.

The side walls were closer now—a hallway, as long as you didn't mind the ceiling still out of reach of the light—standard glow-strips, and none too many of them.

Cantra glanced down at the status lights on her cuff. Dark, they were, which she'd expected, but still wasn't pleased to see. Well, it'd been a long shot. Usual rules applied.

They passed through two more rock doors, crossed a couple of corridors and finally took a right turn onto another. Abruptly, there was rug over the rock, the glow-strips became whole panels and the ceiling, revealed at last, was a faceted vein of rose colored quartz. There were green plants there, too, like she remembered—maybe the same ones for all she knew—flanking a portal ahead.

That next door didn't open at their guide's approach. He put his hand on the plate in the center, breathed a word Cantra thought might have been his name.

The door slid aside, and the guard stepped back, waving at her with an impatient hand.

"The Uncle will see you."

The room—it was the same room, with its shelves of neatly rolled books, the tables groaning under their burdens of tech, art, logic tiles, and best-to-not-knows. Brocades were hung to hide the rocky walls, and the footing was treacherous with layers of carpet and pots and what-not holding plants.

There were more plants than there'd been, the last time she was here—some held in wall sconces where they might benefit from being closer to the ceiling lights, others were shown off in tiered stands. Might be she was more alert this time, but it seemed there were far more flowers than she remembered. Certainly the room smelled as much of flowers as of rock and people.

A man sat at one of the tables, heedless of the languorous blue blossom hanging a couple hand spans over his head while he carefully fit tiles into a logic-rack. He glanced up as they entered, smiled and rose to his feet.

Sweeping 'round the table, he came forward to meet them—a young man, tall and lean, his long dark hair swept into a knot at the back of his head and fixed with two porcelain sticks. He was dressed in a crimson robe heavy with embroidery, with here and there a wink of gold—smartstrands.

"My dear Pilot Cantra!"

His voice was deep and musical, the hands stretched out in greeting a-glitter with rings inset with strange stones. His eyes were a cool and calculating gray; his face beyond all reason familiar. "How delightful to see you again!"

You heard rumors, when you ran on the edge. Rumors of devices and techs that made possible what maybe shouldn't be within grasp. You heard rumors—but hearing and seeing were two different things.

Cantra felt her stomach clench, and her throat tighten. Reflexively, she bowed, low and slow—no more nor less than what a simple pilot owed a man of power and learning—and by the time she straightened her stomach and her face were under control.

"Uncle," she said, keeping her voice nothing but respectful. "You're looking well."

He folded his hands before him and inclined his sleek head.

"I thank you. I feel well. Certainly more well than when last we spoke."

She drew a deep breath. It would gain nothing to tell the man before her that they had never met. The smartstrands—she figured it was the 'strands; *hoped* it was the 'strands and not some other, more terrible technology—made it seem to him that he was the very Uncle she had known, with that Uncle's memories and manner of speaking. Even the same voice, made young and vibrant.

She drew another breath, careful and close. Best to get her errands over with, get back to *Dancer*, and get *out*.

"I believe you told Karmin that you have something which belongs to me?" The Uncle said delicately.

Right. Errand number one.

Forcing herself to move smoothly, she turned and motioned Dulsey to step up.

"Belongs here, she says, and I don't say she's wrong."

The Batcher threw her one half-panicked gray glance before obediently going forward to make her bow, so deep it looked like she was trying to sink into the rock floor beneath the patterned rug. Behind her stood Jela, legs braced, hands at his sides, face specifically noncommittal. Errand number two.

Dulsey straightened, cleared her throat. Said nothing.

The Uncle smiled, wide and delighted. Reaching out, he captured her hands in his, the rings winking balefully in the pale light.

"*Welcome*, child," he said gently, looking down into her eyes. "What is your name?"

She swallowed, and seemed to wilt just a little, her fingers clenching the Uncle's hands like her last hope of aid.

"Dulsey, sir," she whispered. "Dulsey..." and here Cantra thought she might be adding her Batch number...but if she was, she swallowed it, and stood up straight and bold.

"Dulsey," he murmured caressingly. "You are home now. All your cares are behind you."

"Thank you, sir."

"What is your specialty, child?"

She took a deep breath and it seemed to Cantra that she stood a mite straighter still.

"I'm an engineer," she said, and there was no mistaking the pride in her voice.

"An engineer," the Uncle repeated, and smiled wider. "We are *most* happy to welcome you." He squeezed her fingers and let her go, folding his hands against his robe.

"We will send you to the infirmary, first, so that the tattoos may be removed. Trust me, you will feel immensely better when that is done. Then—"

"Pardon me, sir," Dulsey interrupted, fingers suddenly busy at the fastening of her sleeve. "But the tattoos were erased on ship."

The Uncle lifted an elegant dark brow and looked to Cantra.

"Were they, now?"

Cantra shifted her shoulders—not yes and not no, ambiguity being the best defense against the Uncle. According to Garen.

"I can't see 'em," she said. "'Course, I ain't got a deep reader."

"Of course not." The Uncle swayed a slight bow. "But I do."

"Thought you might," Cantra allowed. She had a feeling she might want to glance over at Jela, standing quiet and ignored just inside the door. She fought the urge, figuring it was none too soon to break herself of the habit.

Dulsey had her sleeve shoved up past the elbow now, showing a pale, unscarred arm.

The Uncle considered the offered appendage for a moment before he stepped to a table laden with weird tech, gesturing her to follow him.

"Step over here, if you will, child. It will be the work of a moment to discover if you are in truth free of the marks of your slavery." He picked a long tube up from the general clutter and thumbed it on.

It began to glow with a vivid orange light.

"Extend your arm, if you please," he said to Dulsey. "You may feel some warmth, but the process should not hurt. If you experience any pain, tell me immediately. Do you understand, Dulsey?"

"Yes, sir," she said, eyeing the tube with more interest, Cantra thought, than dismay.

"Very good. Now hold out your arm. Yes…" Delicately, he ran the reader down Dulsey's arm.

From the corner of her eye, Cantra saw Jela shift—and fall again into stillness.

"Ah," the Uncle breathed. He lifted the reader away, thumbed it off and put it back in its place among the clutter.

He looked at Cantra over Dulsey's head.

"You will pleased, I know, Pilot, to learn that the tattoo is indeed gone. Completely."

"Good news," she said.

"Indeed." He moved his eyes, and added a caressing smile for Dulsey.

"Since you have already been relieved of your burden, you may proceed to the second phase, child." He turned toward the door and raised his voice slightly.

"Fenek?"

The door opened to admit a dainty dark haired woman with eyes the color of the flower hanging over the Uncle's worktable.

"Sir?"

The Uncle placed a kindly hand on Dulsey's shoulder.

"This is our sister, Engineer Dulsey, Fenek. She requires clothes, a meal, a hammock and an appointment with the teams coordinator. Please assist her in obtaining these things."

Fenek didn't exactly salute, but she gave the impression of having done so. "Yes sir!" She positively beamed at Dulsey and held out a slender hand.

"Come, sister."

The Uncle gave her a gentle push. "There are no bounty hunters here, Dulsey."

She turned her head to stare at him.

"You knew?"

He smiled indulgently. "Certainly, I knew. We pride ourselves in getting all the latest news and rumors, child! You'll see."

He waved then, and a trick of the smartstrands—or of some less-savory technology—cast a pale sparkling gleam toward the side of the room. "Now, go through the house door there with your sister Fenek and tend to your needs."

"Yes," Dulsey said, and stepped forward.

Fenek dropped back, holding the door open with one slim arm. On the threshold, Dulsey turned, and held out her hand.

"Pilot Jela."

He blinked, as if suddenly called to a realization that he wasn't the pile of rock he'd been imitating so well, and put his hand out to meet hers.

"Dulsey." He smiled his easy smile, squeezed her fingers lightly and let her go. "Remember an old soldier now and then, eh?"

"Yes," she whispered, and turned.

Cantra raised a hand and smiled, hoping to forestall another episode like the one on the ship. Not smart to let the Uncle think there was divided loyalties in his house.

"You take care, Dulsey," she said, deliberately casual.

A pause, then a brief nod—*Good girl*, Cantra thought. *Bright as they come.*

"Yes. And you take care, Pilot," she replied, and turned, walking between a pair of tall purple plants with delicate pink fronds, and through the door, Fenek following.

TWENTY-FIVE

Rockhaven

THE DOOR CLOSED, and the Uncle turned, the smile slowly leaving his face, which was fine with Cantra. She could have done without the intent, we're-all-believers-here stare, which had been a feature of the former Uncle, too, and even more unsettling on the face of a young man.

But now his eyes lit on the plants Dulsey had just passed and he went to one of them, only half looking at her as he groomed it, letting the pink fronds flow over his hand as he made tiny noises and dropped bits of browning leaf to the carpet.

"I wonder, dear Pilot Cantra," he asked over his shoulder, "do you believe in fate?"

"Fate?" *Now what?* she wondered—then figured she'd find out soon enough. "I don't believe there's some megascript that makes us all act in certain ways," she said carefully, not wanting to move into the scans of those things it was better not to think on too close— or at all.

"Ah," the Uncle breathed. "Well, you are young and doubtless have been busy about your own affairs." He finished with the plant and turned to face her full again, left hand flat against his breast.

"I, however, am old, and I have seen sufficient of the universe to consider the existence of that script, as you have it—probable. For instance—"

His left hand was suddenly outstretched, fingers pointing at a place approximately halfway between her and the silent Jela, rings a-glitter.

"You, dear Pilot Cantra. I had never expected to see you again. You must tell me, how has the receptor flush served you?"

"No ill effects," she said.

"Good, good. I am delighted that our little technique provided long-term satisfaction. We had been using it for some time in aid of those in our community with need, with no ill effect. However, we had never had the opportunity to test it on a natural human. The lab will be pleased. But, as I was saying—I had no expectation to ever see you again, my dear, and yet here you are come to me by your own will, in company…"

The Uncle smiled gently, not at her. She risked a glance out of the side of her eye. Jela wasn't smiling back.

"Companied…" the Uncle fair crooned, "by a True Soldier. Nothing could be more fortuitous!"

Well, that sounded ominous enough for six. And Jela was decidedly disamused. Funny 'bout that, Cantra thought abruptly. Along the course of their time together, she'd certainly seen Jela use force, and he wasn't shy about making those he deemed would be improved by the condition dead. But he was rarely out of temper. This cold stare into the teeth of the Uncle's smile was—worrisome.

Like she needed something else to worry about.

"Well," she said brightly, drawing the Uncle's eyes back in her direction. "I'm glad you're pleased, Uncle. I wouldn't say us being here proves fate so much as wrongheaded willfulness on the part of certain pilots. It does put me in mind of a thing, though." She touched the seal on her leg pocket and drew out the gel-pack.

"Saw something a few stops back that I thought might interest you."

The light eyes considered her.

"You've brought me a gift?"

Cantra smiled. "That's right. I was raised up to be civilized."

The Uncle laughed. "You were raised up, as you care to style it," he said, sweetly, "to be a dissembler, a thief, and when need be, a murderer."

No argument there. Cantra let her smile widen a bit. "Where I come from, that's what passes for civilized."

He allowed her to approach and took the packet from her hand.

"Indeed." He ran his finger under the seal, and the pack unfolded, revealing the three little ceramic toys.

Behind her, she heard Jela take a long, careful breath.

The Uncle stood as if transfixed, long enough for Cantra to begin to think that she'd made a bad mis—

"Why, Pilot Cantra," the Uncle purred. "You have managed to surprise me." He looked up. "Where did you get these?"

"A couple stops back," she repeated, agreeably. "Teaching devices, is what the trader told me."

"Did she, indeed?" The Uncle used the tips of his fingers to turn the ceramics over. "And did you test them, to be certain that they were what was advertised?"

No reason not to tell the truth. "I tested the ship," she admitted. "It prompted me for a basic piloting equation. Emitted praise and warm fuzzies when I gave it."

"Ah. And the others?"

"I didn't test the others," Cantra assured him. She'd meant to, but in retrospect the interaction with the toy ship had been more disturbing than pleasant—a good deal like the Uncle himself.

He gave her a long, penetrating look, which she bore with open-faced calm.

"The directors breed marvels, indeed they do," he said softly. "And you the last of your line, more's the pity." He lifted the gel-pack on his palm, and looked past her, to Jela.

"You have seen objects like this before, I think, sir?"

"I have," Jela said, and it was the same hard, perilous voice he'd used when she'd showed him the first aid kit. "They're not toys. They're *sheriekas*-made and they're dangerous."

"Not necessarily," the Uncle crooned. "It is true that they mine information from the unwary and send back to the Enemy when and as they might. However, we find that minds trained to a specific agenda may not only gain more information from the devices, but can feed them—let us call it *misleading*—information to pass on—to the confoundment of the Enemy." He smiled gently. "Which I am certain that one such as yourself would allow to be worthy work."

"The *sheriekas* are outside of our knowledge," Jela replied forcefully. "We barely understood what they were when they retreated at the end of the last war. Now…" He moved his big shoulders. "The best thing to do with those devices is destroy them." He sent a quick black glance to Cantra. "And send the name of the trader who sells them to the military."

The Uncle *t'sked*, turned and put the gel-pack down on the cluttered table.

"I would have thought the military would take a bolder stance," he said, meditatively. "It is well that we have taken this work to ourselves, I see."

"I'd think the work best left alone," Jela said forcefully. "Unless you have a reason for wanting a world-eater's attention."

"One might," the Uncle said with a smile. "One might. Think of what might be learned about the nature of the Enemy, should one of their mightiest engines be captured!"

He raised a hand suddenly. "But stay, I don't wish to raise such controversial topics so soon in our partnership."

Cantra felt a flutter along her nerves, and deliberately reposed herself to stillness.

"Partnership?" asked Jela.

"Surely." The Uncle smiled, cold enough to raise a shiver, though the room was a thought over-warm for Cantra's taste. "I am offering you a place, M. Jela. Here, your talents will be appreciated and well-rewarded."

Well, thought Cantra, specifically not looking at Jela. *This might work out all by its lonesome...*

"No," Jela said, shortly.

Or maybe not. She cleared her throat, the Uncle's gaze moved to her face.

"Truth is, Uncle," she began, and looked casually at Jela where he stood, solid and reassuring and—

Lose it, she snarled at herself. *He ain't your partner—never was—and while he sat your co-pilot, that ends now, and good riddance.*

Jela shifted at his post, his face tightening, eyes widening and focusing somewhere beyond the Uncle's room.

"Tell your operative to stand away from the tree," he said sharply.

The Uncle tipped his head. "Your pardon, M. Jela? Do you address me?"

"I do. Call off your operative. *Now.*"

"What operative?"

Jela didn't bother answering that, only said again, in a voice nowhere near patient—

"Tell your operative not to touch the board and not to approach the tree. There's nothing hidden in the tree, and if she doesn't stand back, I can't tell what it might do to protect itself."

Intruder on the ship. Cantra gritted her teeth, glanced down at the tell-tales—still jammed, blast it to the Deeps. *Dancer* was on her own, and if the fool did touch that board...

"Your operative is regarded as a threat, Uncle. Your operative is in danger."

"Come now, you can hardly be in touch with your ship, which lies quietly at dock. For our own security we smother all ship communications..."

"I'm not in communication with our ship," Jela said then. "All my comm systems are dead in here, and I'm betting the pilot's are the same, or she'd have triggered something unpleasant already, being a lady who isn't fond of strangers on her ship. However, I am in communication with the third crew member, who stands within striking distance of your operative, and who is prepared to act."

An alarm blared, and the Uncle's robe briefly blazed golden as the smart-strands took receipt of info.

"What's that?" Jela asked, perfectly calm.

The Uncle took a hard breath, and smoothed his hands down the front of his robe, eyes closed.

"Hydroponics alert," he murmured, eyelids fluttering. "An anomaly in the release gasses. These things happen, which is why we have alerts."

"Ah," said Jela with a grim smile.

Cantra concentrated on keeping her breathing even, though her lungs wanted to gasp at the notion that the tree—Jela's damn' tree, that he insisted told him jokes and that he talked to like an old friend or comrade-in-arms...

Well, why not? she asked herself, and took another deep breath, specifically not thinking about what was going to happen if the Uncle's snoop tried to gimmick the board—

Jela casually tapped his wrist chronometer.

"You're the one who has to pass the word. Or take your chance of surviving whatever comes next. It's all the same to me."

It wasn't quite all the same to Cantra, but there wasn't anything she could do except wait, and swear, and hope—

The plant beside the Uncle shivered, and the pink fronds began to curl, as if closing for the night, or...

For a moment the Batch leader was clearly nonplused; he went so far as to peek at something half hidden in his sleeve.

He glanced then at Jela, who was studying the plant with a sort of detached interest as the fronds coiled toward the core.

The Uncle raised his hands, rings glinting, and spoke into the air.

"Chebei, please do not touch either the piloting board or the tree. Return to your station and inform Arin that we are found to be poor hosts."

There was quiet then. Cantra breathed concentrated on breathing calm and easy, the while keeping one eye on Jela—who was still watching something beyond the Uncle's study—and the other on the Uncle, who appeared to be in like state.

"Thank you," he said abruptly to the air, and sent a sharp glance toward Jela.

"Chebei has cleared the ship, touching nothing save those things she had already touched. Do you confirm, M. Jela?"

No answer for a heartbeat...two...

The wayaway look faded, the broad chest expanded, and the shoulders rolled.

"Confirmed," he said, and sent Cantra one of his more unreadable looks.

"If you would please to pass my compliments on to your crew member?"

Jela's expression was unreadable, but his eyes went distant. A fleeting grin passed over his features, and then his face was like stone again.

"Understood, Uncle," he said then, looking not at the Batcher but at Cantra.

"Business concluded, Pilot?"

No and yes, Cantra thought. Though she wasn't such a fool as to refuse Jela's back-up on a port that had gone from risky to downright dangerous.

"We did what we came to do," she said, giving him a smile. "If you got nothing more to say, then we'll just ask the Uncle for a guarantee of safe passage and be on our way."

The Uncle pressed a beringed hand over his heart, his face showing an expression of pained gentility which was notable for its sincerity.

"Guarantee of safe passage? Dear Pilot Cantra, surely you don't believe anyone here would seek to harm you?"

She smiled, seeing his sincere and raising it to wounded innocence.

"You did send a snoop onto my ship," she said, as mildly as possible.

The Uncle looked pained. "A mere inspector, child. We only wished to assure ourselves that nothing overtly dangerous had been—

inadvertently, of course!—brought to dock at our poor habitat. And
we see you are as careful as ourselves and could not be more pleased.
We count your visit among our most pleasant in decades!"

Right.

Cantra gave him another smile and nodded to Jela.

"Let's go."

He swung forward a step, clearing her way to the door, and
coincidentally putting himself between the Uncle and that same door.
Much good it would do, with all the smartstrands the man was
wearing. On the other hand, she didn't think it likely that the Uncle
would try to detain them. His habitat was fragile and he couldn't
know what they were carrying by way of plain and fancy explosives,
for instance, nor what that vegetable on the bridge might take into
its...branches...to do if Jela came to harm.

That being the case, there wasn't any need to be rude in their leave-
taking. She mustered up a bow, just as respectful as she could manage.

"Uncle, good fortune to you."

He smiled and inclined his head.

"Pilot Cantra, you must come and see me again. In the meanwhile, fair fortune to you."

He tipped his head.

"M. Jela, may I not convince you to enter my employ?"

"No," Jela said shortly, and the Uncle smiled, soft and regretful.

"How," he said gently, "if you were to know that even now it is
whispered that soldiers are being bidden to forsake the emptiness
of this arm for the comfort of the center? You, however, can still
indulge your soldier's soul. You can be here, at the edge of decisive
action, where matters of importance to all humankind will be determined. You may be a hero to Dulsey and all her..."

Jela shook his head, cutting off the Uncle in a way that likely
wasn't too polite.

"This was a waystop for us," he said, "a balancing of accounts
with someone who risked her life for us. I've been a hero and
found it far more trouble than you might think. I'll continue traveling with Pilot Cantra and we'll all part safely."

The Uncle seemed to take it well, all things considered and, if he
thought the warning a bit plain-faced, he hid it well. "Then I will bid
you, too, farewell and fair fortune." He dropped back a step.

On Cantra's right hand, the door slid open.

TWENTY-SIX

Rockhaven

THERE WAS NO Karmin waiting to guide them to the dock, which absence set Cantra's trouble-meter to twittering.

Jela came up on her right side, angling his shoulders awkwardly, though it wasn't so cramped as that, his fingers dancing at belt level: *Stay close, stay alert*, he signed, and passed on, taking point.

So, she wasn't the only one who was worried.

Dutifully, she fell in behind, which gave her a fine view of attentive shoulders.

The Uncle hadn't exactly promised that safe passage Jela'd given as his expectation, nor it wasn't like him to be disinterested in a telepathic talking tree, much less whatever other goodies Chebei had happened to take note of during her tour. The fact that the board was rigged for oblivion, she didn't figure would give him more than pause. And truth told, there were likely enough pilots 'mong free and equal Batcher-kind that the rig wasn't so certain a thing, giving them time to study on the problem.

The more she considered it, the more nervous she got and by the time they made it back to the hall where the doors had tried to cut Jela off from the rest of them, her palm was outright itching for the feel of a gun.

She fought the inclination, for the reason that she didn't know what the station might employ by way of safeguards and that getting fried by a watch-bot for pulling a hideaway wasn't likely to improve her mood any.

Ahead, the big doors were sliding back, and she let herself breathe a quiet sigh of relief. Another few minutes and they'd be aboard *Dancer*, and fortified, if not precisely safe.

Jela was through the door, and she was right behind him—

A shadow moved in the near dimness. Cantra paused between one step and the next, but the movement—if it had been a movement—didn't repeat.

Jumpy, she scolded herself and moved on—

Toward a door that was very nearly closed, with Jela on the far side. She threw herself into a run—and there was noise from the shadows now, the sounds of boots moving fast.

Swearing, she jumped, got a shoulder through the narrowing crack, felt the pressure of the doors grinding against her chest and her back...

She squeezed through somehow, popping out into the docking area with a yell.

"Ambush!"

Weapon in hand, Jela spun, taking his attention off the number of armed people between him and *Dancer's* ramp.

Behind her, she heard the door work.

"I'll hold 'em!" she yelled at Jela, snatching one of her hideaways out of its pocket and thumbing the charge. "Get to the ship!"

The last thing she saw before her own problems overtook her was Jela charging the half-formed line of attackers.

Something hissed past Cantra's ear and she spun, gun rising— and sent a dart into the attacker's shoulder. Bad shooting: She'd been aiming for the throat.

His fellows raced past him and Cantra fired again, missing all available targets, as near as she could tell.

Another dart went by her ear, but the two leaders were on her now, and the gun was useless.

She fell back, slipping the slim glass blade from its special pocket and dropped into a crouch.

The first was over-confident—a kick and a thrust took care of her. The second was timid—a kick sufficed there, just in time for the arrival of the rest of the six, and it was a brawl then, with knives and knucklebones and a nasty something that filled the air with crackling waves of force.

The owner of that particular toy tended to stay well back, not wanting to catch her mates in the field. Cantra had a singed sleeve out of her near encounter with an energy-wave and didn't want to risk another.

The others were keeping her busy, and it was starting to look bad—then she saw an opening, slid in with the knife, and came out slashing, which took both out of the dance with one move, snapped off a shot in the direction of the energy-bearer and spun.

Between her and her ship were four prone bodies. Further on, there was Jela, visible through the transparent walls of the gang tube, wasting no time.

Behind her, she heard a shout and looked over her shoulder to see the door standing open and a dozen more combatants racing into the docking area.

She got her legs moving and bolted for the—

A wall of fire slammed into and through her.

She screamed, scarcely hearing her own voice through the crackle of energy and dropped to the stone floor, rolling. Her 'skins—her 'skins were on fire, which wasn't possible, and she was gagging on acrid smoke, rolling—and then not, as she was hauled to her feet by one arm.

Karmin grinned, his grip on her arm lost in the other, larger pain, and hefted his knife, the point darting toward her face.

She jerked back, stronger than he'd been expecting. She broke his hold; the knife notched her ear; and she fell heavily to the floor. She was baking, suffocating; she could feel her dermis crisping in the heat of her 'skins destruction.

*Jela will have made the ship by now...*she thought with absolute clarity.

There was a gurgling sound, quite near at hand, followed by yells, shouts, curses, and a peculiar whistling. Cantra was kicked—and kicked again where she lay.

The heat from her 'skins seemed somewhat less—or her nerve endings were overloaded; she opened her eyes—and took in the sight of Pilot Jela, three down and bleeding, and himself wielding something that to her dazed sight seemed to be a long ceramic whip.

As she watched, Karmin leapt back from the hiss of the whip, then feinted in, knife flashing—

The whip snapped; the knife and a finger fell away.

Karmin shrieked and whirled aside, the remainder of those still standing following. Jela let them go, and dropped to one knee beside her.

"Can you walk?" he asked.

"...not sure..." she managed in a voice ravaged by smoke.

"Right." he said. "I'm going to carry you. It's probably going to hurt."

It did.

She passed out.

TWENTY-SEVEN

Rockhaven Departure

CANTRA HAD LOST consciousness and that was good, since the best he could do for her was a rough-and-ready shoulder-carry.

The Batcher recon squad was off the field, which was good as far as it went; and he was willing to bet it went less far than he'd like.

They were in. The hatch was down and sealed against trouble— and that was very good, though an immediate lift was in order.

Which was a problem, given the pilot's state and the fact that the board had been closed—and likely gimmicked and he had no idea what she'd done.

Well, he'd figure it out or he wouldn't. First order of business was his pilot's health. He didn't want to think too closely about the damage she'd likely taken. The energy generated from the shorted circuitry and support systems would, he hoped, have mostly dis-charged outward, and the fact that she was still breathing was an indicator that her injuries weren't too serious.

He hoped.

The hatch to the piloting tower stood open, the tower itself on dims. The board was showing a sprinkling of orange stand-bys. The tree sat snug in its corner, leaves still.

Jela received an impression of wariness as he swept past on his way to the cubby and the *sheriekas* regeneration unit.

His boot broke the beam, the door slid back, releasing an eddy of cooler air. Cantra over his shoulder, he sank to one knee by the side of the chill black box, and triggered the release.

The hatch rose silently to reveal the unsettling green-lit interior. Jela got Cantra down on the pallet as gently as he could, straightened her, and got to his feet as the hatch began to descend—

Stopped. And reversed itself. The interior green light shifted to an even more unsavory violet, and it didn't take a Generalist to parse the fact that the unit found the offering not up to spec.

Horrified, he bent forward, fingers on her throat. If she'd died...

The pulse under his fingers was sluggish, her breathing shallow and raspy—but she was alive.

"Object to pilot 'skins, do you?" he muttered, but it made sense. The blasted remains of the internal systems might still interfere with whatever process the regenerator used to effect its healings.

There wasn't much room to work, and he had a bad moment when it looked like the magseals had fused, but he managed to get the 'skins off her. She moaned once or twice during the process, but mercifully didn't float back to the here-and-now.

He worked fast—if she went into shock, he'd lose her quick— and tried not to think about the damage he was doing. Not all the energy had dissipated outward. Not nearly all. Tears rose and he blinked them back.

"You've seen worse," he told himself, shakily, and kept working.

Behind his eyes—an image: A halfling dragon stretched along a bed of dry leaves, its long neck at too sharp an angle, one wing twisted and vane-broken, the wide eyes dull.

"No," he said, out loud, and the image faded.

It was done. He threw the blasted 'skins to the deck and knelt there, unable to look away from the ruin of his pilot until the hatch came down and locked her away from him.

Another image formed behind his eyes—thunder heads boiling over the distant shoulders of mountains, lightning dancing between the clouds.

"On my way," he whispered and got his feet under him.

He approached the orange-lit board, and frowned. It had been locked all the way down to deep sleep, on the pilot's own orders, the last time he'd seen it.

There were a number of ways to gimmick a piloting board, some more fatal than others. He wished he had a precise reading on how much Cantra had distrusted the Uncle. He sat himself down in the pilot's chair, engaged the webbing and studied the situation.

The status lights showing stand-by were main engine, weapons, and navigation brain. The combination tickled a pattern at the back of his untidy mind. He closed his eyes and tried to visualize a blank screen, but instead of a clarification of the thought, he got thunder heads again, augmented this time with an evil, edgy wind that snapped mature branches like twigs—

"Not helpful," he muttered. "If I don't get this right, my guess is that neither of us will see a thunderstorm again."

The wind died; the storm clouds dissipated. The internal screen went blank—no.

Another image was forming—lightning again, one single orange bolt, blazing into and merging with a second, the doubled force striking down into water.

"Not—" he began—and the image repeated, with an edge of impatience to it: One bolt, two, one, strike.

Jela blinked.

"She wouldn't have…"

But she might have. A pilot's first care was her ship, after all. And to what length might a pilot who dared not let her ship fall into the hands of someone who was a little too fond of *sheriekas*-made goods go?

His fingers, apparently placing more faith in tree-born intuition than his thinking mind, were already moving across the board, taking them off-line in deliberate order: nav-brain first; then the main engine; lastly, the guns.

Satisfyingly, the stand-bys went dark. Jela sighed—and jumped as the board came abruptly live. The internal lights came up; blowers started; and behind him the door to the tower slid shut.

Screens came on-line, showing him cannon in the docking area; and the comm opened, admitting a man's breathless voice.

"Surrender yourself and the ship, and you will be well-treated. Attempt to lift and this habitat will defend itself."

If a pair of quad cannons was the best they could field, leaving wasn't going to be a problem.

He reached to the weapons board, pulled up the ranging screen, acquired the target—and stopped, finger on the firing stud.

"Dulsey," he said, and saw a flicker of green at the back of his eyes. Hole the habitat, which *Dancer's* guns were fully capable of doing, and there was a chance Dulsey wouldn't live through the experience.

He thought of Cantra, dependent for her life on alien technology that was itself dependent on the well-being of the ship it traveled in.

"Surrender yourself!" The demand came again; a woman's voice this time, sounding more angry than scared.

"Well," Jela said to the tree. "I think we can take what they've got to dish out."

Quickly, he put the weapons to rest and slapped the shields up. He thought of the defenses his former ships had carried, and was briefly sorry. He thought of Cantra again—and engaged the engines.

Dancer leapt away from the dock. In the screens, the cannon flared, the shot so hopelessly bad that he reflexively checked the scans—and thereby discovered bad news.

The route outspace—and there was only one reasonable route outspace, as there had only been one reasonable route in—was crossed and re-crossed with what appeared to be ribbons of colored light.

Particle beams.

"This might be rough," Jela told the tree, as he brought the shields up high. "We've got a field of charged beams to get to the other side of."

A legitimate merchanter would have foundered, its shielding shredded by the beams before it had passed the halfway point.

Dancer, with her up-grade shields and her quick response to con, had a better chance of surviving than that legitimate merchanter, not quite as good a chance as a real military craft.

He brought the guns up, knowing he might be needing them as soon as he was clear of the defenses...and now they were ready.

The field wasn't extensive, just enough to be nerve-wracking, and they lost a layer of shielding before they got through it, but through they came, guns at ready—and the pilot in the mood for a scrap.

He was unfortunately disappointed. There was no *sheriekas*-built battle cruiser—or even an armed corsair—awaiting them at the maze's end, only the dust and the emptiness of the Deeps.

"Now what?" he asked the tree, but no answering flash of images appeared behind his eyes.

Scans reported no beacons, even the chirping that had guided them in was silent. And he was no Cantra yos'Phelium, able to pilot blind and—

"Fool!" he snapped at himself, his fingers already calling up the nav-brain, hoping that for once in her life she'd followed a standard protocol and recorded the—

She had. Jela sat back in his chair with an absurd feeling of relief.

"All we have to do," he told the tree, like it was going to be easy, "is follow our own path back out."

He had never done such a bit of piloting himself, but he had talked to pilots who had.

And what else did a generalist need besides knowing that something could be done and a bit of luck?

TWENTY-EIGHT

Spiral Dance
The Little Empty

HE WATERED THE tree, ate a high-cal bar and drank a carafe of hot, sweet tea.

He slept, webbed into the co-pilot's chair, one ear cocked and one eye half-open.

He cleaned house, thinking unkind thoughts about the Uncle the while, and retrieved his belt and the captured disruptor from the lock, throwing the hand into the recycler, and swabbing the deck clean of blood.

He consulted the charts and he consulted the tree.

He tried the comm.

He checked the first aid kit. Several times.

He went over the charts again, ate a high-cal bar and had another nap, during which he debated with himself—maybe—weighing ship's safety against the necessity of reporting in.

When he woke, he compromised. He set course for Gimlins and locked it, but did not initiate. Instead, he kept her shielded and quiet in the Shallows, pending the pilot's accepting the route.

That done, he sent his query again.

No ack from his primary.

No ack from the back-up.

No ack from use-this-only-in-extreme-emergency.

Growling, he extended a hand to sweep the comm closed— and pulled up sharply as the incoming dial lit.

Hope rising, he watched the message flow onto the screen—

My very dear Pilot Cantra, and esteemed M. Jela—

Please accept my sincere apology for the inconvenience surrounding your departure from our humble habitat. I hope neither of you has taken lasting harm from the incident.

I do very much thank you for your assistance in identifying certain of my children who have become somewhat over exuberant in their pursuit of our common goal.

*Dulsey asks that I send you her warmest personal regards, to
which I will add my own hope that you will consider my family as your
own.*

Uncle

Jela closed his eyes, tasting dust in his mouth. Wearily, he sent the
message into the pilot's queue, then shut down the comm and went
to check the first aid kit.

The smooth black box sat as it had for the last four ship-days,
lid down, doing whatever it did, however it did.

He had to take it on faith that the thing was working, that it
would have given some notification, had Cantra died in the course
of its treatment. Her injuries had been terrible. He had seen that
for himself; he didn't dwell on the question of whether they were
survivable.

He'd taken counsel of the tree, which was wary, but willing to
wait. Himself, he was getting impatient, and had decided to give the
thing two more ship-hours to finish up or at least provide a status
report, before he opened the lid himself.

Standing over the damned box, he admitted to himself that he
might have made a mistake. What he could have done instead—that
was the sticking point.

"Damn' M's," he muttered. "Always know better."

Except when they didn't.

He was wasting time, hovering over the box. It would open in
its own time, or he would open it in his. Meanwhile, there was this
and that of ship minutiae to occupy himself with and, for a change,
he could worry about not being able to make contact. He turned
and left the alcove, heading for the galley to make tea and maybe a
real-meal.

He hadn't reached the door when the chime sounded and he
spun 'round so fast he almost tripped on his own feet. An image
flashed inside his head—one of the youngling dragons tumbling
wings over snout down a long mossy slope.

Grinning, he went back to the first aid kit—not running.
Not quite.

Perfect, whole, neither happy nor unhappy, she lay swathed in light.

Gently, the light parted, admitting a crystalline whisper, bearing
choices. Perfect though she now was, there existed an opportunity.

She might be made *more* perfect, exceeding the arbitrary limits set by her original design. Smarter, quicker, more accurate—these things were but minor adaptations. The ability to bend event to her will, to sculpt the forces of the mind—those might also be attained—if she wished.

The cusp was here and now: remain perfect and perfectly limited or embrace greatness and be more than she ever dreamed. How did she chose?

Bathed and supported by the light, she considered. And as she did, a breeze sprang up, bearing scents of living green, while across the light fell the shadow of a great wing.

Startled, she looked up—and the light faded, the voice withdrew. She heard a chime, and opened her eyes.

Lean cheeks, black eyes, mobile mouth—doing his best not to look worried and making a rare hash of it. She made a note to herself to remember that look. For some reason, it seemed important.

"Cantra?" letting the worry leak into the voice, too. Deeps, but the man was going to bits—that's what came of talking to trees.

"Who else?" She looked up, saw the hatch above her leaking sickly green light and took a breath, tasting ship air—and that quick memory came back on-line.

"You hurt?" she snapped.

Jela blinked and gave over a half-smile. "I'm hale, Pilot."

"Good. The ship?"

"Ship's in shape and we're well away," he answered. The half-smile twisted a little. "There's a note in queue from Uncle, apologizing for any inconvenience and thanking us for smoking out his insurgents."

She snorted a laugh. "I'll send him a bill," she said, which pleasantry got a genuine grin from Jela and an easing of the muscles around his eyes.

"So." she said, swinging her feet over the side of the pallet. "Got tea?"

Tea was had and a bowl of spiced rice mixed up by her co-pilot, who insisted that he'd been on his way to make the same for himself when the chime sounded and that doubling was no problem.

So, she'd leaned against the wall, wearing a robe she carefully didn't ask how he'd gotten out of her quarters, and sipped her tea, watching him work. She smiled when he handed her a bowl and followed him to the tower.

The bowls were empty now and they sat sipping the last of the tea, companionably silent.

She rested her mug against her knee and waved her free hand at the board.

"I imagine you got a course set."

Jela looked wry. "It's my intention to raise Gimlins."

"Never come up on my dance card," she said. "What's to want on Gimlins?"

"Maybe contact," he answered, slowly, and looked at her straight. "I've been trying to report in, but I'm not getting any answers to my signals." That bothered him—and it bothered her that he let her see it.

"It could be," he said, but not like he believed it, "that we're too far out."

"It could be," she agreed, seriously. "The Deeps do funny things to comm sometimes—even the Shallows can play tricks on you." She finished her tea, slotted the cup and sat up straighter in her chair before meeting his eyes.

"We gotta talk."

He gave her a nod, face smooth and agreeable, which return to normal behavior she observed with a pang. Might be she'd taken a bad knock on the head, back on the Uncle's dock.

"First off—" She raised a hand and pointed at the tree, sitting quiet and green and for all the worlds like a *plant* in its pot. "What *is* that thing? And I don't want to hear 'tree.'"

Jela glanced over his shoulder at the tree in question, settled back into his chair and sipped tea.

Cantra sighed. "Well?"

He lifted a hand, showing empty palm.

"You said you didn't want to hear 'tree,' Pilot. Since that's what it is, I'm at a loss as to how to answer without violating my orders."

"That coin would spend better," she told him, "if I had any reason to believe you ever once in your life followed orders."

He grinned. "I've followed my share of orders. It's just that I have a bias against obeying the stupid ones."

"Must've made you real popular with your commanders."

"Some of them, yes; some of them, no," he said, easily, and flicked his fingers over his shoulder.

"That, now—that's a tree, and if it has a personal name or a racial one, it hasn't shared them with me."

"A telepathic tree is what I'm hearing," Cantra said, just to have it down on the deck where they could both consider it at leisure.

"Why not?"

"It's not exactly usual," she pointed out. "Where'd you get it? If you don't mind saying."

He sent another over-the-shoulder glance at the subject of the conversation. When he looked back, his face was serious.

"I found it on a desert world; the only thing alive in a couple days' walk. We'd seen some action and it was my misfortune to be shot down. By the time I found the tree, I was in pretty bad shape. It saved my life and I promised, if rescue came, that I'd take it with me." He glanced down, maybe into his mug.

"Promised I'd get it to someplace safe."

"Safe," she repeated, thinking of Faldaiza, Taliofi, the Uncle, and of a dozen chancy ports between.

"It's probable," Jela said, "that 'safe' is a relative term. The tree was in danger of extinction when I found it. When things are that bad, someplace else is pretty much guaranteed to be better. Safer." He looked down into his mug again, lifted it and finished off his tea.

"I'd hoped," he said, slotting the empty, "to find a planet where it would have a chance of a good, long grow..."

"Which doesn't," Cantra said when he just sat there, eyes pointed at the empty mug, but clearly seeing something else, "address what it *is*—or how it was able to tweak the Uncle's hydroponics long-distance."

He glanced over his shoulder and then gave her an amused glance.

"I don't know how—or what—the tree did," he said; "but I'm not surprised it was able to act in its own defense—and in defense of its ship."

Cantra closed her eyes. "Now its official crew, is it?"

"Why not?" Jela returned, damn him. And, no matter its vegetative state, the tree *had* acted to protect the ship and made it stick when both pilot and co-pilot were cut off and helpless.

"All right," she said, opening her eyes with a sigh. "It's crew." She stretched in her chair to look past Jela to the end of the board.

"Done proper," she said to the tree. "The captain commends you."

The top leaves moved, probably in the breeze from the circulation system, but looking eerily like a casual salute.

In that breeze there was a sharp snap; a branch carrying two small pods fell to the deck, and bounced once.

Jela laughed, picked up the branch, and felt the pods relax, almost as if they ripened in his hand.

"Here," he said, smiling. "The tree commends the captain and the crew!"

She looked at them askance.

"What'll I do with it? Plant it?"

His free hand fluttered pilot talk—*Eat up, eat up.*

She lifted an eyebrow, watching him carefully as he approached, teasing, as she read it, and leaned conspiratorially toward her.

"You've never tasted anything quite like this," he suggested in a mock whisper.

"You sure it's good?" she asked, not so much playing as seriously wanting to know.

The tree's top branches waved slightly—she was really going to have to check those fans soon if they were creating that much disturbance.

"Edible? Yes! Good? Really good..."

He broke the pods into sections. She took them into her hand to avoid him hand-feeding her, which it looked like he might.

He challenged her then, holding a piece to his lips while watching her expectantly.

She looked to the fruit, caught a bouquet reminiscent of half-a-dozen high-end eats she could name.

Damn' thing smelled good—

"Not very big, is it?" she asked, by way of buying time while she sorted past the inviting smell. She knew all about nice smells, now, didn't she?

"You'll like it," Jela said, suddenly serious. "I promise." He popped the piece into his mouth then and, not to be outdone or seen to be timid, so did she.

He was right. She liked it.

She'd eaten the pod, cleaned her fingers, and studiously did not
give herself over to considering Jela's person, though there was
that urge. She noticed it on the two previous occasions she'd had
to make use of the first aid kit. It was like the unit brought everything right up to optimum...

"If it can be told," Jela said, breaking her line of thought, "Where
did you get those devices you gave the Uncle?"

She sighed. "Like I said, a couple ports back. A lucky find,
since the Uncle has this interest in *sheriekas* artifacts."

"Do you remember," Jela persisted, "the name of the trader or
company who sold them to you?"

Well, she did, as it happened, the directors having done them all
the favor of breeding for extra-efficient memories—and she was
damned if she was going to share the news.

"I'm gonna tell you so you can report trading with the enemy
and send somebody out to pick 'em up?" she snapped. "No point
to it. A lot of weird drifts in from the Deeps and catches up against
the Rim. Depend on it, somebody bought a box-lot or a broken
pallet somewhere and the toys were in it. There's a lot of *sheriekas*
tech on the Rim; people trade 'em as oddities or collect 'em."

"Like the Uncle?" Jela asked, and Cantra laughed.

"The Uncle ain't collecting; he's using. Figures he can beat
the enemy by mastering their machines and turning them against
their makers."

"Then he's a fool," Jela said, with a return of the stern grimness
he'd given the Uncle, "and an active danger to the population of the
Spiral Arm."

Cantra frowned. "Might be. In point of fact, though, what the
Uncle exactly ain't is a fool, nor any of his folk. The Batchers who
make it out to the Uncle, they're tough and they're smart. Seems like if
anybody was going to be able to figure how to use the enemy's equipment against them, it's the Uncle's people." She considered Jela's face,
which was no more grim or less, and added—

"Understand me, I ain't the Uncle's best friend by any count."

That got a real, though brief, smile, and a roll of the wide shoulders.

"I don't doubt that they're smart," he said slowly. "But they're
not the only ones who've thought of using the *sheriekas* weapons
against them—and come to grief for it. I've seen battle robots
based on captured *sheriekas* plans which have gone mad, laying waste

to the worlds they were built to defend—a flaw in the design or are they performing exactly as the *sheriekas* intended them to?"

He leaned forward, elbows on knees, warming to his topic.

"Another case—out there in the Tearin Sector, they've been building battle tech based on plans captured from the last war— fleets of robot ships, under self-aware robot commanders who've been fed all the great battles fought by all the great generals. They've turned them loose, I hear, to roam out into the Beyond and engage the *sheriekas*."

Cantra tipped her head. "So—what? They join the enemy when they make contact?"

"They might," Jela said, sitting back. "The reports I've seen have them turning pirate and holding worlds hostage for their resources."

"And you're thinking this is also in the plan?" she persisted. "To seed us with tech and proto-machines that'll attack us from inside while the world-eaters take bites outta the Rim?"

"Like that," he said, and gave her one of his less-sincere half-smiles. "Old soldiers have their crochets. No doubt the Uncle's harmless."

Cantra laughed. "Nobody said so. And that thing that fried out my 'skins sure wasn't harmless." She hesitated, wondering if she wanted to know—but of course she did.

"How bad?"

He glanced aside. "Bad," he said, and sighed. "You needed nothing less than a *sheriekas*-made heal-box—and I wasn't sure it was enough."

Well. She closed her eyes, then opened them.

"My 'skins?"

"Sealed inside a sterile pack," he said. "What's left of them."

She shivered, took a breath—

"I owe you," she said, and her voice was a little lighter than she liked. She cleared her throat. "Owe you twice."

His eyebrows went up, but he didn't say anything, only made the hand sign for *go on*.

"Right. You were clear—I saw you on the ramp. No reason for you to come back—you could've got away clean."

He snorted. "Fine co-pilot I'd be, too, leaving my pilot in such a mess."

She glanced aside. "Well, about that…" She took a hard breath and made herself meet his eyes.

"The thing is, I went in thinking that the Uncle might enjoy having himself a soldier and that selling you might net a goodly profit."

Something moved down far in those Deeps-dark eyes, but his face didn't change out of the expression of calm listening.

"Say something!" Cantra snapped.

He raised his hands slightly, let them drop onto his lap.

"I'll say that I don't blame you for wanting me off your ship," he said. "And I'll point out that, intentions aside, you didn't sell me to the Uncle." He moved his shoulders against the back of the chair.

"No bad feelings here, Pilot," he said, which was generous, she allowed, and precisely Jela-like. She wondered if it came of being a soldier, his giving the greater weight to the action done and the lesser to the reasons behind it.

For herself, she was unsettled by her intentions and her actions, both. She knew—none better—that Jela wasn't anything like a partner, nor did she owe him anything as a co-pilot, being as he had forced his way into the chair and the ship.

Yet, when decision came to action—

Mush for brains, she growled at herself.

"Meant to ask you," Jela said. "Why did your directors decide to retire your Series? If it can be told."

She blinked, it being on the edge of her tongue to tell him it *couldn't* be told. But, dammit—she owed him…

"Pliny," she said, and cleared her throat, "…he'd've been a half-brother. So—Pliny come home from an assignment, reports to Instructor Malis for debriefing—and slapped her." She paused, feeling Garen's hand hard 'round her arm, yanking her into a run—

"So," Jela said softly. "He slapped a superior. In the military, that might be good for getting him shot, but not his whole unit."

She looked up and met his eyes.

"He'd been delayed," she said, just telling it, "and by the time he came in, he really needed that debriefing. Add that Instructor Malis…liked to hear us beg for the drug. The sum of it all being that he killed her—and the directors aren't about to tolerate a line that bites the hand that's fed it, housed it, clothed it, and taught it." She paused, considered, then shrugged. It wouldn't do him any harm to have the whole tale of it.

"The Uncle come into it because some level of Batchers're kept in line by binding—happy-chems, mostly—to certain receptors. Close enough to how the directors keep *aelantaza* in line, except the directors didn't figure to waste any happy-chems. Uncle's lab techs gimmicked an unbind process, which Garen knew, and figured it was worth the trip to find out would it work."

"I see." Silence, while Jela glanced over his shoulder at his damn' tree, sitting still and green in its pot.

"So the line was ended because it showed independence and self-reliance," he said. "And you're the sole survivor."

"By luck…" she muttered. *And by Garen.*

He smiled at her—a wholly real smile.

"That's all any of us can claim," he said, and stood, gathering his empties into a broad hand and reaching for hers.

"What I propose," he said, looking down at her, his face serious. "If you agree, Pilot. Is that we do make for Gimlins. I've got a good chance at a contact there, which will get me off your ship and out of your life."

For one of the few times in her free life, her mind went blank and she stared at him, speechless.

"And I'll apologize," Jela continued, "for putting you in harm's way. I *am* a soldier; the risks I find acceptable aren't what a civilian ought ever to face."

Almost, she laughed, wondering what he thought her life had been—but he was gone by then, the door sliding closed behind him while she sat in the pilot's chair and for the first time since Garen died blinked away tears.

TWENTY-NINE

Spiral Dance
Shift Change

JELA HAD GOTTEN his log-book out, meaning to bring the entries current. An hour later, there he sat, the book open on his knee, pen ready—and he'd done no more than note down the date.

It happened that the date was of some interest to him, it being something over forty-four Common Years since the quartermaster had assigned M Strain Jela to Granthor's Guard crèche, despite the fact that the proto-soldier was smaller than spec. That he'd been the single survivor of an enemy action focused on the lab which had killed every other fetus in the nursery wing—that had weighed with the quartermaster, who'd noted in the file that a soldier could never have too much luck.

He'd been lucky, too—or as lucky as a soldier could be. Despite a certain reckless disregard for his own personal welfare, and what some might call an argumentative and willful nature, he'd outlived crèche-mates and comrades, commanders and whole planets.

And now he was old.

Worse, he was old while the enemy continued to advance and wrongheaded decisions came down from the top; his mission was in shambles and—

The last—that rankled. No, it *hurt*.

That this would be his last mission, he had accepted, the facts being what they were. That he would fail—somehow it had never occurred to him that he would fail, though he'd certainly failed enough times in his life for the concept to be anything but new. This mission, though, assigned by this particular commander...

He'd been so sure of success.

And there was worse.

He'd promised—personally promised—the tree that he would see it safe, which he should never have done, a soldier's life and honor being Command's to spend.

It weighed on him, that promise, for he had made it with true intent, between soldiers; and the tree was as much his comrade-in-arms as any other he'd fought beside, down the years.

He told himself that the tree knew the realities of a soldier's promise, that the tree, comrade and hero, didn't fault him for putting duty before promises.

The fact was that he faulted himself, for what increasingly seemed a life misspent and useless. Yes, he had followed orders—more or less—which was all that was required of a soldier, after all.

And duty required him, right now, to plan for the best outcome of the mission, since success was not within his grasp.

Sighing, he shifted against the wall, sealed the pen, closed the book and put both on the hammock by his knee. He closed his eyes.

Gimlins, now.

Gimlins was a risk. It might even be an unacceptably high risk. He wouldn't know that until he did or didn't have someone on the comm who did or didn't have the right sequence of passcodes.

There'd been a corps loyal to the consolidated commanders on Gimlins. Some time back, that would have been, and he was the first to realize the info was old. His big hope, in a narrowing field, was that the corps was still there. His smaller, more realistic hope, was that the corps had moved on to fulfill its duty, leaving behind a contact for those who might have lost their way.

If there was neither corps nor contact at Gimlins, then he'd—

He wasn't precisely sure what he'd do then, in the cause of the consolidated commanders—which unsettling thought spawned another. He'd promised Cantra he'd clear off her ship and that was a promise he *did* intend to keep. Duty might have required him to find quiet transport out of the range of fire, but duty hadn't required that he continue to impose his will—*his* will—upon her once he'd gotten clear.

He could have picked up a ship at any of the ports they'd passed through on their way to settle Dulsey with the Uncle. The truth was, he hadn't chosen to. Like he'd chosen to sign on as Dulsey's escort to safety, forcing Cantra onto a course she'd never have charted for herself, and for which audacity she'd determined to sell him to a ruthless man who she might have had reason to believe could keep him occupied long enough for her to lift, regaining her life and her liberty.

He understood her motive and didn't blame her for the intention. A fully capable woman, Cantra yos'Phelium, and as good as her word—when she gave it. He'd enjoyed being her partner in trade. And he'd learned something about piloting from her, which he wouldn't have thought was possible.

He smiled a little, remembering her yawn for the X Strain's display of prowess—and the smile faded with the more recent memory—looking down to the dock where she was surrounded, smoke billowing from her 'skins and the scream—

He'd never thought to hear Cantra yos'Phelium scream—and hoped never to hear it again. The sound of her laughter—that was a memory for a soldier to take away with him and treasure.

Memories…Well, a soldier had his memories—which shouldn't, in the normal way of things, interfere with his duty or his planning.

Sighing, he shifted again against the wall, settling his shoulders more comfortably, and engaged one of the focusing exercises.

The sound of the air being cut by wings disturbed his concentration; sunlight flickered in strange patterns across the barely visualized task screen, which melted, morphing into a wide band of blue, arcing from never to forever over the mighty crowns of trees.

Again came the sound of wings and there, high against the canopy sky, two forms, necks entwined, danced wing-to-wing.

"Not likely," Jela muttered and started the exercise from the beginning, banishing the dancing lovers from his mind's eye.

The exercise proceeded, task screen came up—and was again subverted by the tree's will.

This time he saw the now-familiar green land, gently ridged by the great roots of trees. Against one giant trunk a nest sat a little askew, with bits and pieces of it strewn about, as if it had fallen from a higher branch, unmoored perhaps by the wind.

In the nest was a dragonling, its tiny wings still wet and it was crying, as any baby will, for food and for comfort.

As he watched, a seed-pod fell into the nest, and the baby set to with a will; another pod was given and devoured; and a third, as well, after which the baby curled 'round in its battered nest, eyes slitting drowsily…

Leaves sifted gently downward, filling the nest softly. The dragonling sighed and tucked its head under its wing, slipping off into sleep.

A flash of the task-screen then and a shift of scene to doleful, dusty wasteland, the sun pitiless overhead, and below, nested in the sand, a creature soft and dun colored, its snout short, its eyes reflective...

In the hammock, leaning against the wall of his quarters, Jela snorted a laugh.

"And a pretty sight I was," he said aloud.

The tree continued as if he had not interrupted, displaying now an unfamiliar green land touched by soft shadows—and there, curled against a trunk he somehow knew for the tree's own, despite its greater girth, a small and soft dun-colored creature was peacefully asleep.

In the now of Cantra's ship, Jela frowned.

"Is that real?" he asked the tree, but his only answer was a flicker of shadows and the sound of the wind.

She checked their location, and gave Jela full points for finding his way out of the Deeps and into the relative safety of the Shallows.

For old time's sake, she called up reports from weapons and from the ship-brain, opened the comm logs, read the Uncle's note, laughed, and scanned the long list of sends which had raised no answers.

She went down the list again, frowning after call-codes familiar from her previous audits of Jela's comm activity, through a complicated skein of unfamiliar—and increasingly untraditional codes.

The man's worried, she thought, and caught herself on the edge of starting a third time from the top.

Mush for brains, she growled, and banished the log with a flick of a finger.

She should, she thought, get dressed, pull up the charts and do some calculations, checking Jela's filed route to Gimlins.

The sooner you raise it, she told herself when she just sat there—*The sooner you raise this Gimlins, the sooner you've got your ship back*.

True enough and a condition she'd yearned for since shortly after shaking the mud of Faldaiza off of *Dancer's* skin.

Despite which, she stayed in the pilot's seat, pulling her feet up onto the chair and wrapping her arms around her knees, the silk robe sliding coolly against her skin.

The Little Empty was in the forward screen, the few points of light showing hard against the endless night. She leaned back into the chair...

Don't stare at the Deeps, baby, Garen muttered from memory. *The empty'll fill up your head and make you's crazy as your mam, here.*

No use explaining that Cantra knew her pedigree down to multiple-great-grandmothers and that Garen yos'Phelium was nowhere in the donor list. Garen believed Cantra to be her daughter—the same daughter who had been annihilated—along with the rest of Garen's family, acquaintances and planet—by a world-eater, some many years before the directors of the Tanjalyre Institute commissioned Cantra's birth.

Garen'd told her the story—how her ship had come home from a run, excepting there wasn't any home there. Told how they'd checked the coords, gone out and tried to come back in. How they'd done it a dozen times, from a dozen different transition points until finally the captain put them in at Borgen, cut the crew loose and sold the ship.

She told that story, did Garen; and as far as Cantra'd ever determined, she'd seen no inconsistency in admitting her daughter dead and destroyed while at the same time believing Cantra to be that same daughter. Not the least of Garen's crazies, and the one that Cantra ought by rights to have no argument with, it having saved her life.

The question now being, Cantra thought, tucked into the pilot's chair of a ship she could never fully trust, staring out over the Deeps— *saved it for what?*

Life wants to live, baby. That's just natural.

True as far as it went. But life—life wanted to accomplish, too; to make connections; to trust; to be at ease and off-guard for some small moments of time...

That's a powerful gift you've been given, baby. A weapon and a boon. You can have anything you want, just for a smile and a pretty-please.

A curse, more like, and a danger to her and to those who fell under her sway. The best course—the safest—was to keep herself to herself and to stand as cantankerous and off-putting as possible when human interaction came necessary.

The meager stars danced in the screens. She closed her eyes, which didn't shut the empty out.

Five years since Garen'd died. Five years of running solo, keeping low, with nobody except herself to talk to.

And for what?

"Habit," she whispered, and in the Deeps behind her eyelids she saw Dulsey, her stolid face animating as she talked about the Uncle and his free and equal society of Batchers. Jela, the joyful gleam of anticipated mayhem in his eye as he squared off in front of an opponent twice his mass.

...and other images—Jela half-way up the ramp and more; Jela parting the killing mob around her; Jela's face, worried and relieved and cautious all at once, the first thing in her eyes when the 'kit opened up.

Jela, who had a mission and a reason to live his life as he did, and who had promised to take himself and his tree off at Gimlins, which was, damnitall, what she wanted.

Wasn't it?

Should've sold the man to the Uncle and had done she told herself—and laughed. Selling Jela would have solved more than one problem, the way she figured it now.

So you owe him, she said to herself, but it was more than that. She'd *gotten used* to him; gotten used to his back-up and his good sense. Worse, she'd gotten used to having him on her ship, in her daily routine. Gotten used to regular sleep shifts, and not running half-ragged. Hadn't touched a stick of Tempo in—

Well, she was going to miss him, that was all.

Nothing else but what you traded for.

Right.

Deliberately, she put her feet down on the cold decking and pushed out of the chair.

Behind her, the door cycled.

She turned and considered him, the tight ship togs showing the shoulders to good advantage.

He paused just inside the door, his face open and a little unsure, hands quiet at his sides.

"Occurs to me," he said, quiet-like and as serious as she'd ever heard him. "That I put you off more than one course at Faldaiza. I'm no redhead, but I can try to make it up to you." He gave her a smile that was nigh heart-stopping in its genuine wryness. "If you're interested."

Well. Yes, as a matter of fact, she was interested.

So she smiled and walked toward him, knowing she was going to regret this, too, at Gimlins.

He tipped his head, the black eyes watching her with a certain warm appreciation. She felt her smile get wider and let it happen while she held out a hand.

He met it, his fingers warm, his palm calloused, his grip absurdly light for a man who could crush another man's fist.

"My cabin's bigger," she said softly, and they left the tower together.

THIRTY

Spiral Dance
Gimlins Approach

GIMLINS HUNG IN the second screen, where it had been for some time while Jela played with various comm-codes, his face slowly settling into an expression of grim patience, tension coming off of him in waves.

Cantra busied herself with the piloting side of things, pulling in such feeds as were available; checking her headings for the sixth time; and riding the scans harder than need be.

The tension from the co-pilot's side continued to build, to the point where the pilot started to itch. Sighing, she released the straps and stood.

"I'm fixing tea," she told the side of Jela's face. "Want?"

Not even a blink to show he'd heard her. His fingers moved on the comm-pad, paused—moved again.

Give it up, she thought at him. *Anybody who's hiding this hard can't be anything but trouble.*

"One more string," Jela said, his voice as distant as his profile. "Tea would be fine, thank you."

"Right."

She took herself off to the galley, put the tea on to brew and leaned against the cabinets, arms crossed over her chest, feeling something like grim herself.

"Cantra yos'Phelium," she said aloud, "you're a fool."

Worse than a fool, if she was going to start talking out straight to herself while there was still another pair of ears on-board to hear it.

She sighed heartily and closed her eyes.

The man's leaving at Gimlins, she told herself, counting it out by the numbers. *He's taking his tree and he's going; it's what he wants and, if you had a brain in your head—which you don't—it's what you want. Yes, you owe him—he's done everything and more that a co-pilot should, to keep his pilot hale and steady. So pay him up even and set him down where he says. It's not like he can't take care of himself. And his damn' tree, too.*

The tea-maker squawked, startling her. Grousing, she pulled open the cabinet, unshipped mugs, poured, stuck a couple of high-cals into her sleeve as an afterthought and went back to the tower.

Jela was on his feet, expression now forcibly agreeable, tension still evident but of a different quality.

Cantra raised an eyebrow, deliberately nonchalant.

"Contact," he said. "We go in."

"Great," she answered, like she meant it and showed a smile as she handed him a mug.

He dressed in trade leathers, rolled up his kit and stood for a moment staring down at it: a moderate pack, the tough coderoy scarred and travel-worn—not the sort of thing a trader would be carrying on his back to a business meeting.

It would have to stay.

Sighing lightly, he bent, rummaged briefly, pulled out the log book and slid it into an inside vest pocket, straightened the pack and lashed it to the wall. Nothing there that couldn't be replaced, and it could be that Cantra would find use for some bits. After all, it wasn't the first time he'd had to abandon what was his in the course of obeying orders. And it wouldn't be the last.

Not quite the last.

The tree, too, was going to have to stay and take its chances with whatever care Cantra could give it. He'd tried to express this and his reasons, though he couldn't tell if he'd actually gotten through. He hoped he had and that the tree understood—though it couldn't make any difference if it didn't.

The voice on the comm had been furtive and something less than knowledgeable, though they'd had the pass-codes ready enough. And while that wasn't conclusive, it was better than no answer at all. His guess was that the voice on the comm was a local who had been paid to keep an ear on the old feed, with no expectation that a call would ever come in. The only thing he could reasonably expect was to be passed up the line as quickly as the contact could manage.

He closed his eyes, trying to feel out the tree, but all he found in the back recesses of his skull was a cool and distant greenness.

Right, then.

It was time to take his leave of the pilot—a thought not as comforting as it could be.

She'd stood at his back and tolerated his infringement of her life without either shooting him or selling him; she'd been more than generous in bed; and he was going to miss her—vile temper, sarcasm, and all.

Well.

He straightened his vest once more, needlessly, and settled his belt 'round his waist, making certain his *shib* was in place and drew easily. The flexible ceramic cutting edge felt cool against his fingers and he smiled. All in order.

Then he went out to the tower to take leave of his pilot.

"With me?" Cantra repeated, with a glance over her shoulder at the tree sitting calm in its pot. "I thought you two were partners."

"We are," Jela answered, trying to sound like there was agreement on all sides. "But it's time to split up. I can't take it with me to the meeting and—" He stopped because she had raised her hand, palm out toward his nose.

"You risked your life—and mine, too—getting that tree off Faldaiza; you took it with you when I set you down at Taliofi. It guarded your back while we was visiting with the Uncle and now you're leaving it with me?" She shot another glance over her shoulder. "Why?"

A fair question, and trust Cantra to ask it. He moved his shoulders, easing out some of the tension.

"The contact I've got—is deep. Likely the only thing they'll be able to do is pass me up-line. I'll have to go quick and I'll have to go light." He sent a look to the tree himself, absurdly pleased to see how tall and how full it was now.

Looking back to Cantra, he saw her eyeing his vest.

"No 'skins?" she said, and held up her hand again. "I know they ain't proof against all evil, but they're something better than trade leather."

"I don't want to draw attention to myself," he said. "The meet's up in the city and I don't want to compromise my contact."

Cantra closed her eyes and took a deep breath.

"Jela," she said, flat calm, which meant he was in for a tongue-lashing.

"Pilot?"

She opened her eyes and glared at him.

"This smells bad to me. Say it smells sweet to you."

Truth told, his nose for trouble detected a decided odor about the business, too. On the other hand, he wasn't getting any younger, and none of the usuals—none—had answered.

"They had the right codes," he said mildly, into Cantra's glare.

She sighed. "Would Pilot Muran of late lamented memory have had those same codes?"

The woman had a wonderful mind for a detail, Jela thought and stifled his own sigh.

"Yes," he said, keeping in calm and friendly. "Muran would have had the same codes. And if they are using Muran's codes, then—I need to know that, too. My orders are clear."

"And this time you feel like following them."

There wasn't any real answer to that, so he just stood there, bearing her scrutiny, until she sighed again and lifted a hand to push her hair back from her eyes.

"You don't," she said, softly, "need to be this desperate to leave on my account. If there's a less chancy place to look for news of folk gone missing, *Dancer's* good for the trip."

Of the things he might have expected to hear her say, an offer of continued passage was last. The brain in his fingers, quicker than the one in his head, came up with a reply first.

Condition is?

She glanced aside and if he hadn't known her, he'd have judged her to be embarrassed.

"I don't have anything on the screens that can't wait," she said huskily.

The offer warmed him, but nothing could be said about his next-best-hope but that it was riskier still.

He smiled, to let her know he appreciated the offer, and flipped his hand, palm up, palm down.

"I've got to try here," he said.

Green eyes considered him. "Got to, is it?"

"Yes."

"All right, then," she said briskly. "I'm coming with you."

He blinked. "Cantra—"

"You can be *sure* that the pilot of this ship ain't taking her orders from the co-pilot, current *or* former," she interrupted. "You can wait for me to get dressed up all pretty like a trader, or you can leave now. If you leave, I'll follow you, which could be awkward for you. If you wait, I'll cover your back and follow your lead."

She was serious.

"The ship," he said, playing the one argument that was sure to sway her. "The ship would be at risk, with her pilot on the port and maybe headed for rough ground."

She smiled, which was bad.

"Ship's safety comes under the pilot's care," she said, voice serious. "And the pilot judges the risk to the ship is acceptable."

He had, thought Jela, done Cantra yos'Phelium a disservice. She could step outside of the boundaries she'd made for herself and take a decision that risked her and her ship, if needed.

Damn everything, that she thought it was needed now.

"I once let my pilot go outta here to a meet maybe a little less hazardous than the one you're on course for," Cantra said, her voice still carrying that note of complete seriousness. "Wasn't much choice about it—she was my pilot and she made it an order. And she come back on-ship in a body-bag."

She gave him another straight-on glare. "I don't expect to let my co-pilot walk out into clear and present danger without back-up," she said. "*Damn* if I will, Jela. You hear it?"

He heard it. It might have been that he heard more of it than she wanted him to hear. Or she might have intended it all.

In either case, he was running out of time to argue, and he didn't doubt she'd make good on her threat.

So.

"All right," he said. "I'll be grateful for the back-up, Pilot."

The meeting place was away up in the city, beyond yard and port—which was yet another thing not to love about it, in Cantra's opinion.

Jela'd flagged down a robocab at the port, directing it to a point somewhat to the east and north of the final destination, according to the city map she'd hastily memorized. From there, they walked, two traders taking in the sights, of which there were a few.

As a general rule, Cantra avoided cities. Garen had never gone beyond the port proper, contending there was more than enough trouble to be found right there—and mostly she was right.

The last time Cantra was inside a city had been during the course of a training run, about a half-year before Pliny put paid to them all. That city had been vertical, rising bone pale and fragile out of the depths of a tumultuous planetary sea. Cylayn, that city had been named, and it was a triumph of bio-engineering. The fragile-seeming and extremely tough shell in which the city was housed had been spun by sea creatures designed for that single monumental task—who then died, dried and blew away on the constant winds, precisely on schedule, leaving behind a marvelous habitat for the imported human population.

It had also been a marvel of security regulations and law, the habitat being, in its way, as risky as any space station; and it had been lessons in circumventing those safeguards of the common good that had occupied Cantra's time there.

This city, now—this Pluad—was level, its streets laid out in a grid—north-south, east-west—dusty, and heavier than she liked. Then there was the noise, and the smells, and the sheer press of people.

She was watching for anything from armed ambush to pickpockets, so it was the people took most of her attention. They weren't on a Closed World, or even close Inside, so there was a spacer's dozen of types on the street—long, short, thick, thin; pale, dark, and in-between.

Her own type, with the high-caste golden skin and the slim, deceptively frail-seeming build, was nothing to notice in this, or almost any, crowd.

Jela made a little bit of stir, but if she was to judge from various interested glances, the reasons would be the shoulders and the hips.

The clothes were as varied as the people wearing them—gowns with sleeves so long they trailed on the dusty walkway, daysilks and sandals, Insider formals, a couple of spacer 'skins, trader leathers, and the inevitable tunics, sleeveless so the Batcher tats showed.

Jela turned into a wide space in the walk and stopped. She swung in beside him. Overhead, suspended from a thin silvered arc, hung an inverted ceramic bowl. As they came to rest beneath, its color changed from pale yellow to bright red.

"'nother cab?" she asked, which was the first thing either had said to the other since leaving the ship.

He glanced at her. "Are we being followed?"

She sighed lightly. "Not that I've noticed."

"Right. So we'll go further in and then take another walk." He looked around at the wide crowded walk and busy street, the low, featureless pastel buildings shining in the full light of the local sun.

"Nice city."

"If you say so," she answered, as a flutter caught the edge of her eye and she turned to look up the walkway.

The next building up was a domed affair, pale pink, with a striped yellow-and-blue awning over the door. Coming out of the door were a dozen or more people in long, cowled robes striped to match the awning, bearing pale pink baskets. As they reached the common walkway, they separated into pairs, each pair taking off at a tangent. The pair walking toward their position at the taxi stand were pressing something from their baskets into the hands of those they passed, with a murmured phrase she couldn't quite pick out at this distance in the general city din.

Cantra moved her eyes, checking the moving people and assuring herself that they still weren't being followed. Near as she could tell, which wasn't as near as she'd like.

"Here comes our cab," Jela said from beside her.

She turned face forward, spying the thing as it cut across four lanes of traffic, not much more than a bench seat mounted behind the hump of a nav-brain, enclosed in plas-shielding, the whole vehicle scooting along on three wheels.

She took a step forward, felt someone too close to her right shoulder and spun, nearly knocking over one of the striped-robes— she had an impression of pale eyes, and a glint of teeth in the dimness of the cowl, and something cool pressed into her hand.

"Die well, sister," the soft voice murmured and they were gone. The cab had arrived and Jela was already on the seat, the door coming down, the shielding already starting to opaque—

"Cantra!"

She jumped, ducked under the descending door and fell heavily onto the bench, banging into Jela's shoulder.

"Sorry," she muttered.

"No problem," he answered, most of his attention on the map panel. He jerked his head toward the sealed door.

"What was that about?"

"Couple of crazies, giving me a—" She opened her hand, and blinked down at the plain square tile in her hand.

"Looks like one of the toys I took to the Uncle," she said.

Destination chosen and accepted, the cab accelerated. Cantra breathed a small sigh of relief for the now-completely opaqued dome as Jela sat back and held out a broad hand.

"Mind if I take a look?"

She dropped it in his palm. "It's all yours."

His fingers closed over the tile and he sat with his eyes slitted for one heartbeat, two, three—

He hissed, fingers flying wide. The tile fell to the deck of the cab.

Cantra threw him a look, seeing true anger on his face.

"Not impressed, I take it," she said, and he pointed at the fallen tile.

"Did you listen to what it was saying?"

"Didn't say anything to me," she answered, "but I'd only had it a couple seconds and I was occupied with something else, besides."

"Try it," he said.

"If it's got you this riled, I think I'll pass. Whyn't you just tell me about it?"

He took a hard breath, and then another, as their cab leaned sharply to one side, obviously taking a corner at speed. Cantra banged into Jela's shoulder again, grabbed for the strap and pulled herself right.

"It asked me to embrace the sacrament of suicide," Jela said, stringently calm. "It told me to pause to remember those I love, to have compassion and include them in my death."

"Oh." Cantra looked down at the decking, but the tile was out of sight, having doubtless slid away under the bench during the last hard turn.

"*Sheriekas*-work, you're thinking," she didn't ask.

"What else?" he answered and turned his attention to the map and the rapid green line that was the graphic of their journey across the city.

He tapped the display with a broad forefinger and she bent to look.

"We'll be getting off in another couple turns—" A grin, though not up to his usual standards—"if we survive the trip. We'll walk into the meet place from above, check it out before we go in, right?"

Relieved that he was being sensible, she gave him a smile, though she had the feeling it wasn't one of her better efforts, either.

"Right."

So far, the timing was good. They were within a block of the meeting place—a shop called Business as Usual, which rented guaranteed secure meeting rooms by the local quarter-hour.

His plan was to reconnoiter, then take up a position and watch the front door. He figured he'd be able to spot his contact well enough and take a reading before committing.

If it read bad, he had promised himself, or even a little over-risky, he'd back off, retreat to the ship and regroup.

Having Cantra with him complicated things, but she *was* fully capable, as she'd demonstrated numerous times now.

Besides which, he was just glad to have her with him.

A soldier, even a thorough rogue of a generalist, was a pack creature, accustomed to having his comrades about him. It warmed him now to have a comrade at his back, with action maybe looming.

The streets on this side of the city were thinner and less peopled; the buildings tending to monochrome-colored blocks, rather than the rounded pastels on the northeast side.

Cantra was walking on his off-side, a long step behind. Out of the corner of his eye he watched her scanning the street, the buildings, the people.

Fully capable woman, he thought again, and there was the worry again, because time was getting tight. If he didn't make a good contact today, it might come down to leaving the tree and his mission, both, in the fully capable hands of a woman who had for so long cared only for herself and her ship that she might not be able to make the leap to a larger duty.

Leave it alone, he told himself. *Mission first. Worry later.*

"Coming up," he said, pitching his voice so Cantra could hear him, but likely no others. "We want to take the right turn, go down 'til the second right and take that. That'll—"

"Put us in the service alley," she finished, with more of a laugh than a snap in her voice. "I did take a look at that map, like I said I would."

He glanced over and met her foggy green gaze.

"I thought you weren't worried," she said.

He shrugged. "Having a civilian in it worries old habits," he said, surprising himself with the truth.

"Let's think of this as the pilot backing the co-pilot," she answered. "That ease old habits, any?"

"It does," he said, keeping with the mostly-truth. "It's good to have a comrade at hand."

"Strangely easeful," she allowed. "This our turn?"

It was and they took it, passing out of full sunlight and into dense shade. Jela motioned and Cantra stretched those long legs to come up shoulder-to-shoulder.

"If there's any trouble—and I don't expect it—what you want to do is get out of it and call for back-up," he said and gave her as hard a look as he had in him.

Her face showed bland and pleasant—not a good sign.

"Cantra?"

"My idea," she husked, and her voice did fall sweet on a soldier's ear, "was to stand as your back-up. That's why I'm here."

"There's a time when you've got to cut your losses, retreat and regroup," he said, in the easy voice he'd used to coach countless newbies. "If it starts to look bad, remember that I'm built to take a lot of punishment with minimal damage, and get clear of it."

"I'll do that," Cantra said insincerely.

He sighed—and gave it up as a lost battle.

"Next turn upcoming," she said and shot him a grin. "Might have some trouble getting those shoulders in there."

The alley was thin, but not that thin. It was even dimmer than the shaded street, and crowded with all the unglamorous bits of business—trash compactors, delivery crates, wagons and storage sheds.

Cantra slipped 'round the corner, hugging the wall, and paused in the shadow of a recycling bin.

Jela slid in beside her, arm touching arm.

"Our target," he murmured, scanning what he could see of the clutter, "is in the middle of the left side of this alley. Which," he added as he felt her draw a slightly deeper breath, "I know you know. I'm just checking to see if our info agrees."

He heard the ghost of a chuckle.

"It agrees."

"Good. I'll go first. You cover me."

No argument there—which didn't surprise him. As good as her word, Cantra yos'Phelium. She'd volunteered to be his back-up—back-up is what she'd be.

So, he eased out from cover of the recycler and moved on down the alley, keeping to what cover was convenient, scanning the likely places and the unlikely ones, too, going soft-foot and unhurried—which was how he managed to come on them unaware.

Four of them—soldiers all—checking their weapons and settling into quiet positions, not deep concealment, from which he deduced that they were waiting for a sign from inside.

He hesitated, weighing the odds and the need for info—and the fact that there was a fully capable civilian—a pilot!—giving him back-up, which tipped the balance to retreat.

Soft and careful, he sank back into the shadows, turned, slipped around his cover—

And ducked back as three more came walking down the alley toward him.

Jela slipped around the edge of the equipment and disappeared into the general clutter.

Cantra counted to twelve, then eased forward, gun in hand, sinking down onto a knee in a relatively dry bit of cermacrete. Cheek against the side of the recycler, she peered out—and bit off a curse.

Three people, two of the taller new-style soldiers Jela was so impressed with and one probable natural human, some fair bit shorter than the others. The natural was wearing a uniform with enough shiny stuff on the sleeves to make Cantra blink. Women that impor-tant were hard to find.

They were armed but not at ready, and they were heading straight for Jela.

"You wanted to do back-up," she muttered to herself, and went after them, keeping tight against the side of a storage shed. Not that it mattered. From the way they walked, the three soldiers thought they owned this alley and everything in it.

Swaggering, three abreast and looking neither to the right nor the left, they passed a tall stack of delivery crates—which promptly fell on them. Cantra caught a glimpse of trade leather among the back shadows and grinned even as she dropped to her knees, gun up, sighting on the nearer of the two big soldiers, who'd managed to keep his feet, despite the crate wedged over his head.

The other two were roaring and flailing on the alley floor—and suddenly the second big one was up, throwing a crate with forceful malice and going for his side arm.

The one on the ground had used her eyes, though, worse luck. "That's him! Take him out!"

Cantra changed targets and squeezed off a shot at the one with his pistol already out.

She'd gone for a back shot—something to slow him down—and for a second she thought she'd missed entirely.

Then the soldier slapped his right hand to his upper left arm and spun, staggering as the crates shifted around his legs.

"Gun at the rear!"

Great.

She got her feet under her, snapped off a shot at the second big guy and angled across the alley, keeping low.

A plentitude of shots, now, more than she thought could be produced by three disoriented soldiers.

The map she had memorized had the alley intersecting with another side street several hundred paces beyond the current action, so Jela had an out—may have already taken it, for all she could figure from the noise and the movement. Her immediate problem was the three soldiers, all on their feet now and just as irritable as they could be.

"There!"

The not-so-tall soldier flung forward, gun out, face grim.

Cantra brought her weapon up and fired.

The charge hit the leaping woman in the chest, knocked her off her feet and back into the tumble of crates.

Cantra sprinted for cover—

There was a roar behind her, she spun, dodged the big fist descending toward her head, tucked and dove for the floor between his feet, coming up behind him, facing the confusion of downed crates—and the other big soldier, who had his gun out now and aimed at her.

She fired at his face, missed, and threw herself backward into a somersault between the first soldier's legs.

Close by, there was a shot; she snapped to her feet, spun—

The first soldier was down, his right leg under him at a bad angle and bleeding copiously. The soldier with the gun moved it, sighting beyond his downed comrade.

Cantra took her time, sighted and fired.

The charge took him in the throat. He fell noisily into the crates, his weapon discharging harmlessly into the air.

Slowly, Cantra straightened. The alley was eerily quiet. Right, then. Jela had taken the back way out and—

A shout, the voice too familiar, and the sound of more boxes falling with energy.

Swearing, Cantra moved forward, picking her way across the downed crates with care.

Jela'd got himself into a bit of a conundrum. He taken up position in a relatively clear spot in the alley, the sides formed by the privacy fence at his back, a storage shed to the right and a heavy-duty conveyer to the left. There was room to maneuver, but not much opportunity to bring firearms into play.

One of the big soldiers was down already—an added hazard to footing already made risky by the tumble of crates. Three more soldiers were trying to get a grip on the man who kept moving, dodging, feinting, a knife in each hand.

Cantra slid into the shadow of a lorry and considered the action. Watching, it came to her that the big soldiers were operating under a handicap. They seemed to be trying to capture, while Jela was basically pursuing kill-and-maim.

Right.

She brought her gun up, checked the charge, and considered her options.

She'd about settled on the back of the guy nearest her position, when a shadow moved across her vision and she looked up, frowning…

Atop the storage shed was another soldier, stretched long and secret across the flat roof, a rifle against his shoulder.

So much for the capture idea. Jela's playmates had just been keeping him busy until the rifleman got into position.

It was a risky shot with a hand gun, though even if she missed, her shot would serve as a warning—for whatever that was worth.

At alley level, Jela's three opponents suddenly let out simultaneous roars and rushed him.

On the roof, the rifleman took his sighting.

Cantra brought her gun up, acquired her target—fired.

The secret shooter jerked, the rifle releasing its round into the blameless conveyer.

In the alley, the fight was a confusion of movement and shape. She glimpsed Jela, dancing like a lunatic, one knife gone, the sleeve of his pretty trader's shirt hanging in bloody ribbons. There was no possibility of a clear shot, and no doubt but that things were going bad for her co-pilot, built to take punishment or not.

The time had come to take a more personal interest.

Gun in one hand, knife in the other, howling, Cantra charged.

A soldier looked up at her noisy approach, an expression of stark disbelief on his tattooed face, and a battle knife roughly as long as she was in his hand.

Leaving Jela to his mates, he swung to face her, grinning.

Fine.

She stretched her legs, bent nearly double, aiming to get *inside* that long reach, where she could do some damage and his absurdly long blade would be a handicap.

He grabbed for her, she dodged, saw the blade, flung an arm up.

The gun deflected the thrust and flew out of her hand. Her arm fell, numb, to her side, but she was inside now—inside his guard; and she jumped, using the momentum to drive the knife up between the rib—

Her legs were in a vise; she was upside down; the was knife lost; and she was spinning, her hair whipping across her eyes. She knew with utter clarity that in another frenzied heartbeat her brains would be running down the side of the shed—

The spinning stopped.

Her legs were released and she fell, remembering at the last instant to get her arms out and break the fall.

She was panting. There was no other sound in the alley—wrong. A groan.

She rolled to her feet, turned, saw her late opponent standing as if frozen, his eyes fixed on something…else.

Across the alley, Jela's two admirers were likewise frozen in mid-combat, and Jela himself was climbing warily, and none-too-steadily, to his feet.

"Both of you!" snapped a high, feminine voice. "Come here! Quickly!"

Slowly, Cantra turned, squinted—and there at the edge of the conveyer unit stood a lady in the grey robes of a philosopher, her red hair blazing in the murk like a torch.

"Well." That was Jela arriving at her side. He began a bow, bloody hand outstretched, staggered—Cantra grabbed his arm and yanked him upright.

"Thank you, ma'am," he said hoarsely to the lady.

"You are quite welcome," she replied coolly. "Attend me, now. At the far end of this alley, you will find a red-haired man holding a cab for you. Go with him. I'll finish dealing here."

Cantra glanced at the three huge, frozen figures, thought about the dart gun in her inside pocket—

"Do *not* kill them," the lady snapped. "Just *go!*"

"Go it is," Jela said placatingly. He turned in the indicated direction, feet tangling, and Cantra got a supporting arm around him.

"Take it easy," she said.

"No time," he muttered. "I'll be ready in a few—your board, Pilot."

She set a steady, if not precisely brisk, pace, half holding Jela up—no small weight, that, despite his size. He kept the pace, though he seemed not exactly connected, which got her worrying about how much blood he'd already lost and what she'd do if he went down.

Worry and stagger aside, they made the end of the alley without disaster; and he seemed a little more alert by the time she pushed him up against a wall and had a long look out into the street.

All clear on the straight, and on the right, to the left—

Stood a slender man in formal black tunic and pants, one elegantly slippered foot braced on the floor of an open cab. He was holding a watch in his hand, and smiling at her.

"I see that all proceeds according to plan," he said merrily, and stepped away from the cab, sweeping a flawless bow of welcome. "Please. Your carriage awaits you, Pilots."

She glanced at her co-pilot, saw his eyes full open in a face paler than she liked.

"Well?" she asked.

He sighed and appeared to do some quick math.

"Not well," he growled after a heartbeat. "But I think we'd better take the kind ser's offer."

"All right, then." She eased back and he stood away from the wall, moving with something like his accustomed certainty.

Good enough.

She strolled out to the cab, and bowed to the red-haired man.

"My co-pilot and I are grateful," she murmured, and stood back to let Jela get in first, then went after him.

Behind her, the door began to descend. The red-haired man ducked inside, slipping onto the half-bench facing them, his back to the forward screens.

"Pilots," he murmured, as the cab hurtled into motion. "I beg you acquit me of poor manners, if I am short of conversation this next while. I am called to aid my lady. There is a field kit under your seat." He closed his eyes and settled his back against the opaque plas shielding.

Cantra blinked and rummaged under the bench, locating the field kit and pulling it onto her lap.

"Do you know who these people are?" she asked, as she sorted out dressings and lotions.

"No," Jela said tiredly, holding his arm out so she could get at the worst of the blood. "I don't know who they are, but I know what they are."

"What's that, then?" Cantra asked, breaking out an antiseptic swab.

"They're *sheriekas*."

THIRTY-ONE

On Port
Gimlins

THE ARM WAS patched as good as she could make it, which wasn't near as good as it needed.

She said as much to Jela, now apparently recovered from the woozies, but he only shrugged and asked her to cut off the remains of the bloody sleeve.

That done, the kit repacked and returned to its spot beneath the seat, she joined him in staring at the cab's on-board map.

"Don't seem to be working," she said after a moment, and heard him sigh.

"That it doesn't."

She considered their rescuer, slumped, to all appearances unconscious, on the jump-seat.

He was a pretty little man, his bright red hair artfully cut and arranged in loose ringlets. He wore it long and carelessly caught over one shoulder with a twist of jeweled wire. The tunic's long sleeves were cross-laced with black ribbons, and the elegant slippers were heavily embroidered with black silk.

He looked, Cantra thought, like a high-caste member of a High House on one of the Inmost worlds—a supposition borne out by his accent, bearing, and bow. His face was a shade too pale for proper high-caste, but she thought that might be an effect of whatever induced state he was presently in. Awake, she thought he'd be as golden-skinned as any pure-blood or deliberate copy.

"You're sure this guy is *sheriekas*?" she asked Jela.

"Yes," he answered shortly, his attention still on the non-functional map.

"Hmm," she said, eyeing him. "How're you doing mostwise?"

He looked up from the map, black eyes speculative.

"I'm up for some action, if you are."

"Fine," Cantra said firmly. "Then there's no reason to stick around until the ser finishes his nap."

She reached into her vest, slipped a length of smartwire from the inside pocket, and shifted around on the bench to face the hatch.

"Get ready to jump," she said over her shoulder. "The door likely won't go up all the way, and it might be something of a tumble, but we should be out of here—"

The red-haired man on the jump-seat took a sudden deep breath, straightened, and opened his eyes. They were, Cantra saw, a deep and vivid blue, initially focused on something on the far side of the next sector, sharpening quickly on matters closer to hand.

"That's done then," he murmured, and his voice was light and cultured. He sent a glance to Jela.

"Indeed, sir," he said, as if they had been engaged in cordial conversation. "It is my very great pleasure to correct you. Neither I nor my lady are *sheriekas.*"

Jela snorted. "Tell me you've never destroyed a star system."

The little man smiled with gentle reproach. "But I am not such a fool, dear sir. Of course I have destroyed star systems. I hope you won't think me boastful if I admit to being uniquely equipped for such work. Much as you, yourself, are uniquely equipped for fighting. Will you tell me, M. Jela, whose mandate is to protect life, that you have never killed?"

Jela smiled—one of his real ones, Cantra saw.

"No," he said softly. "I'm not such a fool."

The little man inclined his head, acknowledging the point. "Well answered, sir. We stand on terms." He turned his eyes to Cantra.

"Lady," he murmured. She held up a hand.

"Hate to disappoint you," she said, watching his eyes, "but I'm no lady, just a Rimmer pilot."

A flicker of amusement showed in the eyes, nothing else.

"Lady," he repeated, courteously. "Please allow me to be at your feet—your most humble and willing servant in all things. Your well-being is more important to me than my life. There is no need to resort to such things as pick-locks while you are in my care."

She considered him, admiring the way he blended irony with sincerity. Whoever had the training of this one had drilled him well.

Unless of course he was the genuine article, in which case she wasn't wholly certain that she wouldn't rather have fallen into the so-called care of Jela's *sheriekas.*

"If my well-being means so much to you," she said, bringing the Rim accent up so hard it rang against the ear. "Open the door and let us out."

"In time," he said, lifting a slim forefinger. A ring covered the finger from knuckle to first joint—an oval black stone in a black setting, carved with—

"In time," their host-or-captor said again. "I would be careless indeed of your well-being, not to say that of the most excellent Jela, if I released you now, with enemies on the watch and information yet to be shared."

She sighed, and slipped the smartwire back into the inside pocket. "You got a name?"

He inclined his head. "Indeed, Lady, I have a name. It is Rool Tiazan."

"And you can blow up star systems," she pursued, since Jela wasn't saying anything.

"I can destroy star systems," Rool Tiazan corrected gently. "Yes."

"Right—destroy," she said, amiably. "And you ain't *sheriekas*."

"Also correct."

"If you're not *sheriekas*," Jela said, finally joining the fun, "what are you?"

"Excellent." He placed one elegant hand flat against his chest. "I, my lady, and all those like unto us, are *sheriekas*-made, M. Jela. We were created on purpose that we should do their bidding and hasten the day when eternity belongs only to *sheriekas*; the lesser-born and the flawed merely distasteful memories to be forgot as quickly as might be."

"If you're *sheriekas*-made, in order to do the bidding of your makers—" Jela began and Rool Tiazan held up his hand, the carved black stone glinting.

"Forgive me, M. Jela," he murmured, and his pretty, ageless face was no longer smiling. "You—and also you, Lady—are surely aware that choice exists. We no longer choose to perform these certain tasks on behalf of those who caused us to be as we are. We are alive, and life is sweet. There is no place nor plan for us in the eternity toward which we were bade to labor."

He moved his hand in a snap, as if throwing dice across a cosmic cloth.

"We of the *dramliz* cast our lot in with those who are also alive, and who find life sweet."

"That's a fine-sounding statement," Jela said calmly, "and you deliver it well. But I don't believe it."

"Alas." Rool Tiazan tipped his head to one side. "I sympathize with your wariness, M. Jela—indeed, I applaud it. However, I would ask you to consider these things—that my lady and I have preserved your lives and now assist you to evade those who wish you ill."

Jela held out his hand, palm up. "The first is probably true," he said, and turned his palm down. "For the second, we have only your word, which I'm afraid is insufficient."

"You do not trust me, in a word," Rool Tiazan murmured. "May I know why?"

"You do," Jela said, mildly, "destroy star systems, as and when ordered by the *sheriekas*."

"The correct verb is 'did.' I have absented myself from the work for some number of years. However, I understand you to say that there is no ground upon which we might meet in trust because I have done terrible things during the course of my training and my duty. Do I have this correctly, M. Jela? I would not wish to misunderstand you."

"You have it correctly," Jela said.

"Ah." He turned his head, and Cantra felt the dark blue gaze hit her like a blow.

"Lady—a question, if you will."

She held up a hand. "Why bother? Can't you just grab what you want out of my mind?"

He smiled—genuinely amused, as far as she could read him.

"Legend proceeds us, I see. Unfortunately, legend is both accurate and misleading. Under certain conditions, I can indeed siphon information from the minds of others. It is not difficult, it does no harm to those so read and may provide some good for myself and my lady. However." He raised his jeweled forefinger.

"However, there are some individuals whom it is very difficult to read—yourself, for an instance, and M. Jela for another. And even if I could siphon the answer out of your mind, M. Jela cannot, and it is for him that I would ask the question."

He was good, Cantra thought. And she was intrigued.

"Ask."

"You are, I believe, full-trained as an *aelantaza*, to deceive and destroy at the word of those who caused you to be as you are. I would ask if, in the course of those exercises necessary for you to gain competence in your art, you ever took a blameless life."

"For Jela, is this?" She faced her co-pilot. "We had—rabbits, they were called. We practiced all our kills on live targets."

"Rabbits that ran on two feet," Rool Tiazan murmured.

"Batch-bred?" Jela asked.

She inclined her head. "What else?"

There was a short silence, then Rool Tiazan spoke again.

"M. Jela, do you trust this lady, whose training and acts run parallel to my own?"

"I do. She's proved herself trustworthy."

Accidents all, but it warmed her to hear him say it anyway, praise from Jela being coin worth having—and keeping, if she was being honest.

"Ah," Rool Tiazan murmured. "Then I see I shall need to continue upon my path of candidness. So—"

He gestured gracefully toward the roof of the cab—or perhaps beyond it.

"While it is true that I have destroyed star systems, I must confess that those which fell to my thought were chaotic and incapable of supporting life. The more life-force—shall we call it *will*?" He paused, apparently awaiting their agreement.

"All right," Jela said, with a shrug of wide shoulders.

"Will, then. The more will that exists within a system, the more difficult it is to bend the lines of probability into a conformation in which the extinction of the system is inevitable.

"Similarly, though I may alter probability on a less epic scale, the subsequent ripple of unanticipated changes make the practice somewhat less than perfectly useful."

Cantra raised an eyebrow. "You're trying to say that the *sheriekas* made a design error and that you're really not worth their trouble?"

"Not entirely, Lady. Not entirely. There is, after all, some benefit to be had from the mere reading of the lines and by observing the congruencies of various energies. Indeed, observation of an anomaly in the forces of what we shall, I fear, have to call 'luck' is what brought my lady and me here to pleasant Gimlins."

"Just in time to save our necks," Jela commented. "I'd call that lucky—or planned."

"You misunderstand me, M. Jela. It is neither I nor my lady who are lucky. It is you—" the slim, be-ringed forefinger pointed for a moment at Jela's chest, then swung toward Cantra—

"And most especially *you*, Lady—about whom the luck swirls and gathers."

"Lucky!" Cantra laughed.

Rool Tiazan smiled sweetly. "Doubt it not. Between the two of you, the luck moves so swiftly that the effect—to those such as my lady and myself—is nothing short of gravitational. We were pulled quite off of our intended course."

"I'd be interested to hear how you'd reconcile our being lucky with coming within two heartbeats of getting killed back there," Cantra said.

"The luck is a natural force, Lady Cantra. It is neither positive nor negative; it obeys the laws binding its existence and cares not how its courses alter the lives through which it flows."

"So you—and your lady—" Jela said slowly, "were pulled here against your will."

"Ah." Rool Tiazan moved his hand as if he would hand Jela a coin. "Not quite against *our* wills, M. Jela. The *dramliz* have long been aware that if we are to win free to life, we will require allies. We have further understood, through an intense study of probability and possibility, that the best allies life has against the *sheriekas* is random action. It is *our will* to take part in the chaos resulting from your necessities, from your..."

"Luck, in a word," said Jela.

Rool Tiazan inclined his head. "Precisely."

"And you think, do you and your comrades," pursued Jela, "that the *sheriekas* can be defeated."

The little man gazed at him reproachfully.

"No, M. Jela. The *dramliz* have come to the conclusion—as you have—that the *sheriekas* may not be defeated."

"Then what use are allies?"

Rool Tiazan smiled.

"Because, though the *sheriekas* may not be defeated, they can be resisted, they may be confounded, they might be *escaped*," he said softly. "Life may go on, and the *sheriekas* may have their eternity, each separate from the other."

"Escaped how?" Cantra asked, and the blue gaze again grazed her face.

306   *Sharon Lee and Steve Miller*

"There are several possibilities, Lady, of which we most certainly must speak. I would ask, however, that we put the discussion of how and may be into the near future, when my lady may also take part." He paused, his head inclined courteously.

"Whatever," she said, deliberately discourteous, but he merely smiled as if she'd given him proper word and mode and turned his attention back to Jela.

"Regarding your mission, M. Jela. You are aware that the consolidated commanders are effectively defeated, are you not? They have been routed in most of their bases and are hunted—with more fervor than the proper enemy! Or do you believe the late contretemps in the alley a mere coincidence?"

Beside her, Jela—seemed to loose some breadth of shoulder. He sighed.

"I had hopes that my commander..." he murmured, and let the words trail away into nothing.

Rool Tiazan lifted his head, pointing his eyes toward—*beyond*, Cantra thought—the roof of the cab.

"Your commander is at liberty," he said, in a distant voice. "She has eluded those the High Command sent against her and commands a small force of specialists. Their apparent course is for the Out-Rim, vectoring the area of increased *sheriekas* attacks." He blinked and lowered his gaze to Jela's face.

"I do not find a probability or a possibility, not a likelihood at all, in which she survives beyond the turning of the Common Year."

Thirty Common Days, as Cantra did the math.

"If it does not offend," Rool Tiazan said quietly, "my lady and I offer our condolences, M. Jela."

Silence. Jela's eyes were closed. He took a breath—another. Sighed and opened his eyes.

"I thank you and your lady," he said softly and with no irony that Cantra could detect. "My commander would wish to die in battle, doing proper duty."

"So she shall," the *dramliza* assured him. "That she extends the fight acts to disguise events wonderfully. Your commanders may lose, but *your* mission...continues."

Another small moment of silence passed before Jela straightened, visibly throwing off grief.

"Where are you taking us?" he asked Rool Tiazan.

"Ah. To your ship, where my lady will meet us."

"What?" Cantra demanded, but Jela only nodded.

"Good. I want another opinion of the two of you."

Rool Tiazan smiled. "We will be delighted to accommodate you, sir."

"If you will excuse me once more, my attention is wanted elsewhere," the *dramliz* Rool Tiazan murmured.

He apparently took their permission for granted. No sooner had he spoken than he was slumped on the jump-seat again, in a trance so deep he hardly seemed to breathe.

Jela took a moment to consider the extreme vulnerability of the man's situation, then shook the thought away. He *looked* vulnerable, did Rool Tiazan, but it would be beyond foolish to assume that he allowed himself to be at the mercy of his enemies.

Or of his allies.

Jela sighed to himself, and put thoughts of mayhem on hold, pending the tree's judgment.

He glanced over and saw Cantra watching him. Her fingers moved against her knee, flicking out—*Condition is?*

Now there was the question, he thought—wasn't it? Trust Cantra to ask it, and he'd better be accurate in his assessment, because only she knew what course she'd plot from the data.

Condition is, he signed slowly—*double usual rules.*

She gave a slight nod, indicating receipt of the message, and settled herself silently into her corner of the bench. Apparently neither one of them wanted to start a conversation that their host could retroactively snatch out of the air when he came to.

What thoughts might occupy Cantra, he didn't know, though he might guess it had to do with the prospect of allowing strangers possessed of peculiar talents onto her ship and strategies for holding them harmless.

For himself—well, for the first time in his generalist's life, he had too much to think about—and on subjects he'd rather not consider.

That the consolidated commanders had been discovered and were in the process of being destroyed—he'd suspected the worst when his usual contacts had failed him.

The situation of his commander—if he believed the report of Rool Tiazan—and he had no reason, given his own direst fears, to doubt it...

The report that Commander Ro Gayda would soon be dead in action grieved him more than he could quite assimilate. He had lost comrades before—countless numbers of comrades—and commanding officers, as well. And yet this death, despite that he believed it to be one that she herself would embrace with a soldier's fierce joy—this death pained him in places so deep and private he hardly knew how to deal with it.

Had his arm been caught in a man-trap, he might have hacked it off and kept on fighting; had his ship been breeched, he might have rushed the enemy and with his last breath made the pain meaningful.

But this—there was no getting at the wound; no assessing the level of function disturbed...

A flicker out of the corner of his eye—Cantra's fingers, asking— *Condition is?*

He sighed, and watched his fingers spell out—*Old soldier hit bad*, which might've been more truth than he would have willingly given, but a pilot learns to trust his fingers—and besides, it was too late to unsay it.

Cantra reached out and put her near hand on his knee, then leaned her head back against the bench. She didn't say anything else, or even look at him, really, but the pressure of her hand eased the tightness inside his chest. His commander might be dead, her unit destroyed, but he had his duty, his mission—and a comrade. It wasn't much—maybe, maybe. But when had a soldier needed more than his kit and his orders?

The cab was slowing. He glanced at the map before he recalled that it was off-line, then at the *dramliza*.

Rool Tiazan opened his eyes and straightened in his seat, the rich color returning to his face.

"We will be leaving the cab very shortly and joining my lady," he said in his smooth voice.

Jela felt Cantra's fingers tighten on his knee, but she unexpectedly held her peace, leaving him to ask—

"I thought we were returning to our ship?"

"Indeed we are, M. Jela. But not directly to your ship, I think? Four people walking across the yard may—no, I must say, *will be*—

unremarked. We have not the same assurance of anonymity, riding at leisure in a cab." He paused, head tipped to one side.

"If your wounds pain you, sir, my lady will be pleased to assist you."

He meant the arm and the various other scratches from the late action, Jela thought, to keep the hairs that wanted to rise up on the back of his neck where they belonged.

"Thank you for your concern," he said politely. "They are hardly noticeable; I've fought long days of battle with worse and not faltered."

"Surely, surely." The *dramliza* smiled and moved his slender hand, stroking the common air of the cab as if it were a live creature. "I meant no insult, sir. The prowess of the M Series is legend even among the *sheriekas*, whom we must thank for the original design."

The hairs did stand up then.

"Explain that," he said, and heard the snarl in his voice. Cantra's fingers, still resting on his knee, tightened briefly, then relaxed.

"Don't tease him," she told the *dramliza* in the lazy voice that meant mayhem wasn't too far distant. "He's had a trying day."

Rool Tiazan inclined his head in her direction, his face smooth and urbane.

"Lady. It was not my intention to tease, but to inform." He paused.

"The prototype of the M Series," he said, with care, Jela thought, "was developed at the end of the last war by those now known to you as *sheriekas*. The design was captured, modifications were made, and when the *sheriekas* returned to exercise their dominion over the Spiral Arm, the M Series was waiting to deny them the pleasure."

Jela grinned. "I hope they were surprised."

"By accounts, they were just that," said Rool Tiazan. "They had abandoned the design as flawed, you see." He smiled, as sudden and as feral as any soldier about to face an enemy.

"Over and over," he murmured, "they make the same error."

"The *dramliz* are flawed too, I take it," Cantra said, still in her lazy, could-be-trouble voice.

"The *dramliz*," Rool Tiazan said softly, "are multiply flawed, as the *sheriekas* had no wish to create those with abilities sufficient unto the task of destroying *sheriekas* without—appropriate safeguards."

A chime sounded inside the compartment and the sense of motion ceased entirely.

"Ah! We are arrived!" Rool Tiazan moved a hand as the door began to lift.

"Please, after you, Lady and sir."

They were on a narrow and sparsely populated street in the upper port. The shop windows of the stores lining the blue cermacrete walkway were uniformly opaque, the sell-scents and light-banners quiet.

"Ah, excellent," Rool Tiazan murmured, as he stepped out of the cab. "Our timing holds." Behind him, the cab's door descended, the window darkened, and it sped off up the street.

"Come," the *dramliza* said, moving down the walk toward the cross-street "my lady awaits us."

They turned right at the corner, Rool Tiazan walking with something like a soldier's proper stride, for all he looked so fragile. The few people they passed spared them no glance, though surely the three of them were a sight worth—

Four of them, Jela corrected himself, catching the flutter of grey robes from the edge of his eye as a lady stepped from the doorway of a closed bookshop and fell in silently beside Rool Tiazan, placing her hand lightly on his arm.

The lady was—diminutive, a fact that had not been readily noticeable in the alley. The top of her cropped red head barely reached her mate's shoulder.

Her gray robe was embroidered in gray thread. Jela squinted after the design—and found himself looking instead at the shop windows, the traffic, and the few pedestrians they passed.

"Interesting robe," Cantra murmured from beside him. "I wouldn't look too close, though."

"I *can't* look too close," he complained, and heard her throaty chuckle.

They came to another street, turned right and were abruptly in day port, the walk busy with people, the banners and signs in full attraction mode, the street filled with cabs and lorries and cargo carriers.

And still no eyes turned their way, even in idle curiosity.

"Invisibility has its uses," Cantra muttered.

"But we are not invisible, Lady Cantra." Rool Tiazan's voice drifted lightly over his shoulder to them. "We are merely—of no interest."

They crossed the busy mainway carefully, and were soon among the ships. Jela felt Cantra growing tense beside him.

"Pilot?" He murmured.

She sighed. "This visit really necessary?"

"Yes," he told her regretfully. "Pilot, it is."

"Right."

Dancer was coming up on the next row and Cantra stretched her legs to come even with Rool Tiazan.

"I'm captain of yon ship," she said. "It's mine to go up first and open her."

"Of course," he said with an inclination of his bright head.

His lady lifted her hand from his arm and fell back beside Jela. He looked down into her sharp, solemn face.

"The configuration carries the suggestion," she said, answering the question he hadn't asked.

"So if we walked down the street four abreast, people would notice us?" he asked.

"Not necessarily," she replied. "But such a configuration might require Rool to somewhat exert his will, which might in turn catch the attention of those with whom we would rather not deal."

"The *sheriekas* are looking for you, then?"

The lady turned her head away. "What do you suppose, M. Jela?"

"That, if the *sheriekas* were hunting me, I'd think very hard about where I led them."

"We have thought—very hard," she returned, giving him a haughty look from amber eyes. "We and those who are like us. The consensus is that, while success is not assured, we must nonetheless act. It is true that we may fail and all the galaxy—indeed, all the galaxies!—go down into the empty perfection of the *sheriekas* eternity. But if we do not try, we shall certainly embrace that doom."

They were at the base of *Dancer's* ramp. Cantra went up, light-footed as always, Rool Tiazan pacing silently at her side.

Jela would have waited a moment on the cermacrete, to avoid a crowd at the hatch, but his walking companion placed her tiny hand on his wounded arm and urged him forward.

"I regret that you have taken hurt," she murmured, as they moved up the ramp.

"I've been wounded before," he told her shortly, and was surprised by a stern glance from those amber eyes.

"We have all of us been wounded, M. Jela. It is still possible to regret the occasion."

He bowed his head. "You're correct, Lady. It was a rude reply."

"It is not the rudeness which is dangerous," the lady said, as they hit the top of the ramp. "But the assumption that pain may be discounted."

Ahead of them, the hatch rose, and Cantra ducked inside, Rool Tiazan her faithful shadow. Jela and the lady followed them into the narrow lock, the hatch reversing itself the instant they stepped within.

Cantra turned away from the control panel, waited until the hatch was sealed, then slithered past the crushed three of them to lead the way down the corridor to the piloting chamber.

Rool Tiazan extended a hand and his lady moved forward to take it. So linked, they followed Cantra.

Jela took a step—and paused, lifting his wounded arm. It felt—odd. He snapped the seal on the dressing Cantra had so painstakingly applied, pulled it off—

The wound had been—non-trivial. He'd done what he could, and Cantra had done what she'd been able. Still, it would have—should have—taken time and a medic's care to fully heal.

And now—there was no wound, no sign that he'd been wounded. His tough brown hide didn't even show a scar.

Neck hairs prickling, he threw the dressing into the recycler and moved after the others.

The corridor was dim with emergency lighting, the doors along it dogged to red. Cantra hadn't wasted her few seconds with the control panel, Jela thought, and approved.

The door to the piloting chamber was dogged, too. Cantra placed her fingers on a certain spot along the frame and the door opened.

Inside, it was no brighter than the corridor, the board a blot of darkness along the far wall. Taking no chances, was Cantra yos'Phelium, canny woman that she was.

At the far end of the room, in the corner formed by the end of the co-pilot's board and the curve of the interior wall, leaves glowing in the light from the emergency dim above it, was the tree.

Cantra walked to the pilot's station and stood, tense but calm, her hand on the back of the chair. Rool Tiazan and his lady, however, had stopped only three steps into the room, and stood as if caught in an immobilizer beam.

Jela moved to one side, so he stood between them and the tree without obscuring their view of each other. After all, it was the tree he had wanted them to see; the tree who should make the judgment, here. The tree—

Its branches were moving slightly, though the blowers were off, and the whole tower was suddenly filled with the aroma of fresh seed-pod.

"Ah," Rool Tiazan's lady breathed, and glided forward on silent gray slippers. Her mate went after her, one respectful step behind.

Though this was the meeting he had wanted, Jela twitched, suddenly not sure he wanted these...*sheriekas*-made in position to damage—

Two steps from the pot itself, the lady sank to her knees on the decking, gray robes pooling about her, head down, tiny hands upraised, as if in supplication—or prayer.

Rool Tiazan, a step behind, went gracefully to one knee, and bent his head.

The tree...

There was a tumble of images in Jela's head—of a world seen by dragon-eye, the crowns of trees so thick that the sea was barely visible as a glint in the pale light of the star. Sounds filled his ears— water rushing, waves crashing, rain striking the earth, and the wind, moving through countless millions of leaves...

The dragon-eye blinked, and the wind shifted—became dry and pitiless, scouring rock, stirring the dust in the dead sea-bed, moving the sand in long waves, burying the skeletons of trees were they lay...

Jela's eyes filled with tears. He blinked them away, shot a glance at Cantra, standing with her slim shoulders bowed, her hair shielding her down turned face.

Before the tree, the lady raised up her head.

"We were not the agents, but we accept the guilt. We have committed crimes against life, actions so terrible that there can be no forgiveness.

"Have pity on us, who had none. Allow us to make amends. We pledge ourselves to you; we give you our lives—use them or end them. It is with you."

A blast of hot wind rocked the inside of Jela's head. He saw the young dragons, tumbling into the air, rolling on the soft, dry leaves at the base of a stupendous tree—and pushing out of the sheltering deadfall, hopeful new leaves on a tender trunk...

"Yes," Rool Tiazan's voice was ragged. "We have children and they are kept as safely as any may be. End us now and they will end with all else, when the *sheriekas* have had their way." He drew a hard breath.

"I have lain down my shields; you may do what you will. It will be necessary to end me first, for I may not allow harm to befall my lady."

Another breeze, this one scented with the hint of rain.

At the pilot's station, Cantra suddenly straightened and shook her hair out of her face.

"My opinion, is it?" she said, and laughed on a wild note Jela had never heard from her before. "I don't have one. Best I can bring you is something Garen used to say, that made more sense than most." She took a breath and closed her eyes, reciting in a voice a bit deeper and a fair amount slower than her normal way of speaking:

"*In the matter of allies, you need to ask yourself two things: Can they shoot? And will they aim at your enemy?*"

She opened her eyes and nodded at the tree. "That's my opinion, since you asked for it."

There was a stillness in the chamber and among the leaves of the tree. The air grew warm, which was just, Jela thought, that the blowers weren't on...

The *dramliz* didn't stir from their attitudes of supplication, save that the lady lowered her hands and folded them against her robe.

Then, as if the threat of storm had passed off; the air freshened, the top-most branches of the tree moved; and Jela, prompted by an impulse not his own, walked forward, the aroma of tree-fruit in his nose.

He slipped past the kneeling *dramliz*, and held his hand out under the branches. Two seed-pods dropped into his wide palm; he began to close his fingers—and two more dropped, attached by a branch no thicker than a thread.

Well.

Turning, he touched Rool Tiazan lightly on the shoulder, and when the man looked up handed him the two attached pods. Passing on, he gave one of the remaining two to Cantra and stood by her, his own fruit cupped in his palm.

Across the field of his mind's eye a dragon swept by, hovering on effortless wings above the crown of an enormous tree. As he watched, the dragon lowered its mighty head and a branch lifted to meet it. The dragon selected a pod, swallowed it...

The image faded.

At the base of the tree, Rool Tiazan broke one pod off the tiny branch, and handed the second to his lady.

"I, first," he murmured, and held the fruit high in his palm, where it fell into sections, releasing its aroma into the chamber.

He ate without hesitation, as a man might savor a favorite treat, and as if no suspicion—or hope—of poison clouded his heart.

His lady waited with bowed head for three heartbeats, then ate her own fruit, neatly.

"Us, now?" Cantra asked.

"It seems so," he answered.

"Right." She ate; and he did; and he closed his eyes.

Overhead, he heard the sound of dragon wings.

THIRTY-TWO

Spiral Dance
Gimlins

The gray-robed lady was in the jump-seat, Rool Tiazan standing behind her like a paladin, or a servant.

Cantra lounged at her ease, arms folded on the back of the pilot's chair, keeping her expression pleasantly neutral. She hadn't offered the ship's guests tea or other refreshment, which was her call as captain. If either noticed the lack, they didn't mention it.

Jela was in the co-pilot's chair, on his mettle and letting it show, face hard, eyes hooded. Having second thoughts about accepting the decision of a vegetable in the matter of allies, Cantra guessed, and carefully didn't think about her moment of contact with that same vegetable, its question as clear as if it had whispered in her ear.

"The *sheriekas,*" Jela said, breaking the longish silence. "According to Ser Tiazan, they can't be defeated, but they can be escaped. I'd like to hear more about that particular assertion, such as how the escape plan is configured, and what exactly you expect from your allies."

"Ah." That was the lady, sitting straight-backed and prim, gray slippered feet swinging some inches above the decking, her hands folded in her gray lap.

"Perhaps we ought better to have said that it is the fervent hope of many of the *dramliz* that the *sheriekas* may be escaped. We who have refused to serve are numerous, and varied, and not entirely of one mind."

Jela frowned. "There's no plan, then," he said, flatly.

The lady raised a tiny, ringless hand.

"There are several plans, Wingleader Jela. There is, for an instance, the plan formulated by our esteemed colleague Lute and his dominant. They—"

"Hold it," Jela was frowning hard now. "Explain dominant."

The lady sighed sharply and it was Rool Tiazan who answered.

"Lady Cantra had previously raised the question of the flaws which insure that the *dramliz* pose no threat to their makers," he said, as calmly as if they were discussing the possibilities of a proposed trading route. "Each *dramliza* is composed of two units. While each unit is possessed of those odd talents which the *sheriekas* find good, there is a selected-for disparity between them.

"The dominant unit's talents are the lesser—" He inclined his head to Jela. "You understand, sir, that we speak in relative terms of value."

"Right," said Jela.

"Yes," murmured Rool Tiazan. "So, the dominant unit holds the lesser powers, except that she may command and direct the subordinate unit and he may not withhold himself. The subordinate is also required to defend the dominant with his life."

"Must make for an interesting situation," Cantra commented, "if they ever wanted to shut one of you down."

The vivid blue gaze came to rest on her face and he inclined his head.

"Indeed. The dominant carries the seeds of her annihilation within her. When the *sheriekas* wish to terminate a *dramliza*, they merely trigger the implanted doom; and the dominant expires. Unable to regulate himself, the subordinate soon follows, unless speedily paired with another dominant."

"Nasty," Cantra said, and meant it. She looked directly at the lady. "So, why're you still walking, if it can be told? From what Jela tells me, I don't expect the Enemy likes deserters none."

The lady smiled tightly.

"This pairing is a—miscalculation, Pilot. When we realized the extent and nature of our abilities, we used them to liberate as many of our kind as possible. However, the *sheriekas* have other means of disposal at their beck, and time grows short—" she sent a swift glance to Jela—"for all."

He nodded. "I'm sorry to interrupt, Lady, and glad of an explanation of how your corps operates."

"Ah. Then I may proceed?"

"Please."

"So. Our colleague Lute and his dominant have determined that it may be possible for them and for those *dramliz* of like mind to insert themselves into the fabric of the universe as it decrystallizes and to exert their wills in such a way as to—form a bubble universe in which life might thrive, surrounded, yet apart from, the *sheriekas* eternity."

There were few enough times when Cantra had reason to think kindly on her schooling—and this was one of those rare occasions. She neither blinked nor laughed and was confident that her face hadn't changed expression. A quick glance to the side showed Jela doing pretty well, too, though he did raise a hand, signing *clarification*.

"Yes?" the lady said, none-too-gentle.

"I wonder why they think this is possible," Jela said mildly, which was as fine a bit of understatement as Cantra'd heard lately.

The lady glared, apparently finding Jela too dim for conversation, for it was once again Rool Tiazan who answered.

"They see it merely as a return to a more efficient former state, M. Jela, and anticipate little difficulty in re-crystallizing a life-friendly universe from some portion of decrystallized matter."

"I...see," Jela said carefully. "What about you—do you think this is a reasonable plan?"

There was a short pause, then the lady sighed.

"Wingleader, you must understand that what the *sheriekas* attempt—what they are accomplishing at an ever more rapid rate—is...unprecedented. The *dramliz*—we are pushing the edge of what we know to be possible, and while we may be closer to the enemy in kind and talent than any living thing, we are as children."

"That being so," Cantra heard her own voice ask, "you're still talking in terms of escape?"

The lady turned to look at her, amber eyes serious.

"We—Rool, Lute, my sister and I—we seek escape. We believe that escape, in one form or another, is possible. There are others of us who believe that the *sheriekas* can be defeated."

"Can they?" Cantra asked, fascinated despite herself. Deeps knew, the Enemy was a threat to everything in the path of themselves or their works—had been for all her life, and all of Garen's too. But the notion of descrystallizing—whatever that was meant to say—the known galaxy in the hopes of creating one better, out of will and cussedness alone—

"M. Jela," Rool Tiazan said, so soft he might have been a part of her thoughts, "has a good bit of the math which describes the process, Lady Cantra."

She glared. "Read that right out, didn't you?"

He smiled at her and glanced down at the top of his lady's head.

"Neither I nor the majority of the philosophers among the free *dramliz* believe that the *sheriekas* may be defeated," the lady said in her prim, serious voice. "Not by the *dramliz*, nor by the forces of humanity, nor even by those forces combined." She glanced aside, down the room to where Jela's tree stood tall in its pot, leaves at attention.

"Had we a dozen worlds of *ssussdriad* at the height of their powers, with legions of dragons at their call—we do not believe even that would be enough to defeat the *sheriekas*."

"But there are *dramliz* who are going to engage the enemy, even knowing they'll fail," Jela said, more like he was checking facts than questioning the sanity of the proposition.

"There are those who *must* fight, M. Jela," Rool Tiazan said gently. "As to failure—all we attempt, as a force and individually, may yet end there."

"We hope that it will be otherwise," his lady added.

"Right." Jela shifted a little in his chair, eyes on the farthest corner of the tower.

"What I see, from soldier's eyes, is that your corps has a dual-pronged campaign on the board: a group of fighters to draw the enemy's attention and forces while those with Ser Lute attempt to capture and keep a reduced territory. The question comes back: what do you want from us?"

He moved a hand, enclosing himself, the tree and Cantra in the circle of "us," which was check—or maybe not. She'd eaten the damn' nuts, hadn't she?

There was a small silence, as if Rool Tiazan and his lady took lightning counsel of each other on a level not available to the rest of them.

"Wingleader," the lady said, "we have, in fact, a *three*-pronged plan. For our part, Rool and I have determined to liberate the mathematician Liad dea'Syl, whose work has continued to evolve and now transcends that with which you are familiar."

She closed her lips and refolded her hands, as if that explained all.

Cantra sent a glance to Jela, only to have it bounce off ungiving black eyes. Right.

She looked back to the *dramliza*.

"I'm not following," she said to the lady.

The prim mouth opened—and closed. Her thin red brows pulled sharply together.

"Rool?"

"Indeed," he murmured. His eyes were open, but Cantra was willing to lay steep odds that he wasn't seeing anything like *Dancer's* piloting tower.

"What is it?" That was Jela, quiet, so as not to startle the look-out.

"A hound has discovered us," the lady said softly, shifting around on the jump seat so that she faced her mate. "It may be possible—"

"Neutralized," Rool Tiazan said, in a flat, distant voice. He took a breath, his focus coming rapidly back to the present, the tower, his lady.

"The absence will be noted," he murmured, looking down into her eyes. "Soon."

"What did they see?" the lady demanded.

He moved a hand, the stone on his forefinger throwing out flickers of black lightning.

"The maelstrom of the luck. Our ally the *ssussdriad* obscured much, but in the final moment the lady knew me."

"So." The lady squared her thin shoulders. "We to play decoy, then. Locate an appropriate scenario."

"Yes." He closed his eyes, and Cantra was abruptly aware of a sense of absence, as if the essence of the being known as Rool Tiazan had departed the common weal.

The lady twisted, coming off the jump-seat in a flurry of gray and spun to face Jela.

"Wingleader—your mission!" she snapped, a mouse giving orders to a mountain.

Jela moved his shoulders, but—"Tell me," was all he said.

"You, the pilot and the *ssussdriad* will proceed to the world Landomist, where Revered Scholar Liad dea'Syl is confined with all honor to Osabei Tower. You will gain his equations which describe the recrystallization exclusion function. You will then use them as you see fit, for the continuation and the best interest of life. We will draw off the *sheriekas* lord who now has our enterprise under scrutiny. The hound did not see you—only us." She paused, her thin form seemed to waver, to mist slightly at the edges—then she was as solid as the decking on which she stood. Solid as Jela, who sent a long black glance at her, and said nothing at all.

"Wingleader, I require your word," the lady said softly.

Jela spun his chair to face the tree; spun back to face the lady.

"You have my word. I will do my utmost to liberate Scholar dea'Syl's equations and use them in the service of life."

The lady turned to face Cantra, who pushed up from her lean, ready to resist any demands for her oath—

"There are two," Rool Tiazan said, in that flat, distant voice, and held out a hand.

The lady altered her trajectory, and landed at his side, her hand gripping his.

"We will diminish," he said.

"*Diminish* holds a hope that *extinction* does not," the lady answered. "Proceed."

"Nay, look closely..."

"I see it," she snapped. "Proceed!"

Wreathed in mist, he opened his eyes.

"M. Jela—your choice! A death in battle or of old age?"

Jela was on his feet. "What are you doing?" he demanded, but Rool Tiazan merely repeated, on a rising note.

"A choice, M. Jela! Time flees!"

"Battle, then," Jela said, calm as if he was deciding between beer and ale.

Across the chamber, Rool Tiazan smiled, and raised his lady's hand to his lips.

"So," he said softly. "It is done."

The mist was thicker around the two of them. From the midst of it, came the lady's voice, calm and sounding distant.

"This world is tectonically active and there will soon be an earthquake of major proportion. It would be well if you were soon gone. The confusion will cover your departure."

There was a sudden toothy howl of wind, harrying the thickening fog, the temperature plummeted, the mist shredded—

The *dramliza* were gone.

Cantra spun to the board, slapped it live, initiated a self-check, and spun back to glare at Jela.

"Tell me you saw that," she snapped.

"I saw it," he answered, and gave her a long, deep look. "I believe it, too."

"So, you're for Landomist."

"I am," he answered. "I thought we all three had our orders."

The board beeped readiness; the tree sent an image of dark clouds and lightning, with more and worse towering behind...

The ship trembled a moment, rocking on the tarmac. Alarms lit the board in yellow, orange, and red.

Swearing, Cantra hit the pilot's chair, yanking the webbing tight.

"Strap in," she snapped at Jela, "this is gonna be rough."

CAST OF CHARACTERS

Soldiers

Bicra, Corporal
Contado, Chief Pilot
Harrib, Commandant
Kinto, Corporal
Loriton, Commander
M. Jela Granthor's Guard, Generalist
Muran, Pilot
Ragil
Ro Gayda, Commander
Tetran, Junior Pilot
Thilrok, Corporal
Vondahl, Under Sergeant

Batchers

Arin
Chebei
Dulsey
Fenek
Karmin
Ocho
Seatay
Uno

Dark Traders

Rint dea'Sord
Efron
Qualee
Cantra yos'Phelium Clan Torvin
Garen yos'Phelium Clan Torvin

Others

Danby
Liad dea'Syl
Ilan
Keon
Malis, Instructor
Pliny
Timoli

Ships

Spiral Dance, a.k.a. *Dancer*
Trident
Pretty Parcil

Planets

Ardega
Borgen
Chelbayne
Daelmere
Faldaiza
Gimlins
Horetide
Kizimi
Landomist
Phairlind
Scohecan
Solcintra
Taliofi
Vinylhaven

Cosmography

Bubble, The

Deeps, a.k.a. the Beyond, *also* Outspace or Out-and-
   Away

Far Edge

In-Rim

Inside

Out-Rim

Outer Edge

Rim, The

Shallows, The

Spiral Arm, a.k.a. the Arm

Tearin Sector

GLOSSARY

aelantaza —A specially-bred human

Batch —humans made to order

Batcher —an individual grown as part of a Batch

bounty hunters, 'hunters, also *charity agents*

candesa —a vapor which, enclosed and compressed, emits a cloudy
white light, at once too bright and hard to see by

carolis —next coin down from qwint

coderoy —tough fabric from which soldier kit packs are constructed

demi-qwint —small change

dramliz —an enchantment of wizards

dramliza —a single wizard

dueling stick —a cross between a cattle prod and a stave

fastflame —chemical fire that dies out after it consumes its own fuel

flan —next coin up from qwint

galunus, two-headed —a mythic creature of loathsome aspect and
third-rate thought process

jumping-jack(s) also 'jack(s) —cheap rooms for rent

Level One shielding —lowest level energy shield

logic tile —the smallest component of a computational device

lumenpaint —luminescent paint

OS-633 —Overhead Shields Series 633

phantom lover —a punishment device

Pilot's Undernet —pilot information network

pin-laser —sneak weapon

Pod —a Batch

qwint —coin

sadiline —a gemstone

SATA —Spiral Arm Trade Association

Ser —"Sir" "Mr."

sheriekas —the Enemy

skileti —naturally occurring lycra

'skins —protective suit for pilot wear on-planet

smartstrands —computational media

smartwire —binding wire

starsilk —expensive fabric

Tanjalyre Institute —a school for *aelantaza*

telomite —rock, for carving

Tempo —a drug that increases mental acuity and reduces the need
to sleep. For a while.

undertrade —black market, specifically trade with the *sheriekas*

viezy hide —tanned hide of an extremely rare and poisonous reptile

world-eaters —*sheriekas* doomsday machines

ON GROWING OLD, OR AT LEAST, OLD ENOUGH

We started writing *Crystal Soldier* in 1986. Sharon was working at the University of Maryland's Modern Languages and Linguistics Department at the time and the overruns and too-light copies came home with her to become "first draft paper." First draft paper was something we needed when using actual typewriters, if you want to know how far back that really was.

We still have three attempts at a beginning for what we were then calling *Chaos and the Tree*, typed on the backs of dittoed Spanish 101 vocabulary sheets and mimeographed Russian Lit exams.

To place this as nearly as possible: We'd already written *Agent of Change*, *Conflict of Honors*, and most of a third novel, pieces of which would become *Carpe Diem*; as well as an astonishing number of fragments, sketches, scenes, and word lists. It was a time of frenetic creativity, where one idea would smack into another, and dozens of child-ideas would spin off in all directions, like some cosmic game of pool. Needless to say, darn few of those ideas sank neatly into side pockets and waited patiently for retrieval. It was all we could do to note down trajectories and intentions, and hope to be able to get back at some less frenzied future time for more details.

It was during the pool game phase of our careers, then, that we realized we were going to have to write the story of Val Con's many-times-great-grandma, the smuggler, and the origins of Clan Korval, so, with the brass-plated confidence of complete ignorance, we began...

...and stopped.

And began...

...and stopped.

And began...

...and realized that we were too young in craft to do justice to the story we could feel building, like a long towering line of thunder heads, just beyond the ridge of our skill.

Having realized that we were yet too young to write about Jela, Cantra, and what befell them, we put the story aside, with a promise to the characters that we would not forget them; that we would come back when we were old enough and tell their story as it was meant to be told.

We had plenty to keep us busy in the meantime, what with one thing and another. There was a delay in the publishing, a major move, cats to feed. Along the way we'd have requests from readers wanting to know more about Clan Korval's roots. So we made a promise to the readers that we'd try to tell the beginning of the story, if we could.

Over time, we finished out the story arc concerning Cantra's trouble-prone descendants, and, when Stephe Pagel asked us what we'd be writing for him after *Balance of Trade*, we said that we thought we were now old enough to make good on certain promises of our youth.

Herewith is the first of two installments which will fulfill those promises. We hope you've enjoyed it.

Sharon Lee and Steve Miller
August 3, 2004

ABOUT THE AUTHORS

Sharon Lee and Steve Miller live in the rolling hills of Central Maine. Born and raised in Baltimore, Maryland, they met several times before taking the hint and formalizing the team in 1979. They removed to Maine with cats, books, and music following the completion of *Carpe Diem*, their third novel.

Their short fiction, written both jointly and singly, has appeared or will appear in numerous anthologies and magazines, including *Such a Pretty Face*, *Stars*, *Murder by Magic*, *Absolute Magnitude*, *3SF*, and several incarnations of *Amazing*.

Meisha Merlin Publishing has or will be publishing twelve novels cleverly disguised as ten books in Steve and Sharon's Liaden Universe®—*Partners in Necessity*, *Plan B*, *Pilots Choice*, *I Dare*, *Balance of Trade*, *Crystal Soldier*, *Crystal Dragon*—*The Tomorrow Log*, first of the Gem ser Edreth adventures, and the anthology *Low Port*, edited by Sharon and Steve. Sharon has also seen a mystery novel, *Barnburner*, published by Embiid in electronic and SRM Publisher, Ltd in paper.

I Dare, *The Tomorrow Log*, and *Balance of Trade* have been Locus magazine bestsellers. *Pilots Choice* (including novels *Local Custom* and *Scout's Progress*) was a finalist for the Pearl Award. *Local Custom* took second place in the 2002 Prism Awards for best futuristic romance, while *Scout's Progress* took first place. *Scout's Progress* has also won the *Romantic Times Bookclub* Reviewer's Choice Award for the best science fiction novel of 2002.

Both Sharon and Steve have seen their non-fiction work and reviews published in a variety of newspapers and magazines. Steve was the founding curator of the University of Maryland's Kuhn Library Science Fiction Research Collection, and former Nebula Award juror. Sharon served the Science Fiction and Fantasy Writers of America, Inc. for five years, as executive director, vice president and president.

Sharon's interests include music, pine cone collecting, and seashores. Steve also enjoys music, plays chess, and collects cat whiskers. Both spend 'way too much time playing on the internet and have a web site at: www.korval.com.

ABOUT THE ARTIST

Donato Giancola balances modern abstract concepts with realism in his paintings to bridge the worlds of fine and illustrative arts. He recognizes the significant cultural role played by visual art, and makes personal efforts to contribute to the expansion and appreciation of the science fiction and fantasy genre that extend beyond the commercial commissions of his clients. Since beginning his professional career in 1993 Donato's list of clients has continued to grow. From the major book publishers in New York to design firms on the West Coast, his commissions include companies such as LucasArts, National Geographic, DC Comics, The Free Masons of Philadelphia, Microsoft, Amazing Stories, Bantam Books, Ballantine Books, HarperCollins Publishers, Penguin, Playboy Magazine, Scholastic, Sony, Tor Books, Warner, Random House, Danbury Mint, Discover Magazine, The Franklin Mint, Milton-Bradley, Hasbro, and Wizards of the Coast.

Donato was born and raised in Colchester, Vermont. He moved to New York City shortly after graduating Summa Cum Laude with a BFA in Painting from Syracuse University in 1992 to begin his stellar art career.

Success as a science fiction illustrator has taken Donato around the world as a guest of honor at numerous events such as Magic: The Gathering tournaments in Santiago, Chile, to the Lucca Comic Book Convention in Italy, the Essen Toy Fair in Germany, and the Lisboa Comic Book Convention in Portugal. Donato is a frequent exhibitor at the Society of Illustrators and shows at many conventions around the states, including World Science Fiction Convention. He was given a Jack Gaughan Award for Best Emerging Artist in 1998, seven Chesley Awards including one for Artistic Acheivement 2002, and has been nominated five times for the Artist Hugo Award. Donato's work can also be seen in *Spectrum: The Best of Contemporary Fantastic Art*, whose juries have awarded him multiple medals from the recent Silver in Advertising Illustration in 2003 to a 2001 Gold in Editorial Art. He was also included in *Infinite Worlds*, a compendium of notable science fiction illustrators of the 20th century authored by Vincent DiFate.

In addition to a lucrative freelance career he has also taught at the School of Visual Arts, and in 1999 was an instructor at the Fashion Institute of Technology. He has served as Guest Lecturer at Syracuse University, Pratt Institute, Virginia Commonwealth University, and Pennsylvania School of Art and Design, and was a co-chair of the 1997 Student Scholarship Committee at the Society of Illustrators in New York.

Donato appears at various colleges, institutions, Magic tournaments and science fiction conventions, where he interacts with fans, performs demonstrations in oil paint, and displays original paintings. A comprehensive listing of his work, technique, and in depth biographical information is available on his website at www.donatoart.com.

Donato lives in New York City with his wife and two daughters. Any time away from his studio is spent in the museums, with his family, playing soccer, or attending various cultural events around the city.

Here is a special treat for our readers. Meisha Merlin Publishing, Inc. would like to give special thanks to Donato Giancola for

supplying us with his preliminary scketch for the cover of
this book, *Crystal Soldier*. We hope you enjoy!
—Meisha Merlin Publishing, Inc.